MURDER AT THE PENTAGON

MARGARET TRUMAN

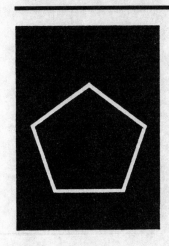

MURDER AT THE PENTAGON

 RANDOM HOUSE NEW YORK

TO THE MEN AND WOMEN OF THE ARMED FORCES,
EACH AND EVERY ONE

"The Constitution is like the Bible; it ought to be read again and again."

—PRESIDENT FRANKLIN D. ROOSEVELT

"Everybody knows that corruption thrives in secret places, and avoids public places, and we believe it is a fair presumption that secrecy means impropriety."

—PRESIDENT WOODROW WILSON

"They're stealing our country right out from under us. They're our own people, and every last one of them is a traitor."

—SENATOR HENRY "HANK" WISHENGRAD

MURDER AT THE PENTAGON

CHAPTER

ONE

 The upper quadrant of a sun that would scorch the desert blossomed on the horizon, livid red and rising fast into an inky sky. Black-browed, graceful bedouin in kaffiyehs and burnooses who had not received the warning—or who had chosen to ignore it—fed their feisty camels and prepared to serve the Prophet for yet another day.

In a bunker dug into the sand, men waited and watched, their attention focused on a steel skeleton six miles away that jutted up into the now-brightening sky. They wore special dark glasses, and powerful field glasses dangled on leather straps from their necks. A bank of electronic equipment was in front of them, LEDs fluttering, row upon row of red, green, and yellow lights blinking. A stocky man in a military uniform the color of earth counted down, his concentration on a digital clock that advanced silently—and incessantly. Other men aimed video cameras at the skinny metal aberration in the middle of the vast desert.

"Minus two," the clock-watcher said.

"Stand by."

"Minus one," the keeper of the clock said, precisely one minute later.

"Cameras."

"Rolling."

"Glasses on."

"Thirty , . . twenty-nine . . . twenty-eight."

The bunker was pungent with anticipation. And fear.

"Three . . . two . . . one."

It started slowly, a barely discernible rumbling of the earth. Then a brilliant white light erupted from atop the metal stand, its intensity reaching those in the bunkers slightly ahead of the sound. And in a second, no more than two, the awesome potency of energy equivalent to twenty thousand tons of TNT drove down and up and out—sending smoke and fire and acres of the desert itself into the heavens, its courier and its cap a mushroom cloud of devastation.

The video cameras captured every perverse second of the sequence—from the rumble to the fulgent light to the grimly familiar mushroom. Monitoring stations around the globe registered it on their sensitive meters. The meters and accompanying apparatus told a striking story. The Russians immediately knew the first fact. A weapon with the approximate power of America's first atomic test had been detonated somewhere in the Middle East. Others knew, too. The Danes, the Japanese, the French . . . and several select groups of Americans, who converged like smaller clouds.

In the Hybla Valley Federal Building on Telegraph Road, south of Alexandria, Virginia, members of the Defense Nuclear Agency's Operations Division gathered for an emergency meeting.

In the Pentagon the Joint Chiefs of Staff huddled in a closely guarded conference room within the National Military Command Center, across the hall on the E ring's third floor from the offices of the SecDef, the secretary of defense, who, at that moment, was in the White House conferring with his president, David Beardsley, and a dour Cabinet. The hastily drawn report by DOD's nuclear-monitoring section had been read to them in somber, flat tones.

"Then he's got it," Beardsley said.

"It appears that way." Secretary of State Warren Smith's face was expressionless.

"Jesus," said Vice President Joe Fletcher.

President Beardsley took in the other faces of his Cabinet. Then, in an uncharacteristic display, he slammed his fist on the table. "He's got it. That madman has got the bomb."

CHAPTER

TWO

The desert test that had awakened the world to the renewed potentials of war had occurred in early July. Now, on a hot, sticky day in late August, air force major Falk sat on one of many benches in the Pentagon's center court, a five-acre magnolia-lined park caught within the building's five walls. The morning sun did to her silken black hair what sunshine always does to such hair—brought out its underlying copper tones. She wore khaki Bermuda shorts, pristine white sneakers, and a pink T-shirt with green lettering on its front that said "I'M A WHIRLYBIRD . . . AND PROUD OF IT." Margit Falk, named after her German-born mother who'd died when Margit was five, was usually called Margaret by those to whom she was introduced, and who did not listen carefully. There was a time when she considered changing her name to the American version, but got through that short period of insecurity and proudly, almost compulsively, spelled out Margit to the confused. Naturally, people were prone to call her Peg, or Peggy, but she unfailingly, and pleasantly, shifted them back to the name she preferred.

She was beautiful, no dissenting votes. Hers was the sort of beauty that warmed the winds of romance for certain men and fueled the fires, the sexual fantasies, of adolescent men of any age eagerly awaiting their next copy of *Playboy*. She was, in living color, what publisher Hugh Hefner had promised would be "the girl next door" and seldom was, unless you lived next door to a . . . well, never mind.

In fact, a *Playboy* photographer once had visited Lowry Air Force Base intent upon developing a photo feature about military women. When he spotted Margit, he knew he had his centerfold—until, spotting the flash in his eye, she politely told him that once past infancy, she took off her clothes for only a few human beings, most of them doctors or nurses; that her military career meant more than all the money Mr. Hefner had ever possessed or even had lost; and that she found the idea of standing around in the nude rather silly. Besides, she said, her smile an entire sunrise in itself, she had no apple to peddle.

No pox on the photographer's artistic judgment, however. Five feet seven inches tall, long-legged and nicely tanned in midyear, naturally melanous in other seasons, Margit Falk was, by strength of character, a more likely candidate for the cover of *Prevention.* "Tight" was a word sometimes used to describe her figure. "Athletic." "Healthy." All those things and more.

Sometimes, she was mistakenly assumed to be French. In fact, her paternal grandparents were French, and she'd spent much of her youth with them, resulting in a fair working knowledge of the language, at least conversationally. Her father had been a line-maintenance chief in the air force, which made Margit a military brat. She'd enjoyed her childhood despite the frequent moves. Her father worked as hard at raising her as he did at ensuring that the aircraft in his charge were safe for their pilots. He'd lived long enough to guide her into the early innings of her adult life. She missed him, sometimes painfully.

The large eyes were surprisingly blue for someone with such dusky skin tone, unexpectedly bright, direct eyes that exuded, at once, intelligence along with a natural friendliness.

She did not dress or walk provocatively, but no matter. Whatever Margit wore—a T-shirt that suggested nicely proportioned bosom and distinctly female hips, dress blues, or a pilot's fatigues—she turned heads. As she did that morning, swiveling not her hips but the heads of a dozen men who were also there for the Pentagon's T&E annual picnic. Those men from the Office of Test and Evaluation who weren't with wives or girlfriends were the most overt in their admiration. Those with short-term or long-running attachments were more furtive evaluating what they'd never test.

He waited by the purple watercooler in the Pentagon's subbasement. There are 685 drinking fountains in the Pentagon, but only one is purple. Why? No one knows. He looked at his watch: 11:05 A.M. Five minutes late. Lateness was a form of arrogance. People kept waiting for "the arrival." A bad trait.

"Having fun in the sun?"

A heavyset man plopped his large bulk down beside her on the bench, a pleasant smile on his round, wet face. Tiny drops of perspiration on Margit's upper lip and brow were her only acknowledgments of business-as-usual summer conditions in the nation's capital.

"It's a beautiful day," she answered.

"Too hot for me," the man said, sweeping his face with an already soggy handkerchief. "I'm Joe Maize. As in corn." He offered the hand that held the handkerchief, laughed, and switched hands. She shook it. "Margit Falk."

"I haven't seen you around," Maize said.

"I haven't been here very long," she replied. "I was transferred last month."

"T and E?"

"No," she said. "SecDef's general counsel staff."

"A lawyer?"

"Yes, and I haven't been at that very long, either."

"Well, welcome to the Puzzle Palace."

"Thank you." The classic nickname for America's center of national defense, the Pentagon, was one of several. Fort Fumble, the Fudge Factory, the Five-Sided Wailing Wall, were used less frequently.

Margit didn't ask, but Joe Maize offered the information that he was a civilian GS-15 in DCAA, the Defense Contract Audit Agency. An average of fifty thousand contracts are signed each day in the Pentagon. They were kept busy. He said, "That's my wife over there." He pointed to a substantially made woman standing with a small group of people near a horseshoe pit created for the picnic.

Margit nodded. He was sizable, sweaty, married, and not especially interesting. But he seemed nice enough, Midwestern friendly. What was there to say?

Maize stood. "Well, welcome aboard, Ms. Falk." He leaned forward to read the lettering on her T-shirt. "A club?" he asked.

"Not really," said Margit. "I'm chopper-rated. Some other women pilots and I got together and had these made up."

"Cute," Maize said. "And pardon me for calling you 'Ms.' Military, huh?"

"Major."

"Glad to meet you, Major."

"Thank you." Funny how men like to read our T-shirts so intently, she thought. Maybe we should have had shoulder patches made instead.

Although Margit had never met Maize, she knew who he was—the lead auditor on a controversial air-force weapons system known as Project Safekeep, based on the X-ray laser and funded by DARPA, the Defense Advanced Research Project Agency. Safekeep's technical development had been contracted to Starpath, Inc., a low-profile, high-tech California company. The theory behind the new weapon, as Margit understood it from scuttlebutt, was that small nuclear devices, carried by combat aircraft, could be detonated in the air, their nuclear energy sending out radiation sufficient to destroy enemy missiles. No working model had been field-tested, as far as Margit knew, although Starpath claimed successful laboratory tests. DARPA, and the air-force section of the Pentagon charged with overseeing the new weapons-system project, had recently told Congress that significant progress had been made. Others in the scientific community cast doubts on the testimony, citing their knowledge of the state of the art in X-ray lasers, which, they claimed, was still in its infancy—at best.

She watched Maize join his wife, the tall, fair, square woman with short blond hair and cheeks flushed with heat. After a time Margit got up and casually strolled in her direction. As she passed, she heard Mrs. Maize say to others in the group, "Saturdays, Sundays, it never stops. Now *that's* an agreement the president ought to hammer out with the Russians. One day a week when it's illegal to even think about national defense." She laughed lightly, but there was discernible seriousness in her voice.

Margit didn't know many people at the picnic. She was the only person there from SecDef's general counsel. She'd been invited because her first assignment upon reporting to the Pentagon was to act as legal liaison with Test and Evaluation's Project Safekeep. She'd considered declining the invitation, especially when Jeff had begged off. She and Jeff Foxboro had been law students together at George Washington University, Jeff studying full time, Margit using nights and weekends during a tour at Bolling Air Force Base just outside Washington. Upon graduation, he had taken a job with a highly visible liberal senator from Wisconsin, Henry "Hank" Wishengrad, now in his fourth term in the Senate, and Congress's leading Pentagon critic.

Their relationship had blossomed in the classroom under the watchful eye of law professor Mackensie Smith, who, in addition to teaching Margit the law, served as her adviser. Not long after graduation Margit was reassigned to Lowry AFB in Colorado, which put a decided, although not fatal, crimp in her relationship with Foxboro. Her returning to Washington via her new Pentagon assignment was good news on three fronts: first, of course, being closer to Jeff; second, a chance to renew contact with Mac Smith and his wife, Annabel, with whom she'd become friendly beyond ordinary student-professor status; and third, the obvious allure of a Pentagon assignment. A stint at the Starch-and-Salute Factory, her name for it, didn't guarantee military career success, but a successful tour there couldn't hurt.

Even though Jeff Foxboro hadn't been able to accompany her to the picnic that morning, he'd encouraged her to attend. "Good chance to meet people outside the office," he'd said. "Knowing people on a personal level, especially in that zoo, will help smooth the way when you've got a problem."

He was right, of course, and though alone, she was glad she'd come. There, in the tranquillity of trees and grass, surrounded by one of the world's largest office buildings—83 acres of offices on 175 acres of land—and within whose walls decisions of the gravest consequence were made, one experienced the distinct and pleasant feeling of an old-fashioned family picnic. Children ran and stumbled in three-legged races and tag-team competition. The more competitive of the adults had gone to the Pentagon Officers' Athletic Club

(POAC) to compete in gymnastic and swimming events. The POAC building had been built during World War II as a bomb shelter for FDR. No bombs had fallen on it, but it began to deteriorate of natural causes until athletic-minded officers found the funds to spruce it up.

Others at the picnic vented their Pentagonesque competitive natures in less strenuous games of horseshoes, volleyball, and badminton. Margit preferred to compete with herself, to stretch her endurance, increase her strength—no need to prove it to someone else—and so she contented herself with observing the competitions, the fun, and enjoying the warm sun on her face.

He heard footsteps on the hard floor, checked his watch again. Nine minutes late. About time.

"Margit."

She'd been on her way across the center court to the kiosk in the middle from which hamburgers, hot dogs, watermelon, soft drinks, and beer were being dispensed. She stopped and turned.

"Good to see you again." Bill Monroney. So it wasn't true that Margit didn't know anyone at the picnic. She knew Lieutenant Colonel William Monroney from years back, right after she'd completed helicopter training and had been certified to fly the tricky, unwieldy, wonderful aircraft. They'd met in Panama, where Margit—military directives against women in combat be damned—had flown a UH-60 "Blackhawk" on clandestine supply missions from a CIA-funded airstrip in Costa Rica to support the invasion. Monroney was the air-force intelligence officer assigned to their unit.

"I heard you were at the Pentagon," he said pleasantly, narrowing the gap between them and extending his hand. Margit scrutinized his face. He'd grown older—no surprise in that—but was even more handsome than she remembered him to be, tall, imperially slim, a new dash of gray at the temples adding a touch of wisdom to his patrician good looks. Like Margit, Bill Monroney had enjoyed keeping fit, and his sinewy frame attested that he still did. He wore white slacks and loafers, and a shirt the color of Pepto-Bismol with the top two buttons left open. One thing certainly hadn't changed; his smile was infectious.

Margit briefly took his hand and then disengaged. "Yes," she said.

"Arrived about a month ago. Funny I haven't bumped into you in the building." If I were honest, she thought, I'd admit that I had hoped not to see him. Unrealistic, of course, even in the mammoth complex. Monroney was assigned to the Air Force Directorate of Engineering Services (DE&S). Margit's assignment to the X-ray laser project ensured that they would come in contact at some point.

"It's a big building," he said. "And I've been away most of the month. I suppose that's why we haven't run into each other. How have you been?"

"Fine. Really good."

"Still flying choppers as if born to it?"

"Sure. When I get the chance."

"And a lawyer, too," he said with a sense of slightly exaggerated respect. "What's next for Margit Falk, brain surgery?"

"I've been considering that," she said. "Need any work? You look good. The Pentagon must agree with you."

Monroney laughed. "As long as you don't take it too seriously. Actually, I've been enjoying the assignment. Nothing like rubbing shoulders with the purple suiters." Pentagonese for top brass. "Good for the career, if not for the morale."

"How's your wife?" she asked.

Monroney looked to where his wife was sipping a lemonade while chatting with another woman. He returned his attention to Margit. "Celia is fine. Still living the single life?"

"Yes, and enjoying every minute of it. Excuse me. It was good seeing you. I'm thirsty." She resumed her path toward the kiosk, aware that Monroney was watching her every step. She skirted Celia Monroney and reached the kiosk where volunteers wielded long black forks that pierced frankfurter skins and slid easily between charred ribs. Fat dripping from hamburger patties hit the flame of the barbeque pit with the searing hiss of a snake pit. Margit ordered a diet cola.

Unpleasant memories flooded her, but she willed them away. To her right, lined up along a counter, were military officers who somehow wore their profession and rank even in civilian clothing; lobbyists invited to the picnic by their Pentagon contacts; and a member of the House of Representatives whom Margit recognized from pictures.

"I know one thing," one of the military men said in an authoritative, commanding voice (did he sound that way to his wife and children? Margit wondered), "that son of a bitch had better be put in his place now before he takes a notion to use that bomb he's ended up with."

"It sure as hell got Israel's attention," said a lobbyist. "What did I hear yesterday, that they've voted an emergency two billion for weapons?"

"Can't blame them," another officer in mufti said. "That head case drops one bomb on Tel Aviv, good-bye Jewish homeland, bonds for Israel, and conventional warfare."

Margit continued to sip her soft drink and eavesdrop. The demonstration by the leader of an Arab nation that he had, in fact, developed nuclear weapons had dominated virtually every conversation since videotapes of the test were released. Until that fateful moment the world had been drifting, albeit slowly but surely, into a rumbling but comforting peace. Relations between the United States and what had been the Soviet Union had continued to develop into one of mutual cooperation. Gorbachev and his policies of revised *glasnost* had started the process. The Wall had tumbled in Berlin. Eastern bloc countries had flexed their muscles, to the extent they existed, and sought to enter the mainstream of free enterprise and free elections. Then, the failed coup against Gorbachev and, of all things, the collapse of Communism within the Soviet Union, set in motion the dismemberment of the Russian nuclear superpower itself, at least as it had been known.

Saddam Hussein's audacious takeover of Kuwait, and subsequent rout on the battlefield under Stormin' Norman and the hundred-billion-dollar Desert Storm operation—give or take a billion or two—had rendered Iraq impotent, at least for the time being. Negotiations between Israel and the PLO had taken what appeared to be a few positive steps forward, although they were far from achieving a definitive resolution.

And then, with a push of a button, the world once again faced the prospect of a nuclear outburst. What governments had always feared was now a fact. Not that a superpower would unleash nuclear devastation, but that the technology would end up in the hands of a renegade, a rogue, an uncivilized and unreasonable despot who would view the use of such a weapon not as a threat to humankind but as a means of achieving commanding power. And, of course, depending upon the depth of his religious convictions, a hallowed place in heaven.

The testing of the nuclear device had detonated the Pentagon into a frenzy of round-the-clock activities. Weapons systems that had been put on hold were dragged off the shelf and viewed as viable again. Members of the House and Senate appropriations committees, who'd pushed hard to turn the world's calm into a moderate peace dividend—unleashing funds at least temporarily freed from defense to rebuild America's infrastructure, to help ease the growing, grinding rate of poverty and close the widening gap between rich and poor, and to fund needed educational programs to bring America up to par with its leading economic competitors—now seriously rereviewed cuts in the military budget.

A crew in a Russian missile silo outside St. Petersburg lounged on couches provided for their long, boring shifts. American and Russian negotiators had made considerable strides in reducing the arsenal of nuclear weapons on both sides, but the day had not yet been reached when all such weapons were abolished. Three members of the crew played cards. A radio broadcast Mussorgsky orchestrations of Russian folk themes into the large, windowless room that was the central control for the launching of the silo's deadly instrument. The word to launch would come by telephone, a simple black instrument on a desk near the much more complex technological apparatus that, once activated, would send the missile into the sky, across the ocean, and, if everything went right, to a direct hit on its still-designated target, a kiosk in the center of five acres of trees and grass surrounded by five walls, a target consisting at the moment of Coke and Pepsi, burgers and dogs, potato chips and popcorn, coffee and tea. The kiosk had, for decades, been Ground Zero, the chosen target for the first Soviet missile launched in the event of war. The bags of potato chips and the walls around them would become, in a flash, indistinguishable.

"I have a headache," one of the Russians said.

"Too much vodka last night," a major said helpfully.

"Deal the cards," an enlisted man at the table said.

And so it went, shift after shift, week after week, waiting for a phone to ring that had never rung before, and that was less likely to ring with each passing day of détente.

Unless, of course, the missiles under the Soviet crew's control were to be turned, from a kiosk in the center of the Pentagon to a white-walled city in the Middle East.

Margit continued to wander the park, stopping occasionally to introduce herself to people who looked accessible to overtures from a stranger. A sadness had come over her. It wasn't profound, just there, a moment of melancholy not unknown to her, usually triggered by being alone in a setting in which families prevailed. Being married and having children certainly appealed to Margit, although she wasn't driven by that need, as evidenced by the proposals she'd declined in her adult life. Her thoughts went to Jeff. Would their relationship develop to the point that they might marry one day? You didn't push those things; at least, you shouldn't. If it happened, it happened. Meanwhile, she had work to do.

She noticed another woman who seemed to be alone. Should she introduce herself or leave the picnic, which was her first inclination? She looked a little more closely. The other woman had . . . well, a sensual aura about her as some women do, not so much a matter of dress or makeup, but through an inherent sense that it is their birthright, almost their duty, to flirt and to be coy, to attract and to seduce, men or women. The woman was approximately Margit's height and wore beige slacks and a flowered shirt. An abundance of gold hair was loosely curled, the heat and humidity causing it to relax more than it should. Her features were ordinary (in the sense that none stood out as wonderful) except for lips that were fuller than average. Superb, pouty lips. Sexy lips.

The woman leaned against a tree away from the crowd. Margit approached her. "Hi," she said, "I'm Margit Falk. New here." The woman had not seen her coming, and she seemed startled before saying, "Hello. I'm Christa Wren. I'm not."

Margit gestured to the picnic. "Fun," she said.

"Yes, it has been. Are you going to work in the Pentagon?"

"I'm an air-force major assigned to the General Counsel's Office. Do you work here?"

"No. I'm with someone."

"Oh." Margit didn't ask who he was, or where he was. Why assume it was a *he*? Maybe she was with a girlfriend. No, it would be a man.

Christa offered the explanation Margit hadn't asked for. "I'm here with Dr. Joycelen. He had to go inside for something."

"Dr. Joycelen. I certainly know of him, although I've never met him. He's with DARPA."

"Deputy director."

"A brilliant man, yes?" Margit said.

"Very smart. A genius."

"So I've heard. Well, nice meeting you. Maybe I'll see you again. At another picnic. Or the Christmas party. Surely we have a Christmas party." Margit laughed softly.

"Maybe," said Christa, who looked back again to a door leading from the center court into a wing of the Pentagon.

Not a word was spoken where the two of them met by the purple watercooler. One started to speak, but then there was a sound, a ridiculously tiny 'pop' considering the damage that followed. The bullet shattered eyeglasses and pierced skin and bone directly between the eyes. A word formed on the dying person's lips but was never uttered. Sudden. Quick. Dead.

There was only one witness on the scene. The killer. No one else to see.

Except for a silent eye, one of hundreds of surveillance cameras peering down. Perpetual, unrelenting vision when they worked, hopelessly blind when they didn't.

Another fifteen minutes, Margit told herself as she left Christa Wren and watched Bill Monroney step up to a microphone on a small wooden platform near the kiosk. "Ladies and gentlemen," he said, "time to announce the winners of the athletic competitions. We'll start with the kids' events." A younger man holding a box containing medals and ribbons joined Monroney on the platform. Margit had been introduced to the younger officer during a meeting. Mucci? Yes, she seemed to recall that was his name. A major, like herself. Major Anthony Mucci. All spit and polish, she remembered. An officer out of a recruiting poster, brown hair cropped close; intense, steady eyes; good posture; few words. Even in his civvies, he was the quintessential young military man. Impressive.

The children who'd won their events proudly stepped up on the platform to receive their recognition. In truth there were medals for every young person—fourth place, sixth place, eighth place, whatever, and it took time to get through them. Once Monroney had, Mucci brought up another box, medals now for the adult competitors. Monroney had started to announce the first few when Margit became aware that two men had come out of the Pentagon and were walking at a brisk pace toward the platform. Others saw them, too, including Monroney and Mucci. Monroney came off the platform, and he and the two late arrivals engaged in an animated, hushed conversation. When they were through, Monroney returned to the platform, took the microphone in his hand, and said, "Ladies and gentlemen, there's been an accident inside. Sorry to say so, but the picnic is over. Medals for the rest of the winners will be delivered to them on Monday. Please, disperse now. Go home. Thank you for coming."

Monroney motioned to Mucci and another staff man to join him, and they followed the two who'd brought news of the accident back into the Pentagon through the same doors.

The crowd, dispersing, was abuzz. So suddenly. So quickly. What happened? What *kind* of accident? Who?

Instinctively, Margit turned to look at the spot where Christa Wren had been leaning against the tree. She wasn't there anymore. Margit stood on tiptoe and looked over the crowd, saw Christa walking quickly from the center court and through the designated entrance/exit being used by slower-moving picnic-goers.

Margit joined the crowd as it filed toward the exit, heard the talk around her, the questions, the speculations. She had no one with whom to join in such conversation. No sense in playing the speculative game anyway. She'd find out soon enough—along with everyone else.

Monroney, Mucci, the third officer who'd joined them, and the two security men looked down on the body. They were in a subbasement of the Pentagon, a storage area reached by a set of stairs and an elevator, both heavily guarded one floor above. Dr. Richard Joycelen was slumped against the watercooler. The bullet that took his life had passed cleanly between his eyes, and blood had drained freely from the wound, over a prominent hump in his nose and down one side of his face. Much of it was already congealed, and was reddish brown rather than oxygen-fired red.

"Has the building been secured?" Monroney asked one of the security men. "Medics called?"

"Yes, sir."

"Good." To Mucci: "Let's go upstairs. Looks like we'll have the rest of the weekend here, and it sure as hell won't be any picnic."

CHAPTER

THREE

 "Okay if I leave?" Jeff Foxboro asked his boss, Hank Wishengrad.

"Hell, no." Wishengrad grinned. "You've only been here for three days and nights, and you look it. Go home."

"Not directly. A dinner date, but I'll hit the sack early, unless I fall asleep in my soup. You could use some rack time yourself."

The Wisconsin senator sat back in the tall red leather chair and slid his hands behind his head. His hair was silver, and he wore it longer than would be expected of a man in his sixties, a U.S. senator to boot, almost long enough to be termed "flowing." Coupled with half-glasses that spent most of their time perched on top of his head and a penchant for bow ties, he had the look of a 1960s intellectual, a professor, a radical lawyer, or a senior beatnik, an appearance pundits on the Hill mocked as affectation. Which was only half true.

The senator closed his eyes and asked absently, "Who you having dinner with?"

"The woman I told you about, Margit Falk."

"The major?"

"One and the same. Actually, it's a foursome. Mackensie Smith, my former law professor, and his wife, Annabel, invited us for dinner."

Hank Wishengrad opened his eyes, and a smile curled his lips. "Mac Smith. How is he?"

"Just fine, I hope. Haven't seen much of him since we graduated.

We keep in touch once in a while by phone. Great man, and married to a wonderful woman. Actually, Margit choreographed this dinner. She's been trying to mount a mini–class reunion ever since she got posted back to Washington."

Wishengrad stood, stretched, yawned. "Well, Jeff, if you pick up any pearls from the distinguished professor, or from your Pentagon sweetheart, be sure and pass them on in the morning. We can use all the smart thinking we can get around here. Sometimes I think we gave up thinking after the Marshall Plan."

Foxboro took his tan raincoat from an antique coat tree and put it on over his brown tweed jacket. He went to the window and looked outside. A light rain had begun to fall. Maybe it would cool the city, drop it down a few degrees to a slow boil. He saw his image in the glass and patted the top of his head to rearrange hair that was not out of place. It made little difference. Foxboro's sandy hair had the consistency of brushes used to thin out the undercoat of dogs and cats. Each individual hair made its own statement, pursued the direction it wished to go in, and he'd never been able to properly prune the bush until running across a stylist in Georgetown of the sort who had replaced barbers and who promised to "tame the beast"—and did, sort of. Foxboro carried his five-feet-eleven-inch frame straight-up: oddly, a distinct military posture, although he had not served in any branch of service. His face was squared-off and his brow was usually furrowed, set in an angry look that did not accurately reflect the quick, dry wit that could send that same face into a kaleidoscope of laugh lines. He lifted weights, but only for muscle tone, not for bicep bulge, and he'd developed into a pretty good Chinese cook after taking an extension course in D.C.

"My best to Mac Smith," Wishengrad said as Foxboro made for the door.

"Sure thing, Senator. I'll tell him you have a new plan to get our nonexistent railroads to run on time—the Mussolini Plan. Have a good night. Get on home. Chances are, the United States government will still be in business in the morning."

Foxboro had intended to walk from the Dirksen Senate Office Building to Mackensie Smith's house on Twenty-fifth Street in Foggy Bottom, but the fact that he was already late prompted him to jump into the rare, blessedly empty, rainy-night cruising taxi.

As fatigued as he was, the contemplation of an evening with

Margit and the Smiths energized him. He grinned as he projected what dinner would be like. While a law student at G.W., he'd been to his learned but streetsmart, practical professor's home for dinner on a few occasions. Those evenings invariably ended up in raucous debate among the students invited for the evening and their teacher, who seemed very much at ease moderating the conflicting points of view that flew around the table. That Smith had a remarkable mind was without question, but it was often Annabel who capped off an issue with a pointed, insightful, usually witty comment, smiling sweetly at her husband when their viewpoints clashed and his ended up on the floor. Foxboro sometimes wondered after leaving their house whether they continued disagreeing, whether they ever fought. Probably not the latter; the Smiths seemed blissfully suited to each other, to say nothing of looking good together: he a craggy, rugged-looking man behind whose heavy horn-rimmed glasses, the beard-line was always reappearing minutes after a close shave; she a stunning female with a complexion like half-and-half, a thick mane of copper hair, and a figure that left scant doubt to which of the two major sexes she belonged.

Foxboro bounded up steps in front of the narrow, two-story taupe brick house with the Federal blue shutters and door, and announced his arrival with a sharp rap of the brass knocker. Annabel answered. She held Rufus, their Great Blue Dane, by his collar to keep him from planting large paws on Foxboro's shoulders. "Hello, Jeff," she said pleasantly. "Come in. We were getting a little worried about you."

"Sorry I'm late," he said. "Been a hectic couple of days at the office. Or years. I forget which."

"Decades," said Annabel, taking his coat and leading him to the living room, where Margit sat, a glass of white wine in her hand.

"Hi, honey," Foxboro said, kissing her cheek, lingering a little. To Annabel: "Where's the prof?" Foxboro was never sure how to address Mac Smith. In his student days, of course, it was Professor Smith. Now that Foxboro was a full-fledged attorney and a senatorial aide, he'd been asked by Smith to call him Mac, which he did but always with a modicum of unease.

"Where else?" Annabel replied. "In the kitchen whipping up another culinary triumph. Something to make Burger King limp with envy. Drink?"

"Yes, please," Foxboro said. "Scotch on the rocks would be help for the needy."

Annabel returned with a large glass filled with ice and Knockando. Few blends in the Smith household, Jeff thought appreciatively. All the scotch was single blend, and the bourbon came from a single barrel. Smith poked his head out of the kitchen to shout a greeting. He wore a long apron over a blue button-down shirt and red paisley tie. The illustration on the apron was a stream running through a forest. Two oven mitts shaped like trout were attached to the apron with Velcro.

Annabel sat next to Margit on a love seat, Rufus sprawled at their feet and halfway into the next room. Foxboro wandered into the kitchen, where Smith was busy rubbing a beef tenderloin with soy sauce. He further seasoned the meat with fresh pepper, then placed the platter on top of the refrigerator. "The last time I cooked a beef tenderloin, I made the mistake of leaving it on the counter," Smith said. "One swallow, and Rufus enjoyed another hors d'oeuvre."

Foxboro laughed. "A Big Mac for him."

"And Chinese takeout for us. How have you been, Jeff?"

"Pretty well, although I feel as though I've taken up residence in Senator Wishengrad's office. By the way, he sends his best. I didn't know you were friends."

Smith looked up from a large cast-iron skillet into which he'd placed a tablespoon of olive oil. "We're not friends. I spent some time on the senator's commission on the cities, and I got to know what a good man he is. Not much came out of the commission, I'm afraid. Your boss is in the minority where federal aid to cities is concerned, but we did what we could. You have a drink. Good." Smith picked up a heavy cut-crystal glass filled with ice and a velvety brown liquid, raised it to his lips, and sipped slowly and noisily. "Excellent. I know the trend these days continues to be wine spritzers, or bottled water with little bubbles, but a good single-barrel bourbon is a lot more soul-satisfying. At least for me. Rufus doesn't much care for it." He turned on the oven, adjusted the temperature dial to 450 degrees, and leaned against the counter. "I haven't caught up on the news yet today. Anything on the Joycelen murder?"

Foxboro shrugged. "About the only thing Rufus *doesn't* care for, except burglars. Not much talk about the murder where I've spent the last few days. Oh, there was some speculation right after it happened, but our Arab friend with his new toy is center stage."

"Damn shame," Smith said. "Any movement on the UN resolution to condemn him?"

"Not enough. Everybody seems to have their own notion how to deal with it, which means it probably won't be dealt with, at least for a while."

Margit appeared in the doorway, and Foxboro put his arm around her waist. Annabel joined them, causing Smith to ask, "Why is it that everybody always ends up in the kitchen? My sexual magnetism?"

"In this case it's not your cooking prowess, or any other. It's four fierce appetites," Annabel answered. Smith enjoyed cooking, although he didn't do much of it. He considered himself an able chef, but it was the quiet consensus of those who knew him best that the key to his success in the kitchen was in the markets, buying the best ingredients, and keeping the menus simple.

"What's the scuttlebutt at the Pentagon on Joycelen?" Smith asked Margit.

"Not much that I know of, though we seem to manufacture gossip with greater productivity than anything else. Well, maybe with the exception of paperwork. The Defense Criminal Investigation Service is in charge. Whether they've gotten anywhere isn't being broadcast outside their offices. Strictly information blind for the troops. Which, of course, must be driving the press crazy. It's all over TV, radio, and the papers, but they just keep repeating the few facts they know, which are damned few."

Annabel felt a chill that was not the result of the central air-conditioning that pumped cool air into the house. She wrapped her arms about herself and said, "Eerie, the whole business of Dr. Joycelen being murdered inside the Pentagon." She said to Margit, "You must feel on edge being there."

"A little. But there's more than twenty thousand of us. I suppose that the victim was a man of Dr. Joycelen's stature contributes to it."

"To say nothing of how it could have happened in one of the most secure buildings in the world," Smith added. "Gives credence to the adage that you can never make anything completely secure. Or anyone."

Margit said, "What I imagine we're all thinking is that because security is so tight—and there's no doubt that it is—the murderer obviously had to be someone with clear access to the building."

"Which means, of course, that Joycelen was done in by one of your own," Foxboro said.

"I'd rather not think about that," Margit said.

"Hard not to," Foxboro said.

Margit glanced at him; was he about to take a dig at the military establishment? He was fond of doing that, and they'd had words in the past, resulting in his promise to curtail the tendency. He knew what she was thinking, smiled broadly, and pulled her closer to him.

Margit, Jeff, Annabel, and Rufus watched with appropriate respect as Smith browned the beef on all sides in the skillet. He then transferred it to the oven: "Should take about twenty minutes," he said, "just enough time to enjoy a relaxing drink together. Old American custom, although we allow young Americans to play, too."

Glasses refilled, they repaired to the living room, where, for no apparent reason, Margit started to giggle. The others looked at her. "I feel like I'm back in law school," she said.

Annabel smiled. "I wouldn't mind being back in law school." She'd been a tough-minded but fair divorce attorney when she met Mac Smith after his wife and son had been killed by a drunk driver on the Beltway. Smith was, at the time, one of Washington's most respected trial lawyers. Not long after meeting Annabel, and after many long, soul-searching conversations with her, he closed his practice and accepted his present post at the university. Annabel had enthusiastically supported his decision, which certainly made it less taxing, and taxable, for him. Then, about a year later, they had a similar series of conversations, only this time it was Annabel voicing her desire: to stop practicing law and to pursue what had become a fervent interest in pre-Colombian art. She disposed of the cases she had and rented a small, pretty storefront in Georgetown in which she established a gallery devoted to her passion. It did well, and she eventually took over adjacent space to accommodate the growing number of pieces she'd successfully obtained. Of course, not only Mac's but their combined income was dramatically cut, but as Smith often said, the first debt to be paid was the one they owed themselves, and now and then to society. Not only criminals should do so, he pointed out. Neither of them ever regretted the decision.

"How about you, Mac?" Annabel asked. "Still view Margit and Jeff as students?"

"Certainly not, although I do feel a little older sitting with former students, one now a major in the air force and a helicopter-flying lawyer of all things, the other a trusted key aide and brain-truster to one of our country's prime legislators."

As in Washington it's wont to do, the conversation turned to local gossip. Each of them had enough contributions to that theme to make it lively, and there was much laughter until Smith raised his nose in the air, sniffed, stood, and said, "Enough! I don't want to overcook the beef."

They were soon seated at a nicely laid table in the dining room, and Smith opened a bottle of "house red, by the glass or bottle." "Gallo by the gallon," Annabel put in helpfully.

Mac asked, "Anybody ever meet Joycelen?"

They hadn't.

"I heard him speak once," said Smith, enjoying the garlic-touched mashed potatoes. "As brilliant as he obviously was, I had the impression he wasn't the sort of fellow you'd want to end up sitting next to on a long plane trip."

Foxboro laughed. "His personality didn't seem to turn off the ladies. Married twice, and engaged, I understand."

Margit said, "I'd completely forgotten about a conversation I had at the picnic. There was a woman there. Christa Wren was her name, I think. She said she was at the picnic with Dr. Joycelen, although I never saw him with her. The minute they brought the news out of the building that there had been an accident, she left. But then, everybody was leaving."

Smith said to Foxboro, "You say he was engaged? Maybe that was his fiancée."

"Yes, it was," Foxboro said, returning his attention to what was left on his plate.

"How do you know her name?" Margit asked.

"I heard someone mention it once," Foxboro replied without looking up.

Smith sat back, dabbed at his mouth with his napkin, and said,

"Jeff, I get the feeling you know more about Joycelen than you're willing to admit."

"Why do you say that?"

"Well, it makes sense that Senator Wishengrad and his staff would have a distinct interest in Joycelen. After all, as deputy director of DARPA and the brains behind that advanced weapons system . . . what is it called?"

"Project Safekeep."

"Right. Project Safekeep. Your boss has been criticizing that program since it was first announced. Did the senator have dealings with Joycelen?"

"Not that I know of. Maybe before I joined the staff."

Smith looked at Annabel and Margit, whose faces mirrored what Smith was thinking. Foxboro did not wish to discuss Joycelen on any level other than what the papers were saying. Fair enough, Smith decided. Drop the subject. After they finished the main course, with much lip-smacking and noisy commendation for the chef, he went to the kitchen and returned with a platter of four cheeses—a Tuscany Caciotta, an English Somerset Cheddar, the French Fourme d'Ambert, and an Italian Toma. Smith's fondness for cheese rivaled Annabel's love of pre-Colombian sculpture.

The evening was extended into the living room, the topics of conversation changing with regularity and rapidity. The discussion would have gone on longer had Foxboro not announced his fatigue, saying that if he didn't get home to bed, the Smiths would have an overnight houseguest on the couch. Margit had driven there and had found a parking space—as rare as Jeff's taxi—relatively near the house. "Come on, let me get Senator Sleepyhead home," she said, taking Foxboro's hand and pulling him from the couch with exaggerated difficulty.

"How are your quarters at Bolling?" Smith asked at the front door.

"Wonderful," Margit said. "Not only does Bolling have the best commissary, PX, and gas station in the area, I wake up each morning to a stirring pageant. The Air Force Band is headquartered there and rehearses every day, and the Presidential Honor Guard goes through its drills. I love it. I only wish it were still an active flight center. I'm going to have to get in my chopper time at another base." Despite its rich history—Lindbergh's *Spirit of St. Louis* was housed there following his historic 1927 flight to Paris, its hangar now the commissary—no aircraft had landed at the air-force base since 1962. An F-105 Thunderbird cemented in place at the base's entrance was the only plane to be seen. Bolling's role since 1962 had been strictly support.

"I'm sorry you're so exhausted," Margit said to Jeff as she drove to his apartment in Crystal City, an area in Virginia just across the Potomac that owed its rapid growth to its easy proximity to Washington and to the presence of the Pentagon, with all its related activity and personnel.

"Goes with the game, I guess," he said sullenly.

"Nice evening," she said. "They are a terrific couple."

"Yes, they are, only I wish the professor didn't have a need to probe as though you were on a witness stand."

Margit laughed. "I don't think he does that. He's just an intensely interested man who picks up on what people say and who wants to know more."

"Maybe. Anyway, the food was good."

They sat in silence in front of his apartment building before she said, "I hope we can find more time together, Jeff. Even though I'm back in Washington, our lives seem to drift further apart."

"We'll have to work on it," he said. "Look, Margit, I'm a noncontributor to any further conversation. Damn, I'm beat. Hate to end the evening, but I have to."

"I understand," she said. She leaned over and kissed him lightly on the lips. For a second she thought he was about to leave it at that, but then he shifted in the passenger seat and put his arms around her. This round of affection was conducted with considerably more fervor, and went further and lasted longer.

As she watched him enter his building, she realized how much he meant to her. Did she mean as much to him? She liked to think she did, and with that thought she headed for Bolling and a good night's sleep.

CHAPTER

FOUR

 The twenty-eight-passenger blue air-force bus that traveled Route 15B every thirty minutes between Bolling AFB and the Pentagon was almost full when Margit boarded it in front of Building 1300. She'd driven her red Honda Prelude to work the first few weeks, but decided that the bus was a better bet. Her rank entitled her to a Pentagon parking space roughly in the middle of the sixty-four acres designated for such use, which meant she had a quarter-mile walk from her car. Those of lower rank faced a half-mile hike each morning. The parking, coupled with a chaotic traffic situation (though in a capital city of high tech, not a traffic light is to be seen within the Pentagon's grounds) caused her to leave her car at the base most mornings, unless she had evening plans that called for its use. Of course, she could have joined the "Bolling Blasters," a club of runners who jogged to the Pentagon each morning. But that sort of sweaty start to the workday didn't appeal.

As she joined a long line of men and women flashing badges at security guards, she felt a familiar exhilaration at entering the building. Military and civilians alike seemed to share a sense of urgency that, Margit reasoned, had nothing to do with whether their daily tasks were urgent. It was the pace of the Pentagon that caught you up, a briskness, the crisp uniforms and close haircuts, the sheer numbers of people, many of them extraordinarily intelligent and dedicated, aside from the predictable corps of pay-promotion-pension types, the knowledge that the security of the country rested in your hands (sort of), all of which generated a cadence that even the slowest-moving found impossible to deny—except, perhaps, for the cleaning crew, who seemed to find a more deliberate gait to be more appropriate.

The offices of SecDef's general counsel were located off corridor 9, on the third floor of the D ring. Margit's office was 3D964; a visitor could find her if he knew that the 3 designated the floor, that D designated the ring, and that the first numeral specified the corridor off which her office was located.

"Five" seemed to have been the rule for the designers of the building back in 1941, when fifteen thousand workers went about the task of constructing a center to house America's military establishment—fragmented into fiefdoms under what was then called the National Military Establishment, unified six years later into the Department of Defense. The building's five sides went with five floors, each floor connected by wide ramps to allow for quick evacuation in the event of an emergency. There were five interior rings marked by the first five letters of the alphabet. The A and E rings were most prized; offices in the A ring looked out over the center court. The E ring, which circled the exterior of the building, gave views of the river, the city, Arlington Cemetery—depending upon which side you were on. Most offices in the B, C, and D rings lacked windows through which the sun could brighten space or spirits.

It was claimed that no two offices in the Pentagon were more than a seven-minute walk from each other, assuming, of course, you knew where you were going. Margit now felt secure in finding her own office; she made sure to take the same route each day. She'd been successful locating a few other offices in the month she'd been there, but had once become hopelessly lost when searching for one on the fifth floor of the B ring. Lots of jokes about strangers entering the Pentagon and finding their way out days later, all undoubtedly apocryphal, but then again . . .

She'd been moving smartly along seemingly endless vinyl hallways, heels clicking out her rhythm, until she reached the Arnold corridor, the air-force executive run named after Hap Arnold, taught to fly by the Wright brothers and eventually the only air-force five-star general. Here, carpeting muffled footsteps; it was a relatively calm area, at least in the hall.

Then, back to vinyl and click-click-click, more people, all in a rush. Margit had learned to stick to the middle of the wide corridors to avoid being run over by someone racing out of an office. Ahead of her a young marine enlisted man led a dozen people on a tour. He walked backward, as he would throughout the hour-and-a-half tour, his eyes never leaving those in his charge, an occasional glance over his shoulder his only acknowledgment that something could be in his way.

A horn startled her from behind, one of many battery-powered buggies driven by enlisted men delivering mail and intrabuilding correspondence. She stepped aside, and he passed. " 'Morning, Major," he said. Despite Margit's nickname for the Big P, there was no saluting indoors; even the open center court had been designated "indoors" for some reason, which contributed to its informality.

She reached her office. "Good morning, Jay," she said to the man with whom she shared the cramped space. He was reading that day's edition of *Early Bird*, a compilation of media clippings having to do with defense that was put together in the middle of the night and widely circulated each morning. *Early Bird* was read by everyone in the Pentagon. High-level officers and civilians had it delivered to their homes, and read it in the backseats of the limos that brought them to work. Most morning staff meetings, at every level, began with comments about what *Early Bird* said the press had reported over the past twenty-four hours.

Major Jay Kraft glanced up, nodded, and went back to reading. Kraft represented the only unpleasant aspect of Margit's Pentagon assignment, at least to date. He was a dour person who, in their tight confines, did nothing to lighten the atmosphere.

Margit perused her calendar. It promised to be a busy day, beginning in fifteen minutes with the arrival of Samuel Caldwell. Unlike most lobbyists who operated under the same theory of successful public relations—keep the profile low and do your work behind the scenes—Caldwell enjoyed the spotlight. It hadn't, however, affected his ability to shape opinion within branches and agencies of government about the clients who paid him handsome retainers, including Starpath, Inc. The small, controversial, high-tech California company currently developing Project Safekeep paid him well. Margit knew something about Caldwell through Senate hearings into Safekeep, chaired by Jeff Foxboro's boss. Caldwell had testified to Hank

Wishengrad's committee on more than one occasion, and Margit had watched portions of the hearings on C-Span. From what she remembered, Caldwell was as comfortable in the witness chair fielding questions from senators and their counsel as if he'd been sitting in a living room, or in a xenophobic men's club.

Caldwell had called Margit a few days ago, saying he wanted to "meet and greet" the new member of SecDef's legal team. Margit had told him while she would enjoy meeting him one day, her schedule was such that it was impossible to find the time, at least in the near future. Her rebuff didn't dismay him. He pleasantly thanked her for taking the time to talk to him on the phone, and said he looked forward to when her schedule eased up and they had a chance to get to know each other.

The next afternoon Margit received a call from an assistant to the assistant secretary of defense for legislative affairs. After introducing himself as Colonel Watson, he suggested that it might be to Margit's benefit, as well as helpful to the team involved with Project Safekeep, to get to know Caldwell.

"Why?" Margit asked.

"Because, Major Falk, Caldwell is an integral part of the process to get this system off the ground. He can be a good source of information."

Margit started to ask a new question, but Watson cut her off. "Major Falk, please find time to see Mr. Caldwell, and extend every courtesy."

She and Caldwell sat across a desk from each other in a small, often empty office maintained for such meetings. He was an affable man, about sixty, Margit judged, blocky in stature, ruddy and fit, and possessing a hint of a southern accent that Margit decided did not come naturally. As far as she knew, Caldwell was a native Californian.

"Well, Major Falk, I certainly do appreciate this chance to meet you personally. I understand you're acting as legal liaison with T and E on Safekeep."

"Yes, that's right."

"They started you off with a tough assignment," he said, laughing.

"I haven't learned enough about it yet to know how tough it's going to be. Right now, I'm trying to soak up everything I can about the project."

"In your sponge phase," he said. "Well, that's one of the reasons I thought we should meet. I want you to know that I am at your disposal at any time, for any reason, and to encourage you to call upon me if you need anything."

"That's very generous of you, Mr. Caldwell. I'll certainly keep it in mind."

He leaned forward in his chair and became slightly conspiratorial, an old friend giving good advice. "You know, Major Falk, this project is vitally important to the defense of this nation, especially now that we have that psychopath in the Mideast showing off his nuclear muscle."

Margit said, "It seems every weapons system has taken on new importance since he detonated that bomb."

"For good reason," Caldwell said.

"What's the testing status of the system?" Margit asked, not sure it was her business.

Caldwell narrowed his eyes and nodded his head. "Things are going very nicely, Major. A few kinks. Like anything involving so much technology. But real progress is being made. Of course, it's important that the process keep flowing smoothly, like a river without any dams."

Translation: Keep the money flowing to Starpath. Margit had nothing to do with funding the system. That was up to Congress, but she reminded herself that as a lobbyist for the defense contractor, Caldwell was obliged to touch base with anyone and everyone who had anything to do with it, and to attempt to shape the legion of people, civilian and military alike, to some consensus. Fair enough. She'd given him his shot, gave of her time that morning, had followed orders. She checked her watch; she had another meeting to get to and needed time to gather up papers for it, and to find the meeting site. "I'm afraid I'm going to have to run out on you, Mr. Caldwell. Another meeting. Always a meeting, it seems. We could defeat any enemy on earth by bombing them with minutes from our meetings." She stood and straightened her khaki skirt.

Caldwell stood, too, and extended his hand. "It was gracious of you to see me, Major Falk. I hope we have the chance to do this again. Maybe in more social, relaxed circumstances."

A slight nod of Margit's head was the extent to which she committed to that suggestion.

"Some lawmakers amaze me sometimes," he said.

"Oh?"

"No matter what the facts are, Major, some of them just don't see things the way you and I do. Take Wishengrad, for example. He just can't see real threats to this country, no matter what facts are laid in front of him. It's a shame. Every man and woman in uniform sees it, and that's why we all have to work together, help people like the senator from Wisconsin, and others like him, to realize that instead of cutting the defense budget, they ought to be finding ways to boost it, get it up to where we don't have to fear people like this Arab Hitler."

Margit resented being lumped into a common group—lobbyists and military personnel—but she didn't express it. She escorted him back to her office and said she'd call down for an escort to accompany him out of the building. No one wandered the halls of the Pentagon without an escort unless he worked there and had a badge to prove it, or had special status that entitled him to a No Escort I.D.

Which, of course, Caldwell had. "I've got to stop down at DE and S. I promised some folks there I'd drop in this morning. I'm still all shook-up over what happened to Dick Joycelen. Can't believe it. That man—and I knew him pretty well—that man's genius laid the groundwork for Project Safekeep. A hell of a loss to this nation. Well, I'd better get downstairs. Don't like to keep my friends waitin'."

If he was trying to impress Margit with the depth and breadth of his contacts, he'd succeeded only slightly. She wondered in passing whether one of the people he would see in the Directorate of Engineering Services was Colonel Bill Monroney.

From the time Caldwell left until Margit walked out of her final meeting of the day at five-thirty, time had passed quickly. The meetings had been focused and well managed, an achievement on the part of those in charge that Margit admired. She'd received lots of informal advice from those she met in the Pentagon, including that superiors looked for the sort of leadership that resulted in meetings being choreographed to achieve the desired result in the shortest amount of time. "Elevator speeches" they were called, getting your points across in the time it takes for a typical elevator ride. That specifically did not include "tap dance meetings," Pentagonese for slick, quick meetings lacking in substance. She'd been exposed promptly to a few of those since assuming her new post. Sometimes, like most people, she resented meetings; they got in the way of her real work. On the other hand, they served to get her out of the cubbyhole she shared with Kraft. Aside from being, apparently, a naturally sour human being, Jay Kraft was transparent in his resentment. He'd been working on Project Safekeep but was taken off it upon Margit's arrival and assigned to less demanding, and certainly less important, duties. His resenting her was, she knew, only human, but his disappointment and anger were misdirected. Kraft was someone who'd obviously not made his mark since being assigned to the Pentagon. You could spot them, hear it in their voices, see it in their walk. The Pentagon was a career opportunity. You either ran with it or it ran over you, as seemed to have happened to Kraft.

When she returned to her office late that day, he had gone home. "Something to do with a sick kid," one of the civilian administrators said.

Margit closed the door to her office. She had a half hour to kill—*spend* is more like it—before going to a meeting of DAC-WITS, the Defense Advisory Committee on Women in the Service, which was being held in one of the building's auditoriums. Margit had joined the organization at Lowry and intended to stay active. Early in her air-force career, she'd questioned the wisdom of getting involved with organizations that stood for women's rights in a predominately male domain—220,000 women on active duty worldwide, 11 percent of America's military force—and growing in proportion each year since those 1991 figures. But she'd soon got over those feelings. While career opportunities for women in the service had improved over the years, there were still areas of male prejudice that Margit felt should be corrected, not only in the interest of a more unified service, but out of fairness. She certainly was not, nor had she ever been, a strident feminist. She liked the fact that there were two sexes, and that they were set apart by defined physiological and psychological factors. But *la différence* shouldn't have any impact upon the ability of members of either sex to do their jobs to the best of their ability, and to be compensated unequivocally. The military's prohibition on women engaging in any combat role had not only, in Margit's opinion, been wrong, it was hypocritical. She knew the helicopter missions she'd flown in Panama placed her in extremely dangerous situations. She knew other women who'd flown missions in Vietnam and in the Persian Gulf that exposed them daily to every bit as much peril as their male counterparts. She recognized the concerns, even the considerations, that had led to such a prohibition. But times had changed—the world had changed—and it was time to recognize that every man and woman in uniform was in it together and should share the risks together. Differences could be dealt with.

She'd packaged up materials to take home to read, and was about to leave the office when there was a knock at the door. "Come in," she said.

A young lieutenant with a boyish face poked his head around the door. Max Lanning was a personal aide to the general counsel. A horse-holder, as young officers were called when their duty was to serve the personal whims of purple suiters. He and Margit had liked each other from her first day there. Among many things she enjoyed about him was his simple, wide-eyed awe at working in the Pentagon. He was also an incorrigible snoop and gossip, and a great deal of the semi-facts Margit had been privy to had come from him.

"Hey, big news, Major," he said, stepping inside and closing the door.

"Really? They're changing the menu in the cafeterias? No more mystery meats?"

"Nah, nothing that important," he said, grinning. He lowered his voice. "The word is that they're about to come down with a suspect in the Joycelen murder."

"That *is* big news," Margit said. "Any idea who it is?" While she found the rumor interesting, it also sent a twinge of apprehension through her. It was bound to be someone involved with the Pentagon, possibly a uniformed member of the military. She didn't like that.

"No name yet, but I hear it's an officer out of CIA."

"CIA?" Margit's screwed-up face reflected her puzzlement.

"Some liaison officer. That's all I know—I think they're planning to break the news in the morning."

Margit exhaled, causing a faint whistle. "You're sure they're that close to announcing it?"

Lanning shrugged. "I've given you everything I know, Major."

"I doubt that, Max. But you've given me quite a lot," she said. "Well, have to run to a meeting."

He looked at his watch. "The day is over."

"Not for the hardy. Thanks for the gossip, Lieutenant. See you in the A.M."

CHAPTER

FIVE

 Margit got back to Bolling too late for the week-
night social hour at the Officers' Club, but had a
drink with some chaplains attached to the Air
Force Chief of Chaplains Office who were cele-
brating a birthday—chief topic of conversation,
the Joycelen murder.

After a quick and quiet dinner by herself in the club's Washington Room restaurant—Jeff had accompanied Senator Wishengrad
to Wisconsin for the weekend—she sat in her quarters until after
midnight reading Project Safekeep files, the all-news radio station
WTOP kept on low volume beside her in the event there was an
announcement of a break in the Joycelen case. No such announcement was made, although the murder led off each twenty-minute
news round. If a suspect had been identified, the media hadn't got
wind of it.

She awoke before her alarm clock did its job, thanks to a torrential
downpour and the stiff wind that erupted with it. The weather
posed a transportation question for Margit—car or bus? She'd get
soaked walking to catch the bus. On the other hand, if she took her
car, she'd get soaked walking from her parking space. Always some
major decision to make, Major. One of the things Margit enjoyed
about being in the military was that the choice of what to wear each
morning depended only upon the seasons. No need to debate
whether this scarf went with that blouse, whether this skirt matched
that jacket. There was summer and there was winter, with dress
versions of each to be worn as appropriate for the occasion.

She sat next to a captain with whom she'd become acquainted on previous bus rides. Assigned to the Office of Special Investigations (OSI), whose headquarters was at Bolling, he was a pleasant, open sort of fellow, not the investigator type. She couldn't resist: "Anything new on the Dr. J. murder?"

"I don't think so. Why do you ask?"

"Just curious. Do you think they'll ever solve it?"

" 'They'll?' "

"The investigators. Your office."

"I'm not involved with it," he said. "I've spent the last two months investigating commissary theft."

"Oh. Mice?" She smiled and turned to a Dick Francis paperback mystery that had been her bus companion the past few days.

Jay Kraft was out again, which didn't displease Margit. She had settled at her desk and started to write a report when Max Lanning motioned for her to join him in the hall.

"What?" she asked.

"It's coming down in an hour."

"The Joycelen case?"

"Yes, ma'am. His name is Cobol. Robert Cobol, captain, United States Army."

"The CIA liaison officer you mentioned?"

"I think so." He looked up and down the hall, waited until a battery-powered cart passed them, then leaned into her ear. "Can I tell you something strictly off the record? QT? For your ears only?"

"As long as it's not classified."

"I would never tell you anything classified, Major Falk. The word is that this Captain Cobol killed Dr. Joycelen over a personal matter."

"Death's always pretty personal," Margit said.

They stopped talking. A tour led by a backward-peddling army corporal rounded the corner and came in their direction, the tour leader spouting a canned speech they all used. After they'd passed, Lanning said, "They were lovers."

"Joycelen? This Cobol?"

"That's the word."

Margit leaned against the wall. "Joycelen was married twice. He was engaged to be married again. I met his woman. She was no transvestite."

"That's what I heard, which makes the story seem stupid. Right?"

She looked directly into his eyes. "Right."

"I'm just passing on what I heard. They're making the announcement at ten."

"Where?"

"Here. In the building. I don't know any more than that."

"You seem to know a lot."

"I keep my ears open. Hey, you don't mind that I share this with you, do you? I mean, I figured you'd be interested, that's all."

"No, I don't mind. It's nice of you. I suppose we'll all know the real story at ten. I have to get back. A heavy-duty report to get out. Can I offer you a suggestion?"

"I'd be honored."

"Be careful who you tell things to."

He looked hurt. "I just tell you, Major Falk. I'm the original Tight Lips, believe me."

"I believe you." She didn't, of course. Just as it is impossible for anyone to have only one phobia, gossips are constitutionally unable to limit themselves to a single listener.

The press conference was held in the large room used for the Pentagon's daily press briefing. This morning, augmenting reporters assigned to the Pentagon, who had only to stroll across the corridor from their newsroom, were crime and beat reporters, gossip columnists, free-lance magazine writers, foreign press, and the producer of a popular network TV show that presented true-crime stories each week.

The conference started promptly at ten. By ten-fifteen the first reaction to the announcement spread through the building. Like a joke that changes in the telling from person to person, the recounting of what had been said was altered as it traveled. But the basic facts were evident: Army captain Robert Cobol, a CIA officer assigned to the Pentagon as liaison with the Joint Chiefs' Compliance Testing and Space Division, had been charged with the murder of Dr. Richard Joycelen. The murder weapon found at the scene, an army-issue, Italian-made Beretta 9-mm automatic handgun, belonged to the accused. This was confirmed through the weapon's serial number. In addition, his initials were engraved in the weapon's handle. No motive had been established, at least not in the reports that reached Margit's office, nor was there any mention of homosexuality. The investigation had been conducted by a special unit established by the secretary of defense, and included close cooperation with the FBI. Cobol was in custody at an unnamed location. End of statement. *"No questions at this time."*

The rain made it impossible to enjoy the center court for lunch that day, so Margit brought back to her office one of the seven thousand sandwiches and thirty thousand cups of coffee that would be purchased that day from the building's six cafeterias and nine stand-up snack bars. She considered going to POAC for a quick workout, but decided her time would be better spent at her desk.

Lieutenant Max Lanning was out of the building all afternoon driving SecDef's general counsel to meetings across the river. He returned just as Margit was packing up to leave. "Well, what do you think?" he asked her.

She shrugged. "Have you heard anything that hasn't already been around this building a hundred times?" she asked.

"No. I had an hour to kill waiting for him and popped into a bar with a TV. They ran the press conference again. Pretty short. Didn't say much."

"Well, I'm heading home," Margit said. "I'm sure they'll be repeating it every hour on TV. Have a nice evening, Lieutenant."

"You, too, Major."

She stopped at Building P-15 before going to her quarters, and worked out on a Nautilus and enjoyed the sauna. Refreshed, she went to her BOQ and flipped on the television. It was only minutes before a newscaster led into another rerun of portions of the Joycelen news conference. The announcement was made by Lieutenant General Morris Paley, director of the Defense Criminal Investigation Service, who'd been assigned by SecDef to spearhead the Joycelen investigation. He was joined at the podium by Frank Lazzarus, director of the Federal Bureau of Investigation.

"As unfortunate as this incident has been, we can take some solace in the speed with which the accused has been apprehended. A special task force that included selected members of the uniformed services, and special agents of the FBI, have worked round the clock to bring this phase to a quick conclusion. A brilliant and dedicated man, Dr.

Richard Joycelen, has been taken from us. I can assure everyone that justice will be pursued to its fullest extent under the Uniform Code of Military Justice. I can also assure you that the accused, Captain Robert Cobol, will be fairly tried under that same code."

The anchor reappeared and said that reporters' questions had not been answered, including those about the motive for the murder, the circumstances that had led investigators to Captain Cobol, whether he'd confessed to the crime, and whether legal counsel had been chosen. *"Stay tuned."* A commercial for a thirst-quenching, or thirst-inducing, soft drink filled the screen.

Her phone rang.

"Hello, Major. Mac Smith."

"Hi, Mac. We had a very nice time with you two."

"Good. And thanks for the flowers. How are you?"

"Fine. Annabel's prettier than any flower. Me? I just came back from working out."

He laughed. "So did I. You know what they say about a healthy body. Next I'll try for a healthy mind."

"To what do I owe the honor of this call?"

"Annabel and I were thinking of having a bite out. We know Jeff's away, and wondered if you'd care to join us."

It was tempting. It was Friday night, and she was off-duty until Monday morning, but she declined the offer. Things had been piling up on her lately—letters to write, reading to finish, a manicure to get to. "Another time, I hope," she said.

"Sure. I assume you've heard the news about Joycelen."

"Hard to miss."

"Anybody bring up the rumor of a homosexual slant to it?"

She thought of what Max Lanning had said but decided not to repeat it. He was the only person who'd raised it, and considering his penchant for gossip . . . "No, no facts on that. Have you?"

"Locker-room blatherskite. Doesn't make sense, considering Joycelen's long marital history." Before she could respond, he added, "Of course, being married doesn't necessarily mean a lifelong pledge to heterosexuality. Nasty business, those kinds of rumors. They can be misleading. Say 'gay,' and some people think all motives fall into place. If I've heard them, I'm sure it's all over town by now, replacing cocktail chat about nuclear bombs, aid to the Russians, and who

Beardsley will nominate for the Supreme Court vacancy. Well, wish you could join us, Margit. Annabel sends her best."

"And mine to her. It's nice—and therefore typical—of you two to think of me. Thanks for the invitation."

She changed into pajamas and robe, pulled the ingredients for a simple, healthy dinner from the refrigerator, and sat at the window. She missed Jeff. She wished they could spend time together that weekend. She thought of her father, with whom she'd been very close, and of her mother, whom she hardly knew at all. She was sad; it could turn into a depressing weekend if she allowed it. She looked at her nails and considered working on them. Looked as if they could use some rehabilitation. She picked up the phone and made an appointment with the base beauty shop for a haircut, manicure, and pedicure at eleven the next morning. Sometimes, you just had to do those things. They might not contribute to the security of the United States of America, but they'd do quite a bit for hers.

CHAPTER

SIX

 Under ordinary circumstances Margit would not have been required to keep the base locator informed of her whereabouts while off-duty. But because recent events in the Middle East didn't fall into the ordinary category, many Pentagon commands and offices had instructed their personnel to do just that. Margit felt slightly foolish informing the duty airman that she would be at the beauty parlor, but she did. As it turned out, it was just as well she had. The result, however, was one she could have done without.

Work on her fingers and toes had been completed. The polish on her nails was still wet; she was afraid to touch anything. Tiny pieces of white cotton separated her toes; her feet rested in paper sandals designed for such artwork. Her hair had been cut, and the young woman who'd wielded the scissors with considerable skill now held a dryer to Margit's shorter-shorn head.

"Phone call for Major Falk," a woman at the reception desk announced.

Desperation was painted on Margit's face. The woman laughed and said into the phone, "Major Falk is indisposed at the moment. Can she call you back in a half hour?" The reply was obviously negative. "Hold on," she said, placing the receiver on the desk and crossing to Margit's chair. "He says it's important."

Margit shuffled to the desk and picked up the phone between her thumb and middle finger as though it were contaminated. "Major Falk," she said.

"Major, this is Lieutenant Lanning."

An instant anger flared in her. She enjoyed their office banter, but to call her at home—even worse, here at the body-and-fender shop—was inexcusable.

"Sorry to bother you, Major, but this is no for-fun call. The boss told me to get ahold of you right away." The boss was Colonel James Bellis, general counsel to the secretary of defense.

"Why?" she asked, feeling less angry.

"He wants you at the office at two this afternoon," Lanning said.

"What for?"

"Major, I don't know. I'm just following orders."

"Is it a general staff meeting?"

"I don't know any more than what I'm telling you. But no. Two o'clock sharp."

"All right, I'll be there. Thank you for calling, Max."

"Hey, Major."

She sighed and rolled her eyes. "What?"

"I think it might have to do with the Cobol thing."

"Cobol?"

"Nothing tangible, except I heard his name mentioned yesterday afternoon, and I heard your name mentioned in the same breath."

She was not about to pursue this latest line of speculation, thanked him again, and hung up.

Being summoned to the General Counsel's Office set up several reactions in Margit. She suffered them simultaneously as she returned to her chair and waited for hair, hands, and feet to dry. Had she done something wrong to be summoned on a Saturday? Weekend duty wasn't unusual in the military, but this sounded serious. Could Max Lanning, Pentagon scandalmonger, be correct in his assessment? It was inconceivable that her meeting with Colonel Bellis could have anything to do with the murder of Dr. Richard Joycelen. She kept that thought in mind as she returned to her quarters and prepared for the meeting, paying particular attention to her uniform and shoes.

The Pentagon parking lot was only a quarter full. Still, she parked in her designated slot lest some overzealous security guard be called upon to boost his weekend summons tally. She went to her office and pretended to be busy, but her thoughts focused exclusively upon what she might face twenty minutes from now.

At 1:55 she entered the general counsel's reception area. The door to his office was closed, and she wished his secretary were there. She paced, checked her watch: two o'clock straight-up. She knocked. His familiar gruff voice barked, "Come in."

Colonel James Bellis was a contradiction in style. Very much the career soldier, exhibiting some of the rough edges career soldiers seem compelled to adopt, his law training—Harvard, and a stint at Oxford—spoke of considerable intellectual depth. He was a marine. The hair on the side of his head, and what was left on top, had been red but was now accented with gray. Freckles covered his forehead and spread up into his bald pate. He had the complexion of a redhead; Margit had heard that he'd had dozens of basal-cell skin cancers removed over the years. He liked to talk informally, off-the-cuff, but there was a military formality that could not be ignored. On this Saturday, seated at his desk, he had no rolled-up sleeves or tie pulled loose from the collar. He was in full uniform and sat erect in his chair.

"Major Falk, thanks for coming in. Sorry to screw up your Saturday."

"No problem for me, Colonel. A free weekend."

"Sit down. That chair."

She sat where he indicated and watched him rummage through a desk drawer. He didn't find what he was looking for and slammed the drawer shut. Then he looked at her as though surprised that she was there. "Sorry I haven't been able to devote much attention to you since you arrived," he said.

"That's all right, Colonel. I've been taken good care of. The staff has been extremely helpful."

"Glad to hear that." It was common knowledge that Colonel Bellis was not particularly pleased with several of his staff, particularly the civilian contingent. He preferred military attorneys, they said, and could be unnecessarily harsh on those who did not wear a uniform. His temper was well known. Margit had not, at least as yet, been victim of it, although once she had heard him bellow through the oak door that separated him from the rest of the free world. A tough boss, one to be understood and accommodated.

"I'd offer you coffee, or tea," he said, "but I don't have any made. Helen usually does that for me." He was referring to Helen Matthei, his administrative assistant, who performed myriad tasks far more important than filling the coffeepot in the morning.

"I've had coffee, Colonel, but thank you for thinking of it."

It was evident that Bellis, blunt as a bombardier, was having trouble getting to the point. Why? He was her superior. Did he want to assign her something unpleasant? Then do it. Along with making the choice of clothing in the morning easy, the military also made Margit appreciate its straightforward command process. No need to cajole, convince, even con, an employee to take on a task. Give the order. That simple, unless the order was clearly illegal, in which case the employee—someone of lesser rank—could balk on the basis of its illegality. He'd called her here. Tell her what to do, and, unless it *was* illegal, she'd do it. It was known as following orders.

Maybe Bellis sensed what Margit was thinking, because he leaned his elbows on his desk and said, "Let me get to the point, Major Falk. I have an important assignment for you."

"Yes, sir?"

"You've heard that Dr. Joycelen's murderer has been apprehended."

Margit withheld a smile. Did anyone *not* know that? "Yes, sir, I have."

"What have you heard?"

"That his name is Robert Cobol. That he's an army captain assigned to the CIA but stationed here at the Pentagon. I heard on the news that it was his weapon that was used to kill Dr. Joycelen." She paused. "I think that's all."

"There's more."

"Oh?"

"It's full of twists and turns, some of them not very pleasant."

She said nothing.

"Look, Major, let me ask you a couple of questions. Have you had much experience with military law?"

"No, sir, not much. Not enough, anyhow. I was assigned the defense of a couple of airmen at my previous assignment."

"How'd you do?"

She smiled. "I won both cases."

"Beat the system, did you? Beat our employer?"

"I never viewed it that way. In both cases the Command was wrong in its charges. They weren't cases involving serious crime, just infractions."

"Murdering the deputy director of DARPA is no infraction."

"I would agree with that."

"Would you have trouble defending a fellow officer who gunned down somebody like Joycelen?"

She didn't know how to respond. My God, Lanning had been right. She was being interviewed for the role of defense counsel for Captain Cobol. If there was a right moment to beg off, this was it. He was giving her an out.

"Trouble defending such a person?" she asked. The question filled the gap in her thinking.

"Yes, for you. Philosophical difficulties. Outraged at the crime and unable to mount a decent defense." He cocked his head. "Afraid defending such a person wouldn't be good for the career."

His last comment nettled. "I'm very secure in my military career, Colonel," she said. "I think I'm a good officer. I also think that the air force recognizes ability and dedication and rewards it accordingly."

He sat back as though she'd slapped him. Then he laughed. "No offense, Major, but we do have military lawyers who shy away from cases because they think taking them on might upset someone up the chain of command. Obviously, you don't fall into that group."

"No, I don't think I do."

They scrutinized each other in silence for a moment. She broke the quiescence. "Why me?"

"A lot of reasons. I'm told you're bright. Maybe even better than bright. I've got a bunch of bright boys who can't find the door. I'm told your law training was top-notch. Law Review at G.W. A protégé of Mackensie Smith. Smart as a whip, I'm told. Impressive."

Margit had been doing some hard thinking for the past minute. She drew a deep breath before saying, "Colonel Bellis, may I be direct with you, sir?"

"I'd welcome it."

"Sir, I don't wish to defend Captain Cobol."

"Why not?"

"Because I don't think I'm qualified."

"Nothing to do with the career?"

"No, sir!"

"Sorry, Major, but I've made a decision while sitting here. I like what I see. I like what I hear. I am assigning you to the defense of Captain Robert Cobol, charged with the murder of Dr. Richard Joycelen, deputy director of the Defense Advanced Project Research Agency."

"May I have time to consider this?"

"No, ma'am."

She broke the stare between them and looked at photographs on his wall. The assignment made no sense. The Trial Defense Service was rife with qualified military lawyers whose job it was to defend members of the armed forces before military tribunals. She was not part of that service. Since earning her law degree, she'd been immersed in a perpetual flow of paper, contracts, regs, position papers. Her desk was heaped with contracts relating to Project Safekeep. "Party of the first part" stuff. Nothing murderous, aside from the hours spent in search of vague paragraphs and misleading statements. She'd never tried a murder case in her life, civilian or military.

Why me?

She asked.

Bellis stood. "Major Falk, the murder of Dr. Joycelen has ramifications beyond what might be apparent at this moment. Let me ask you another question. How do you feel about homosexuals?"

There it was. The rumor—first from Max Lanning, then from Mac Smith. It obviously had some validity. Or at least life. She shrugged. "I think they lead a difficult life because society makes it so," she said flatly.

"Nice sentiment, but you aren't working for the ACLU. We have military regulations that say that if you're a homosexual, you're out."

"Yes, sir, I'm aware of that. Why are you asking me this?"

"Because it is possible that Captain Cobol is a homosexual, and that he killed Dr. Joycelen over a purely personal matter between them."

"Dr. Joycelen was gay?"

"I prefer the original meaning of the word. He evidently was bisexual. Now, how do you feel about all of this, Major?"

She'd become exasperated. She wanted to get out of there, to take a long walk, to think. His questions were premature, and she felt singularly ill equipped to answer them with even a measure of intelligence. She said, "Sir, if I am being assigned to the defense of Captain Cobol, I will have to accept that assignment. I understand that. If Captain Cobol is a homosexual, and if the motive for the murder revolves around that, I will have to deal with that circumstance as any attorney would, in any criminal case. I do not want this assignment. I am not interested in defending Captain Cobol because I am ill equipped, and anyone accused of murder deserves experienced counsel. I respectfully ask you to reconsider your choice."

He nodded. "Yes, Major Falk, I will give it some additional consideration. But don't count on me changing my mind. I'm not famous for it like some presidents and secretaries of defense."

She stood. "May I go?"

"Of course. Look, Major, I'm sorry that we have had our first substantive conversation under these circumstances. I could have done without being given this assignment by SecDef. This is a no-win situation for me . . . and it probably will be for you . . . provided I don't change my mind." He smiled. "Major Falk, I don't intend to change my mind. Sorry. You're it. Give him the best defense you're capable of, which, I'm confident, will be considerable. I'd like to meet with you Monday morning at eight, here, in this office."

He walked her to the door. "Foul up your weekend pretty good?" he asked.

"Oh, yes, sir, you certainly did." She couldn't help but laugh. With all his exterior gruffness, Bellis was a nice man. She liked him, despite the fact that he *had* truly screwed up her weekend.

He had a final word before she left. "Let's keep this between us, Major Falk, at least until an announcement can be made next week."

"I wish you hadn't said that, Colonel Bellis."

"Why?"

"Because I intended, the minute I got back to my quarters, to call Mackensie Smith and become a law student again."

Bellis laughed. "You want to discuss it with your former law professor? Go right ahead, Major, but keep it at that. The one thing

I don't want is the media to get hold of this until we've decided how and when to give it to them."

"Understood," Margit said.

"Good. By the way, a question off the subject. What do you think of Lieutenant Lanning?"

"Think of him? He's a capable young officer."

"He's like a little old lady, a gossipy young man."

"I wouldn't know about that, sir. He seems to have your best interests at heart."

"Glad to hear it. One thing we don't need around here is a tale-teller. Thank you for coming in on your leisurely Saturday, Major. I look forward to working with you."

She wished she could say the same and, of course, did.

"Annabel?"

"Yes."

"Margit Falk."

"Margit. How are you? Sorry you couldn't join us for dinner last night. We ended up having pizza at Belmont Kitchen. You might have saved us."

"I'm glad now I didn't join you. It takes two hours in the gym to get rid of a Belmont pizza."

"How is Jeff?" Annabel asked.

"Still off in Wisconsin with Wishengrad. I had a simple weekend planned, but I ended up in a meeting with my boss at the Pentagon."

"I hope we aren't going to war this weekend," Annabel said.

Margit laughed. "No, but from my perspective, that might be preferable to what I've been handed." As far as she was concerned, flying night missions over Panama's jungles, with snipers boring holes in her Blackhawk helicopter, was a less daunting assignment than what she had just been given by Colonel James Bellis.

"Sounds heavy," Annabel said.

"Yes, it is. Is the professor around?"

A lilting laugh from Annabel. "Somehow, I don't view him as a professor on weekends. More a grouchy home handyman who hits his thumb too often. Yes, he's here. He just came back from walking Rufus. Or vice versa. Hold on."

"Hello, Margit," Smith said.

"I need to talk to you, Mac."

"Missed you last night. We had pizza."

"I heard. Mac, I need some informal consultation. I'm defending Captain Robert Cobol for the murder of Dr. Richard Joycelen."

There was silence on the other end. Then Smith said, "Get on over here."

CHAPTER
SEVEN

 Most of Consulnet's board had trickled into Vienna during that Saturday, although some had arrived the night before. They'd gathered for dinner in a small private dining room at Korso, the elegant restaurant in the Bristol Hotel, on the Kärntner Ring, in which they all were staying.

They'd dined sumptuously on specialties of the house—some enjoying *Schweinsjungfrau*, commonly known as "pig's virgin," others eschewing pork for fish dishes like *Fogosch* and *Krebse*. Two of the eight men stuck to less adventuresome schnitzel. The Dutch member of the group selected an Austrian wine, Gumpoldskirchen, which the others agreed had been a good and tasty choice, although the French representative had muttered something about its fruitiness being carried to a criminal extreme.

It was almost midnight; dishes had been cleared, and dessert and coffee delivered. Sacher torte was served to all. Most preferred simple black coffee—*Schwarzer*—with a few opting for a touch of rum in theirs, the *Mokka gespritzt* version. One of those choosing the alcoholic rendition was an American, Paul Potamos, who sat at the head of the table not by chance, but because he projected a leadership persona. He wasn't a big man—no more than five feet eight inches tall—nor did he have the Central Casting look of a captain of industry. He was quite bald, and there was a sheen to the swarthy skin atop his head. His parentage was Greek, although he'd been born in the United States. Sixty years old, heir to his family's shipping company, he'd guided it to even greater success. Business associates, especially those with whom he'd butted heads, considered him arrogant. He preferred to view himself as self-confident, a character trait helped in no small degree by money.

Potamos yawned and looked at his watch. "Unless there is further business to discuss," he said, "I suggest we call it a night."

"There is further business," the Brazilian Consulnet representative said.

"Which is?"

"Payments. He's behind, too far behind to ignore."

Potamos looked to the German member of the board, Hans Keller, who'd been pleased that Potamos wanted to end the evening. Keller had someone waiting in his room. He knew she wouldn't leave; she'd been paid for the night. But to waste such pleasurable time was anathema. "How much does he owe, Hans?" Potamos asked.

Keller, a large, fleshy man whose shirt collar was too small, shrugged. "He paid thirty-three million. He owes another thirty."

"Just for the yellowcakes," said the connoisseur, Sidney Cheval. "Raoul is right. He's too far in arrears. Thirty million for the yellowcakes alone. Our Japanese supplier is asking questions. Who can blame him?"

"Other payments?" asked Potamos. "Other debts?"

Keller laughed, then coughed on smoke from his cigar. "I told you when we entered into this contract that we were asking too little in advance. The vacuum pumps are a good example. Twenty percent as a down payment? Absurd. He hasn't paid another Ostmark." Keller was a former East German who hadn't needed the Wall to come down to prosper. Germany was all one now; it had always been for him.

"The lathes and milling machines," said the Brit at the table, Sanford Sheffield. "And the nickel alloy. If I recall correctly, he put up nothing for those items."

"He made a small payment against those invoices," Keller said. "Very small."

Potamos stood. "Gentlemen," he said, a smile on his small face, "I'm afraid I'm too weary to deal with such high finance. Perhaps tomorrow, if you feel it's necessary. These are really pennies. I remind you that when Consulnet took on this challenge, it was done with the understanding that shortfalls would be guaranteed."

"Yes, but . . ."

"I prefer to wait and see to what extent our client decides to ignore his financial obligations. When that is clear, the guarantees will kick in. I think we're premature in assuming that we'll encounter a problem being paid for our work. It's made him, as we say, the talk of the town." He looked to Keller again. "When will you be meeting with the client again, Hans?"

"The talk of many towns. The talk of the world. In a few days."

"A firm date?"

"Nothing is ever firm with him."

Potamos sighed. "Well, I suggest we wait until you have that meeting. Get together with Walter, establish what is owed, and report back to us after you've met with our client. Our next meeting is the end of September, I believe. Where?"

Raoul Cinsere, the Brazilian, answered. "London."

"Good. The financial report will be first on our agenda. Good sleep to all. Are we gathering for lunch tomorrow?"

Walter Munch said, "At one. At Glacisbeisl. I left directions in your mailboxes."

"Splendid," said Potamos.

As he left the private dining room with Keller, he asked, "A redhead this time, Hans?"

Keller blushed and forced a laugh. "Tea. A cousin. Brunette. I haven't seen her in a long time."

"How nice seeing family again. Enjoy your reunion."

Two waiters started to clean the room in which Consulnet had met. "Important men," one said.

The other grunted. "Yes, important men. Expensive rooms and meals, small gratuities. I did better in the coffeehouses."

CHAPTER
EIGHT

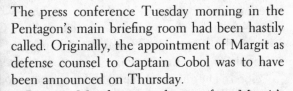

The press conference Tuesday morning in the Pentagon's main briefing room had been hastily called. Originally, the appointment of Margit as defense counsel to Captain Cobol was to have been announced on Thursday.

But on Monday, two hours after Margit's 8 A.M. meeting with Colonel Bellis, the Armed Forces News Division, an office reporting to the assistant secretary of defense for public affairs, received a call from a *Washington Post* Pentagon reporter. The journalist wanted to confirm whether a Major Falk had, in fact, been assigned to defend Captain Robert Cobol, and wanted permission to speak with her. The duty officer promised to get back to him and immediately contacted Bellis.

"How the hell did they get this?" Bellis bellowed at three members of his staff who had the misfortune to be within a hundred yards, which included Margit. His hard stare at her made her wonder whether he was assuming that her conversation with Mac Smith had resulted in the leak. She knew it hadn't. She hadn't had to impress upon Smith the need to keep it under wraps until the official announcement was made, and she had faith in his discretion.

Bellis called the officer who'd reported the press inquiry. "Tell that reporter there'll be a press conference tomorrow morning at ten. Set up that conference. Get the word out to the rest of the vultures, so we get credit for announcing it."

He hung up, sat back, and shook his head. "If a leak came out of this office, the person who did it will be a former member of this office." And of this planet, Margit thought. He dismissed everyone except Margit. When they were alone and his door was closed, he sat on the edge of his desk. "Did you have your discussion with Smith?" he asked.

"Yes, sir, I did."

"Did you tell him the need for secrecy?"

"Whatever we talked about never left his house. Among other things, he's a master of discretion."

Bellis nodded. "I would tend to have that same confidence, although I know Smith only by reputation. Any ideas who leaked it?"

Margit shook her head.

"I meant what I said. If it came out of this office, I'm going to lop off that individual's head and roll it down the hall like a bowling ball."

Margit couldn't help but smile, and Bellis seemed pleased that she'd found humor in it. He sat behind the desk. "Plans for lunch, Major?"

"No. I assume any eating today will be done at my desk."

"Wrong, Major. Any eating you do today will be done at *my* desk. We have a lot to go over before tomorrow morning. I suggest you go back to your office and take care of whatever matters are pressing. When you're free, call Helen and tell her you're ready to meet with me. I have appointments this afternoon that I'll cancel, at least those that don't bear upon this case." Margit stood. "Ready for a long, tough haul, Major?"

"Do I have a choice?"

"None whatsoever. See you in a couple of hours."

Margit canceled appointments for that afternoon. Her final call was to Foxboro at Senator Wishengrad's office. They'd made a tentative date for a drink and early dinner. "Jeff, I'm not sure what time I'm going to be out of here tonight. Something broke that could tie me up for a while."

"Like what?" he asked, sounding distracted.

"I really can't discuss it on the phone. In fact, I can't discuss it at all until tomorrow morning after it's been announced at a press conference."

Now, his attention seemed more focused. "Don't tease, Margit. It's annoying. What's up?"

She was sorry she'd called, or at least she should have begged off the evening without hinting that something extraordinary was taking place. She said, "I know, it isn't fair, but my hands are tied. Please understand. If I see that I'll be able to leave at a decent hour, I'll call, and we'll meet as planned."

"Call either way," he said. He sounded angry.

"If I get a chance." She hung up and felt unsettled. There had been these minor tugs and strains lately. She chalked them up to the pressure of their jobs, and had recently considered taking a few days' leave, suggesting to Jeff that he take time off, too, and maybe they'd get away together for an extended weekend. But this was no time to be thinking about leave. She called Helen Matthei, Colonel Bellis's administrative assistant, and said she was ready to meet. Helen buzzed him, then came back on the line and told Margit to be there in a half hour. It was twelve-thirty. She was suddenly hungry. Would he order in some lunch for them? She hoped so, because she didn't have time. They may say that no two offices are more than seven minutes apart in the Pentagon, but you couldn't prove it by her. Going downstairs to the nearest snack bar would take at least fifteen minutes. More if she took a wrong turn.

"I have two hours before I have to meet with SecDef," Bellis said to Margit. "That means we have two hours to choreograph the press conference." Margit wasn't sure she liked his choice of words.

Bellis continued. "Aside from making sure that the military justice system is followed to the letter, we have two other things to accomplish. First, the public must be assured that Captain Cobol will be prosecuted to the fullest extent. He's not only been accused of murder, the victim was a well-known expert in the field of military weapons research. It also happened on military property." His laugh was sardonic. "The Pentagon, peacekeeping HQ, no less. Second, the public has to be assured that the accused receives the fullest and fairest defense available." He sighed. "In other words, Major, this had better be a textbook trial on both sides."

Margit had formulated a list of questions. Before asking them, however, she said, "In my defense, Colonel, is there any chance of getting something to eat?"

"I've always admired pragmatic lawyers. I'll have Helen order something up. What's your pleasure?"

"Chicken salad on whole wheat," she said. "And coffee."

They got back to the topic at hand. "Does Captain Cobol know I've been assigned to his defense?" Margit asked.

"Yes."

"Does he accept me as his counsel?"

"Evidently."

"Considering the seriousness of the charge, I would think he might invoke his right to civilian counsel."

"As far as I know, he hasn't asked for that. Sure, he's entitled. We'll make sure he understands that it's one of his rights. How would you feel about being co-counsel?"

"Fine with me," Margit said. She'd been hoping it would end up that way. She'd feel considerably more comfortable defending an accused murderer with a savvy civilian criminal attorney at her side.

She asked where Cobol was being detained.

"McNair."

The army base, Fort Lesley J. McNair, sat on a strip of land south of the U.S. Capitol in the District of Columbia, just across the Anacostia River from the Anacostia Naval Station and Bolling Air Force Base. Its history as a detention center was long and colorful. The oldest active military post in America, it was where, on July 7, 1865, four men were hanged for their conspiracy in the assassination of President Lincoln, and where the body of John Wilkes Booth was secretly buried until removed two years later. These days, its stately grounds housed the National War College, the armed forces' most prestigious training center for senior military officers.

"Will I have a chance to talk to Captain Cobol before tomorrow's press conference?" Margit asked.

"That was part of the plan when the announcement was to be made—on Thursday. I don't want to rush you out there. If you're asked whether you've conferred with the accused, say that you will be doing that within the next forty-eight hours."

Margit said, "I'll have to take a close look at what evidence against Cobol Command has accumulated. By the way, who is Command in this case?" She was referring to the concept under the Uniform Code of Military Justice in which the commander in whose jurisdiction a crime has been committed assumes ultimate responsibility for the prosecution and defense of an accused.

Bellis said, "The chairman himself."

"If the chairman of the Joint Chiefs is the commander under which this court-martial takes place, that creates a conflict of interest for me." She waited for a response. When Bellis said nothing, she added, "Doesn't it?"

"How so?"

"Well, the UCMJ spells it out pretty clearly that defense counsel is not to be drawn from the command in which the crime took place."

"Right, Major, but you aren't assigned to the Joint Chiefs. You're assigned to SecDef."

"I suppose you're technically correct, Colonel, but it does seem to be splitting hairs."

He shook his head. "No, I've run this past the Chiefs' staff judge advocate. He's overseeing this for the chairman and sees no conflict."

"I just thought I'd raise it," Margit said.

"That's why we're sitting here. Raise anything and everything you want. Let's just make sure we're not cutting each other's legs off at the conference."

Margit asked, "To what extent am I to participate in tomorrow's conference?"

"As little as possible. I've prepared a statement that includes you in it, your military background, legal training, qualifications to undertake the defense of Cobol, all the things the assembled will want to hear."

She hesitated before saying, "Including the fact that I am a relatively new military attorney and have never tried a murder case before?"

"I don't intend to make a point of that. No need to. You have defended in military courts. Period. If the question comes up, answer it truthfully, but keep in mind that while you're the attorney-of-record, you'll have the support of my entire staff. If you need more than that, we'll arrange for you to go out and get it."

They spent the next hour forecasting and examining every detail that might arise at the conference. Bellis handed Margit a folder containing Cobol's military records. "Familiarize yourself with what's in there before tomorrow," he said.

That meant some heavy reading that night. She'd already packed into her briefcase as much legal background as she could find to help prepare a credible defense for an accused murderer in the military system of justice. What she really wanted to do was to bolt from Bellis's office, from the building itself, and run to Mackensie Smith, sit at his feet, and soak in his wisdom as she'd done so many times as a student. But she knew she couldn't do that. He'd been generous with his time on Saturday, listening mostly, asking questions, probing her feelings, assuring her that she had what it took to face the challenge of defending an accused murderer. When she was leaving, he encouraged her to talk things out with him at any time. But she couldn't—wouldn't—take advantage.

It was quarter to three. Fifteen more minutes with Bellis, then back to her office. She should go directly to her quarters and read, but decided to call Foxboro just to see if she could resurrect their dinner plans. She needed the break, felt she would be better equipped to digest what she was reading after a few hours' respite.

"Jeff, Margit."

"Congratulations," he said.

"For what?"

"I just heard on the radio that you're defending Cobol."

"You heard it on the *radio*? We're having the press conference tomorrow at ten."

"An academic exercise, I suppose. Jesus, how did you get roped into that?"

"I've been asking myself the same question. Feel like that drink and dinner? Maybe you could help me come up with an answer."

"You should have turned it down."

"I tried. No luck."

"Margit, you don't have much of a legal background."

She stiffened at the comment; it seemed unnecessarily broad. He sensed it, adding, "I mean, you have a good background, but have you ever defended anybody charged with a crime of this magnitude?"

"You know I haven't. I brought that up, but it doesn't seem to make any difference. Besides, Colonel Bellis assures me I'll have the total resources of his office available to me. Jeff, there's no sense in beating to death whether I should be in this position or not. I am.

That's the unfortunate reality. I have a lot of catching up to do before the press conference tomorrow, but I would love a relaxing drink and dinner with you." She paused. "I really need that, Jeff."

"Okay. When you called earlier, I figured we were off for tonight, and I decided to hang in here to finish a project. It can wait until tomorrow. Where are we meeting?"

She flushed with relief and pleasure. "You name it," she said.

"Feel like Thai?"

"Sure."

"Thai Taste, the Georgetown one."

"What time?"

"Six?"

"See you there. And . . . thanks, Jeff."

They ate charcoal-grilled marinated chicken, a platter of *satays,* and talked for three hours. Foxboro did most of it once Margit had exhausted her comments and thoughts about being assigned to the Cobol case. On most social occasions Foxboro was more of a listener than a talker, but when he was obsessed by something, he could launch into a long and detailed monologue on the subject. This night, it was the effect the detonation of the nuclear device in the Middle East was having upon military budget hearings on the Hill, and on the atmosphere in the Pentagon. A vast army of lobbyists, military and civilian alike, were coming down hard on Congress to restore massive cuts that had taken place over the past two years. "If only they'd stop at restoring the cuts, maybe we could live with some of it, but they not only want to bring the budget back up to where it was, they want millions more tossed into it."

"He does pose a much more substantial threat now that he has nuclear capability," Margit said.

"Sure, everybody understands that, but it shouldn't mean that two years of domestic social reform have to go down the drain. Christ, you people have been running this country for years."

" 'You people'!"

She hated it when he did that, lumped her into the giant military bureaucracy instead of viewing her for what she was, a human being who happened to have chosen a career in the military, a woman who knew she was falling in love with him, not without reservations, certainly not as a cognitive act; rather, it was a purely emotional, visceral reaction of a woman to a man.

She reached across the table and touched his hand. "Jeff, let's not end the evening in a debate over the military budget. I know you feel deeply about it, and I respect that, but when you say 'you people,' you stop viewing me as an individual."

"An individual who happens to be a major in the air force."

"Yes, but so what? I don't set policy. I'm a lawyer, like you, and I also happen to love flying. That doesn't make me part of some military conspiracy you seem to be reacting to."

"You're right, Margit. You're a lawyer, just like me. The difference is how we apply our legal training."

She thought he was referring to the fact that he was in the civilian sector, while she was military, that he applied his legal training and mind to what he considered more worthwhile social issues. But then he said, "I can't believe it, Margit, that you'd defend that fag."

She sat back and frowned.

"That doesn't sound like the Jeff Foxboro I know."

One of the many things that had attracted her to him was his concern for, and commitment to, social justice, especially for what were called society's disenfranchised and minorities.

He knew he'd gone too far. His emotions had run away with him. He drew a deep breath and smiled. "Sorry, Margit, I know we were having dinner to let you get this thing off your chest. I also know that you don't want this assignment but that you don't have a choice because you're in the military. You take orders. I guess that bothers me a little because I don't believe anybody should have to blindly follow orders when what they're being told to do runs contrary to what they believe." He held up his hands. "But I understand. I even know the cure. Feel like some ice cream?"

She tried to match his sudden turnaround in mood but had difficulty. He'd deflated her, and she was resentful. Still, she put on a smile. "I would love some ice cream," she said, "but not tonight. I really have to get back and dig into this reading."

His car was parked a block away. She hadn't been so lucky; hers was three blocks away.

"I'll walk you to your car," he said.

"No need, but thanks for offering. I may take a roundabout way. I could use some exercise after that meal."

He pulled her to him, and they embraced. She realized she was on the verge of tears but also knew she would not allow them to flow. They kissed, and she felt a physical yearning for him—and dismissed it.

"Sure you have to do all this reading tonight?" he asked.

"Afraid so."

"We need some time together, Margit. Quiet, personal time."

"Yes, I know. I was thinking maybe we could arrange to get away for a few days, a long weekend, maybe go down to the shore."

"From the sound of this case, you're not going to see leave time for quite a while."

"I promise I'll find time."

"How about this weekend? It's Labor Day."

She hesitated. "All right. We'll try. Let's put it on our calendars, book the time. I'd better stay in town, though. Saturday night, Sunday? Just hang out?"

"Sounds good." He kissed her again, then watched her walk away, turn the corner, and disappear.

CHAPTER

NINE

Margit stood on the platform next to Bellis. On her other side was the Joint Chiefs' staff judge advocate, Colonel Thomas Detienne, whose responsibility, among others, was to act as legal adviser to the command. Detienne was a tall, pudgy man whose uniform bowed out in front, yet who carried himself well. His curly hair was the color of pewter. He wore horn-rim glasses. Margit had noticed during their first meeting that he had a slight stammer. Detienne was an inveterate golfer; his large, carpeted office included a long felt putting green. He almost had room for nine holes.

Margit judged the number of press present to be in excess of fifty, although she hadn't taken a head count. She was too nervous.

Detienne spoke first, confining his short remarks to his role in the proceedings. He announced that a general court-martial would be convened in the near future, and that trial counsel for the command and defense counsel for the accused had been chosen. He turned the podium over to Bellis.

Bellis spoke from a neatly typed script: "As you all know, a commissioned member of the armed forces has been charged with the murder of Dr. Richard Joycelen. His name is Robert Cobol, captain, United States Army. He is currently being held at army detention facilities at Fort McNair. An arraignment proceeding will be held later this week under the rules of the Uniform Code of Military Justice, and the *Manual for Courts-Martial.* Counsel has been assigned. I will introduce one of them to you in a moment."

Margit smiled. It was a reflex, and a nervous one at that. Heat from the TV lights outgunned the room's AC. Let me out of here, she thought.

"The purpose of military law, as it was conceived in the Articles of War used during the American Revolution, is best stated in the 1984 *Manual for Courts-Martial*. The manual states, 'The purpose of military law is to promote justice, to assist in maintaining good order and discipline in the armed forces, to promote efficiency and effectiveness in the military establishment, and thereby to strengthen the national security of the United States.' The general court-martial of Captain Cobol will be conducted under, and will adhere to, every tenet of the military system of justice.

"At his arraignment Captain Cobol will be permitted to enter a plea. He will be represented at that proceeding by his defense counsel. It is, of course, obvious to each of you that this case has significant ramifications. The victim was a highly esteemed member of the scientific community. Dr. Joycelen was deputy director of the Defense Advanced Research Project Agency, known to most of you as DARPA. Dr. Joycelen's contributions to national security through his untiring efforts to maintain, and to improve, this country's military capability to defend itself, are well documented. We have lost a valuable member of the community, and his loss will be felt for a long time."

A still photographer crouched low as he approached the podium. He stopped directly beneath Margit and trained his lens on her. *Click. Click.* She thought of the *Playboy* photographer and winced. At least she had her clothes on.

"At the same time, while Captian Cobol has been accused of this crime, he has not been convicted of it. While the military system of justice differs in certain areas from the civilian system of justice, the basic rights of the accused are as steadfastly protected as those of any alleged criminal tried under the civilian system.

"There have been a number of rumors surrounding this case that only add to its unpleasantness. I would suggest that those rumors be dispelled until the facts are brought out through a proper tribunal. For that reason I respectfully request that your questions following the prepared statements deal only with substantive facts." He glanced up and smiled. "You might as well heed my suggestion.

Questions outside the appropriate aspects of this case will be ignored anyway."

"Ignoring those questions won't make them go away, Colonel Bellis," a reporter yelled.

"It certainly will accomplish that during this meeting," Bellis shot back.

He returned to his prepared text: "Because of the seriousness of the crime being charged here, and the severity of the possible punishments should a conviction be obtained, the court-martial of Captain Cobol will be held under regulations governing a general court-martial. A minimum of five commissioned officers shall sit on the court. In addition, a military judge assigned by the U.S. Army Trial Judiciary, and appointed by the judge advocate general, will sit with the other chosen officers. Although this case will be tried under the command of the Joint Chiefs of Staff, the military judge will be chosen from another command. As some of you may be aware, military judges are rated by other judges, not by commanders, to ensure their independence."

Margit considered Bellis to be a short-and-to-the-point man. Why was he going on so long, and in such detail? The press didn't want a primer on military law. They wanted the juicy parts of the murder.

"Trial counsel for the command, the military's equivalent of a civilian prosecutor, has been assigned by the chief of criminal law under the guidance of Colonel Detienne's office. That officer will be made known to you later today, and will be present at the arraignment."

She now understood. He was going on for several reasons. First, by dragging it out, he was giving the journalists the impression of a full and fair briefing, and making the parallel point that he respected the fact that they had their jobs to do, too. Second, he was keeping the heat off her. By taking up time with the practices and procedures of military law, he held the press at bay from questioning her, and he could end the conference without it seeming premature. For this she was grateful. Third, he almost surely did want them to understand the law, at least to the extent it could be explained in so brief a time, and under such circumstances.

Sometimes in Washington things were done for the announced purpose, and individuals actually meant what they said.

"Defense counsel for Captain Cobol stands next to me, air force major Margit Falk. Major Falk has an outstanding record as a commissioned officer in the United States Air Force. She is a flight-rated officer, and has served with distinction in that capacity in a number of previous assignments. She is also an attorney, having received her law degree with honors from George Washington University. Her current assignment at the Pentagon is to the secretary of defense's general counsel. While she has been designated as lead defense counsel, she will have at her disposal the full resources of my office, as well as support from outside my office should she deem it necessary in order to properly represent the accused." He looked at Margit and smiled, then turned to the microphone. "I have asked Major Falk if she wished to present any prepared comments. She declines to do that, although she will remain with us for a brief question-and-answer period. I remind you that in the interest of justice and fairness, many aspects of this unfortunate event will not be open to discussion by either defense or trial counsel. That said, I invite your questions."

The media representatives in the room had plenty of questions to ask. Throughout, those regarding the allegations that Dr. Joycelen and Captain Cobol had been engaged in a homosexual relationship were firmly set aside by Bellis.

One reporter asked about the propriety, to say nothing of legality, of keeping Cobol in detention without formal charges having been brought. Bellis replied that the duration of his detention was well within defined military law, and that the formal arraignment would take place within the next few days.

"Major Falk, have you met with the accused?"

Margit stepped to the microphone to field her first question. "No, I have not, although I will be doing that well in advance of the arraignment."

"What is your background in defending accused murderers?" she was asked.

"If you're asking whether I have ever defended an accused murderer, the answer is no."

"Colonel Bellis, you talk about making sure Captain Cobol gets the best possible defense, yet you assign someone without prior experience. How does that jibe with your previous statement?"

Bellis stared down from the podium at the young reporter and asked in measured tones, "Have you ever written about an accused murderer from the armed forces?"

There was some laughter in the room. "The point I'm making," Bellis said, "is that a good journalist, given the proper amount of material, should be able to write about anything. The same holds true for a good attorney. Major Falk's academic background, as well as her performance in her military duties as an attorney, are exemplary. She has experience in military courtrooms. Next question."

"We've been told that the murder weapon belonged to Captain Cobol, that there is no doubt about that. How do you intend to handle that piece of incriminating evidence, Major Falk?"

"That particular allegation, along with others, will be dealt with at the appropriate time and, as Colonel Bellis has said, in an appropriate tribunal. Now that I have been assigned to the defense of Captain Cobol, it would be unprofessional to discuss specific aspects of his defense."

"Do you feel that being a woman played any role in being chosen to defend Captain Cobol, considering the alleged personal spin that's been put on this case?"

"No comment," said Margit.

Other questions were asked in flurries, some worthy of response, others pushed aside by Bellis. Eventually, after glancing at his watch, he announced the conference was over and left the room with Detienne and Margit. Once in the sanctity of a small room behind the podium, Bellis said to her, "You did nicely, Major. You handled yourself well."

"Thank you, sir."

"I've arranged with the authorities at McNair to have you meet with Cobol at four this afternoon."

It struck Margit that it was presumptuous of Bellis to arrange such a meeting without first conferring with her. Now that she was defense counsel, it should be up to her to set schedules, to determine where and when such meetings occurred. She didn't express those feelings, however. In this festival, there wouldn't always be time for the niceties. Actually, she was pleased that she would get to meet her client that day. It was the first, and potentially most painful, step she would have to take as she embarked on a course she never would have dreamed a week ago would be hers to navigate.

. . .

As the press conference at the Pentagon was taking place, Senator Henry "Hank" Wishengrad called to order a special closed-door hearing of the Senate Armed Services Committee in the stately, old-fashioned Senate Hearing Room in the Russell Building. Wishengrad sat in the chairman's position at the raised table. Flanking him were other members of the committee. Seated directly behind him were Jeff Foxboro and a young woman also on the senator's staff.

In front of the senators was a long witness table at which four men sat. They had not been subpoenaed to appear; their presence was voluntary. The meeting had been called by Wishengrad in the hope that these four, all experts, would shed some needed light on the recent events in the Middle East, particularly as applied to the intense pressure by the military to obtain billions more for the defense budget.

Facing Wishengrad, from left to right, the four were director of the Central Intelligence Agency, Thomas Hickey; the staff coordinator for the Nuclear Weapons Council Standing Committee (NWCSC), Colonel Paul Burt; Bruce Massingill, DOD's undersecretary for policy; and the vice chairman of the Joint Chiefs of Staff, General Walker Getlin. Familiar faces to Wishengrad because they'd testified before his committee in the past. Of the four, he personally disliked only one, the civilian Massingill, the Pentagon's undersecretary for policy. It wasn't his abrasive, curt personality that bothered the senator as much as the evident power he wielded, and the blatant pleasure he took in exercising it. Massingill's office was unofficially called, in Congress and in the White House, "the Little State Department." Much to the chagrin of Warren Smith, the administration's "real" secretary of state, Massingill often conducted matters of state under a cloak of Pentagon security that ran contrary to the long-term programs and goals of State itself. That the Pentagon engaged in numerous and far-reaching covert operations, with its "black budgets" and secret joint operations with the CIA, was no secret to anyone within the Beltway. It was, Hank Wishengrad often thought, like two separate governments—the military with its seemingly unlimited funds and penchant for taking action anywhere on the globe without conferring with other elements of the administration and Congress, and the civilian, elected element of government, too often kept in the dark about such things and, when driven to probe, often rebuffed under the claim of national-security considerations.

Wishengrad adjusted his microphone, cleared his throat, and said, "Good morning, gentlemen. I'm sure I speak for my colleagues on the committee when I thank you for taking your valuable time to share your knowledge and insight with us. As you know, recent events in the Middle East have pressed upon this committee the need to quickly and thoroughly reevaluate in the coming days levels of defense spending.

"It is not, of course, defense spending. It is the spending of tax dollars earned and sent to us here in Washington by our citizenry. It is the people's spending—or, to be more precise, spending done for them and in their names.

"We have had testimony behind these closed doors from a number of people, all of them dedicated to the preservation of this nation's security, yet many of them disagreeing on the extent needed for an enhanced military capability. Frankly, I personally have heard so many conflicting opinions that I walked into this room this morning hoping, for purely selfish reasons, that a few hours spent with you would shine a welcome light of reason, honesty, and good old-fashioned common sense on this situation."

Wishengrad asked each committee member if he or she (Martha Carlisle was on the committee) had any preliminary comments. A few did, but they kept them short. The absence this day in the room of C-Span's live television cameras brought about a welcome brevity on the part of the politicians seated at the raised table.

Two of the witnesses—NWCSC's Colonel Burt, and JCS's General Getlin, delivered prepared statements. No surprises, nor had Wishengrad expected any. The four witnesses represented the military side of the debate, including the CIA's Hickey, who although not a member of the military always made it obvious that his sentiments were with it.

After the opening statements Wishengrad was the first to question by virtue of his position as chairman. "Let me be up-front with you gentlemen about the thing that has me most puzzled. When the military budget was last brought before this committee and serious debate took place about it, the consensus seemed to be that things were in pretty good shape around the world. Don't get me wrong. You gentlemen, and others representing DOD, presented a strong, persuasive case for not letting down our guard despite relative peace in the world. What I especially remember was the testimony concerning the state of relations in the Middle East. I went back over transcripts from those hearings, and what I keep reading is a conviction, based upon our intelligence gathering, that none of the Arab states were within five years of developing nuclear capability. You gentlemen, and others, have repeatedly pointed out that many of the nations in that region were actively seeking the ability to manufacture such weapons, but that because of a combination of circumstances, it would be many years before they would succeed. Now, just such a nuclear device has been detonated. My question is: How could we have been so wrong? What happened to allow this Arab leader to suddenly devise, manufacture, and otherwise put together all the complex ingredients to make a bomb?"

Each witness presented theories to answer Wishengrad's question, but it was CIA director Hickey who offered what Wishengrad considered the most reasonable explanation. "Senator Wishengrad, our previous intelligence reports were accurate. When they were submitted, no leader of any Arab nation was within five years of developing the internal capability to produce a nuclear device."

Wishengrad raised his large eyebrows. "And?"

"What we are convinced has happened is that an arms dealer, more likely a consortium of arms dealers, handed such a device to him on the proverbial silver platter. After all, if you're *given* a pie, there's no need to whip one up in the kitchen."

Wishengrad was not a fan of metaphors, but this one made certain sense. The other witnesses elaborated on what Hickey had said until committee member Senator Martha Carlisle asked, "Are we so ineffective in our overseas intelligence-gathering capabilities that we are not able to discern which arms dealers might be engaged in such activity?"

"Far from it," said Hickey. "Over the past dozen years we've identified and curtailed more than two hundred such operations. We work in extremely close concert with intelligence organizations from other governments. The German authorities are currently investigating more than twenty German firms suspected of attempt-

ing to feed Middle Eastern nations the various components necessary to develop a bomb. We've successfully shut down arms dealers
in Brazil, Switzerland, and Japan."

"That's impressive, Mr. Hickey," said Senator Carlisle, "but it
doesn't address the scenario you brought up earlier. If an arms
dealer, or group of them, has handed over a bomb, intercepting and
shutting down those others seems academic to me."

General Getlin, vice chairman of the JCS, broke in. "I've been
sitting here thinking exactly the same thing, Senator Carlisle. It is
all academic now that he has demonstrated the bomb for the world
to see. Of course, we should keep looking to identify those dealers
who seek to do business with unprincipled nations, but the fact is,
the bomb is there. We've all seen the video of it a hundred times
or more. I get the feeling that what's being attempted here is to
close the proverbial barn door after the horse has blown up in our
faces. The bomb is reality. It completely upsets the balance of power
in the Middle East, and threatens to have severe impact upon the
rest of the world, including this nation. I respectfully submit that
this is not the time to second-guess how it happened. Instead, we
need to have reinstated immediately that money that was cut from
the defense budget last year, and to add to it."

They talked for another hour, chewing on the same sour food,
Wishengrad and some of his colleagues pressing the need to know
how the Arab leader obtained the bomb, the witnesses at the table
dismissing that as a wasted exercise and pushing for funds to ensure
a strong counter to the threat.

It was Bruce Massingill, undersecretary for policy at the Pentagon, who made the final statement from the witness table. "I certainly recognize the need for this committee and for all of Congress
to gain a better understanding about why this unsettling event has
happened. But while this process drags on, each day brings us closer
to the use of a second or third bomb in that region that could render
it, and eventually the rest of the world, unrecognizable as we know
it today. I appreciate the efforts of the secretary of state and others
in the administration to seek some political negotiation, but I suggest that while the State Department fiddles, Rome will most certainly burn. Or explode! By Rome, of course, I mean Israel. Or
Egypt. Or Cleveland—or the District of Columbia."

Wishengrad was glad the hearing was over. Massingill's final comment stuck in his throat like a large vitamin pill that didn't wash down. He'd intended to hold a staff meeting immediately following the hearing but canceled it.

"Not feeling well, Senator?" Foxboro asked after they'd returned to their offices.

"I've felt better, Jeff," Wishengrad responded. "I suppose what's really bothering me is that they make sense. That son of a bitch with a rag around his head has the bomb in his hands, and we have to do something about it. Sorry to sound anti-Arab. I'm not, as you know, but I sure as hell am antinuke. I think I'll take a twenty-minute catnap. I have a headache."

CHAPTER

TEN

"You were great, Major," Max Lanning said when Margit returned from the press conference. She had the feeling he'd been lurking in the hall for her arrival.

"Thank you," she said. Jay Kraft was hunched at his desk over a thick file. He didn't acknowledge her arrival, nor did Margit extend her usual morning greeting.

She sat behind her desk and glanced up at Lanning. Her raised eyebrows asked, "Well? What?"

"I've been assigned as your driver for the rest of the day, Major Falk," Lanning said, a pleased smile on his face.

"My driver? I didn't know I had a driver. I didn't know I had a car."

"Those are my orders," said Lanning. "I was told you're going to Fort McNair this afternoon at four."

Someone else who knew about the meeting with Cobol, maybe before she did? She'd bring that up the next time she met with Bellis.

"Fine," she said. "I'd like to leave in plenty of time."

"I'm at your disposal all day," Lanning said.

"I won't need you until I go to McNair. We'll leave at three."

Her attempt to make good use of her time before heading for McNair was thwarted by a succession of phone calls. Some of the press, including a few in the downstairs pressroom, had bypassed the Information Office and reached her directly. After three such interruptions, she called the Armed Forces News Division and requested that something be done about it. Within an hour a new telephone with a private number had been installed on her desk. Simultaneously, the building's telephone command center, which links the Pentagon's offices through 100,000 miles of telephone cable, handling over 200,000 calls each day, arranged for Margit's publicly listed number to be routed directly to AFND.

At three that afternoon Margit got in the backseat of a blue air-force four-door Ford with DOD markings on its doors. As Lanning headed for McNair, her thoughts hopscotched, and she struggled to focus upon a list of questions she'd scribbled on a yellow legal pad. The first was not on the pad. Who was Cobol, and what was he like?

They reached a dead end on P Street, turned left, then took an immediate right through the main gate. Margit put the pad back in her briefcase, drew a deep breath, and said to Lanning, "Building Forty-One. I'm to check in with Trial Defense Service."

Lanning jumped out of the car and came around to open the door for her, but she was quicker. She had the feeling he wanted to escort her inside. "Lieutenant," she said, "I have no idea how long I'll be with Captain Cobol. Please stand by here."

Twenty minutes later, at precisely four o'clock, Margit was ushered into a large, tastefully decorated and furnished office within Trial Defense Service. "Am I meeting Captain Cobol in here?" she asked her escort.

"Yes, Major Falk."

"This is someone's office," she said.

"That's right."

"I assumed I would meet my client where he's being detained."

"We thought you and your client would appreciate more comfortable surroundings."

"Why?"

"I didn't make the decision, Major."

Margit went to the window and looked out. Parked in front was a military police van surrounded by six armed soldiers. The rear doors opened, and a manacled prisoner was helped down. He wore green fatigues and black slippers. Following him out of the vehicle were two more armed soldiers. The prisoner looked up at the building; although Margit knew he couldn't see her, she felt his eyes.

Captain Robert Cobol.

Her client.

The officer who'd brought her to the office pointed to a couch in the corner. A glass-topped coffee table in front of it was flanked by two lemon-yellow wing-back upholstered chairs. "We thought you and Captain Cobol might be most comfortable over there, Major Falk."

Margit looked at the desk, then to other parts of the large room. "That will be fine," she said.

A minute later there was a sharp rap on the door. "Come in," the officer from Trial Defense said. The door opened, and military policemen stepped aside to allow Cobol to enter. He stood passively, his arms secured behind his back, and Margit took the opportunity to study him. She'd seen photographs of Cobol in his file, but here he looked different. In pictures, he was a handsome young man; his records indicated he was thirty-one; in person, he looked ten years older. He had the disheveled, unkempt look of someone who'd been in confinement, although Margit wondered why that should be. Military prisoners are expected to maintain a daily standard of discipline, including attention to their appearance. Why not Cobol?

His face was squarer and heavier than she had seen in the photos. Remnants of teenage acne pitted his cheeks. His features didn't seem to go together. His nose was square and somewhat flat, like a prizefighter's, yet his mouth was thin and delicate. His posture was noncombative, not aggressive, docile—someone resigned to whatever would come next.

Margit crossed the short distance between them and extended her hand. "Major Margit Falk, United States Air Force. I've been assigned as your counsel."

Cobol glanced down at her hand, which was the only one there. His were secured behind his back. A small smile came to his lips. Margit, too, looked at her solo hand and laughed, then said to one of the guards, "Please remove the handcuffs." The guard glanced at the Trial Defense officer, who shook his head.

"Captain, if I am to confer with my client, I do not wish to do it with him in that uncomfortable position."

The captain replied, "Major Falk, considering the nature of the crime Captain Cobol is charged with, I think . . ."

"I understand your concerns, Captain, but I insist upon this. You

have enough military police around here to ensure that should
Captain Cobol decide to do something foolish, he wouldn't get very
far." She snapped her head in Cobol's direction: "You wouldn't do
anything foolish, would you?"

"No, ma'am," he said, surprised that he'd been asked.

"Please, Captain," Margit said.

When Cobol's handcuffs were removed, he slowly brought his
hands to the front, stared at them, rubbed each wrist.

Margit said, "I'd like to get started." Before there was a reply, she
said to Cobol, "Please sit over there in one of those chairs." To her
escort: "Thank you for your courtesy."

"The security detail will be right outside the door, Major Falk,"
he said.

"Good."

When they were alone, she sat on the couch, opened her briefcase, and placed two legal pads on the glass table, one with her
questions, the other blank. She withdrew a pen from the case,
uncapped it, looked at Cobol, and said, "You're accused of having
murdered Dr. Richard Joycelen."

Cobol, who'd been staring down at his shoetops, slowly raised his
head. "If there's one thing I know, Major Falk, it's that."

"Do you accept me as your defense counsel?"

"Yes."

"Do you know anything about me, about my legal background
and experience?"

"No, ma'am, I do not."

"I am relatively new to the legal profession. I have defended
people who've been accused of breach of regulations, but I have
never defended an accused murderer. How do you feel about that?"

"I . . . no offense, Major Falk, but I have a feeling it really doesn't
matter who defends me. I'm sure you'll do the best you can, which
is all I can ask."

"You have a number of options, Captain. You can ask for other
counsel, you can request a civilian attorney, or you can decide that
you want a civilian co-counsel."

"Do I have to decide this now?"

"No, but I suggest you make a decision as quickly as possible.
Assuming I am your counsel, let's proceed with this initial meeting."

She glanced down at her handwriting on the yellow page. "Did you kill Dr. Richard Joycelen?"

"No."

"I want you to understand that if I question you as though I'm skeptical, it's not because I doubt you. It's important that you be totally honest with me, and that I satisfy myself that I fully understand the circumstances of this charge."

"I understand. Ask whatever you wish."

"You say you did not kill Dr. Joycelen, yet your weapon was found at the scene, and the bullet that killed Joycelen came from that weapon. How do you explain that?"

"I can't."

"You'll have to do better than that."

"How can I? Should I make up a story? I used that weapon on the firing range three days before Joycelen was killed. I don't routinely carry it. I put in my firing-range time, cleaned the weapon, and put it in a dresser drawer in my bedroom. I checked that drawer just before leaving for duty at the Pentagon Friday night, and it was there. At least I thought it was. They say it wasn't. They say mine was used to kill Joycelen, and that the one in the drawer didn't belong to me. Someone swapped them is all I can figure out."

"Who might have done it?"

"I haven't the slightest idea. I wish I did."

"Who had access to it?"

"Very few people. My roommate did, but I know he didn't take it."

"Your roommate? You live on the economy?"

"Yes."

"Most single officers live on area military installations."

"I like the military, Major Falk, but it's nice to get away from it at night."

Margit smiled to herself. He was right; she sometimes wished she'd opted to live in an apartment rather than at Bolling.

She wondered, of course, whether his decision not to live in military surroundings had anything to do with allegations that he was homosexual. She would get into that subject, of course, but decided to leave it until the end of their meeting. "Is your roommate in the military?" she asked.

"No."

"You were on duty in the Pentagon at the time of Dr. Joycelen's death?"

"Yes, I was."

"Were you in the basement area where his body was found?"

"No. I was in the security office on the floor above."

"Directly above where he was found?"

Cobol narrowed his eyes. "No, not directly above, but on that side of the building."

"You saw or heard nothing?"

"Nothing."

"What about the surveillance monitors? There's a camera right where the shooting took place."

"That camera was down that weekend. At least that's what they told me."

"I see," Margit said, referring again to her notes. "Did you know Dr. Joycelen?"

Cobol shook his head. "I'd been at a few briefings he gave at the Company. I was introduced to him once, along with the others at the briefing. We shook hands. That's all."

"That was the extent of your connection with him?"

"Yes, ma'am."

Time to get into it. "Have you heard the rumors that you killed Dr. Joycelen because you'd been lovers?"

She expected an emotional response. Instead, she got his answer in tones that mirrored the flat expression on his face. "Yes, I've heard them."

"Any truth to them?"

"Absolutely not."

"Are you homosexual?"

"Yes."

Margit wasn't sure where to go next with her questions. Once she'd become aware that Cobol was rumored to be gay, she'd researched military law where homosexuality was the issue.

Until 1981, regulations governing the subject had been ambiguous. Unstated. Then, in 1981, DOD passed regulation 1332.14, which stated flat-out that "homosexuality is incompatible with military service." Anyone in uniform discovered to be homosexual was to be given a dishonorable discharge, that prerogative upheld by the

Supreme Court in 1990. The regulation could be bent, however. In wartime homosexuals facing a dishonorable could have it "deferred" if they were willing to fight for their country. Hostilities cease— dishonorable discharge goes through.

Army captain Robert Cobol had openly acknowledged that he was homosexual. She asked was this the first time he'd made such an admission to another officer?

"No, it isn't," he said.

"You're aware of Reg 1332."

He smiled. "Of course I am. Every gay in the service is aware of *that* reg."

"Who have you shared this with before me?"

"I wouldn't exactly say 'share' is accurate. I know what you're getting at. Naturally, I was more comfortable admitting it to others like me." He raised his chin defiantly. "There are more of us in the military than you probably imagine."

"Maybe, but that doesn't interest me. You've been in the army for nine years. I gather that you've lived a homosexual life for those years. It must have taken a great deal of discretion to keep it from your superiors."

"I've been in my share of closets."

"And no one—no superior—ever became aware of it?"

"Not true."

"Then why . . . ?"

He'd been sitting on the edge of the chair and leaning forward. Now, he sat back and appeared to relax. "I'm a good officer," he said, "and there are others—maybe not many, but at least some, who are willing to ignore the regs in order to keep a good officer."

"That happened to you?"

"Yes, about six months ago. It was when I met my roommate, the one I've been living with recently. Someone—and I have no idea who it was—became aware that I'd entered into this relationship and reported it to my superior at the CIA, Major Reich. Reich called me into his office and dressed me down, not so much because I was gay but because I'd not been discreet enough. He told me that because my record was outstanding, he was going to forget he ever heard about it. Of course, he also warned me that if my sexual life was reported again, he couldn't continue to protect me."

"An enlightened major," Margit said.

Cobol smiled warmly. "Very."

And pragmatic, thought Margit. Like Eisenhower when he was in command of our troops in post–World War II, according to a lesbian officer with whom Margit had been friendly during her tour at Lowry. The future president had a large WAC division working directly for him, performing primarily clerical and support duties. One day, he was told that the unit included a number of lesbians. He directed one of his closest aides, a woman, to investigate the rumor and to prepare a list of them for him. His aide said that she would, but also told him that her name would be first on the list. She named others whose names would join hers, and pointed out that their military service had been outstanding, and that they played a critical role in helping him discharge his awesome responsibilities.

"Cancel that order," Eisenhower is reported to have said. "Forget I ever mentioned it."

Margit wrote Reich's name on her pad, then asked Cobol to capsulize his military career for her.

He responded slowly, thoughtfully. When he was finished, Margit asked how he ended up assigned to the CIA.

"Beats me," he replied. "I have to admit I was excited about it. Little Bobby Cobol working for the spooks, cloak-and-dagger, the spy who came in from the cold." He shrugged.

"What about your family and friends?"

"My father is dead," he said. "My mother is alive and lives in the house where I was brought up on Long Island."

"Have you had any contact with her since you were arrested?"

"No. I understand she's telephoned a number of times, but I haven't been allowed to speak with her."

"Would you like to speak with her?"

"Very much."

"I'll see what I can do." He gave her his mother's phone number. "Is there anyone you can suggest I talk to who might be helpful in your defense?"

"You mean somebody who can provide an alibi? No. I was alone in the security office when he was murdered."

"That aside, I'll need character witnesses."

"I can give you some. Characters. I mean, some of them are."

"Captain Cobol, the evidence against you, as I understand it at this point, is circumstantial but substantial. The atmosphere, the environment, of this case doesn't help. A leading member of the scientific and government community has been murdered in cold blood. I'll be honest with you. I don't know how successful I'll be in defending you."

"I understand that, Major Falk, and I'll appreciate every effort you make. I guess the only thing I can say to you is that I did not kill Dr. Joycelen. I have never killed anyone in my life."

Margit stood. She didn't know whether to believe him or not, but knew she had to give him the benefit of the doubt. She said, "I don't know whether I'll speak with you again before the arraignment on Thursday, but I'll be there. We'll enter a plea at that time, which, I assume, is Not Guilty."

He stood. "That's right. Not guilty."

"How did it go?" Max Lanning asked when they were on their way to Bolling.

"Fine, Max." She knew he wanted to hear more but was not about to feed his penchant for gossip. He made small talk during the ride, to which she responded to the extent of not being considered impolite. When he pulled up in front of her BOQ, he said he would stand by.

"No need," she said.

"Shall I pick you up in the morning?"

"Are you assigned to me for the duration?"

"I don't know, but they told me to drive you wherever you wanted to go tomorrow."

"No, you don't have to pick me up in the morning. If I need you during the day, I'll let you know. Have a nice evening, Max."

Once inside, she changed into a pink sweat suit and went to the kitchen, where she did something unusual for her when alone—made a drink. Someone had given her a bottle of pepper vodka as a gift, which she mixed with spicy V-8 juice.

She sat by her window and watched the comings and goings of men and women assigned to the base. There were many people she considered calling: Jeff, Mac Smith, friends around the world she'd made during her air-force career. But the phone stayed in its cradle.

Talking about the Joycelen murder, about Cobol, about any of it, would only further depress her. She needed to forget, at least for this night, about the whole affair, and so she turned to what she usually did to clear her mind. She worked out at the gym to the point of exhaustion, returned to the BOQ, and fell into a deep sleep that she wished could last for a month.

CHAPTER

ELEVEN

 "Mrs. Cobol, this is Major Margit Falk. I've been assigned as your son's defense counsel."

"Yes, I know who you are. He pleaded Not Guilty this morning. I heard it on the radio."

"That's right. I know you've been trying to speak with him. I apologize that you haven't been able to, and I arranged after the arraignment for you to do that."

There was silence. Not total. A hushed sob?

"Mrs. Cobol, I understand that this is painful for you, but I want you to know that I am committed to presenting the best possible defense for Robert. I would like to meet you. Could we combine that with a visit to him?"

Flo Cobol pulled herself together. "I'll meet with you at any time. Robert is not guilty. I know he didn't kill this Dr. Joycelen."

Margit didn't commit herself to that view. She simply asked, "When do you think you can come to Washington?"

"I could come this afternoon."

"I think it would be better to wait until tomorrow. That will give me time to make sure there's no hitch in your visit. If I can arrange a meeting at one o'clock, would that be all right with you?"

"That would be fine."

"If you could arrive in Washington at noon tomorrow, I'll pick you up, and we'll go together to visit him."

Flo Cobol agreed to that, and they established a place to meet at the airport.

Margit sat back in her chair. Jay Kraft was at his desk, and Margit made an immediate decision. She could not effectively conduct Cobol's defense while sharing an office with Kraft—or anyone else, for that matter. She needed privacy, and decided to seek it through Colonel Bellis, whom she was to debrief at noon about the arraignment.

The arraignment had been a simple legal procedure. Trial counsel assigned to prosecute Cobol by the chief of criminal law, under the command's staff judge advocate, was an army captain, William Higgins. He introduced himself to Margit. "A pleasure to meet you, Major."

"Thank you," she said, surprised at his open pleasantness.

"Looks like we'll see quite a bit of each other."

"Looks like it, Captain."

The charges were read to Cobol, and he was asked to enter a plea. "Not Guilty," he said in a strong voice. He was immediately led from the spartan room.

"Sir," Margit said to the trial judge, air force lieutenant colonel J. K. Washington, a tall, lean, balding black man whose expression was one of almost constant bemusement, "Captain Cobol has been denied the right to receive visits from family members, including his mother. I understand the sensitive nature of this case, as well as its grave seriousness, but I respectfully request that Captain Cobol be given the same visitation rights as any other accused military prisoner."

Washington looked to Captain Higgins, who said, "I have no objection, sir."

"And I see no reason for such visitation to be denied. So ordered."

At noon Margit sat across the desk from Bellis.

"Do you believe Cobol?" Bellis asked.

"That he didn't do it? To be perfectly honest with you, sir, I don't know. I do know, however, that if I am to be a successful advocate, I have to put a certain amount of faith in him."

"Right," Bellis muttered.

"Colonel, I've made a list of needs."

"Your needs?"

"Yes, sir." She referred to a note on which she'd listed them. "First, I need a private office. It's inappropriate, I think, for me to be sharing office space during the course of this procedure."

"Office space is tight."

"Not so tight that the defense counsel to an accused murderer should be hampered by it. Surely, there must be some spare office I could use."

"I'll check. What else?"

"I need an assistant, and an investigator."

"What kind of assistant?"

"He or she doesn't have to be an attorney, but should have some knowledge of military law. A noncommissioned paralegal will do nicely."

Bellis wrote something on a pad. "Go on."

"I would like to have an investigator assigned to me."

"For what purpose?"

"To interview people that I obviously will not have time to interview."

"I'll see if Investigative Services can assign someone on a temporary basis."

"I appreciate that, Colonel. I also would like to be able to bring in civilian co-counsel."

"Has Cobol requested that?"

"No, sir, he hasn't but . . ."

"You know that the accused has to arrange for outside legal counsel."

"Yes, sir, I do, and I intend to suggest it to Captain Cobol when I see him tomorrow."

"I'd hold up on that, Major."

"May I ask why, sir?"

"Because of the sensitive nature of this whole affair. SecDef wants to keep it in the family, so to speak."

"In the family? Family as in military?"

"Yes. Remember, Cobol was CIA-assigned. He's enjoyed a top-security clearance until now, and has been exposed to a hell of a lot of sensitive material."

"But military law clearly states that the accused has the right to bring in civilian counsel."

"I know what the law says, Major Falk, and what I am suggesting to you is that you not push the idea on Captain Cobol. Why are you meeting with him tomorrow?"

"His mother is flying in from New York. I've arranged for her to see him and intend to spend some time with her myself."

"Anything else?"

"No, sir." Margit glanced up at the ceiling, then back at Bellis. "You said you were suggesting that I not push the idea of civilian co-counsel on Captain Cobol. Did you mean that? Are you suggesting it, or was that an order?" She knew, of course, that when a superior suggested something, wise and prudent subordinates took it as an order. In this case, however, she wanted clarification.

"No, it's not an order because I haven't been given any orders in that regard. May I suggest to you, however, that it is the prevailing thinking upstairs that this should be kept within military channels as much as possible. If you'd like, I'll check with SecDef to clarify whether what they told me should be considered an order. I'd rather not do that. I'd rather make you aware of the thinking around here and have you exercise your obvious good judgment."

She'd made him angry. She wished she hadn't.

Margit left Bellis's office and tried to sort out the conversation they'd had. His message, as veiled as it might have been, did not come as a surprise. Her years in the military had taught her many things, including the inescapable observation that there was an unstated but clearly defined animosity between the military and civilian sectors of society. Because much of the media was in the civilian camp, the Pentagon was viewed with considerable and consistent suspicion. Given a choice, the military preferred to keep its operations to itself, good and bad—particularly the bad. In the case of Joycelen's murder—especially with the rumors that homosexuality might be at the root of it—it was natural that the military command would make every attempt to keep it "within the family."

Margit respected that, as she had from the beginning of her career in uniform. But there had to be exceptions. As she sat at her desk and pondered the morning's activities, she became increasingly convinced that this should be one of them.

Bellis acted quickly on her requests. In less than an hour a crew arrived and moved her to a small, private office directly across the hall from him. It was one of three rooms in a small suite; Margit would share with the other two occupants the services of a secretary who sat in an anteroom.

As she was leaving her old office, she said pleasantly to Kraft, "Good news, Jay. Looks like you have your own place now. At least for a while."

He managed a weak smile and returned to the contracts on his desk. The hell with you, Margit thought as she scooped up the last remaining files and headed off to her new digs.

At three that afternoon she received a call from a civilian, George Brown, who was in charge of the Defense Criminal Investigation Services's Investigative Support Directorate. After introducing himself, he said, "I understand you need an investigator."

"Yes, sir, that's correct."

"I spoke with Colonel Bellis a short while ago, and he outlined your needs. I can temp-duty one of our people over to you."

"That would be much appreciated, Mr. Brown. Will it be someone with a background in criminal investigation?"

"Of course. Maybe not in the investigation of murder, but a trained person."

"Will this investigator be military or civilian?"

"Military," Brown answered.

"When can I expect him?"

"Might be a her."

"Doesn't matter. When can I expect him—or her?"

"It will take a few days. Let's see, today is Thursday. We've got Labor Day coming up this weekend. How about next Wednesday?"

Margit had hoped for help sooner, but realized that with the holiday weekend, not much would be accomplished anyway. "Fine," she said.

She was summoned to Bellis's office at four.

"Major, what do you think of the marines?" he asked. He now seemed in good humor.

Margit laughed. "I've really never thought about it, sir."

"I've sprung a warrant officer from Quantico's Legal Assistance Office for you. His name is Woosky, Peter Woosky. He does a lot of the routine legal work over there—wills, powers of attorney, that sort of thing. I'm sure he'll be of help."

"Everything has moved so fast," Margit said. "I received a call from Mr. Brown, who's sending me an investigator on Wednesday."

"Good. How's your new office?"

"Fine, sir. Nice to have it to myself."

"Looks like you've got everything you need."

"Yes, I suppose I do."

"Good." He paused. "A word of advice."

"Yes?"

"Don't get too involved with Cobol's mother. I know the tendency is to want to go out and talk to everybody who ever knew Cobol, but that won't help."

"I don't think I understand, sir. If the evidence against him is as compelling as it seems to be, I'm going to have to depend, to a great extent, upon character witnesses, on people who, although they might not be helpful in the actual defense, could play a role in mitigating his sentence."

Bellis's open good humor seemed to sour. He abruptly ended their meeting by standing and going to the door. "If Cobol is convicted of murdering Joycelen, there isn't going to be much debate about his sentence."

Margit thanked him again for his help and returned to her office across the hall.

The secretary she'd inherited handed her slips of paper. "You received these calls while you were out." One was from Annabel Smith, who left the number of her Georgetown art gallery. The others were from offices within the Pentagon, including requests for interviews by reporters that the Information Office had collected.

Margit ignored the interviews, returned the official calls, then reached Annabel.

"Just thought you might like to use up the raincheck from last week," Annabel said. "Mac and I are going out to dinner and wondered if you and Jeff could join us."

Margit immediately accepted the invitation for herself, and said she would try to reach Jeff. She'd spent enough time alone at night stewing over this new and problematic assignment. Until this day her energy level had been down. Now, for some reason, her batteries seemed fully charged, and the last thing she wanted to do was to hibernate in her BOQ. "One condition, though," she told Annabel.

"What's that?"

"No pizza."

"Deal. Mac was pushing for one of his favorite macho steak

houses, but I convinced him lighter fare was more in keeping with the needs of our waistlines. Japanese okay?"

"Sure."

"I'll make a reservation for seven at Sushi-Ko, on Wisconsin. I'll meet up with you and Mac there. I won't be leaving the gallery until about that time. Table for four?"

"I can't promise Jeff will be there. Want me to call you back?"

"No need. See you at seven."

Foxboro was out of the office when Margit called. She left her number and said she would be at it until six-thirty. He didn't return the call, and she left the Pentagon disappointed. She was not at all pleased with the direction their relationship was taking, and knew that if she were going to get it back on track, it would take extra effort on her part. She also knew that wouldn't be easy with the Cobol case facing her, but pledged to herself to find the time.

"Will you at least think about it?" Margit asked Mac Smith as they left the restaurant.

Smith looked at Annabel, who said, "We'd better get home. Rufus probably has his legs crossed."

"Just think about it. That's all I ask," Margit said.

Annabel kissed her cheek. "Nice seeing you, Margit. Sorry Jeff couldn't make it."

"It was a great evening. Thanks again."

As Smith went to the parking lot to bail out their car, Annabel said, "Margit, you aren't serious, are you?"

"Of course I am."

"He's retired. He's a professor."

It hadn't occurred to Margit that Annabel would react negatively, and she wished she'd been more sensitive. "I hope I haven't done something stupid tonight," she said.

Annabel shook her head. "No, nothing stupid. Mac is like any man his age who falls asleep each night pitching in the crucial game of a World Series, or throwing the winning touchdown in the Super Bowl. There he is, called back into action in middle age, the team's only hope, relying on his cunning and experience to overcome a weak arm. And of course he wins the game in the final seconds."

Margit couldn't help laughing. "How nice to fall asleep with visions like that."

"I agree. As long as they happen in bed. I just hate to see him tempted to get involved again in controversial cases. He did it when Senator Ewald's aide was murdered at the Kennedy Center, and again last year at the National Cathedral when our friend Reverend Singletary was found murdered in a chapel." She shrugged. "I know I'm being selfish when I try to control him this way. It's just that I like him as a professor."

"I understand," said Margit.

Smith pulled up and opened the door for Annabel. As she slid into the passenger seat, she winked at Margit and said in a stage whisper, "I'll get him to think about it."

CHAPTER

TWELVE

"Thank you, Lieutenant, but I won't need you today," Margit told Lanning the following morning.

"But I was told to drive you."

"I think you misunderstood the order," Margit said. "You were told to be at my disposal should I need transportation. I don't. Please close the door after you." Dejectedly, he backed out of her office.

She opened a recently revised telephone directory for the Central Intelligence Agency and turned to the *R* pages. There were two Reichs, neither a major. She called the Central Personnel Locator number, identified herself, and asked for Major Reich. "No Major Reich listed," she was told.

She hung up and made a note to ask Cobol for more details about this superior who, according to Cobol, had bent the rules on his behalf.

Next, she opened a folder in which she'd collected newspaper accounts of the Joycelen murder. There had been something in the press every day; once she'd been assigned to defend his accused murderer, Margit tried to keep up with the clips. She made another note to have the assistant she'd inherit on Wednesday conduct a more thorough search.

She removed one clipping from the file and read it again. It consisted, in part, of an interview with Joycelen's fiancée, Christa Wren. Ms. Wren said she was devastated by the sudden death of the man she was to marry, and that he was the finest, brightest man she'd ever known. She said that although it could never replace him in her life, there was some small satisfaction in knowing his murderer had been apprehended. Her final comment was in response to the interviewer's question about rumors that Joycelen was homosexual. "Utterly ridiculous! Absurd!" Christa had replied.

Margit opened a city phone directory and looked up Wren. There was one—C. Wren. Her address was a new apartment building in the recently completed and fashionable Washington Harbour complex, on Georgetown's waterfront.

Margit had been thinking about contacting Christa Wren from the moment she'd got up that morning. She knew she should include her on a list of people to be interviewed by her investigator, but felt compelled to make the call herself—and to do it today. If nothing else, it would give her a sense of having actually begun the process of defending Cobol. And because she'd met Christa Wren at the picnic, however briefly, it made her feel as though she knew this woman.

Her phone rang a half-dozen times before she picked up.

"Ms. Wren, this is Major Falk. I've been assigned to defend Dr. Joycelen's alleged killer, Captain Robert Cobol."

Christa Wren said nothing.

Margit continued. "I met you at the picnic the morning of his death. Maybe you remember me."

"What do you want?" Wren asked.

"I'm not sure I want anything. I do, of course, extend my condolences. I'm sorry for your loss."

"Thank you." The two simple words were delivered icily.

"Ms. Wren, I know this will be difficult, but I would like a chance to meet with you."

"To help you defend the man who killed my fiancé?"

"Yes, I suppose that is the purpose. As distasteful as it may seem, Captain Cobol, like any other accused criminal, is entitled to a proper defense. I did not choose this assignment. I was ordered to defend him, and I follow orders."

Wren let out a rueful laugh. "How very military. You want to speak with me, interview me about Dick?"

"Yes." Margit considered saying that an investigator might conduct the interview, but she decided to keep the option open.

Christa said, "Sure, why not? If you come in the morning, I'll serve tea. Any time after noon the bar is open. I've been making good use of it lately."

"Thank you, Ms. Wren. I'll get back to you."

Later that morning, as Margit prepared to leave for National Airport to pick up Flo Cobol, she was summoned to Colonel Bellis's office. "How goes it?" he asked.

"I'm not really sure. I'm on my way to pick up Cobol's mother at the airport and take her to see him."

"Sure you want to do that?"

"Yes, sir. Why wouldn't I?"

Bellis, who was in shirtsleeves with cuffs rolled up, raised his hands into the air. "It just seems to me that you should be busy enough without interviewing people yourself. That's why I acted quickly on your request for an assistant and an investigator."

"And I appreciate that, Colonel Bellis. I'm sure once the list of people to be interviewed grows, I'll be happy not to be doing it myself. But, in this case, I feel it would be helpful for me to know more about Captain Cobol's family and early life."

"Suit yourself, Major Falk, but don't get trapped into too personal an involvement with this. I know you don't have a great deal of experience as an attorney, so take it from this warhorse. Approach it the way doctors do with patients they're about to cut open. Do your best professional job, but keep a distance."

"I'll keep that in mind, sir, and I appreciate the advice."

He laughed gently. "I hate to admit it, Major, but I'm developing a sort of fatherly interest in you."

"Fatherly . . . ? I'm flattered."

"I'm getting old, I suppose. I took another look at your service record. Damned impressive. I like the mix, chopper pilot, lawyer. Commendations from the Panama exercise. Your father was career military."

"Yes, he was."

"I don't want to see you take any missteps to sully that fine record." She started to ask him to be more specific, but he waved her off. "Let me finish. Assignment to the Pentagon carries with it a whole set of potential pitfalls that you don't run into out in the field. Missions are pretty straightforward out there. Not here. This is Washington, D.C. Right across the river are the elected officials who pretty much determine what we can and can't do, mostly because they pull the purse strings. Assignment to the Pentagon is considered a privilege, as you know. It can help an officer's career. It can also sink one."

Margit listened carefully. He wasn't giving her the standard inspirational lecture. He was delivering a message. What was it? Whom for? Should she ask? No. That would be accusatory.

"Captain Cobol deserves a good defense," Bellis said in a tone that indicated he was ending the conversation. "But he's only part of a messy situation. Joycelen was important. Controversial. Keep that in mind."

"I'll certainly try, sir. I have to admit that I'm not quite sure what you . . ."

"What about that woman who was supposed to have been Joycelen's fiancée?"

Margit's eyebrows went up. "I was just reading an interview a reporter did with her," she said.

"I've read some of those. I suppose she'll be on your interview list."

"Yes."

"And I'm sure whatever investigator sent you by DCI will take care of that interview."

Was he telling her that she was not to interview Christa Wren? Should she take his previous comments about Flo Cobol to mean the same thing? She didn't ask for clarification because she didn't want to hear an order prohibiting her from doing what she'd already set in motion. As long as she wasn't specifically told not to talk to Mrs. Cobol and Christa Wren, she could justify doing it, at least in her own mind.

"Is that all, sir?" she asked.

"Yes. I'd like to touch base with you on a regular basis. I thought a brief meeting every morning would make sense, and one at the end of the day. That okay with you?"

"Of course." She didn't like the idea of a strict schedule of meetings, but it wasn't her decision to make.

"Check back with me after you've met with Cobol and his mother."

"I'm not sure how long I'll be with them," Margit said.

"I'll be here all afternoon."

Although Margit had never met Mrs. Cobol, she knew her the minute she came through the door from the Delta shuttle. Margit's first thought—and it certainly wasn't meant to be flippant—was that she looked like a typecast mother from a TV situation comedy. She was a tall, plain woman with thin, mouse-brown hair. She was dressed in her threadbare finery, wore wire-rimmed glasses, and carried a small bag.

Flo spotted Margit, who'd said she'd be wearing a tan summer air-force uniform, but approached as though unsure whether she should. Margit closed the gap. "Mrs. Cobol, I'm Margit Falk."

"Yes. I saw you. I saw the uniform." A tic in her left eye confirmed her nervousness.

Margit made small talk as they walked through the terminal: Had the flight been bumpy?; it seemed to be on time; was it full?. Anything to avoid silence. When they were in the car, Margit said, "Mrs. Cobol, I know how difficult this is for you. I'm sorry you were not able to see Robert until now."

"I didn't understand why. I thought . . ."

"You were right in thinking you should have been able to. You'll be free to see him on a regular basis now."

"I don't know how long I can stay."

"Did you book a hotel?"

"No. I thought—I mean, I thought maybe I would just go home."

"Let's play that by ear. I would like to have time with you after you've seen Robert. Is that all right with you?"

Flo nodded, and Margit headed for Fort McNair.

This time they did not meet in a tastefully furnished office. Cobol was led into a bare-bones, bilge-green interview room that contained a table and four wooden chairs. A small window in the door allowed a military policeman to watch, but presumably not to hear.

Robert Cobol looked at his mother, slowly shook his head and gazed down at the floor. "I'll leave you alone for a while," Margit said. "A half hour?" She told the guard she would be in Trial Defense Service's offices.

Forty minutes later she returned to the interview room where mother and son were seated close to each other. "Should I make myself scarce again?" Margit asked pleasantly.

"No, please, come and sit," Robert said. He stood and came to attention, a positive sign to Margit. Perhaps he was returning to the more normal aspects of military routine.

"Anything you'd like to share with me?" Margit asked. Robert smiled at his mother, who said, "I believe Robert. He didn't kill that Dr. Joycelen." When Margit didn't respond, Mrs. Cobol asked, "Do you believe him?"

Margit could have done without the question. The truth was, she didn't know what she believed, only that if she was to mount a credible defense for him, she would have to, at least, not believe that he *did* murder Richard Joycelen. She looked into the soft, blinking, questioning eyes of Flo Cobol and said, "No, I do not believe Robert killed Dr. Joycelen, and I am committed to defending him with every resource available to me."

"Thank you, Major Falk."

Margit paused before saying what she'd been thinking for the past twenty-four hours. "I believe it would benefit you, Robert, to bring in civilian counsel to work with me."

Mother and son stared at her.

"I consider myself a good attorney. My training was excellent, and I have a solid understanding of military law. But defending an accused murderer in any milieu, civilian or military, not only demands knowledge that is gained from years of experience, the ramifications are immense. Your life is at stake. I'm not suggesting I don't want to defend you. I've made a commitment to do the best job I can. But I think you deserve more than that. Would you consider hiring a civilian attorney to work with me?"

During Margit's previous visit with Cobol, he seemed not to care about the quality of his defense, was resigned to whatever happened. This day he demonstrated more of an interest in his fate. "I have faith in you, Major Falk, and I'll go along with any suggestion you make. If you feel having a civilian attorney involved makes sense, let's do it."

"Will that cost a lot of money?" Flo Cobol asked.

"I don't know how much. Good attorneys are expensive, but I have an idea. My professor at George Washington University was a gentleman named Mackensie Smith. Before becoming a professor, he was a brilliant and successful trial lawyer in Washington. I'm not suggesting that he would be an active co-counsel on a full-time basis, but I would enjoy being able to draw upon his wisdom and experience during the trial. Obviously, he would have to be paid for his time and expertise, but he is not a man consumed by money. I may have acted prematurely by broaching the subject with him at dinner last night. Whether he would agree to help us is conjecture, but I'd like your permission to pursue it."

"I don't have much money," Flo Cobol said. "My husband didn't believe in life insurance, and I don't have much in my bank account. But I'll do anything to help Robert. I could sell the house, or take another mortgage on it."

"I don't think we're talking about selling houses, Mrs. Cobol. At least not yet."

Margit convinced Flo Cobol to stay overnight. She booked a room for her at Bolling's Officer Guest Quarters, and arranged for her to visit her son again the next morning, Saturday of the Labor Day weekend.

They had dinner at the Officers' Club, where, surprisingly, Flo relaxed. She could be funny, Margit found, her unsophisticated remarks humorous not because they lacked sophistication but because they were genuine—direct and honest and, therefore, often amusing.

Later they sat in Flo's room, where Margit encouraged her to open up about her son, this army captain who had become—certainly not by choice—her client, and whose life had ended up in her hands.

As Margit and Flo talked—it was eight o'clock in the evening in Washington—Consulnet's Hans Keller left a private club to which he'd been taken by his Arab host. A woman was on his arm, and she helped steady him. It was 4:10 in the morning; Hans had had a lot to drink, courtesy of his host, and of the club owner who preferred to consider the country's ban on alcoholic beverages to be for other, less enlightened citizens.

The woman with Keller was half-Italian, half-Lebanese, slender but with ample hips and bosom.

Keller stumbled into the backseat of a black four-door Mercedes parked at the curb. His nubile companion joined him. Keller in-

structed the driver to take them to his hotel, a glass-and-steel structure that was part of an American chain.

Keller was anxious to get there. Discussions with his host had not
gone well. Alcohol, food, cigarettes, happy talk, and the stroking of
his thigh had substituted for substance. He was tired, disgruntled,
and looked forward to going to bed with the lovely creature seated
next to him. Not that he was in any shape to take full advantage
of her. That could happen in the morning—late morning; she was
his as long as he was in the city.

Even at that hour, the narrow streets of the business sector were
clogged, and the Mercedes moved through them at a snail's pace.

Keller shook his head to stay awake. Her hand was on his leg. She
giggled and touched his cheek. He tried to kiss her, but she turned
her lips from him. "Not now," she said. "Soon."

He looked out the window and dimly realized they were heading
in a direction away from the hotel. He could see it in the distance,
its rooftop neon sign glaring through clouds that had descended
upon the city. He leaned forward and tapped the driver on the
shoulder. "Wrong road, wrong way," he grumbled, pointing in the
direction of the hotel. "Over there. Go there."

The driver nodded and made a turn, then accelerated and sped
down a street that led directly to a deserted waterfront. The car
came to an abrupt stop.

"What the hell are you doing?" Keller shouted. *"Nackter wilder!"*
he snarled in German. *Moron!*

His question was answered by both rear doors opening simultaneously. "Wait," Keller said, looking at faces staring in at him
through the open doors. The woman quickly slid across the seat and
got out. A man took her place next to Keller.

"What do you want?" Keller asked.

From the other door a hand grabbed his collar.

"No, please."

The man beside him pulled a long, curved dagger from his belt
and thrust it between the ribs on Keller's right side. He gasped, and
his hand went to where it had entered. When he pulled his hand
up to look at it, it was wet and red. The pain. Keller's mouth twisted
into a circle; a beached fish gasping for air, he pitched forward. The
man leaning in the door behind him flipped a thin metal wire over

Keller's head and twisted it, the metal slicing through the thick folds of skin covering Keller's throat as though it were a knife. His eyes bulged. Then his head jerked. It was over.

". . . I think Robert joined the army to satisfy his father," Flo Cobol said to Margit as they sat in Flo's comfortable guest room. There was nothing amusing in her manner now. "My husband was always concerned about Robert, thought he wasn't as manly as some of the other boys. Robert joined the army and went through all that difficult training. When he was commissioned, my husband was prouder than I've ever seen him. He beamed, Major Falk. He kept slapping Robert on the back and hugging him.

"Then my husband died. It was only six or eight months after Robert was commissioned. That was when Robert told me . . ."

Awkward silence.

"That he was homosexual?"

Flo nodded. "He'd known about it since high school but was afraid to admit it, even to himself. Of course, he was always easily influenced. That's why it happened. At least, that's what I believe. He started to spend time with them, and he became one of them. I know that's the way those things happen. Some boys are strong. They don't listen to their friends. Unless their friends have the right values. Robert . . . was with the wrong people, and they influenced him. Don't misunderstand, Major Falk. I don't think poorly of all of them. Everyone is different. We should respect that. But when it's your own son . . .

"He would never have told his father. He told me that he was proud to be an officer, and that he didn't see any reason why his personal life should matter as long as he did a good job for his country."

"The military has strict regulations against homosexuals," Margit said.

"I heard that, I told him that. I told him that he would probably end up in a lot of trouble unless he changed, but he said he was convinced he could live his private life quietly, and that no one in the military would ever know what he was. I don't consider Robert's views on sex to be normal, but I love him. I'm very proud of him."

Margit asked, "Did he ever mention a Major Reich?"

Flo wrinkled her face. "I don't think so."

"Did others know that he was a homosexual?"

Another thoughtful pause. "Close friends, maybe."

"Will you give me a list of his close friends?"

"Oh, Major Falk, I wouldn't want to get anyone in trouble."

"I don't intend to get them in trouble, Mrs. Cobol. I just have this need to understand Robert. He is, after all, accused of murder, and I'm supposed to save his life. I need to know who else was in his life—and who might have wanted to put him in this position."

"I'm sorry," Cobol's mother said. "I'll cooperate with you any way I can."

"Good." Margit stood and straightened her skirt. "Have a good night's sleep, Mrs. Cobol. There is a long way to go, and I'm going to need you with me all the way."

Flo leaned forward, her knees spread beneath the fabric of her inexpensive dress. "Please don't let him die," she said.

CHAPTER

THIRTEEN

 Margit woke up Saturday morning and saw her picture in the *Washington Times.*

When she and Flo Cobol had arrived at McNair the previous day, a few press people slouched outside the detention building. By the time they recognized who'd arrived, the women were inside.

When Margit and Flo left the building, however, the press was at the ready. Margit said only "No comment" in response to their questions, and assumed that would be the end of it. But there had been a still photographer in the group, and the photo he took of the two women was on page 6. A short accompanying article pointed out it was the first time the accused's mother had visited her son. From the way it was written, a reader would assume that Flo Cobol hadn't been interested in visiting him earlier. That spin on fact rankled Margit as she breakfasted in the Bolling commissary on juice, toast, and coffee.

The article concluded with a thumbnail sketch of air-force major Margit Falk, defense counsel to the accused. It had been based on a handout prepared by the Armed Forces News Division, and said little more than what Margit would be expected to divulge as a prisoner of war. It briefly touched upon her military career, indicated she was a graduate of George Washington University, and mentioned she was flight-rated.

Margit closed the paper and finished her coffee. In the turmoil of being named Cobol's counsel, she'd almost forgotten that she was, indeed, a chopper pilot. She had two weeks before she had to put in flying time to maintain active flight status, but the thought that morning of spending a couple of hours in the air was suddenly appealing. To get up and away from it all. She glanced at her watch; she was to meet Flo Cobol in fifteen minutes and drive her to McNair, then take her to the airport for a flight home.

This was the weekend she and Jeff had agreed to grant themselves. He had to work all day at Wishengrad's office, but they'd made plans for dinner and to spend the night and Sunday together.

She hurried back to her room and called Flight Scheduling at nearby Andrews Air Force Base in Maryland. Although the military helicopter role now rested primarily with the army, there were enough chopper-rated pilots in the air force to justify maintaining a small fleet at Andrews.

"Any chance of booking time this afternoon?" Margit asked.

"Sixteen hundred hours okay, Major?"

"Sounds good. Put me down for an hour." That would leave time to get back to the BOQ, shower, pack what she needed for overnight, and meet Jeff for dinner.

"You've got chopper four-two-three at sixteen hundred hours."

"Nice number," Margit said. "Thanks."

Flo's mood wasn't upbeat when she emerged from the second meeting with her son. She said little during the ride to the airport. As she was about to leave Margit's car at National, she said, "It's good my husband isn't here to see this."

"I'll do everything I can for Robert, Mrs. Cobol."

"I know you will, although I have a feeling nothing will help. He feels the same way."

"It's natural to be pessimistic at this stage. Did you talk to him again about bringing in Mr. Smith?"

"Yes. We agree you should do what you think is right. I'll find the money."

"Let's not worry about money now. I'll talk to Mac Smith this weekend and see if he's willing, if only in an advisory capacity." That Smith would have an official role, as defined by taking a fee, was important to Margit, because she felt awkward asking for his advice purely on friendship. If he would accept a fee, she would feel less guilty in disrupting his comfortable and quiet lifestyle.

She called Smith from her BOQ but reached his answering machine. She left a message that she would be home until three, and that if she didn't hear from the machine's owner by then, she'd call again during the weekend. She busied herself with household chores for an hour, then called Wishengrad's office.

"I was just about to call you," Jeff said.

"Happy I'm able to keep down your phone budget. Bigger than the army's, I hear. How's it going?"

"Terrible. They've pushed up the date for public hearings on the Middle East. Looks like they'll start next Wednesday, instead of a week from."

Margit knew what was coming.

"Margit," Jeff said, "I know I'll be here until some ungodly hour tonight, and the senator has called a staff meeting for eight tomorrow morning. I just don't see how we can get together this weekend."

Margit tried to muffle her disappointment. She was well aware that her recent schedule had made it difficult for them to spend time together; she couldn't be critical of similar pressures on him. "I understand," she said.

"We'll do it another weekend," he said. "Soon."

When their conversation was ended, her disappointment turned to anger. She wanted to believe that he was as disappointed as she was, but his tone didn't deliver that message. Her reaction was probably based upon an erroneous evaluation of what he'd said—and how he'd said it—but she couldn't shake it. It stayed in her stomach, a tightly knotted muscle she was unable to unravel.

By the time she changed into her olive drab flight suit and gleaming black flight boots and had perused her flight bag to make sure it contained everything she needed, the day's cloudy beginnings had cleared; the sun was strong. Her spirits, too, had cleared, and, corny as it was, she hummed "Off We Go into the Wild Blue Yonder" while she drove her shiny red Honda down the Anacostia Freeway to Route 95, also known as the Capital Beltway, and took it to Exit 9, which led to the main gate of the air base known as the "Aerial Gateway to the Nation's Capital." Its enhanced military security made it the airdrome of choice for dignitaries arriving in the United States whose safety was an issue. Those whose stature was not sufficiently high to invite bodily harm were welcomed at National and Dulles.

Her destination on the forty-two-hundred-acre base was a small section of the flight center at which the helicopter fleet was tied down. She pulled into a parking area reserved for flight personnel and entered the Ops Office. A dozen pilots milled about, some checking out after having flown, others filing flight plans, receiving weather briefings, and reading flight-reg updates and NOTAMs—Notices to Airmen.

"Just filling squares for an hour," she told the enlisted man behind the busy desk, indicating a flight plan in which prescribed maneuvers would be practiced to meet requirements.

"Fat day," he responded, sliding forms across plastic that covered area charts. Margit happily agreed. The weather was splendid.

Twenty minutes later she was cleared for an hour's solo time in a UH-1H model Huey, powered by twin PT6 turboshaft engines, a vintage army utility helicopter that had been transferred to the air force. In its attack mode, slung with an M-5 40-mm grenade launcher, rocket pods, and M-3 forty-eight shot rocket packs, it was known in battle as a gunship because of its heavy, bulky armament hanging below. In its stripped version, the version Margit would fly that day, it was known as a "slick." In war, slicks carried people, not guns.

She'd trained on the Huey, transitioned to the Blackhawk, which she'd flown in Panama, but now spent most of her time in Hueys of various configurations. They were the workhorses of the military helicopter fleet, drab, conventional, "utility aircraft," hardly the stuff writers of romantic military history dwelled upon. But they'd done the job in Korea and Vietnam, Iraq and Kuwait, transporting troops, carrying the wounded back in hospital versions, attacking enemy installations, scouting the front lines, all of it.

She went to the flight line where the Huey assigned to her—AF 66423—was waiting. It sat on the Tarmac like a brooding Buddha, squat and innocuous, its main rotor blades drooping from the rotor shaft like weary, spent arms. Although it now belonged to the air force, it remained in its Vietnam camouflage markings of gray and olive drab.

A line-maintenance sergeant tossed Margit a casual salute and continued to move around the helicopter.

"Ready to go?" Margit asked.

"Yes, ma'am," he said.

She thought of her father. Was this young sergeant as good as he'd been? Margit's father had been the best. She'd heard it said many times that you took off with confidence in any plane Sergeant Fred Falk had maintained.

But that reputation hadn't been good enough to spare him the agony he was put through at the end of his career, a career that concluded prematurely, because someone had lied and had been believed.

The accident had occurred in California on a routine training mission. Margit's father had been in charge of maintenance for a fleet of helicopters at a base in northern California. He was within one year of his retirement, but everyone, including Margit, knew he would never retire voluntarily. They would carry him out in uniform, kicking and screaming.

Until the accident.

The pilot had lost control of his chopper and died in the resulting crash. "Mechanical failure" was the official explanation. His controls had frozen, rendering the craft unmanageable. Why had the controls failed? Repair work on them had been done by a young airman in Falk's unit. Falk knew what had caused the crash because he'd gone over every inch of the helicopter's parts when they were trucked back to the base. Controls had inadvertently been crossed.

"It could happen to anyone," her father had told Margit. "The kid made a mistake, that's all. Damn it! I wish he hadn't, but he did."

Margit's father had made a mistake, too. In the flood of paperwork, he'd signed off on the repair to the chopper's controls because the airman who'd actually done the work was on leave and would not be available for weeks. Falk explained this to the investigating team, and the panel initially accepted it, issuing only a mild reprimand for having certified repairs he hadn't personally performed.

When the airman returned to duty and was called in to account for his mistake, he lied. Knowing he hadn't signed the form, he claimed that Falk had actually done the repairs. "His signature is on the release, isn't it?" he'd told the investigating panel.

Falk was angry at the airman's lie but assumed nothing would come of it. His record had been pristine, exemplary. He was certain that his version of what happened would be believed.

But there was a factor that Falk hadn't counted upon. The investigatory panel was headed by a bird colonel who'd been stationed with Falk at a previous base. The colonel was flight-rated, which brought him into frequent contact with his line chief, Sergeant Fred Falk. One day the colonel ordered Falk to shortcut a maintenance procedure, which, Falk believed, would create a potentially dangerous condition for the unit's pilots. He refused, politely at first, more adamantly as the debate continued. The colonel brought him up on charges of insubordination. When the case was heard, Falk prevailed. His judgment concerning the maintenance was upheld, and the colonel's charges were dropped.

Falk knew the colonel would not forgive him for making him look foolish in front of his commissioned colleagues. He was right. They didn't speak again for the duration of their tours at the base. Their next assignments took them in different directions until, four years later, they ended up together in California. They had little to do with each other until the accident, and the investigation. The colonel's memory was long. The airman's version of what had happened was accepted. Guided by the colonel with a grudge, the panel recommended that Falk be removed from duty as a line-maintenance supervisor. He fought the decision, but his avenues of recourse were narrow. Eventually, he was given the choice of continuing in the service at a desk job or taking early retirement. From his perspective he didn't have a choice. Throat burning with bile, he left the air force.

Those early days as a civilian were as painful for Margit as they were for her father. They were forced to leave base housing and to rent a small house in town where Margit watched him sit in a chair in the living room for days on end, barely speaking, seemingly growing older with each breath. Gone was the spark, the sense of urgency, that he always felt upon getting up every morning and tending to his flock of ungainly helicopters. She became fearful for him, thought he might take his life.

Eventually, a family friend who'd started a small commuter airline convinced Falk to join the company as vice president of maintenance. Margit's father appeared to be proud of his new title and responsibilities, but in retrospect she knew he was putting up a front. He never felt the pride and sense of accomplishment he'd had as a member of the military.

Whatever discomfort he felt being out of uniform was short-lived. He was dead before he could celebrate his first year on his civilian job. A coronary. Premature. Mercifully quick.

"Just came out of her hundred hour," the young line chief said. Every hundred hours, the choppers were taken off the line for regularly scheduled maintenance.

Margit handed him a clipboard she carried in one hand. Her flight case was in the other. He signed off and moved to another chopper.

Margit put her flight case inside the cockpit and proceeded with her own external inspection of the Huey, using a printed list of sixty-three items as her guide. Some pilots were lazy and shortcutted the preflight, taking the line chief's word that an aircraft was fit to fly. Margit's father often told her that certain pilots, particularly young ones, seemed afraid that he might be offended if they double-checked his work, like a patient reluctant to seek a second opinion for fear of alienating the primary physician.

She stood on the cockpit roof and carefully examined the rotor hub that held the blades to the craft. They didn't call it the "Jesus Nut" for nothing. If it let loose, you were in a nonsurvivable accident, straight down, like a rock, no blades to slow the descent. As for parachutes, copter pilots didn't wear them, even in combat. No time to use a chute. Instead, every chopper pilot going into battle carried two flak jackets, one to wear to protect the torso, one to sit on to deflect enemy bullets coming through the floor. Her final action was to get down on her knees beneath the craft and to push the fuel-drain valve, allowing a few ounces of fuel to fall into a test tube she'd carried in her flight bag. It looked clear; no water from condensation in it. She returned the tube to its special compartment in the bag.

Climbing into the right-hand seat, a familiar exhilaration gripped her, as it always did when she was about to fly. It had been that way since the day when, as a teenager, she began training for her private pilot's license.

She'd pestered her father for a chance to learn to fly, and he'd finally agreed, not because he approved of the idea but because he was tired of being badgered. He drove her to a small civilian airport—a grass strip and corrugated-metal building—and signed her up with an old-time crop duster named Pop Mills. Margit never did learn his real first name. It didn't matter. He was a crusty, demanding instructor who smiled not once during the first seven hours of their dual instruction in a Cessna 150.

Then, on a Saturday morning after they'd spent the first half of the eighth hour shooting takeoffs and landings, he instructed her to taxi to the metal building. He got out and told her to continue takeoffs and landings on her own.

"Really?" she'd said, nerves quivering.

"Yup. Just remember, without my weight she'll handle different." His leathery face creased into what could pass for a smile. Then he winked. "Don't mess up. I only got two a' these."

She didn't mess up, and the joyous feeling she experienced that day, alone at the controls and flying free in a vast, pristine sky, had never left her. That was the way most pilots felt, at least the ones she knew. It wasn't the mission you were on; it was the sheer joy of being up there. Once bitten by that beautiful bug, the addiction was powerful, the habit unbreakable.

She carefully adjusted the Huey's seat so that her left hand naturally fell on the collective pitch lever. The cyclic stick rested comfortably between her legs. She tapped her toes on the antitorque pedals. Ready to go.

She strapped the clipboard to the top of her left thigh, shifted papers on it, and ran down the printed pre-start and start checklist, twelve distinct things to do; fingers flicking switches and turning knobs, eyes taking in gauge readings, mind analyzing what she observed. That chore completed, she replaced the pre-start list with the PPC, the Performance Planning Card.

She tuned into ATIS on her radio, the Automatic Transcribed Information Service that gives out a constant stream of recorded information on airport flight conditions. Updated every hour, each version is designated by a letter of the phonetic alphabet. Margit listened to the "Bravo" report and jotted down notes.

"Clear!" she shouted out the open window. She hit the starter ignition trigger switch on the collective. The PT6 kicked in with a whine, and the main rotor began a slow, laborious circle above her. Up to a hover, she matched gauge readings to the PPC. Everything was within parameters; there was enough reserve power to take off from the confined area.

"Huey four-two-three—request permission to taxi to Charlie pad," she said into a microphone that curved out from her helmet and poised in front of her mouth. Through earphones in her helmet she received the permission she sought from ground control.

Margit gave a thumbs-up through the open window, indicating she was about to move.

The line chief gave her a halfhearted salute and stepped back.

Margit closed the window and eased up on the collective, which changed the pitch of the rotor blades. They bit into the air, and the Huey rose from the tarmac.

Hovering three feet off the ground, she gave a final glance at her engine instruments and applied gentle pressure to the right antitorque pedal, which sent the Huey pivoting about the main rotor shaft in the direction of the departure pad a thousand feet away.

She adjusted the cyclic, and the craft moved forward in what tower controllers call a "hover taxi." Still only feet off the ground, she maneuvered the Huey to the pad, a circle outlined in white paint, and with a Maltese cross in its center.

To the tower: "Air Force four-two-three ready for takeoff. I have information Bravo. Proceeding to practice area."

"Roger, four-two-three. Enjoy!"

Margit smiled as she coordinated left and right hands. She adjusted the collective, and she climbed, the ground falling away below. She was higher now, but not too high. One reason to enjoy flying choppers was that there was more reason, to say nothing of regulatory permission, to fly low—very low.

She looked to the practice area, a heavily wooded government preserve at the perimeter of the base. Areas had been cleared for chopper pilots to practice getting in and out of tight spots. Her face lit up as she guided the craft to where she would run through a series of exercises designed to keep her skills sharp.

Every other aspect of her life disappeared—Cobol, Jeff Foxboro, the Pentagon, her BOQ at Bolling. It was at times like these that she questioned her decision to pursue a law degree. She'd had the option to remain a full-time chopper pilot, a role in which she'd been blissfully happy. Law, and becoming a lawyer, had also been appealing; a challenge, an opportunity to test intellect and to grow in knowledge.

But flying was where pure contentment existed. Not only was controlling an aircraft exhilarating, a chopper left you time for only intense concentration on the task at hand. Fixed-wing aircraft virtually flew themselves, as long as you didn't "mess up." You reach cruise altitude, trim up the plane, lock on the autopilot, and sit back.

But there was no time to glide through the air in a helicopter. Helicopters don't glide. You fly every second, and if you don't come back from a flight fatigued, something is wrong. Maybe you don't come back.

She flew "nap of the earth" once she reached the practice area, keeping the craft at "four-and-forty," four meters above the ground and the speed at forty knots, a useful technique in combat. She practiced hovering techniques in the clearings, then went to an open strip on the edge of the area and ran speed runs for the fun of it, the ground racing by but her speed only about three times faster than what Lindbergh had managed more than fifty years before.

She revisited the wooded area and visualized combat situations, responded to them—air evac of wounded, runs on imaginary enemy installations—things she was kept from doing in an actual conflict because of the regs prohibiting military women from flying combat missions. They may not have considered her runs in Panama to be "combat," but the men on the ground shooting at her as she passed over them at treetop level didn't know the regs. Tell it to her extra flak jacket, on which she'd sat and which took seven rounds through the copter's belly skin.

She ran through a running takeoff, the sort of maneuver all military chopper pilots—at least those still alive—found useful in hot jungle spaces where the air was less dense, the gross weight over specs, and the only chance of clearing trees was to pick up as much horizontal speed as possible before lifting off the ground and hope that the fat, wingless bird would make it over the trees—and not go into them.

She chose a point not too far in the distance. Imaginary trees. She adjusted the cyclic and collective and was soon moving horizontally in the direction of her designated spot. When she reached that point, she sent the Huey into a fast vertical climb, the ground falling away, the crisp blue sky enveloping her.

The hour went by fast. Her final practice maneuver was an autorotation exercise from one thousand feet in which the helicopter's transmission design allows the main and tail rotors to rotate freely when the engine is stopped, or comes to an idle.

She rotated the twist-grip throttle on the end of the collective to the idle position, and immediately lowered the collective to maintain rotor rpm. This produced an immediate descent. Margit maintained proper airspeed with the cyclic, and direction control with the pedals, the craft's forward speed producing enough energy in the rotating blades to decrease the rate of descent.

At a precise altitude above the ground, she initiated a flare by moving the cyclic to the rear. But rather than touch down, she decided to make a power recovery. She simultaneously moved the cyclic forward to place the chopper in a landing attitude, applied collective pitch to check the descent, increased throttle to return the engine and rotor to operating rpm, all the while continuing to maintain directional control with the pedals. Her sure and practiced movements brought the Huey to a hover at the exact place she'd intended. Satisfied, she entered a final fast vertical climb before heading back.

If there was one aspect of chopper flying that Margit didn't enjoy, it was the vibration. You learned to deal with it—you had to—but you never liked it. The vibration that suddenly shook Huey 423, however, was beyond normal limits. Margit had been taught to differentiate between types of vibrations, and this one was high frequency, emanating from the pedals, most likely caused by a problem with the tail rotor. She reduced power to compensate for what was happening at the rear. She wasn't concerned about making it back to the tarmac; she'd successfully dealt with tail-rotor problems before. Once she'd landed, however, it meant filling out multiple forms. Paperwork. The military thrived on it.

She approached her landing straight into the wind, and used minimal power changes to put as little pressure as possible on the tail rotor. As she felt the skids touch the ground, she breathed a sigh of relief.

The young line chief was running a visual inspection on another

Huey when Margit approached on foot. She told him of the problem she'd encountered.

"Shouldn't be," he said. "She just came out of her hundred hour."

Margit had heard that before. It didn't matter what maintenance it had undergone. The fact was that the tail rotor posed a potentially dangerous situation for the next pilot.

"I'll write it up inside," Margit said, doing a good job of hiding her annoyance.

"We'll have to truck it," he said, looking to where she'd left the craft.

"Right," she replied.

He didn't bother to salute this time. S.O.B, Margit thought as she went into Ops and found the appropriate forms. Nothing like her father. He would have shown instant concern, would have listened carefully to the pilot's description of the problem.

By the time she was in her car heading back to Bolling, she'd forgotten about the line chief, thought only of what she'd left on the ground an hour before—Flo and Robert Cobol, Jeff Foxboro, and whether she could convince Mac Smith to help her officially.

She took a shower, wrapped herself in a heavy terry-cloth robe, and returned a call Smith had left on her answering machine. No luck. She'd missed him again, machine talking to machine. He said he'd be home later that evening.

There was a second call, this from Colonel William Monroney, who said he was having dinner in the Bolling Officers' Club with some people and invited Margit to join them.

"No thanks," she muttered.

She thought of Jeff and the disappointment of having their weekend plans dashed, and she reminded herself that she had no right to feel anger or bitterness about it. But the portion of her brain giving out that rational message wasn't communicating with the softer side where emotions dwelt.

Monroney had said he would be in the club at seven. She again dismissed the idea, looked at the corner of her desk where the growing file on the Cobol case rested, debated it, and decided she could use a good dinner and some upbeat conversation. Why not?

· · ·

Margit and Monroney sat in the Officers' Club cocktail lounge. With him was an old friend, Lewis—she never did get the last name—who was stationed in Europe and was in Washington for a week of meetings, and an aide to Monroney, Major Anthony Mucci. Monroney's friend Lewis and Tony Mucci were a study in contrasts. His friend was a jovial sort who kept Margit and Monroney laughing with stories about his recent exploits in avoiding a good-conduct medal. He'd had quite a bit to drink, and proposed marriage to Margit at the end of the evening. "It would be great having a chopper pilot and lawyer as a wife," he'd said, "even better than marrying somebody whose father owns a liquor store." Margit had pleasantly declined his offer, and an hour later he departed, leaving Monroney, Mucci, and Margit standing at the front door. "Nightcap?" Monroney asked.

"Can't, Colonel," Mucci said, his face set in stone as it had been all evening. It wasn't that Mucci was sullen. He wasn't even unpleasant. The problem for Margit was that he seldom laughed, as though his life had precluded opportunities to practice. Sitting with someone who doesn't laugh can make you feel guilty for laughing. Too frivolous, too shallow, for the stiff, correct, and handsome young major. But, she'd decided early, that was his problem, not hers, and she'd giggled even louder at Lewis's funny, obviously tall tales. After all, that's why she'd decided to join them.

"Your call, Tony," Monroney said.

"I have to run the duty roster," Mucci said. "Good night, Major."

"Good night," Margit replied.

They watched him leave the club. "You, Margit?"

"Thanks, no. I'd better get back."

"Just a quick one, Margit. Please. For old times' sake."

And so they sat in the lounge, he sipping a gin and tonic, she looking at an untouched Serrana.

"Glad you could join us," he said.

"I enjoyed it. Your friend's a funny guy."

"Almost as funny as Tony."

"Almost," Margit said, enjoying another laugh.

"He's a good officer. Loyal, conscientious, bright. He won't win the Pentagon personality award, but he gets the job done. As for

Lewis, the only problem is, he dominates a conversation. I'd hoped to have more time to talk with you."

"I wouldn't have had much to say."

"You have a lot to say," he said. "You know, Margit, I think a lot about Panama, about the time we spent together there."

She was now uncomfortable, and wondered whether he sensed it. Panama was *then,* in the past, nothing to dwell upon. "I don't," she said, knowing she sounded nasty. It was also dishonest because she *had* thought about Panama many times, especially that aspect of the assignment that had brought her into a brief but close relationship with the handsome man sitting next to her. She hadn't known he was married then; she hadn't asked, nor had he offered the information. She'd found out later about Celia and their two children. It had upset her, although their relationship was over by that time. She'd resented him for not telling her that he had a family. She'd felt used, assumed she'd been just another conquest by a married man who'd undoubtedly conquered many.

As though reading her thoughts, he said, "You know, Margit, I meant what I said in Panama."

"What was that?"

"That you represented something special for me. I'm not a womanizer. I don't play around, take off my wedding band and apply tanning cream whenever I'm on TDY. There was a lot more to my feelings about you than a fling."

She remembered the night he told her that. That was the night he'd admitted that he was married. She didn't believe it then. Now, it wasn't a matter of not believing. It just didn't matter.

"Look, Margit, I'm not suggesting we rekindle what we had."

"Thank you very much."

"But I don't see any reason why we can't be friends now that you're here in Washington. I'd like to feel we could get together and talk, laugh like we did tonight, enjoy each other's company." He smiled and held up his hands. "On a platonic level, of course."

Margit said nothing.

"Is there someone in your life, someone special?" he asked.

She nodded.

"Military?"

"No, another lawyer. On Senator Wishengrad's staff. We met in law school."

"Senator Wishengrad. The bane of the Pentagon. Must make for some interesting dialogue between you and your friend."

Margit laughed. "Well, we do come at the military establishment from different points of view."

"That's probably good," said Monroney. "Keeps things from getting dull."

"Sure does," said Margit. "Look, Bill, I really do have to get back. This was a lovely evening, and I thank you for inviting me." She stood.

He remained seated. "One of the things I wanted to ask you, Margit, was about the Joycelen murder. You've got yourself one hell of an assignment defending Cobol."

"That is putting it mildly."

"I assume you'll be interviewing me."

"Why would I do that?"

"I was there—I went into the building afterward. Remember?"

"I have photos, and the statement you wrote. That should be enough. If it isn't, I know where to find you."

They walked to the club's front door. "Can we get together again, just the two of us, to talk, a couple of air-force buddies?"

"Not for a long time, Bill. The Cobol case will have me tied up for the duration. Thanks again. I enjoyed it." They shook hands.

It was too late to call the early-to-bed, early-to-rise Mac Smith. It would wait until tomorrow. Margit watched television until midnight, then climbed under the covers and lay awake for a long time. Things seemed to be getting out of control, a situation with which she was singularly unfamiliar, and that she didn't like. Maybe that was what happened as you got older, she mused.

If so, who needs birthdays?

CHAPTER

FOURTEEN

Margit came out of a long, dull Labor Day weekend revved up and rarin' to go.

During a long, leisurely run on Monday that worked up a cleansing sweat, she came to the conclusion that she'd been acting wimpish, had allowed herself to become muddled with confusion and afraid to take the reins in the Cobol case. Her assistant and investigator would arrive on Wednesday. They would need immediate direction from her, definitive, sure supervision. She'd seen ineffectual leaders in the military who, because they weren't confident in themselves and in their mission, transmitted weakness to those reporting to them. That wouldn't be the case with her.

She was aware, however, that her newfound confidence was based, in part, on two hours spent on Sunday with Mackensie Smith. Their answering machines had finally caught up with each other and had put their respective human owners together.

Smith had agreed to work with Margit as an unofficial adviser. Yes, he would accept a modest fee from Mrs. Cobol, which would be shared equally with the Washington Humane Society and the Coalition for the Homeless. It didn't matter to Margit who ended up with the money, as long as Smith was a *paid* adviser.

They agreed that Smith would review all materials gathered by Margit for the defense, and would help her structure a strategy to use during the court-martial. "But strictly in the background," he'd said.

"But won't the court have to be made aware that other counsel is involved?" she asked.

"Probably, but you're the trial attorney." Smith laughed. "Just the opposite from when I was practicing law in this city. The other people in my firm often wrote the script. All I had to do was deliver it before a jury, with feeling. In this case, I'll support you the best I can, but you're in the spotlight. You take the heat."

"Fair enough," she'd said.

They'd also discussed specific strategies, each keyed to how the court-martial might progress. As it stood, Cobol had pleaded Not Guilty, and the focus of Margit's preparation would be to counter tangible evidence presented by the prosecution and to create a sufficient level of doubt in the minds of the court-martial board as to his guilt. If the investigation failed to turn up sufficient hard information to render the prosecution's evidence questionable, they agreed that she would have to be prepared to go to another level, perhaps to attempt to point the finger of guilt in another direction if allowed to do so by the court or, as a last resort, to seek to save Cobol's life through an insanity plea.

"That would depend upon whether there was some personal relationship between Cobol and Joycelen," Smith said. "You say Cobol flat-out denies a homosexual relationship with Joycelen. Believe him?"

Margit nodded. "Yes, I do, just as I've come to believe he's innocent."

"Based upon what?"

"A gut reaction. Being with him." She held up her hands in mock defense. "I know, I know, Mac, I'm probably naive. But his answers to my questions have a ring of truth to them. Either he's telling the truth or he's a skilled liar."

"Which would make him a credible witness on his own behalf," Smith said.

"I'm not sure about that."

Margit asked Smith if he would be willing to meet with Cobol. Smith said he would.

"Which takes you out of the shadows," Margit said.

"It can be done quietly. Set it up."

"Okay."

As she was getting ready to leave Smith's house, he said, "You do know that you might be treading on thin ice, Margit, bringing me in like this. You say your boss didn't like the idea. How are you going to appease him?"

"By telling him that the accused requested civilian counsel."

"Which is not entirely true."

"Not entirely a lie, either. All I did was make the suggestion to Cobol and his mother. They decided it was a good idea. I don't think I'll have any problem with Bellis. He's tough, but fair."

On Wednesday morning following the long weekend, Margit sat in her new office across the hall from Bellis. With her were marine warrant officer Peter Woosky, the legal assistant sent her from Quantico, and an investigator from the Army Military Police Operations Agency, Master Sergeant Matthew Silbert.

Margit judged Woosky to be about fifty, a man whose face said "weary." Ashy jowls hung loose from the framework of his long face. His eyes were large, brown, and sad. His gray hair looked tinderbox dry, a brushfire in search of a match.

Silbert, on the other hand, was bright-eyed, intense, and quick to smile. He wore a classic crew cut and was spit-and-polish in his dress, as opposed to Woosky, for whom, rare among marines, uniform maintenance was evidently not a high priority.

"Well, gentlemen, nice to have you here. I can certainly use the help."

Silbert smiled. Woosky did not.

"Have you been filled in on the nature of this case and the person I'm defending?"

Woosky shook his head, but Silbert said, "I know you're defending Captain Robert Cobol in the murder of Dr. Richard Joycelen. Once I knew that, I learned a lot from reading the papers and watching TV. If you can believe them."

"They have it right so far," Margit said. "Captain Cobol denies the charges against him despite physical, if circumstantial, evidence to the contrary. The weapon used to kill Joycelen, according to the prosecution, belonged to Cobol. It has the serial number that was checked out to him, and his initials are carved in the butt. Less tangible, but certainly not insignificant, is that he was in the vicinity at the time of the murder. As you know, it was Saturday morning. And, the papers speculate, he was involved in a homosexual relationship with Joycelen."

"Is that true?" Woosky asked.

"I don't think so. Captain Cobol denies it. Joycelen was married twice, and was engaged to be married a third time."

Sergeant Silbert sat back and shook his head, a small, knowing smile on his lips.

"Yes, Sergeant?"

"You never know. I've investigated a couple of cases where it turned out someone who'd been married started chasing boys."

"Was that the purpose of those investigations, to ascertain sexual preference?"

"Yes, ma'am."

"And . . . ?"

"And, they both got bounced out under 1332."

"I see," Margit said. "I appreciate your experience, but I don't believe there was a relationship between the two men."

"What about Cobol?" Silbert asked. "Is he gay?"

Margit didn't want to answer. Under ordinary circumstances she would have considered Cobol's sex life to be his own business. Of course, had she been confronted with his homosexual acts as his commander, she would have been placed in the same predicament that the mysterious Major Reich had been—whether to allow Cobol his indiscretion and keep a good officer, or to go strictly by the book. She looked Silbert in the eye. "Captain Cobol has acknowledged to me that he is homosexual."

"How did he manage to stay in so long?" Silbert asked.

"Discretion, I suppose," Margit said. She mentioned Reich and his decision not to report Cobol.

"First name?" Silbert asked, writing "Reich" on a pad.

"I don't know. I have to ask Captain Cobol about that. Reich was Cobol's superior at the CIA, but he's no longer there. I'd like to track him down and ask some questions."

"Want me to do that?" Silbert asked.

"Yes, I suppose so."

Woosky, who'd said virtually nothing, now offered, "If this Major Reich didn't report Cobol as a homosexual, he violated regs."

"I know, and I'm not looking to cause him any trouble. On the other hand, I have an accused murderer to defend."

"What could this Reich contribute to the defense?" Woosky asked.

"Background on Cobol. We don't have much at this point to counter the prosecution. Any bit of information or insight might be helpful."

Silbert asked, "Anybody you'd like me to talk to besides Reich?"

Many names flashed through Margit's mind. There were Christa Wren and Joycelen's two former wives. Cobol's roommate; she'd forgotten to get his name. Anyone on the duty roster that Saturday morning who might have come in contact with Cobol, and who could establish that he'd remained on the floor above where the murder took place for a significant period of time. There were others. A cast of thousands. Everyone at the picnic. Joycelen's coworkers who might have held a professional grudge.

As Margit formulated this list over the past week, it became increasingly evident to her that the best chance of saving Robert Cobol—assuming he was innocent—was to find the person who had, in fact, killed Richard Joycelen. That approach always worked for Perry Mason and Matlock during the final five minutes of their television trials. But this was real life. Forget it, Margit, she'd told herself. You're a military chopper pilot and lawyer, not a Raymond Chandler gumshoe. There's no romance in this. Down and dirty. Save Cobol's life and consider that a major victory. At the same time, do a credible enough job to keep your own career in gear. Had she really thought that? Bellis wasn't all wrong in asking her whether that was a consideration.

"Okay if I make a suggestion, Major?" Silbert said.

"Of course."

"I think I should speak with Captain Cobol. I can find out more from him about Major Reich, and maybe identify others to talk to."

"Go to it," Margit said. "Cobol has lived on the economy with a roommate, another homosexual. I didn't get his name, but he should be interviewed. I'll arrange for you to meet with Cobol. Want me with you?"

"No, ma'am, that won't be necessary."

Margit scribbled a note to call Fort McNair as soon as the meeting was over.

"How would you like me to get started, Major Falk?" Woosky asked.

"First, find out everything you can about Dr. Richard Joycelen. There's been a lot written about him since the murder, and I know stories have appeared over the years about his scientific work. I'd like to have as complete a picture as possible of this man."

"Yes, ma'am."

"What about Joycelen's friends and family?" Silbert asked. "Should I start a rundown on them?"

Margit almost told him to go ahead, but hesitated. "No, not yet. We'll talk to them later. Any questions?"

They shook their heads.

"I hope the office assigned to you will work out. Sorry you each can't have your own, but space is tight." An occupant of another office in the small suite had been moved out over the weekend, and furnishings had been moved in for Woosky and Silbert.

Silbert stood and hit a reflexive brace, like a pianist's fingers automatically curling over a keyboard. "I think the office is fine," he said. "I don't figure to spend much time in it anyway."

After they'd left, Margit sat back and sighed in relief. She'd been in command of other people before, including in wartime conditions. But those situations were clear-cut in the military sense. The job of military men and women was to fight, and to be prepared to fight. Chain of command. Rank. So easy to give orders, and to take them when doing what you'd joined up for in the first place. "Fuel that chopper." "Assemble at zero-five-hundred." "All leaves canceled."

But she was in a different milieu now, and she knew it. She was seated behind a desk like any civilian attorney, conferring with staff about a case. Sure, it was still the military; she could order Woosky and Silbert to do things. But in this setting—in this nonprimary military role—things were different—*had* to be different. They *felt* different . . . they were—off center.

The meeting had gone well, she decided. Woosky and Silbert had been just names until this morning. Now, they took on distinct personalities. They were real people, for better or for worse.

The differences between the two men were marked. Woosky, from Margit's perspective, was a career military man content to be in uniform but to stay out of harm's way, to sit in a small office and help other servicemen and women deal with mundane pressures of everyday life—writing a will, settling a bad debt with a car dealer or department store, maybe giving dry advice on how to amicably end a marriage. He wouldn't initiate much action, but would do as he was told.

In contrast, Silbert appeared to truly enjoy what he did as a noncommissioned officer. He was energetic, impatient, and probably needed constant patting and praise. She'd give him that; issuing orders would not be enough to coax optimum performance from him.

She called Flo Cobol in New York and told her about her two military assistants, and that Mackensie Smith had agreed to the role of informal adviser.

"It's nice that they would help Robert," Flo said.

"Who?" Margit asked.

"The army. I thought they might abandon him because of what they say he did, but I guess they won't. That's one of the things Robert always liked about being in the army. People pull together and help each other, he always said."

Margit agreed, although she wasn't sure assigning Woosky and Silbert to her on temporary duty reflected quite that level of altruism. Still, she had to acknowledge a certain truth in what Flo said. Military service did imbue you with a sense of camaraderie and common purpose, especially in the field and on the line in war, where lives depended upon it. Wait a minute. In courtrooms, too. The court-martial of Captain Robert Cobol was a war, words and a gavel the weapons, the potential victim in the trenches of confinement and with a rifle aimed at his head.

While talking with Flo, Margit glanced down at notes she'd taken during her Sunday meeting with Smith. One word had been underlined several times, and a string of question marks followed it. *"Insanity????"* She asked Cobol's mother whether Robert had ever demonstrated signs of mental instability.

Flo hesitated. "No. Robert is a stable young man."

Maybe, maybe not, Margit thought. She asked, "Has he ever been treated by a psychiatrist or psychologist?"

"Treated?" The mother's laugh was nervous, forced. "Of course not. He did visit one in New York but . . ."

Margit sat up and poised a pencil over a blank sheet of paper. "Why?" she asked.

"Why did he see this psychiatrist?" Flo said.

"Yes."

"Robert told me it was routine. Something to do with his assignment to the CIA." Another unnatural laugh. "I suppose every officer assigned to that organization has to be checked in some way to make sure they're stable enough to keep all the secrets. Robert must have been, because he got the assignment."

"He went to see this psychiatrist before he was assigned to the CIA?"

"Yes. Well, maybe not before, but not long after he'd started working there."

Margit had read Cobol's file a number of times. There was no mention of a psychiatrist's evaluation of Cobol's suitability to serve at the CIA. She asked, "Do you have any idea what the psychiatrist's name was?"

"I don't recall it. He was in New York City. Hold on a second, please." She returned a few minutes later. "His name is Dr. Half. Dr. Marcus Half."

"Robert wrote it down?"

"Yes. Major Falk, does this really have to be discussed? I mean, does it have anything to do with defending Robert?"

Margit was not about to raise the issue of an insanity plea with Cobol's mother. She said, "At this point, Mrs. Cobol, I don't know what's necessary and what isn't. Now that I have my two assistants, this phase involves gathering information from everyone and anyone who might be able to help us understand what happened. Did Robert tell you what he discussed with Dr. Half?"

"Of course not. That would be confidential. I remember he laughed about it, though, talked about the 'crazy shrink' in New York. I laughed, too—the patient calling the doctor crazy. He only went three or four times. I'm not sure. He acted strange after he came back each time."

"Strange?"

"Quiet. Not strange. Quiet."

The call completed, Margit busied herself making lists of things she wanted to accomplish. She had lunch at her desk. By three, a wave of fatigue washed over her. She closed her eyes and thought of Jeff, who was with his boss, Senator Wishengrad, at the first day of public hearings into the tumultuous Middle East.

Jeff had called her yesterday. In the brief conversation he apologized for fouling up the weekend's plans, and suggested they try to resurrect them as soon as possible. Then he said he had to run and would call again.

Her phone rang. Yes, it was Jeff. "I was just thinking about you," she said.

"Good," he said. "I was thinking about you, too, which should be evident by this call. Look, Margit, I've been acting like an absolute bastard. It's not because I want to, but because I'm so busy I've forgotten how to be nice, especially to a special person in my life."

She hadn't heard any terms of endearment from him for too long, and they were welcome.

"We just finished today's session. Remember when you were assigned to defend Cobol and you had to see me, had to spend time with me?"

"Sure."

"The shoe is on the other foot. Can we have a drink, dinner, just talk?"

The only commitment Margit had made that evening was to a quick dinner and a read-through of military regs that might be applicable to the Cobol case. They could wait. "Let's do it," she said cheerily.

"Great." He named a romantic restaurant in Virginia. "Let's get out of this crazy town for an evening. Game?"

"Absolutely. Pick me up here at the Pentagon?"

"How about meeting up at my apartment?"

They set a time, and she hung up feeling happier than she had in a while. She might have been filled with internal resolve that day, but a hand caressing her cheek in a candlelight setting, and a husky voice saying nice things, couldn't hurt.

CHAPTER
FIFTEEN

 They sat on a small terrace outside Jeff's bed-room, fingers laced and bare toes touching, watching the sun rise through a mashed-potato sky over the nation's capital. Jeff had thrown on a pair of gray sweats. Margit wore his bathrobe. Empty coffee cups were on a white plastic-mesh table.

"Happy?" he asked.

Her eyes were closed, and she smiled. "Yes, very. We shouldn't let so much time pass again."

"No happier than I am—couldn't be," he said. "Feel like some breakfast?"

She opened her eyes and turned to him. "Don't have time. I have to get home and change."

After she'd dressed in yesterday's clothing, he asked, "What's on today's agenda?"

"Well, let's see. I start off meeting with Colonel Bellis. We're supposed to meet twice a day, first thing in the morning and again in the afternoon. He canceled yesterday's morning meeting, but we're on for today. Then I want to check on the progress of Mr. Woosky and Sergeant Silbert. Silbert saw Cobol yesterday after-noon. I'm anxious to see how it went. And I have to set up a meeting between Cobol and Mac Smith, call Christa Wren and arrange to see her, and . . ."

"Smith really has agreed to get involved?"

"Yes. Isn't that great?"

"So are you."

During dinner at Chardon d'Or in Alexandria, Jeff had started by giving her a play-by-play of the day's Senate hearing. He imitated witnesses and committee members with a series of sarcastic asides, and had her laughing throughout the early stages of their meal. Then, he'd said, "Enough about me and my day. Fill me in, Margit, on yours. Every bit of it."

"I don't do impressions," she'd said.

"No need."

And so she gave him a rundown of everything that was happening in her life, which, of course, meant the Cobol case, and told him of Smith's decision to be an adviser. She'd sensed an initial flash of disapproval from Jeff, but it was fleeting. Instead of second-guessing her—which she'd expected—he'd told her he thought it was a good decision, and asked many questions about what had transpired during her Sunday meeting with their former professor and current friend.

His unexpected agreement with her decision—in fact, a total lack of a challenge from him the entire night about anything she'd been doing—made for an extremely pleasant dinner.

"What about Joycelen?" he asked as they stood in his foyer that Thursday morning.

"What about him?"

"Have you done much digging into his life?"

"I assigned Mr. Woosky that task. Whatever clippings he comes up with."

"It seems to me you'd want to place more emphasis on Cobol, his background."

"Of course. I intend to focus on that myself."

"Could be you're taking on more than you should. That's what help is for."

When Margit didn't respond and poised to leave, he asked, "What's new on the homosexual slant?"

"It's not true."

Foxboro leaned against the wall. "I heard a rumor yesterday that Joycelen went both ways."

"Who did you hear that from?"

"Cloakroom gossip. Probably no truth to it."

"Probably not."

"But, if it *is* true that Joycelen and Cobol had a personal relationship, it would give Cobol a motive, wouldn't it? I mean, after all, it's hard to imagine why an army captain would gun down a leading scientist—unless there was something personal between them."

"If there was, it'll eventually come out," Margit said.

She left the apartment carrying with her the lovely aftereffects of an extended, passionate kiss.

As she drove to Bolling for a quick shower and change of clothing, three cars moved slowly on U.S.-9. They passed the Cape May Ferry and continued until reaching a sign where the road divided. The lead car took the right fork, and the others followed. Soon, they entered a wooded recreation area on the Atlantic Ocean that was part of Cape Henlopen State Park. A small sign indicated they'd entered the Fort Miles recreation area, an off-post military R&R just outside Fort Meade. Forts everywhere, it seems, surrounding D.C.

They stopped in front of a building that looked like any other small apartment complex in the Washington area. The three uniformed drivers remained behind their wheels as six men emerged from the cars, two from each. Some wore military uniforms; others were in civilian clothing.

They climbed a short set of steps to the front door where a sign said NO VACANCIES. The first man, who was dressed in civilian clothing, pushed through the door and went to a desk where two marine enlisted men snapped to attention. "Secured?" the civilian asked.

"Yes, sir," the marines answered in unison.

A navy commander bounded down a set of stairs behind the desk and stiffened. "Good morning, Mr. Massingill," he said to DOD's undersecretary for policy. "Follow me, please."

They followed the navy officer up the stairs and down a hallway to its end. He opened a door and stepped back to allow them to enter. When the last man was inside, the navy officer closed the door and took a position against the wall immediately outside the room. Four armed marines stepped into the hallway through another door. Not a word was spoken.

Apartment 2-G was furnished with military-issue furniture. The men removed their topcoats and tossed them on a couch. In the kitchen fresh-brewed coffee stayed hot in insulated carafes. A tray of pastry was on the counter, flanked by neatly folded paper napkins and plastic utensils.

The six men fell into a seating arrangement that naturally placed Massingill in a leadership position. "Well, where do we stand?" he asked.

"Hard to say." The CIA's assistant director for foreign policy, Joe Carter, was responding. "We're evaluating the situation now."

"Using what methods?" Massingill asked.

"Everything we have at our disposal," Carter replied, "including eyeballing things up close, on the scene."

The disgust and anger Massingill felt colored his voice. "Just how long will this investigation, this eyeball analysis, take, Mr. Carter?"

Carter, a studious man of middle age, whose large horn-rimmed glasses were distinctly old-fashioned, glanced at the others. "We should have a handle on things within a week," he said.

"A week," Massingill repeated flatly. "There were assurances from the very beginning from you, from Mr. Hickey, and from the others in this room that the terms of the agreement would be met without exception."

"They'd better be," Colonel James Bellis said. "You all know that the secretary of defense had grave reservations about this project from the beginning. So did I. I counseled against it based upon the legal ramifications should it go sour, but I was outvoted. Based upon recent events, I'd say those legal ramifications are looking more likely every day. And they're pretty goddamn serious."

"There were safeguards in place," CIA's Carter offered. "As far as we know, those safeguards haven't been violated."

"That isn't the way I read it," Massingill said. "The murder of that German doesn't look to me like safeguards are working."

"That reflects a business arrangement gone bad," said Carter. "It has nothing to do with our deal with him. Strictly a private matter."

Massingill swiveled left and right in his chair. "Jesus, I can't *believe* I'm hearing this," he said. "We went ahead on the assumption that every detail was worked out, every goddamn *t* was crossed." He glared at Carter. "You and your agency assured us that he was the most stable leader in the region. You and your agency assured us that he was in our camp a hundred percent, and that it was his intention to use whatever weapons given him to work for stability and peace in the region. Isn't that what we were told, Mr. Carter? Didn't you and your boss tell us that?"

"And nothing has changed," said Carter. "We are still of that opinion about him."

"Based upon what?"

"Based upon a long-term and careful analysis of the man, his motives, history, intentions, the overall situation."

"The German press is beginning to make something out of Mr. Keller's murder," said an air-force major from DOD's European Sector Analysis Division. "They're investigating his history as an arms dealer, and are probing for connections with others."

"Can they trace him?" Massingill asked. "I mean, all the way back here?"

Carter shook his head. "Absolutely not."

"What if they can?" Massingill asked Bellis.

Bellis was careful and slow in his answer. "Legally, I believe sufficient distance can be put between the active participants and DOD. SecDef is not directly involved, which, you'll remember, I insisted upon."

"But his tacit approval was given," said Massingill.

"Depending upon how you view it," Bellis answered.

Massingill turned to another uniformed officer in the group, an army bird colonel, Arlie "Specs" Praeger, who commanded the Pentagon division in charge of selling American weaponry to foreign countries. Praeger was a short, muscular man with a beaked nose and steady black eyes. "Are you meeting with Consulent soon?" Massingill asked.

"Nothing planned."

"I think you'd better."

"I'll set it up as soon as we leave," Praeger promised.

On the trip back to the Pentagon Praeger and Bellis shared the car that had taken them to the meeting. It was driven by Bellis's aide and driver, Lieutenant Max Lanning.

"Call them off," Bellis said. "Let's get the Cobol business behind us before they make any more moves."

"How does that stand?" Praeger asked.

"Under control, but there's a long way to go. I'm trying to speed it up, but . . . well, I'll keep you up-to-date." Unsaid was the unsettled tension he'd felt in his gut since getting up that morning. He'd thought for years that the biggest problem faced by every busy man was a lack of time to think. Everything these days, it seemed, was reaction rather than reflection. Putting out those proverbial fires, and so many of them. Everyone involved in the meeting from which he'd just emerged could use some quiet think time. Maybe if they'd indulged themselves in it, his advice would have been heeded. Maybe. If. This was not just another little one-alarm blaze to be extinguished; it had all the potential of a raging firestorm.

CHAPTER

SIXTEEN

 Bellis had canceled their regular morning meeting, so Margit began her day by meeting with Woosky and Silbert. She said she wanted to see them separately, citing the tight quarters of her little office as the reason. Somehow, it seemed wise to her to do it that way. Ordinarily, she'd prefer working as a team, but she wasn't sure this was a team—yet. Woosky, whom she saw first, handed her a manila folder bulging with material.

Margit smiled. "I didn't expect so much."

"A lot of it is work published by Dr. Joycelen. Plus a bio, some newspaper clips."

Margit browsed through the material. "I see what you mean," she said. Included in the folder were technical reports issued by DARPA, including a recent one signed by Richard Joycelen on the development of the X-ray laser, the technology behind Project Safekeep. There was also a transcript of testimony given to the House Armed Services Committee's Subcommittee on Research and Development. It was delivered, for the most part, by DARPA's director, but significant portions had been provided by Joycelen.

Margit closed the file. "Looks like I have some reading to do," she said. The folder was thick with photocopies, thin in content.

Woosky did not respond.

She said, "I'd like you to start researching applicable case law."

"Yes, ma'am."

When Silbert had replaced Woosky in the chair across the desk from Margit, she asked, "How did your interview with Cobol go?"

"Okay, I guess. He's uptight, isn't he?"

Margit cocked her head. "I wouldn't describe him that way."

"Well, he was when I was with him."

Margit mentioned her meetings with Cobol. He'd been so placid, so mild-mannered, so accepting. What had changed him? She asked Silbert whether something had taken place to cause this change in behavior.

Silbert shrugged. "Maybe his mother. She surprised him yesterday with a visit."

"She did? I wonder why she didn't call me."

Another shrug from Silbert. "Cobol mentioned it in passing. I was only with him twenty minutes or so. Frankly, I was glad to leave. I started to get uptight, too. I suppose I can't blame him, being accused of murdering a top techno."

"No, we can't blame him," Margit said quietly. "What did he tell you?"

"Not much. He said a doctor had been in to see him that morning."

"A doctor?"

"Yes, ma'am."

"Why?"

"I don't know, Major. He rattled on about they kept his mother from visiting him until you stepped in. I asked him the name of his roommate, and it spooked him. He kept asking me what his roommate had to do with any of this. I told him probably nothing, but that you wanted a name. He finally gave it to me." Silbert slid a piece of paper across the desk. On it was written *Brian Maitland*.

"What else?" Margit asked.

"I got the name of that Major Reich you wanted." Another slip of paper came at Margit: *Major Wayne Reich*.

"Follow up," Margit said. "Locate him and see if you can arrange an interview."

"Shall do," Silbert said smartly. "Want me to contact Brian Maitland?"

"Not yet," Margit said. "How was Cobol when you left him?"

"The same as when I arrived. Anxious."

"Thank you, Sergeant. I'd like you to begin interviewing those who were on duty in the Pentagon the morning of Joycelen's murder. Get ahold of the duty roster. After that, let's try to identify those people who attended the picnic, who knew Joycelen, and who had access to the building."

The moment Silbert left, Margit called Mac Smith. "What day would be good for you to visit my client?" she asked.

"Monday looks good," he replied.

"Morning or afternoon?"

"Afternoon, if possible."

"I'll *make* it possible."

"How's it going, Margit?"

"I don't know. My investigator visited Cobol yesterday and said he was in an agitated state. Hard to believe. Whenever I've been with him, he's been the picture of tranquillity."

"I have Monday written down," said Smith. "What does your weekend look like?"

"Work."

"Well, if you feel like taking a break, give me a call."

"Sounds appealing. I'll keep it in mind."

Her phone rang minutes later. It was Jeff. "I miss you," he said.

"That's the nicest news of the day. I haven't had a chance to miss anyone this morning, but now that you mention it, I do. Miss you, I mean."

"Good. Up for dinner tonight?"

"I don't think so, but thanks. I'm facing reams of reading. Even harder, thinking. Maybe I'd better hunker down and do with a quick sandwich."

"Sounds dull to me," he said.

"If it sounds dull to you, imagine what it is to me. Tomorrow?"

"Sure. I'll call you tonight."

Margit closed her door and read the material Woosky had delivered about Joycelen. The picture that emerged was as advertised, a fascinating, brilliant, and also enigmatic man.

He was fifty-eight when he was killed. Had he lived another week, he would have been fifty-nine. He was born in Argentina to British parents; his father had been an engineer sent there by the British company for whom he worked.

Joycelen attended a church-run school in Argentina until he was eight. Then his parents sent him back home to England, where he attended boarding schools.

After having established himself in England as a young man with a future in the physical sciences, Joycelen was accepted at MIT. His undergraduate years there were outstanding, and he received a fellowship to Stanford, where he obtained his advanced degrees in physics. His dissertation was in what was then the infant field of laser energy. After stints at two private research centers in California, he was offered a position in Washington with the Defense Advanced Research Project Agency. DARPA was a key spot, a center for cutting-edge technology, a high-energy place.

Indeed, charged with the mission of using high-energy lasers to develop advanced weapons systems—and basking in seemingly unlimited budgets authorized by Congress for a time—Joycelen had risen to preeminence within the esoteric scientific realms of national defense and its insatiable needs.

DARPA had been created by President Eisenhower in 1958 in response to the challenge posed by the Soviets' launch of *Sputnik*. Organized as a separate agency under the Office of Secretary of Defense, and reporting to the undersecretary of defense for acquisition, it quickly became the central research-and-development organization for DOD.

Known informally as the "venture capitalists of the Defense Department," DARPA did no research itself. Its 125 employees, working out of the brown glass-and-concrete Architects Building on Wilson Boulevard in Rosslyn, Virginia, contracted out all research and development to private-sector laboratories and research centers, and to American companies.

One clipping in the file was of special interest to Margit. It quoted extensively from Jeff Foxboro's boss, Senator Hank Wishengrad, whose criticism of the Department of Defense was well known. Wishengrad had started pushing for DARPA to devote a portion of its research energies and dollars to technology that could be converted into civilian industry. It was his contention that for the nation's leading military-scientific think tank to focus only upon armament needs was to shortchange the nation by diverting funds that could make American industry more competitive in the world economic arena. Joycelen, to Margit's surprise, while not siding with the senator, indicated in some of his quotes that he could see the future wisdom of slowly shifting funds from military to civilian objectives. He cited research currently being done on high-energy lasers that, while potentially the basis for weapons systems such as Project Safekeep, had even greater potential in the development of esoteric civilian products.

The article, written four months before the detonation of the nuclear device in the Middle East, spoke of recent cutbacks in funding for DARPA, which paralleled the substantial cuts mandated by Congress for all areas of the military establishment. The most vitriolic attacks upon these budget cuts came from the Pentagon's undersecretary for policy, Bruce Massingill: "This nation is being lulled into a defenseless posture by our enemies. When the shortsighted members of Congress come to their senses, every citizen can only hope and pray that it isn't too late."

Margit closed the folder and thought of the conversation at Mac and Annabel's house when Jeff had inadvertently displayed more knowledge of Dr. Richard Joycelen than he'd been willing to admit. Of course he knew more about the man. From what Margit had just read, there had been a running dialogue between Wishengrad's staff and Joycelen.

Her thoughts shifted to Cobol and what she'd been told by Silbert. She picked up the phone, dialed Trial Defense Services at McNair, and was put through to its commanding officer, Major Jenko. "This is Major Margit Falk, Captain Cobol's defense counsel. I understand he received medical attention yesterday."

"That's right." Jenko's tone said that he was not the most pleasant of individuals.

"May I ask what brought that about?" she said.

"He wasn't feeling well."

"Could you be more specific?"

"No, I can't be more specific," said Jenko. "He said he wasn't feeling well and wanted to see a doctor. We accommodated him."

"May I have the name of the doctor?"

There was a deep, pained sigh from Jenko. "I don't know what his name was. Med sent somebody over."

Margit's tone now matched his. "Would you please obtain the

name of the physician who treated my client and get back to me."
She gave him her Pentagon extension and hung up.

Jenko did not return Margit's call that afternoon. She was annoyed, but decided to give him until noon the following day to provide the physician's name.

As she sat in her BOQ room and read case law provided her by Woosky, two men were dining well at the Tivoli Restaurant in Rosslyn. Arlie Praeger, the Pentagon's chief of overseas weapons sales, sat with Consulnet's leader, Paul Potamos, at a secluded table. They'd started with melon topped with thinly sliced Citterio ham, progressed to a Bibb lettuce salad with house dressing, and Potamos was now finishing *calamari alla Livornese* and a veal cutlet garnished only with lemon wedges, Specs Praeger a mammoth bowl of linguine Alfredo.

An empty bottle of white wine sat on the table.

They waived dessert; cappuccino for one, regular coffee for the other.

"As I said earlier, politics is not my concern," Potamos said.

Praeger laughed. "It shouldn't be mine, either, but that isn't realistic. None of us operates in a political vacuum, except for a few people who have a vacuum where their brains should be."

Potamos saw nothing funny in what was being discussed. He toyed with a demitasse spoon and kept his eyes on it as he said, "We provided the services as promised. Frankly, it was more difficult than any of us imagined. This was not business as usual, Arlie. This wasn't simply a matter of selling a piece of hardware. It took coordination with a dozen sources."

"I understand the difficulties you faced, Paul, but the compensation more than made up for it." When Potamos did not reply, Praeger added, "Right?"

Potamos, his eyes focused on the small silver spoon that he twirled between his fingers, offered one of his few smiles. "Compensation is never adequate if it isn't paid. We're not getting paid."

"I understand. I'm sorry about it, but this is not the time to press for payment. It's politically unsound."

Potamos dropped the spoon to the table. "And, as I've been pointing out to you all evening, Arlie, politics don't interest me. One of my people has lost his life because of politics."

"Unfortunate what happened to Mr. Keller," said Praeger. "But that's the point I'm trying to make. His death is focusing attention upon this project. The one thing it can't stand at this juncture is attention from any sector. It's my belief—and I'm confident I reflect the views of my superiors—that if everyone sits back and cools it, if you will, things will calm down and everyone's needs will be met, including your getting paid."

"Please, Arlie, don't patronize me. Consulnet isn't in the business of providing public service. It is a for-profit organization." Praeger started to say something, but Potamos raised his hand. "And, let me add, we are not concerned with saving anybody's political hide."

"Even if those people whose hides you claim not to care about can ultimately put you out of business?"

"Exactly," Potamos said.

Praeger, who'd maintained a determinedly cheerful disposition throughout the meal, angrily looked away in search of their waiter. He caught the man's eye and wrote in the air to call for the check. When it arrived, Potamos grabbed it. "I insist," he said.

"I won't argue," said Praeger. "This check isn't the issue. Think about what I've said. Think about bigger checks. Pull back. Let time pass. Then go after your money. We've backed you every inch of the way, and we'll continue to do so."

"Including making up our losses?"

"If necessary. The stakes are big for us, too. You might lose money. We stand to lose a government."

And, Potamos thought later, getting into the car, jobs, careers, reputations, and life outside of jail.

CHAPTER
SEVENTEEN

"Sounds like you've been busy," Bellis said to Margit during their Friday morning meeting.

"It took a while to get into gear," she said, "but I think we're making progress. The two people assigned to me seem capable."

Bellis, who'd been sitting back, fingers forming a tent on his chest, came forward and put his elbows on the desk. "What's next?" he asked.

Margit hadn't told him that Smith had agreed to join the defense. She was hesitant about bringing it up because, to be honest with herself, she was afraid of Bellis's reaction. He hadn't been pleased when the notion of civilian counsel had initially been raised. Should she have officially cleared Smith's involvement with Bellis before going ahead?

Too late for that now.

She said, "The Cobol family wishes to have civilian counsel work with me. I spoke with Mackensie Smith. He's agreed to come into the case."

Bellis's reaction: "I see."

"Smith is meeting with Cobol on Monday."

"Do you think that visit is necessary?"

"Yes, sir, I do. If he's to play a role, he ought to know the accused."

Bellis leaned back again and closed his eyes. When he opened them, he looked hard at her. "Why Smith? This city is crawling with trial lawyers, good criminal attorneys, many who've been involved before as civilian counsel in court-martials. Does Smith have any background in military law?"

"No, sir, he doesn't, but as you know, he was, among other things, one of Washington's leading criminal attorneys. He was also my professor. I feel comfortable with him. The Cobol family is pleased with the choice."

"You could have done better."

"In my choice of co-counsel?"

"Yes. Smith has been out of the active practice of law for many years. He's a professor."

"And one of the most brilliant men I've ever met."

"Brilliant in an academic sense."

"I thought a lot about it, Colonel Bellis, and decided that he was the best choice. I respect your opinion, of course, but unless you have a tangible reason to order me not to work with him, I would like to proceed."

Bellis said, "I may have tangible reasons."

"What are they?"

"Not this morning." He looked at his watch and stood. "We'll discuss it later. I'll be out of the building most of the day, but I'll be back by five. We'll meet then."

Margit returned to her office and pondered her day. She'd called Joycelen's fiancée, Christa Wren, and had made an appointment to see her at noon. She'd also got hold of Cobol's roommate, Brian Maitland, who worked as a night bartender at Sign of the Whale Bar and Restaurant, a popular M Street mating ground for big D.C. talkers with small foreign cars. He'd agreed to meet her at five o'clock; his shift started at six.

Had she told Bellis about these appointments, he would have questioned why she wasn't using Sergeant Silbert for that task. The honest answer would have to have been that she'd developed a kinship with Cobol and his mother, and had a need—that's all it was, a need—to become more involved with them, perhaps not in a tangible sense, but certainly psychologically. She wanted to meet the young man with whom Cobol had lived prior to the murder, and needed—yes, needed—to sit face-to-face with the woman who was to have become Joycelen's third wife.

Before leaving, she took a call from Major Jenko at McNair Trial Defense Service. He gave her the name of a medical corpsman who'd visited Cobol. When Margit asked again whether Jenko knew what medical services had been provided, she was told, "I suggest you call the medic."

She was on her way out the door when Silbert came up the hall. "I ran down Major Reich for you," he said.

"Good. Where is he?"

"That's the problem. He's on special duty."

Margit looked at him quizzically. "Okay, so he's on special duty. Where?"

"Not available. He's operating under some kind of cover. No information to anyone. Strictly need-to-know."

Margit's exasperation was written on her face. "I just want to speak with him, however briefly. There's an officer accused of murder here, and I've been given the lousy job of defending him. I need to see the officer who was his boss in a critical situation. Who told you his whereabouts can't be revealed?"

"Special Ops at the Company."

"Leave me the name of the person you spoke with," Margit said. "I'm running late, but I'll follow up when I get back."

"Yes, ma'am."

The Christa Wren who answered her door looked different to Margit from the seductive woman with whom she'd chatted at the picnic. There were purple puffy pouches under her eyes, and the blond curls lay flat upon her head. She looked considerably older than she had at the picnic; maybe it was lighting, maybe a lack of makeup, more likely the lingering effects of having lost a fiancée. Lots of things, Margit thought. Maybe she was just older, too, living years in a couple of weeks.

Margit was led to the living room, where a tray of finger sandwiches and coffee cups was placed on a large glass-and-chrome coffee table in front of an eight-foot-long white silk couch. Another woman was there. "This is my friend Peg Johnson," Christa said.

"Hello," Margit said. She gestured at the table. "You shouldn't have gone to this trouble."

"I have to eat. You have to eat. We may as well combine talk and food. Drink?"

"No, thank you," Margit answered.

"Well, I'm ready," she said. "I'm not on duty. You, Peg?"

"No."

She returned from the table with a large glass filled with ice and brimming with a white liquid. Her powder-blue pants suit had a stain on its bosom. Her feet were encased in scuffed leather slippers. All in all, Margit saw a woman who wasn't doing very well.

Margit joined Peggy Johnson on the couch while Christa Wren paced the room, drink in hand. Margit had formulated questions to ask, but Christa immediately launched into a monologue.

"I didn't think it would be this bad. I mean, that I would miss him so much. It all happened so fast. Poof! One minute with me, the next minute gone forever." She continued to walk as she talked. "Maybe it would be easier if we had been married." She stopped and looked at Margit. "Do you know what I mean when I say that? Maybe I'd have some official status. I'd be his widow if we'd been married. What am I? His girlfriend. I didn't even have a ring, because we didn't get around to that." She resumed her pacing. "They call me his fiancée in the papers. That's nice. We were planning to be married. No doubt about that, but there wasn't even a ring to prove it." Her eyes filled, and she excused herself.

The moment she was gone, Peg Johnson turned to Margit. "She's really busted up about this. But frankly, I don't think she lost much."

The harshness of the words stung Margit. "I can't imagine why you would say that," she replied.

Peg said, "He was a bastard, an out-and-out bastard. Treated her like dirt, walked all over her every chance he got. When I watched them together, all I could think of was that my friend here, who I always thought had a backbone, had a spine of jelly when it came to Joycelen."

"Does she know you feel that way?" Margit asked.

"Sure, but it doesn't matter. All her friends saw the same thing, told her she was crazy to get involved with him. He had that air of superiority, always looking down his nose at everything and everybody, especially her. I used to think of Marilyn Monroe and Arthur Miller. You know what I'm saying? The actress and the playwright?" Margit confirmed that she knew the reference. "I always imagined their relationship was the same way, the dumb blonde and the brilliant artist. Spare me that. She deserved better."

"I'm not sure Marilyn Monroe was dumb. Did Dr. Joycelen abuse her? I mean, physically?"

"Not that I know of, but Christa wouldn't tell me if he had. It was more verbal abuse. She couldn't say anything without him making some rotten remark. We'd be at dinner and she'd say something and he'd laugh at her, or tell her she didn't know what she was talking about."

Margit asked, "Why would she put up with that? Why would any woman put up with that?" As she said it, Christa, who'd been standing in the doorway, came to the center of the room. Her eyes were dry. "You want to know why I put up with Dick Joycelen's abuse? I didn't consider it abuse. Sure, I knew he didn't have a hell of a lot of respect for me. As they say, I'm no rocket scientist. He was—and more. But I didn't consider it abuse. That was the way he was, a genius, a famous man who chose me to be on his arm when he went to fancy receptions. How long have you been in this city, Major? Washington is a tough place for a woman. There are too many of us. What did I read? Seven women to every man."

Christa said to Peg, "If you were really honest, sweetie, you'd admit how jealous you were. You mean well, but I've seen some of the losers you've ended up with, the cheap dates, lousy restaurants, dull people. Dick Joycelen was a son of a bitch, but he sure wasn't dull, and he made sure I wasn't bored. God, how *bored* a woman can get in this city when she doesn't have someone."

Margit felt pity for Christa. At the same time, she didn't quite believe everything she was saying. She couldn't pinpoint why she felt that way. She just did. Maybe it was the cold and calculating reasons for which Christa put up with an abusive man like Joycelen. Then again, had he been as abusive as Peg Johnson claimed?

"Had you made definite wedding plans?" Margit asked. Christa had sat in a chair and was taking a long, slow pull on her drink.

"No. He was busy and under a lot of pressure. We were going to go away together on a real vacation, maybe for a week, to some pretty island to discuss our future. We never got to that. This is our future."

"But he *had* proposed to you," Margit said.

Christa looked at her defiantly. "Are you doubting that he wanted to marry me?"

"Not at all. I'm just trying to gain an understanding of Dr. Joycelen and his life leading up to the time he was killed."

"Because you're trying to defend the man who killed him."

"Yes, of course. I was up-front about that with you when I first called."

"You won't get him off," she said.

"That remains to be seen. I certainly intend to try. Frankly, I don't believe he killed Dr. Joycelen."

Christa gave a half-laugh. "That's trash, and you know it, just like the claim that this Captain Cobol you're defending and Dick had some kind of homosexual relationship. I hate those rumors."

"I don't believe those rumors, either," Margit said. "Look, Ms. Wren, I don't want to cause any more grief than you're already experiencing. I have a job to do, and I take my job seriously. Whether or not Captain Cobol killed Dr. Joycelen will be determined by a court-martial."

"If he didn't kill him, who did?" Peg Johnson asked.

"That's something I have to think about, too," said Margit.

Christa laughed nervously. "If you get your guy off, maybe they'll say I did it."

"If I get 'my guy' off," Margit replied, "there's a legion of people who could come into the picture. When you and I chatted at the picnic the morning of the murder, you said he was inside the Pentagon. Do you know why he was in there?"

"No. Dick didn't discuss his work with me."

"Had you been inside with him?" Margit asked.

"Inside with him? I don't have clearance to go into the Pentagon."

"Yes, I understand that, but Dr. Joycelen could have taken you in on a visitor's pass."

Christa twisted in her chair and looked toward a large picture window. She said without looking back, "Yes, I was inside for a while."

"With Dr. Joycelen, of course."

She turned. "How else would I be in there?"

"How long before you and I talked had you been inside?"

"How would I know that? I don't even remember talking to you at the picnic. I just remember waiting for Dick and then having those men come out and announce that something had happened inside. Never occurred to me that the problem had to do with Dick."

"But you left the picnic immediately after it broke up. I was surprised at that because . . . well, if I were in your shoes, I would have waited to see what the problem was. It was like you left because you knew he wouldn't be coming out."

Christa jumped to her feet. "What the hell are you doing, accusing me of knowing he'd been killed? That maybe I did it when I was inside with him?"

"I'm not accusing you of anything. I'm asking a question."

"I'm asking you to leave."

"Fine," Margit said.

"Is this the way you're going to defend that faggot captain, point a finger at somebody else?"

"No. But if in the process of defending him, I run across someone who might have had motive and opportunity to kill Joycelen, I will certainly pursue it. Thank you for allowing me to visit with you." Margit extended her hand to Peg Johnson, who reached up and took it. Margit said, "Please don't bother seeing me to the door. I am sorry for your loss."

When Margit returned to her office, she called the Med Center at McNair and asked for the doctor whose name she'd been given by Jenko. She was told he was on emergency leave and would not return until the following Wednesday.

"What was the emergency?" Margit asked without attempting to disguise her skepticism.

"Personal."

She wondered how Flo Cobol's latest visit with her son had gone. She wished Flo had called her. Maybe it wasn't such a good idea for them to be alone. If Cobol had been as upset as Silbert claimed, and had needed medical attention for whatever reason, I should have gone to see him, she thought. Her next appointment was on Monday, when she and Mac Smith were scheduled to visit. She couldn't wait that long. She didn't have time to go to McNair at the moment, but would go the next day, Saturday.

Jeff Foxboro called to confirm their plans for dinner and for her to spend the night at his apartment. She was torn, actually felt guilt at devoting all those hours to something purely personal and pleasurable. But she wasn't about to interfere with the new momentum their relationship had recently taken. They decided to avoid fancy restaurants and to go to a neighborhood Chinese place around the corner from Jeff's building. That suited Margit fine. All she wanted to do was to curl up with him, watch moronic television programs, and forget everything and anything having to do with murder or court-martials. But come to think of it, television was all lawyers and trials and murder these days. Maybe there'd be a Bugs Bunny festival, or a Groucho retrospective.

Before leaving for her meeting with Brian Maitland, Cobol's roommate, she changed into a skirt and sweater she kept in the office. Walking into a busy saloon in full uniform would not, she decided, be calculated to put anyone at ease.

Sign of the Whale was bustling when Margit arrived. She asked a bartender for Maitland; he pointed to a booth at the back where a young man sat alone. Margit snaked her way through the crowd. "Brian Maitland?" she asked.

"Yes. You must be Major Falk."

"Thanks for seeing me. May I sit down?"

He stood awkwardly and said, "Oh, I'm sorry. Of course."

Margit took him in. He was slender, fair, and had straight hair the color of honey that he wore slicked back in a popular style of the day. His eyes were intensely blue. "How's Bob?" he asked.

"As good as can be expected under the circumstances. You haven't visited him?"

"No."

"Why?"

"I just thought it probably wasn't the smartest thing to do . . . under the circumstances."

Margit silently agreed.

"Would you like a drink?" he asked.

"Club soda with lime."

Maitland waved to a waitress and gave her Margit's order, asked for a Lite beer for him.

After they'd been served, Margit said, "Tell me about Bob Cobol."

Maitland shifted nervously. "What do you want to know about him?"

"Let's start with when the two of you first met. He told me that becoming involved with you caused problems for him with his superior at the CIA."

Maitland was obviously uncomfortable discussing the intimate aspects of his relationship with Cobol, but Margit saw no reason to tiptoe. "Look," she said, "Bob has been open with me. I know that you two are lovers. That means nothing to me. The only thing I care about is helping him, and I'm going to need lots of help myself to do it right."

"I understand that," said Maitland, glancing up at people parading past the booth. "It isn't so much that I care about myself," he said, redirecting his attention to her. "The fact that Bob is a military officer complicates things, if you know what I mean."

"Of course I know what you mean. It's against regulations to be a homosexual. He told me that when his superior found out that you and he had entered into a relationship, he expected to be severely disciplined, probably kicked out of the service. But his superior told him he didn't want to lose a good officer and would overlook the indiscretion. Did Bob discuss this with you?"

Maitland nodded. "He couldn't believe it. He talked for days about what a wonderful person this Major Reich was to have turned his head to what happened. I agreed with him. If there was ever a time to go back into the closet, this was it. His whole career was on the line."

"It certainly was. I've been trying to locate Major Reich, but he isn't—locatable, I suppose is the word. What else did Bob say about Reich?"

"Nothing, aside from the fact that he was a good guy. Bob took his duties seriously. I mean, after all, he was assigned to the CIA. He never mentioned anything about what went on there, or at the Pentagon, where he spent most of his time."

"What about his revolver?"

"I read that it was used to kill Dr. Joycelen. I don't know how that could have happened."

"Bob told me he kept the weapon in the apartment he shared with you. Did you ever remove it from there?"

"Hell, no. I hated the fact that it was even there, but I knew it had to be. No, I know nothing about the gun."

"Did Bob ever mention Joycelen to you?"

"Never."

"You knew who he was?"

"Maybe. I guess I read his name in the papers a few times. I sure know now who he was."

"And Bob never mentioned his name, never indicated that he knew him."

Maitland shook his head.

It had become noisier in the bar, and Margit leaned across the table to be heard without raising her voice. "Did he discuss anything with you about his duties the morning Joycelen was killed?"

"He pulled weekend duty a lot."

"Yes, but what about this particular weekend? That Saturday morning? Were you with him the day before? Friday?"

Maitland rolled his eyes up as though to help recall. "Yes, I guess I was. He—let's see, he came home just as I was about to leave for here."

"That would be around what, four, five?"

"Yeah, about four-thirty maybe."

"That was early for him to come home, wasn't it?"

"No. He usually got off duty at four and came directly home. He might have been a little earlier that day because . . ."

Margit leaned closer. "Because why?"

"I don't really remember. I think he came home early because he'd been assigned Saturday morning duty."

"It was a last-minute assignment?"

"Yes. He was angry about it. That's right, he was mad because he'd made plans for Saturday and had to cancel."

"What plans?"

"It had to do with his car. He'd wanted to buy some things for his car, and I think he planned to do it Saturday morning." Maitland sat up straight, and his face became animated. "Yes, that's right. He wanted to buy some things for his car, and he was going to shop for clothes."

"But he couldn't because somebody threw him a curve and assigned him to duty the next morning."

"Right."

"Any idea who made that assignment?"

A shrug from Maitland. "No idea."

They talked for another ten minutes. "I know you have to start your shift," Margit said. She finished her soda and shook his hand. "I really appreciate this. Anything you want me to tell Bob?"

Maitland's fair complexion turned crimson. Margit averted her eyes. "Just tell him I'm thinking of him," Maitland mumbled as he slid out of the booth. "No," he said, "tell him that I love him." He was lost in the milling crowd.

Jeff was at the restaurant when Margit walked in. They kissed, decided on dishes more substantive than dim sum, and made small talk over steamed dumplings with sesame sauce and scallion pancakes. They shared an order of General Tsao's chicken and shrimp fried rice, washed it down with endless minicups of tea and a complimentary glass of plum wine, and went directly to his place.

They did that evening exactly what she'd hoped they would, snuggled together on the couch watching a couple of silly sit-coms. They took a half-hour break to affirm their feelings for each other, then returned to the couch and watched a documentary on the origins of blues music. They didn't bother leaving the couch for their second affirmation of love, and were asleep in bed by eleven-thirty.

The phone rang at midnight. Jeff answered, confirmed that Major Falk was there, and handed the phone to her. It was the base locator at Bolling. "Sorry to disturb you, Major," the officer said, "but you have a message from Fort McNair."

"A message?"

"Somebody from the detention center says that your client, Captain Robert Cobol, wishes to speak with you."

"Now? He wants to speak with me now?"

"That's what the caller said."

"Who is the caller? What's his name?"

"Sergeant Davis."

"Did he say that something is wrong there?"

"No. All he said was that Captain Cobol wanted to speak with you."

"Thank you very much," Margit said.

She sat up in bed. So did Jeff. She told him what the call was about.

"You aren't going, are you?" he said.

"I don't know. I've been concerned about Cobol." She told him of Silbert's comments, and that a medical corpsman had visited him. "I planned to go over there tomorrow." She glanced at a digital clock-radio. "Which is today."

"Then that's what you should do. Let's go back to sleep. I'm sure there's nothing so important that you have to race there tonight."

She knew he was right, and her feelings were in conflict with her more sober thought. She was drowsy, which made the decision for her. She kissed him. "I love you," she said.

"And I love you," he said. "Come on, back to sleep. World War Three can wait."

CHAPTER
EIGHTEEN

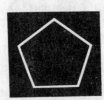

Margit was up at six. She left Jeff sleeping, went to the kitchen and made coffee, and carried a cup of it onto the terrace. The sky was heavy, the clouds gray bordering on black. It had not been a good sleep. She'd awakened many times. Once—it might have been three, maybe four, o'clock—she'd considered getting up and driving to McNair. Silly, she'd told herself. Cobol would be asleep, and the guards at the detention center would not be amenable to a visitor showing up at that hour.

She showered, put on a change of clothing she'd brought to the apartment, and went to the bedroom, where, gently, she shook Jeff awake. He opened his eyes and said in a cross voice, "What?"

"Sweetheart, I'm going to run home, and then go to see Cobol."

"Ah, come on back to bed," he said, attempting to pull her down next to him. She resisted. "No, I really have to go. Will you be here most of the day?"

"I guess so."

"I'll call when I get back."

She changed into a blue jumpsuit at her BOQ and headed for McNair. It wasn't until she was about to turn into the small parking lot across from the detention center that she realized something unusual was happening.

She stopped halfway into the lot and peered out her window. Military police vehicles with roof lights flashing flanked an air-force ambulance. "Wait a minute," she muttered, parking her car in the first available space, leaping from it, and running toward the commotion. The front entrance had been cordoned off with yellow crime-scene tape, the warnings to stay clear in air-force blue. Military police blocked her progress.

"I'm Major Margit Falk, defense counsel for Captain Cobol. He's inside there."

"Sorry, ma'am," one of the guards said. "You'll have to talk to him." He pointed to an army major who stood next to the ambulance. Margit went to him and introduced herself.

"Yes, Major Falk," the major said. "I'm Major Jenko."

He looked as unpleasant as he'd sounded on the phone.

"I'm here to see Captain Cobol. What's happened?"

"There's been an accident," Jenko said coldly, looking beyond her.

"To Captain Cobol?"

"He's dead."

His words had the same impact as if he'd struck her.

"He hanged himself early this morning," Jenko said. "It's under investigation."

"Where is he? The body?"

"Still inside."

"I want to go in," Margit said.

"Sorry. It's off-limits."

"I can't believe what I'm hearing. This man was my client. You can't deny me access to him."

Jenko narrowed his eyes. "You want access to a dead body?"

So much anger welled up in her that the only alternative to striking back at him physically was to turn and walk away. She returned to the front entrance and stood welded to the sidewalk, her brain a series of short circuits that rendered her incapable of processing what she'd just learned.

The sight of a lieutenant coming out of the building cleared those circuits. He was one of the officers in charge of the detention center; she'd dealt with him before.

"Lieutenant!" she shouted. "Lieutenant, please."

He detoured from the direction he'd been walking and came to her. "Major Falk, Captain Cobol's defense counsel. I just heard what happened.

"Yes, ma'am."

"How could it happen?" she asked. "Prisoners aren't allowed anything in their cells to hang themselves with."

"We don't know what happened. His mother was here yesterday to visit. Maybe . . ."

Flo Cobol bringing her son something with which he could kill himself? It was an absurd contemplation. Still, what was the answer? She asked the lieutenant what Cobol had used.

"Looks like a sash, maybe from a bathrobe."

Margit saw Jenko start toward them. The lieutenant saw him, too. "Sorry about your client, Major," he said. "I can't say any more. This is going to be some mess."

Jenko saw them separate and turned away. Margit took the occasion to pursue the lieutenant again. "Lieutenant, please tell me . . ."

"No comment," he said, obviously aware that he'd already said too much.

"Sergeant Davis. Is Sergeant Davis inside?"

"Davis? We don't have any Sergeant Davis."

"Yes, you do. He left a message for me with my base locator last night that Captain Cobol wanted to speak with me. That's why I came here this morning."

"Ma'am, there is no Sergeant Davis assigned to this facility. Excuse me."

"All right, clear the area, clear the area!" someone barked. Margit watched a stretcher, carried by two enlisted men, come through the front door, down the steps, and to the ambulance. Beneath the sheet, Margit knew with deadening certainty, was the body of Captain Robert Cobol. She felt anger again, but it quickly dissolved into despair of such intensity that she wondered whether she could continue standing. She watched the doors to the ambulance close and saw it drive away.

She walked slowly to her car, looking back a few times, tears stinging her eyes, teeth clamped tightly shut. She paused and placed her hands on the auto's roof and took deep breaths. It was inconceivable that this could have happened. It shouldn't have happened. It made no sense.

She drove in the direction of Bolling but changed her mind halfway there and headed for the Pentagon, where she went to her

office and opened the safe in which all materials bearing on the
Cobol case were kept. She removed Cobol's personnel file, placed
it on her desk, stared at it for a while, then opened it. There he was,
his I.D. photo. Smiling. Alive.

Four hours later, after she'd reviewed everything from the safe,
some of it more than once, she picked up the phone and started to
call Jeff. Instead, she dialed a number that rang in Mackensie
Smith's study.

CHAPTER

NINETEEN

 Margit sat in Mac and Annabel's kitchen that night. In the center of the table was a large pot of lamb stew, compliments of the chef.

"Sorry," Margit said. "It's delicious, but I just don't have much appetite."

"I wouldn't either," said Annabel. "It's horrible what happened."

Margit leaned back and rolled her fingers on the tabletop. "I keep going over and over it in my mind. Every time I do, it makes less sense. He would not have hanged himself, even if the means to do it had been accidently left in his cell."

"There'll undoubtedly be a full investigation," Smith said.

"Sure," Margit said. "Full. It'll be behind closed doors, and they'll come to whatever conclusion they want. Like what happened with my father."

Mac and Annabel stopped eating and looked at her.

"I guess I never told you about that." She recounted for her friends the unceremonious departure from the service that had been forced upon her father. "It was a travesty. And it killed him."

"That's very sad, Margit," Smith said. "But you can't extend what happened with him to the Cobol situation. Every bureaucracy—military, civilian, it doesn't matter—likes to keep its dirty laundry from public view. That doesn't mean the results in this case will be less than honest."

"I know that," Margit said, her rising level of exasperation causing her voice to do the same. "I don't want to be cynical. I want to believe that I didn't know Cobol, that he was capable of taking his own life, maybe even had been planning it. I can tell myself that all I want, but it doesn't stand up to what I feel." She became reflective; there was palpable sadness in her voice. "When my father was forced to retire, I hated anything military. The sight of a uniform made me sick. But then you grow up a little, you mature, and you realize that you can't broad-brush any organization because of the actions of one person. This colonel who did my father in could have been a vice president at any corporation, in any branch of government, or in a university. I came to realize that. Maybe that's why I decided to make the military my career. I remember thinking at my commissioning that I was going to make sure that the air force had one officer who wouldn't lie, or hold a grudge, or play dirty pool."

"Whom have you spoken with about Cobol's death?" Annabel asked.

"My boss, Colonel Bellis."

"What did he have to say?" Smith asked.

"He was sympathetic enough. He said he knew this was upsetting to me. But he also said that it meant I no longer had to handle an assignment I didn't want in the first place, and that I could get back to the job for which I'd come to the Pentagon."

"Sounds pretty cold to me," Annabel said.

"I thought it was, too, but I suppose he was only trying to point out the positives."

"What do you think of Bellis?" Smith asked.

"Mixed emotions. He's smart, and from what I can gather, he's an excellent general counsel to SecDef. He's military through and through, but there's a soft side that leaks out on occasion. All in all? I like him."

Smith said, "You received a message last night from your base locator that supposedly came from a Sergeant Davis?"

"Right. Only the lieutenant I spoke with this morning claims there is no Sergeant Davis."

"That doesn't make sense," Smith said, "unless he got the name wrong."

"That's possible, but I did repeat it to him." Margit stood and went to a corner of the kitchen, where she leaned against a large refrigerator. "I should have gone to see Cobol the minute Sergeant Silbert told me Cobol was acting strangely. I should have canceled anything I had to do that day and gone right over there. Worse, when I received the call at Jeff's apartment, I should have followed my instincts, got dressed, and headed for McNair. Woulda, coulda, shoulda."

Annabel broke an ensuing silence. "What do you intend to do, Margit?" she asked. "What *can* you do?"

Margit raised her arms in a gesture of helplessness. "What can I do? I suppose I'll be asked to clean out my desk Monday morning and go back to being legal liaison on Project Safekeep."

"You don't sound especially excited about it," Smith said.

"You're right. I'm not even sure I can do it."

"Why?" Annabel asked.

"Because I wonder if I will ever be able to focus on anything again until my questions about Joycelen and Cobol are answered."

"Maybe they'll put you on the investigative team," Smith offered.

"Fat chance," Margit said. "I said I didn't want to be cynical. I'm trying not to be. But—maybe skeptical is a better word. No, cynical is right. I have this nagging, hurtful feeling that . . . Cobol has been a pawn in this whole Joycelen mess. I don't believe he and Joycelen had a relationship, and I believed Cobol when he said he didn't know the man. I certainly don't believe he killed him, any more than I think he took his own life."

"If your feelings have validity, Margit, you're charging the military with a cover-up," said Smith.

"If that's what comes out of my feelings, so be it."

She rejoined them at the table. "Cobol had his duty assignment changed at the last minute so that he was at the Pentagon the Saturday morning Joycelen was killed. Why? Who changed it? They claim Cobol's weapon was used to kill Joycelen. That isn't very compelling to me. How simple to switch weapons in Cobol's apartment. He didn't carry it routinely, only used it on the firing range, so he wouldn't be checking it on a regular basis."

Mac and Annabel waited for Margit to continue.

She said, "I sat in my office for four hours today going over every scrap of paper in the safe. None of it looked the same. Can you understand that? I've read that material a dozen times, but it all came off the page at me as though it had just been written, and I'd never seen it before."

"Give me an example," Smith said.

"Cobol's personnel file. As many times as I've examined it, I never noticed that someone had written 'HP-5' in very small letters after his serial number."

"What does that mean?" Annabel asked.

"I don't know, but someone made that notation. I went through my *Pentagon Handbook,* which includes a glossary of terms and abbreviations. I couldn't find it there. I checked the Pentagon phone book, which also runs a list, and didn't see it."

"Can you check with Personnel on Monday?" Smith suggested.

"I intend to, provided I'm allowed."

"Why wouldn't you be allowed?" Annabel asked.

"Because, Annabel, I think this entire investigation, beginning with my so-called defense of Cobol, is being slowed, maybe stone-walled. I can't prove that, but my gut says I'm right."

Smith said, "You mentioned this Major Reich. Does it strike you as strange that his whereabouts aren't known?"

Margit thought before replying. "I suppose it does, although obviously the CIA acts in mysterious ways. Lots of their people have to go undercover to accomplish a mission. I assume that's the case with Reich. There's not much chance of pursuing that avenue until he returns to above-ground duty."

"You also mentioned this psychiatrist in New York. What was his name? Half?"

"Yes, Marcus Half. I'd intended to contact him as part of my defense preparation. It's too late now."

Smith took dishes from the table and started to scrape and rinse them. Margit and Annabel moved to help, but he said, "Leave it to me. You two go relax in the living room. I'll join you in a minute."

When he entered the room fifteen minutes later, Margit was sitting silently and Annabel had been consoling her. Smith waited for a moment. "You're between the proverbial rock and a hard place, Margit," he said. "It's obvious from what you've been saying all evening that you know what you want to do."

"What's that?"

"You want to continue investigating Joycelen and Cobol. But if what you say is true about the sense of a cover-up, you're going to be kept from doing that. *Ordered* not to."

"I haven't received that order yet," Margit said coldly. "I honestly don't know what I'll do if I'm told to drop it. All I can think about is something my father repeated to me many times when he was bringing me up."

Mac and Annabel waited.

Tears formed in Margit's eyes. "He told me that no matter what I did with my life, I was to make sure I could always live with myself. He told me to never sell out, never be pushed over, never let myself be bought."

Annabel handed her a Kleenex.

"Would you consider an order to forget Joycelen's murder and Cobol's death as 'selling out'?" Smith asked.

Margit dabbed at her eyes. "Right now—sitting in this living room—I would."

"Then I've got a suggestion. The military can move slowly. They can overlook the obvious. Don't *say* you're continuing the investigation if you decide to do so, and don't hang around asking for orders. Feel like a look at the news?" Smith asked.

"Sure," Margit said.

They were watching a report about alleged police corruption in Washington when the phone rang. Smith answered, held it out to Margit. "For you."

"Margit Falk," she said.

"Major Falk, this is Louise Harrison from *The Washington Post.* The base locator at Bolling gave me this number."

"You're calling about Captain Cobol."

"That's right. I have some questions for you."

"Sorry. I have no comment."

"Just one or two. You were his defense counsel. What was your first thought when you heard the news?"

"My first thought? You mean, was I happy that he'd spared me months of work, and the government a long and costly court-martial?" The reporter tried to refine her question, but Margit forged on. "The fact is, I went to visit Captain Cobol because he asked me to. When I heard what had happened, it sickened me. I am still sick about it."

Smith came around to where Margit could see him and shook his head. She ignored him.

"Does this mean the case is closed?" the reporter asked.

"I suppose it is."

"You don't sound convinced it should be," Harrison said.

"He's dead, allegedly because he killed himself."

" 'Allegedly'? Are you questioning that?"

Margit looked at Smith, who was now reinforcing his advice by waving his hands at her.

"I have nothing more to say," Margit said.

"Could I meet with you?" Harrison asked. "I'd like to follow up on this."

"No, that would be inappropriate at this time. Thank you for calling." Margit hung up.

They settled in their chairs again and sat through a few commercials before the story of Cobol's hanging came on the newscast:

"Army Captain Robert Cobol, the accused murderer of leading scientist Dr. Richard Joycelen back in August, who was shot to death in the basement of the Pentagon, hanged himself in the early morning hours today in his cell at the Fort McNair detention center. Cobol, who'd denied his guilt in the Joycelen murder, and who also denied that he'd had a homosexual relationship with the scientist, used what was described by an army spokesman as a sash of some sort. How that sash ended up in his cell, as well as all aspects of this unfortunate ending to what has been one of this city's most talked-about murders, will receive a full investigation, according to an army spokesman."

Margit's only comment when the segment was over was, "I only hope they got to his mother before she saw it on television. I was going to call her, but I wasn't sure I should."

"Maybe she'll be in touch with you," Annabel said.

"I hope so." Margit's face twisted in anger. "A sash from a bathrobe ending up in a cell with an accused murderer. Nonsense!"

They were interrupted by the ringing of the doorbell. Smith glanced at his watch. "I forgot that Tony and Alicia were stopping by," he said to Annabel. "Tony wanted to drop off a gift."

As Smith left the living room to answer the door, Annabel said to Margit, "Tony is Tony Buffolino. He was a Washington vice-squad cop until he got trapped in a sting. One of his children was sick, and he was desperate for money. He made one mistake, and that was it. Mac defended him and managed to get criminal charges dropped, but Tony was kicked off the force. He owned a nightclub here in town for a while, is a private investigator at the moment, and, among many things, is a real character."

Smith led Buffolino and third wife, Alicia, into the room and introduced them to Margit.

"*Major?*" Tony said. "A lady soldier, huh?"

"That's right," Margit said.

"Every time I turn around, I see women in uniform," Buffolino said, a wide grin on his craggy pugilist's face. "They look cute in their uniforms."

At any other time Margit might have smiled.

"Margit is a helicopter pilot," Annabel offered.

Alicia's eyes opened wide. "I didn't know women flew planes," she said.

"Lots of us do," Margit said.

"Sure," Buffolino said to his wife. "Don't you remember all those women pilots over there when we were kicking butt in the Persian Gulf?"

"Of course I do, Tony," Alicia replied, annoyed at his tone. "I just didn't think they were real. I mean, I never met a real one."

"Join us for a drink, coffee?" Smith asked the recent arrivals.

"Nah," Buffolino said. "Thanks. It's been a long day."

"We have Grand Marnier cream puffs," Annabel said. "Fresh from Watergate Pastry." Buffolino's penchant for sweets was well known to the Smiths.

Buffolino looked at his wife. "Maybe we stay just a few minutes, huh?"

"Whatever you say, Tony."

They talked about many things during the next hour, none having to do with Margit's recent experiences until Buffolino mentioned the Cobol hanging. "How do you figure?" he asked.

"Margit was Captain Cobol's defense counsel," Smith said.

Buffolino sprang forward in his chair. "No kiddin'? You're a pilot *and* a lawyer?"

"I'm afraid so," Margit replied.

"Sure, I read about it," Buffolino said. "The guy must have been real guilty, huh, to kill himself?"

"Not necessarily," Smith said.

"I don't think so," Margit said. "Maybe that's what's so terrible about this whole thing, that the world will now *assume* that Cobol killed Richard Joycelen, and he's not here to defend himself."

"You don't think he did?" Buffolino asked.

"No, I do not."

"That raises the usual interesting question," Buffolino said.

"What's that?"

"If this guy didn't kill the scientist, somebody else did. Am I right?" he asked the room.

"That's a reasonable conclusion," Smith said.

Alicia Buffolino added, "Sometimes people like that can get nasty and do things when they're mad."

"What do you mean?" Margit asked.

"Well, you know, men like that get into a fight with other men like that and sometimes it gets violent. At least that's what I hear. I really don't know any—of them. I did in San Francisco but . . ."

"No different from domestic violence in a heterosexual relationship," Smith said.

"That's right," Buffolino put in. "There's good ones and bad ones, like everything else."

"He wasn't," Margit said.

"He wasn't?" Buffolino said.

"Captain Cobol did not have a relationship with Richard Joycelen. Joycelen was not a homosexual."

"He was married a couple a times. Right?" Buffolino said.

"Right," Smith said, standing. "Well, now that the cream puffs are gone, I guess Tony will have lost all interest in us, and you two will be getting home." Annabel looked away from her husband to shield a smile.

The Buffolinos stood and extended their hands to Margit. "It was a real pleasure meeting you," said Margit.

"Likewise," Alicia said. "The pleasure's all mine."

"Good luck with everything, Major," Buffolino said. "Thanks for the snack, Mac. Talk to you soon." Margit and Annabel heard Buffolino say to Smith when they'd reached the front door, "I almost forgot. Here. The present I got you. Alicia and me went to the shore just to get away, right? We go through this flea market, and I see this. What do I think? I right away think this is perfect for Mac Smith. Didn't I say that, Alicia?" She agreed. "So I bought it for you." Smith thanked him, and the front door opened and closed.

Smith returned to the living room carrying a package. "What is it?" Annabel asked. Smith unwrapped it and held up a framed print from a turn-of-the-century magazine. An elephant dressed in a British judge's white wig and black robes sat behind the bench. Before him were smaller animals—rabbits, birds, cats, and dogs. The caption read, *"Guilty because I say so! Any objections?"*

"Is he making a point?" Annabel asked, laughing.

"No," Smith said. "It was thoughtful of him. We'll hang it over the bed."

"Over Rufus's bed," Annabel said.

"Which is our bed," Smith said.

"We must buy him a convertible sofa," Annabel said.

Rufus, who was asleep on the floor, raised his head at the mention of his name, yawned, and plopped his huge head down with a thud. He'd been sleeping since he discovered that lamb stew was not to be on *his* menu that night.

"Interesting couple," Margit said.

"Putting it mildly," said Smith. "Tony met Alicia in San Francisco after I'd made the mistake of getting involved in the murder of that young woman at the Kennedy Center. Remember that case?"

"Sure," Margit said. "It was in all the papers."

"Alicia was a cocktail waitress at the Top of the Mark. Tony fell madly in love the first night we had a drink up there, and that was it. After he came back to Washington, he opened what he called a Las Vegas–type nightclub. It bombed. Gambling might have helped. He's been doing P.I. work since then. He comes off scruffy and dumb, but he's no dummy. He's got the best natural instincts of any investigator I've ever known."

"I suppose he disarms people with his style."

"Often."

Margit announced she was about to leave.

"Where's Jeff?" Smith asked.

"I called him from the office after I spoke with you," she said.

"I suppose I should have gone to him, but I really needed to speak with you, Mac. Jeff understood. You're both very dear friends. I can't thank you enough for letting me vent my soul and spleen tonight."

"Any time," Smith said. He frowned and looked Margit directly in the eye. "Don't do anything impetuous," he said. "Another reporter calls, stick to your 'No comment' answer. You said some things on the phone to that *Post* reporter that you might regret. And if you decide to go on with this, call me and tell no one."

"I know, Mac. I promise to think first and shoot later. Thanks again."

CHAPTER

TWENTY

 "Good morning, Major," Colonel Bellis said as Margit entered his office early Monday morning. "Close the door." When she was seated, he overtly scrutinized her. "You look beat," he said.

"I didn't get much sleep this weekend. What happened to Captain Cobol has been very upsetting."

"As well it should be. You have time coming to you. Take some and get away from here."

Bellis wasn't suggesting anything she hadn't thought of herself. Yesterday, over coffee with Jeff Foxboro, she'd mused about taking some leave. He'd surprised her again.

She'd told him how upset she was over what had happened with Cobol; that she had trouble buying it; that she felt compelled to seek answers to the questions that nagged at her. She assumed Jeff would be at his pragmatic best, advising her to forget the whole thing and to get on with her life and career. Instead, he was sympathetic and understanding. He actually urged her to follow her instincts and to be true to herself.

Foxboro had left to attend an afternoon meeting with Senator Wishengrad, leaving Margit to lounge in her Bolling BOQ and to ponder what to do next. Leave was appealing; she could hitch a ride on a military aircraft to a pleasant place, relax on a deserted beach, let sun and water bake and wash away her thoughts and feelings. She wished she had family to whom to turn. This would be a perfect time to go home. But there wasn't a home anymore, at least not where family waited with open, comforting arms. The air force was her home, Bolling Air Force Base in Washington, D.C., her habitat—at least for now.

"I may do that, sir," she told Bellis. "Take a few days' leave. You mentioned that I would return to my previous assignment on Project Safekeep."

"If that's what you'd like to do. I can arrange other assignments."

"Here at the Pentagon?"

"Or someplace else. The kind of shock you've just experienced can taint an officer. I'm well aware of that, and I wasn't kidding when I told you I'd developed a sort of fatherly attitude toward you. You're the kind of officer, Major, who makes the United States military the best in the world. I wouldn't want to see you compromise your future."

His words were nice; what was behind them was troubling. Her response was to say that she'd be happy to stay in place for the moment, and to thank him for his concern.

Bellis said, "I came in here this morning committed to putting Joycelen and Cobol behind us. As unfortunate as the whole incident has been, it seems to have resolved itself, maybe not the way we'd all like to have seen it conclude, but resolved nonetheless. Colonel Detienne and General Paley are planning a press conference tomorrow. That will hopefully put it to rest with the press and the public. At least, I hope so."

"Am I expected to attend the press conference?" Margit asked.

Bellis laughed. "No, no need for you to be there. Your role in this is finished." He picked up that morning's copy of the *Early Bird.* "Read this yet?" he asked.

"No, sir."

He directed it across the desk to her. "Read the *Post* this morning?"

"No, sir." Ouch! She knew what was coming without having to read anything. Her imprudent comments to the *Post*'s Louise Harrison . . . She picked up *Early Bird* and flipped through its crudely assembled pages until coming to the Harrison piece. She read it, recognized that Harrison had accurately quoted her, and placed the newsletter back on Bellis's desk.

"I was surprised when I read this," he said.

"I suppose you were," Margit said, sighing. "The reporter took me by surprise. I was tracked down at Mackensie Smith's house. I wasn't very discreet. I talked before thinking."

Bellis waved it away. "No matter. I can understand your feelings. I do suggest, however, that you commit to putting this behind you. We're in the business of defending a nation. That's what we're paid to do." He picked up an official handout that went to the thousands of citizens who took the conducted tour of the Pentagon each week, opened it to the first page, and placed it in front of her. It was the stated mission of the Pentagon:

> To preserve peace, with freedom for ourselves and our descendants. To deter conflict by maintaining Armed Forces that are capable and ready.

Margit resented having been asked to read those familiar words in the presence of a superior—a schoolgirl being reminded of a basic tenet of responsible behavior.

Bellis continued. "I always remember a line from Emerson. 'Not gold, but only man can make a people great and strong.' I may not have it exactly right, but it's close enough."

"Sir, why are you telling me this? I'm well aware of my duties and responsibilities as a commissioned officer." She wished she didn't sound quite so angry.

"Don't take offense, Major. Sometimes we all have to be re-minded—or remind ourselves—of what's important and what isn't. Joycelen's murder and Cobol's self-inflicted death have ended an unfortunate episode, but hardly one that should rank high on our priority list as career soldiers. It's done. See it that way."

Margit's anger now threatened to boil over. She forced herself to look at him.

Bellis came around the desk. "Take a couple of days off, Major. Don't worry about your office. I'll have it moved. Relax, take in a good movie, go out to dinner with your boyfriend."

She went to the door, turned, and said, "Thank you, sir. I may take your advice. By the way, I was wondering whether you know of a designation, HP-5, used on personnel records."

She couldn't be sure, but her question seemed to prick him. He said, "No. Never heard of it. Why do you ask?"

"It was noted on Cobol's records. Handwritten."

"Means nothing to me. Thank you for the excellent job you were doing in preparing Captain Cobol's defense. You were everything I thought you would be when I chose you."

She went across the hall where Silbert and Woosky were preparing to leave. "Thanks for your help, guys," she told them.

"Our pleasure, Major," Silbert said, a rash of file folders under his arm.

"Those are case files on Cobol," Margit said.

"Yes, ma'am. Colonel Bellis wants everything put into a central archive at Trial Defense Service."

Margit looked to the open safe. It was empty. Everything was gone, including Cobol's personnel file. She wanted to protest but knew it was fruitless. She thanked them again, walked briskly down the hall, went downstairs, and started for the building exit. But she stopped, got her bearings, and went in another direction that took her to the Military Women's Corridor, where outstanding military women of history—and the not-so-distant past—were honored.

She stood in front of a photograph of Civil War heroine Dr. Mary Edwards Walker, the only female recipient of the Medal of Honor. Dr. Walker wasn't supposed to be in the army—any army—and she'd had to disguise herself as a man in order to reach the front lines, where she'd nursed the seriously wounded while under intense enemy fire. Her medal had been taken away from her in 1917, but President Jimmy Carter had reinstated the citation that restored it to her.

Margit moved on, pausing at a picture of Lieutenant Colonel Jacqueline Cochran, the first woman aviator to break the sound barrier, and the holder of more official flight records than any other person, male or female.

Before leaving the corridor, she read a plaque devoted to Rear Admiral Grace Hopper, who'd stayed on active duty until she was seventy-nine years old.

I'm proud of you, she thought. I wish I were half as good.

She spent the rest of the morning in her BOQ drinking coffee and reading that day's *Washington Post* cover to cover. The story of Cobol's suicide was boxed on the lower right-hand portion of the front page. There was other news on page 1, of course. The Israeli ambassador to the United Nations had called for an emergency session of the Security Council to discuss the imminent threat of nuclear attack upon his country by the Arab nation that now possessed nuclear weapons, stressing that the one that had been tested was not the only one in the Arab leader's inventory. He said it with all the authority of Israeli Intelligence, which went unmentioned.

President David Beardsley's National Security Council adviser had announced that the administration was considering deploying troops to the Middle East, just as a previous administration had done when Saddam Hussein invaded Kuwait in 1990, and had been poised on the Saudi Arabian border.

She read news of lesser importance on the inside pages, features on neighborhoods, local political jockeying, cooking advice, fashion, gossip, "style," the stuff of which newspapers are made, and forced herself to speed up. She stopped skimming in the business section and read more carefully.

The Senate Armed Services Committee, chaired by Wisconsin senator Henry Wishengrad, had announced it planned hearings into what it termed "the appearance of illegal activity by people involved with the development of Project Safekeep and its California contractor, Starpath, Inc." No names were mentioned, but Margit immediately thought of Starpath's lobbyist, Sam Caldwell, and of Joe Maize, the Pentagon's lead auditor for the controversial weapons system. Were they among unnamed persons about to come under the scrutiny of Wishengrad's committee? Jeff hadn't mentioned anything about such a hearing, although that made sense. Ideally, everyone involved in a planned hearing kept his mouth shut until the official announcement was made. Of course, Washington seldom functions on an ideal footing. Margit admired Jeff's discretion. At the same time she felt somewhat cheated that he hadn't shared it with her. She certainly was sharing everything with him these days. Well, that made him a better person, she decided. "Think first and shoot later" was what she'd promised Mac Smith. She'd better start living that pledge.

After a few false starts she called Cobol's mother on Long Island.

She let the phone ring a dozen times. As she was about to hang up, Flo Cobol answered. "This is Margit Falk. I'm so sorry about Robert."

Flo began to weep. Margit waited, then said, "Mrs. Cobol, is there anything I can do for you?"

Flo said, "He's being buried tomorrow."

"In New York?"

"Yes, in a family plot with his father and my mother."

"What time?"

"Eleven. From our local parish."

"I'd like to be there."

Flo regained her composure. "That would be very nice," she said. "I mean, I would be honored to have you."

Margit received instructions on how to get to the church. She asked, "Who told you about his death?"

"I received a call from his immediate supervisor at the CIA. He's a colonel. His name is Kale. I think it's spelled with a K. Maybe it's C."

Margit talked with her, comforted her with words of belief in Robert, and then said good-bye. She went for a noontime run. It was a lovely day, sunny but crisp, perfect jogging weather. She ran longer and farther than usual, more than ten miles by her estimate as she followed a route along the Anacostia Freeway to the Anacostia River, traced the river to Anacostia Park, ran its length, then doubled back along local streets through Southeast Washington, Fort Stanton Park, and home.

At first she didn't see the envelope that had been slid beneath her door. She'd walked right over it. It was after she'd quenched her thirst some with bottled water, and had sat in a living-room chair to remove her running shoes and socks, that she saw it. A small white envelope. Printed on it in black letters was MAJ. FALK.

Margit picked it up, returned to the chair, and opened it. Inside was a single sheet of white paper with blue lines. The first thing that struck her was that the writing on the paper was not the same as that on the envelope. She started to read:

Friday night

Maj. Falk—I hope this gets to you. My friend said it would. He called and left a message, but I guess you didn't get it. He said he'd deliver this note to you. I know you're trying to help me, but it's no use. I had my friend call because I needed to talk to somebody. I wish I could talk to my mother, but she would only get upset. She got upset when she visited me, and I don't like to do that to her.

They sent a medic to me yesterday. He gave me a shot, and I guess I slept until tonight (it's Friday night). I know they don't want me around to tell anyone what they did. I'm scared. I'm not ashamed to admit that.

If anything happens to me, please let my mother know how much I've always loved her and how much I appreciate her support.

They set me up. I never believed they would do that to me, but they did. I thought I'd wait a few days until they helped me, but now I see they won't. That's why I needed to talk to you. They won't like what I have to say, but I don't like what's happened to me. Maybe if we were civilians, it would be easier.

He had signed it: *Robert D. Cobol, Capt., United States Army.*
Margit dropped the note to her lap and looked around the room as though in search of some tangible answer that might be there, a tablet hanging from the ceiling upon which all truth and wisdom was engraved. There was no such thing, of course, and she left the chair without the slightest idea of what her reaction to the note really was.

She showered, then took a drive—no destination, no purpose—simply fulfilling the need to be in motion. She didn't know how long she'd driven, but she eventually pulled up in front of the Sign of the Whale. It was five-thirty.

CHAPTER

TWENTY-ONE

 It had taken some persuasion on Margit's part to convince Maitland to accompany her to Cobol's funeral. She'd been getting nowhere until she realized he was uncomfortable confronting Cobol's mother. "Brian," she'd said last night, "Robert Cobol's mother is a lot more sophisticated and understanding than you might think. She's a nice person, and has been aware for years of Robert's homosexuality. You have nothing to worry about when it comes to Flo Cobol. Trust me."

And he did, as evidenced by the fact that they drove east together on New York's Long Island Expressway to the church, and to the cemetery that would be Cobol's final resting place.

Margit wore dress blues; Maitland, who would never be voted among Washington's best dressed in a *Washingtonian* magazine poll, wore a blue-and-white plaid shirt with a small collar, a green tie not much wider than a strand of spaghetti, and an oversized sport jacket.

He'd been nervous when they first met up at National Airport, but he visibly relaxed during the short flight. By the time they'd turned off the expressway and had started following local directions to the church, he'd become a pleasant, even witty, traveling companion.

St. James's was in a lower-middle-class, or middle-class, neighborhood in Franklin Square—Margit never had learned how to differentiate. Small, square houses rested on even smaller plots. The houses looked as though they'd been built in the 1930s, although myriad additions and extensions had taken them out of any defined architectural camp, if they had ever been in one. A nice, quiet neighborhood.

As Margit and Maitland walked from their rented car to the church, two other cars parked next to hers. Four men in uniform came out of each vehicle and fell into a loosely grouped formation, as military people tend to do. They headed in Margit's direction. Of the eight men, seven were unknown to her. But one, who brought up the rear of the contingent, was Monroney's aide, Major Anthony Mucci.

She and Maitland waited until the group reached them. "Good morning, Major Mucci," Margit said.

Mucci, whose perpetually sober expression was made for funerals, nodded, mumbled a greeting, and kept in step with the others as they went up the stairs and disappeared through the church door.

"Who are they?" Maitland asked.

"I suppose some of Robert's colleagues," Margit said. "It's nice to see the military sent a group to pay its respects. Come on, let's go in. The service will be starting."

Margit and Maitland sat directly behind the eight uniformed mourners. Flo Cobol was on the other side of the aisle, with people Margit assumed were family. The minister, a chubby-cheeked young man who wore his hair in a ponytail, conducted the service with a minimum of religious rhetoric, but with considerable enthusiasm. He debunked the comforting notion that death brought its victim closer to God. "The fact is," he said, "death stinks, and no matter how many nice things we say, it doesn't make it any different. God is with us, anyhow."

The only lay person who spoke was introduced as Robert's cousin Susan, a slender, pretty girl whose body and voice trembled as she remembered the good times she'd enjoyed with her "favorite cous." As she neared the end of her remarks, her trembling intensified, but her voice became stronger as she looked out over the gathering. "My cousin Robert was one of the nicest people in the world. It's bad enough he isn't with us anymore, and I will miss him very much. I also know that God knows Robert never killed anybody or anything, and that if he took his own life, it was because the pain he suffered recently from the lies was too much to bear."

The minister, whose name Margit didn't catch, concluded the simple, brief service by thanking all those who'd come to pay their final respects, including fellow officers who had traveled from Washington to represent the armed forces. His final words were directed to Flo Cobol: "You raised a fine young man," he said to her, "a loving son, a proud officer, and a citizen who contributed instead of just taking from his society." Flo, who'd cried quietly throughout the ceremony, now completely broke down.

The cemetery, a ten-minute drive from the church, was fittingly small for the community it served. The minister sprinkled traditional dirt on the casket as he intoned, "Man, that is born of a woman, has but a short time to live, and is full of misery. He comes up, and is cut down, like a flower; he flees as it were a shadow, and never continues in one stay . . . ashes to ashes, dust to dust. . . ."

Flo Cobol, who'd had to be supported during the graveside ritual, now leaned against the limousine that had brought her and the immediate family to the cemetery. Margit and Maitland approached. "I'm so sorry, Mrs. Cobol," Margit said. "This is Brian Maitland. He was Robert's good friend."

"Thank you both for coming," Flo said. She seemed in better control of herself now that it was over, at least the official portion. "I hope you'll come back to the house. Nothing elaborate, just some cold cuts and salads. I know Robert would have liked to have you there."

Margit answered for both herself and Maitland. "Of course. We'll follow."

Fifteen minutes later Margit stood in the small, old-fashioned, and tastefully furnished house in which Cobol had grown up. There weren't many people who'd extended the ceremony to include refreshments. Flo was busy in the kitchen, something with which she seemed blessedly comfortable, and Margit and Maitland stood awkwardly in a corner of the living room.

Susan, the cousin who'd spoken at the funeral, came up to them.

"Your words were touching," Margit said.

"Thank you. I meant them. Robert and I were close."

Margit shrugged. "What's to say at this point?"

"Flo says you were doing a good job getting ready to defend him."

"That's kind of her, although I don't know how true it is. I know I was determined to do my best. I didn't do everything I could."

"It's bad enough to lose a son the way she has, but to have it come on the heels of everything else is beyond comprehension. To know that your son has died being accused of having murdered someone— well, it's more than I could take, if I were Robert's mother."

Maitland, who hadn't said much, repeated what the minister had said. "It stinks. It really stinks."

People who'd come back to the house didn't stay long after Flo had served the modest food brought in from her local deli. Soon, only Margit, Maitland, Robert's cousin Susan, and Flo remained. They sat in the living room and talked about things other than death and funerals. Margit asked Flo why she'd visited Robert the day before his death, and hadn't called her. "I didn't want to bother you," Flo replied. "I know you're busy and . . ."

"Never that busy," Margit said. "Did he seem unusually upset when you saw him?"

"Yes. He was very nervous. I didn't stay long because I could see he wanted to be alone."

Margit had grappled long and hard with what to do with the note that had been slipped under her door. She'd shown it to no one, yet knew she had to, at the very least, tell Flo Cobol what her son had written about her. She decided that rather than attempt to paraphrase it, she would show the note to Flo. She also made a decision while there in the living room that she would allow Maitland and Robert's cousin Susan to share in it. They were people who obviously meant a great deal to Cobol, and he to them.

She pulled the note from her purse, went to where Flo sat on the couch, and handed it to her.

"What's this?" Flo asked.

"A note from Robert. I don't know who delivered it to me, but it was obviously written by Robert."

Margit returned to her chair and watched Flo slowly remove the note and unfold it. She knew she'd have to explain Robert's comment about not reacting to the message he'd left with her base locator on Friday night, but that didn't matter. It was done, and she was willing to accept whatever blame assigned to her as contributing to his tragic demise.

There was silence in the room as Flo read what her son had written. She squinted as she read it again.

"What does it say?" Susan asked.

Flo took them all in and said in a low, dry voice, "My son didn't kill anyone. He says he was set up."

Susan took the note from Flo and read it. She looked to Margit for permission to hand it to Brian Maitland; Margit nodded. After Maitland had read it, Flo Cobol stood and looked at Margit with an expression that Margit read as anger. She left the room, returning seconds later with a copy of the local weekly newspaper. On the front was a picture of Cobol, the same photograph that had been in his personnel file. The headline said ACCUSED MURDERER TAKES LIFE.

"I gave them the picture because they asked for it. I thought they were going to write a nice obituary for Robert. Instead, they tell everyone in this community that he was a murderer, that he'd killed someone."

"Not just this community, Flo," said Susan. "The whole country, the world, I guess, has been told the same thing."

If Flo's earlier expression had denoted anger, it was now rage. She threw the newspaper to the floor and went to a window that looked out on the street. "We've always had a good name in this community," she said to the windowpane. "Robert was respected by my neighbors. People who have stores here always asked about him, especially after he got his commission in the army. Everyone was proud of him. And now what do they think?" She turned and looked at the newspaper that still rested on the rug. "They bring up the rumor about Robert having had an affair with this Dr. Joycelen. He didn't even know the man."

Maitland, deep in thought, legs crossed, a frown upon his face, sensed that people were looking at him. "What can we do?" he asked.

"Do?" Margit said.

"Yes. It isn't right that somebody dies like this, painted like some Jack the Ripper."

Flo returned to the couch and asked Margit, "Is there anything we can do to clear his name?"

Margit avoided Flo's eyes. She wanted to be able to tell her that there was a great deal that could be done to clear Robert Cobol's name, that there were avenues to pursue, people to contact who would work together to accomplish it. But she knew—and the realization made her feel like a rock about to sink to the bottom of a murky lake—that there wasn't any avenue, wasn't any person to go to, at least not in the military chain of command. To whom could she give the note? Would it matter if she gave it to anyone? Cobol had made a vague accusation in it that some unidentified person had "set him up." A guilty man grasping at straws was the way it would be viewed.

"You knew my son well?" Flo asked Maitland.

"Yes, I did. We were roommates."

Flo smiled. "Robert never said anything to me about his private life, but he told me he'd met a nice young man and that you were living together. I guess . . ."

"Robert was very special to me," Maitland said. "I didn't want to come here today because I felt awkward about it, but I'm glad I did. He came from a nice family. I can see that."

As Flo and Maitland talked, Margit left the house and stood on the front cement stoop. Small children played in the tiny front yard of a house across the street. That's what happens to neighborhoods, she thought. One generation moves on, and a new, younger one moves in. The children's giggles were shrill and pleasant. Margit looked above them and saw a dog's face in the window, wanting evidently to come out and play, too.

She didn't remember much of her childhood, but there were moments that had stayed with her. One had occurred when she was about the same age as the children across the street.

She and her father had just moved to a new base, which meant making friends all over again. Fortunately, a brother and sister about her age lived next door in Capehart housing, and they quickly became friends. They must have sounded the same way to older people on the block as these children in Franklin Square did, silly little creatures giggling and yelling at the top of their voices as they wrestled, chased each other, and in general played out their natural entitlement to fantasies. At that moment she could actually see herself back in the yard at the base, playing with the brother and sister. And then she looked up and saw her father at the door. He wore an apron because he was preparing dinner for the two of them, and he was smiling broadly. But his face was always more serious whenever he told her:

"Make sure you can live with yourself, Margit. Never sell out. Don't ever allow yourself to be bought."

Now she remembered. He always smiled again after stating that creed, and said, "I know you never will. You don't need this advice from your old man."

Tears flooded her eyes. She wiped them away, returned to the living room, and said, "Maybe there *is* something that can be done to clear Robert's name. I know some people who might be able—and willing—to help. Maybe they can do something I can't."

She said to Maitland, "Come on. We have a plane to catch."

CHAPTER
TWENTY-TWO

Sam Caldwell was not comfortable with discomfort. He never took the red-eye flights that lumbered overnight from west to east, and he always flew first class. Yet here he was, wedged in a coach seat at three in the morning, Washington time, exhausted from a day of unending meetings at Starpath, a belly burning from too much airport booze, and facing more meetings that day without any chance to sleep. His trip to his client in California, and his speedy return to Washington, had been arranged at the last minute, timing that had created his uncomfortable surroundings. First class on the flight was fully booked; something to do with a canceled earlier flight. Ordinarily, he would have waited for a morning departure, but he had to be back in Washington by nine.

At least there was a limo waiting for him at Dulles, courtesy of Starpath. It was in his contract. He was worth it, Caldwell knew, and so did his client. The Washington adage that not the best man but the best lobbyist usually won, even if the product was inferior, wasn't lost on Starpath's board. Caldwell was the best lobbyist. His "Me Wall"—photos on his office wall of himself with Washington power brokers—was the most impressive in D.C.

The product, Starpath's weapons system, was—well, it was still early in the developmental stage.

Caldwell's first meeting of the day was at the Jockey Club in the Ritz-Carlton Hotel on Massachusetts Ave., Washington's most venerable power restaurant, where Supreme Court justices celebrate their appointments, the Reagans celebrated their anniversary, and where type-A personalities from every venue plied their powers of persuasion on others. Buyers and sellers. Of something, and everything.

Caldwell's breakfast companion hadn't wanted to meet at the Jockey Club because he considered it too public a place for sensitive conversation. But Caldwell insisted. "Better to be out in the open," he said. "I don't need reporters with long lenses and parabolic microphones making something out of the fact that we're meeting in some quaint goddamn inn in the sticks."

Although Caldwell was early, Joe Maize, the lead Pentagon auditor on Project Safekeep, was already at a table. He stood as Caldwell approached; Caldwell ignored Maize's extended hand and slid with bulky difficulty into the wine-colored booth.

"Good flight?" Maize asked.

Caldwell looked at him as though he were imbecilic. "Do I look like I had a good flight?" He ran his fingers over the stubble on his cheeks and chin and rubbed bloodshot eyes.

"Just a question," Maize said.

"It was a lousy flight. It was a lousy day and night." Caldwell opened a menu, closed it quickly, and asked, "What's new here?"

Maize said, "You've only been gone a day."

"A day is an eternity in this town," Caldwell said, his voice raspy from a lack of sleep and an overdose of cigars. "One day and we could be a banana republic."

Caldwell watched Maize pick up a glass of water. His hand shook, which pleased Caldwell. Nervous men were more likely to listen to good advice.

A waiter took their orders. Caldwell sat back and closed his eyes. Maize wondered if he were about to take a nap. Caldwell answered the question by opening his eyes and glancing around the room. You get to know a lot of people as a lobbyist, he thought. A top gun with a regulatory agency sat with a prostitute Caldwell had booked out on occasion. At another table a congressman with senatorial aspirations sat with the president of a leading political PR agency. A lobbyist for a large aircraft manufacturer conferred with an air-force procurement officer from the Pentagon with whom Caldwell had had numerous dealings.

Washington, D.C.

Caldwell's early anger had further unnerved Maize. "What time is your meeting with Betterton?" he asked.

Caldwell jerked his head in Maize's direction. "What?"

"Your meeting with the lawyer."

"Eleven."

"How much does he know?" Maize asked, dabbing at perspiration on his brow with a red napkin.

"Damn little at this point. He'll know more once we meet."

Maize stared at the red-and-white checkered tablecloth. His fingers were laced together; he kept unclasping his thumbs. "There's no need for him to know—I mean, to know more than he needs to know to represent you at the hearing."

Caldwell slowly turned and glared at Maize. "Are you telling me what to tell my attorney?"

Maize's smile was conciliatory. "Hell no, Sam. It's just that sometimes these lawyers end up knowing too much. That's all I meant."

Caldwell asked in a low growl, "You've received nothing from the committee?"

"No. Why would I?"

Caldwell's sideways glance said many things, especially that Maize's comment was stupid. "You've heard nothing from your bosses?"

Maize shook his head. He picked up a glass of fresh-squeezed orange juice and was taking his first sip when Caldwell asked, "Do *you* have a lawyer?"

Maize gagged, quickly brought the napkin to his lips, and coughed. He eventually said through the linen, "No, of course not. I don't need a lawyer."

Caldwell strung out his response. "Maybe you do, Joe. Think about it."

They ate eggs and sausage, largely in silence. Over coffee, Caldwell said, "There is no need to panic, Joe. Wishengrad and his committee are fishing, that's all. Wishengrad is a knee-jerk son of a bitch who sees a villain in every defense contractor."

Maize replied, "But he wouldn't hold this hearing without some hard information. I mean, he must have some facts to justify it."

"Maybe. It depends upon how much Joycelen provided before he checked out."

"Maybe there were others."

"Maybe. Were there?"

It took a moment for Maize to realize that Caldwell was suggesting that he might be a source of leaks to Wishengrad and his staff. That upset him. More than anything, he needed the confidence and friendship of Sam Caldwell in the event the committee went beyond probing the activities of Starpath's lobbyist. If it expanded into Caldwell's connections within the Pentagon, particularly in the auditing section, he'd need every friend he could muster. "You aren't suggesting that I might have leaked something," he said.

Caldwell managed his first smile of the morning. "Of course not, Joe. I can't imagine that you'd foul your own nest. Doesn't make sense, does it?"

A shaky laugh from Maize. "Sure doesn't." He sat up straight and forced positiveness into his voice. "A molehill made into a mountain by Senator Henry Wishengrad. Sometimes I question his patriotism."

Caldwell looked quizzically at him. "Why?" he asked.

Maize shrugged, realized he'd made a comment he couldn't support. "He's so antimilitary, so anti–national defense. You'd almost think . . ."

"Wishengrad is as loyal an American as you and me, Joe. He sees things different because that's what the people who put him in office want him to see. Plunk him in Orange County, and you'd have a raging hawk. He's a politician. Nothing more to it."

Caldwell picked up the check. As he was leaving, he said to Maize, "If you hear anything, you'll call me first."

"Of course, Sam. But I don't expect to hear anything."

"Maybe not, but if you do, have my number at the top of your list." He delivered that final order in a voice that said he meant it. He left Maize standing in the Jockey Club's lobby looking gray and worried and old. Good, Caldwell thought. If things got bad, the one thing he didn't need was a civil servant acting with unexpected, unwelcome bravado.

That same morning Margit went to work at the Pentagon at her usual time. Everything had been moved back to her original office. She walked through the door and looked around. Jay Kraft glanced up, smiled, and turned a page of what he'd been reading.

It's as though nothing has happened, she thought. Cobol, Joycelen, the daily meetings with Bellis—it simply never happened. Except that Kraft smiled.

But it had happened, and her memory of it had grown more bitter with each passing hour since the funeral. She'd returned from Long Island, dropped Maitland off at the Sign of the Whale, and had gone directly to her BOQ, where she spent what turned out to be a sleepless night.

She'd no sooner sat at her desk when her phone rang.

"Major Falk, this is Louise Harrison of the *Post.*"

"Hello," Margit said, glancing nervously at Kraft, who seemed preoccupied with what he was reading.

"Major Falk, I would really appreciate a chance to sit down with you."

"I don't think that's possible," Margit said.

"I'll do it any way you wish. Strictly off the record, background only. I'll meet you where and when you say, under any circumstances."

"Thank you for calling but . . ."

Kraft got up and left the office. Margit said, "Look, Ms. Harrison, I'm no longer involved in the Cobol case. He's dead. As far as everyone is concerned, that means the murderer of Dr. Joycelen is dead, too. Case closed."

"I don't believe that," Harrison said. "No, to be more precise, I don't think *you* believe it. Am I right?"

Margit lowered her voice. "Ms. Harrison, your instincts are sound. At the same time, I am a commissioned officer in the United States Air Force. I don't make it a habit of breaching Command."

"I assure you, Major Falk, that no one will ever know we've spoken. I'm not looking to quote you. I'm not looking to get you in trouble. I've been assigned, along with another reporter, to do an investigative piece on this supposed suicide of Captain Cobol. All I'm looking for is a better understanding of what happened. And maybe I can be of help to you. Please. Just a half hour. You pick the woods where we meet."

"Could I have your number and call you back at a more convenient time?"

"Sure," Harrison said. Margit wrote it down. As she was about to hang up, she turned in her chair because she sensed the presence of someone behind her. She was right; standing in the doorway was Max Lanning, typical boyish grin painted all over his face. She placed the receiver in its cradle and swiveled to face him. "Good morning," she said.

"Good morning, Major. I didn't know whether I'd see you for a while. I heard you took leave."

"Just a few days off."

"Boy, that was incredible what happened to Captain Cobol."

"Among other things."

He stepped into the office. "Where's Major Kraft?"

"He left a few minutes ago. Are you here to see him?"

"No. Actually, I came to ask you something."

Margit's raised eyebrows invited the next sentence.

"I was wondering if you'd have lunch with me. Dinner would be even better, but lunch is okay."

Did he want to discuss something with her, or was he asking for a date?

"I hope you don't think this is out of place. I mean, I know I'm a lieutenant and you're a major, but I didn't think there'd be anything wrong in just having lunch or dinner."

To say nothing of age, Margit thought. "I'd like that," she said. "Let's make it lunch. Today?"

"Sure. I meant today. I know a great place on the Metro line. Anna's Gateway. Just a couple of stops."

"What time?"

"Noon?"

"Pick me up here," Margit said.

"Happy to have me back?" Margit asked Kraft when he returned.

"I kind of liked the office to myself," he replied.

"So did I," said Margit. "Looks like we're roommates again. Might as well make the best of it."

"You're back as liaison with T and E?"

"Looks like it. What are you working on?"

"Base closings. Maybe reopenings is more like it. Some of the closings announced last year are on hold because of this Mideast thing."

"Cutting military funds isn't popular these days," Margit said.

"Good for us."

"I suppose so," Margit said.

"Must be dull back on T and E after the Cobol thing."

"Assuming you consider the Cobol 'thing' to be have been exciting. It wasn't. Upsetting is more like it."

"Just as well," Kraft said.

"What do you mean?"

He glanced at the empty doorway before saying, "They tossed you to the wolves."

"They did?"

"Sure," Kraft said, satisfied smile on his face. "They weren't going to deal you a full deck of cards, and you know it. It made sense for them, I guess, to use a woman, considering the circumstances."

Margit's temperature rose. She didn't want to believe what Kraft was saying—and resented him for saying it. Simultaneously, she was angry at her own awareness that what he'd said might be true. "Excuse me," she said.

She went downstairs and out into the center court. The first hint of fall was in the air, which, coupled with sustained sunshine, made for a perfect day, at least where weather was concerned. She stayed outside for a half hour before returning to her office, where she tried to get back, mentally, into Project Safekeep files.

At noon sharp Lanning arrived. "I'll be back about two," Margit said to Kraft, whose expression said that he found their having lunch together interesting beyond reason.

They went to the lobby and rode a long escalator down into the depths of the building to the Metro stop called Pentagon, where they boarded a blue-line car heavy with passengers, most of them military men and women of every conceivable rank except private. After a stop at Pentagon City with its spectacular new shopping mall, they got off at Crystal City. They walked through an underground maze of shops and fast-food restaurants that bustled with shoppers and noontime diners until reaching a large, brightly lit, and appealing window that afforded them a look into Anna's Gateway. Inside, they waited to be seated by *the* Anna. She spotted Lanning and greeted him effusively.

"You must come here often," Margit said.

"I do," said Lanning. "Anna's famous here in D.C. She owned Anna Maria's on Connecticut for years, an institution. She sold it, but they still use her name. That's her husband, Manny." He pointed to a handsome, heavyset man at the cash register.

Margit smiled. "You amaze me, Max. How do you know these things?"

"I listen to people," he replied. "I guess they trust me and like to tell me things."

"I guess so," Margit said.

Over chicken-salad sandwiches and iced coffee, Lanning did most of the talking, encouraged by Margit. She asked him about Pentagon reaction to what had happened to Cobol. He said he hadn't heard much, except that Bellis had commented to someone that she—Margit—was a fine young woman and officer.

"He said that?"

"Sure did. I guess you feel pretty bummed-out about how things ended up."

"Bummed-out is as good a phrase as any. What else has Colonel Bellis said about me?"

"Nothing that I've heard."

"I was very upset when Captain Cobol took his life."

"Do you think he really did?" Lanning asked.

She paused. "No," she said.

"I don't either."

"What do you base that on?" she asked.

"Nothing special. It just doesn't make sense to me."

"That's good enough. By the way, who puts the security-duty roster together?"

"Security."

"Besides the Security Department. The special security details, the ones the sections control."

"Oh. Major Kraft does for our division."

"He does?"

"Sure."

"I haven't pulled security duty since I got here."

"That's because Colonel Bellis told Major Kraft not to put you on as long as you were defending Captain Cobol."

"Oh. What about other divisions? Do you know who's in charge of their security rosters?"

"No."

She'd been trying for the past few minutes to put together something she'd recently heard with the person who'd said it. It came to her. As Major Mucci was leaving the Officers' Club after having dinner with her and Bill Monroney, he'd declined a nightcap because he'd had to "run the duty roster." Was that the same roster that had put Cobol at the scene of the murder Saturday morning?

"Would you be up to doing me a favor?" she asked Lanning.

"Sure."

"Could you—do your contacts include someone who has access to duty rosters over the past month?"

"Major Kraft can . . ."

"Not for our division, Max. For another. T and E, for example."

"I guess I could find out."

"Would you for me?"

"Sure. At least I'll try."

"I'm especially interested in the week Dr. Joycelen was killed."

"Okay, but how come? I thought it was over."

"It is," she said lightly, "but I have to tie up loose ends. You know, for a final report."

"Sure."

"I'd ask my assistants to do it, but they've gone back to their commands. Frankly, I'm overwhelmed being back on Project Safekeep and could use a hand. If it's not too much trouble, of course."

"No, no trouble. I do a lot of sitting around waiting for the elephant to move." It wasn't a particularly disparaging remark about Bellis. In the Pentagon bosses were routinely referred to as "elephants."

"Great," said Margit. "Do it at your leisure, Max, and don't make a fuss about it. Let's keep it between us. Command wants the Cobol case wrapped up quietly, strictly on a need-to-know basis. I'm including you in that list."

"I'll get it done," he said enthusiastically.

"By the way," she said, "in this vast network of contacts you seem to have, do you know anyone in Personnel?"

"Sure. Which Personnel?"

"Army."

"Gee, no, I—maybe I do. Why?"

"Nothing important. I had dinner with a friend, and she was

talking about a designation Personnel uses. I'd never heard of it."

"What is it?"

"HP-5."

"HP-5?"

"Yes. HP-5. Ever hear of it?"

"No."

"Think you could ask your friend?"

"Sure. HP-5. I'll see what I can find out."

"Great. Just a silly bet." He looked at her quizzically. "My friend. She thinks it's an assignment designation. I think it's a category of specialization."

"How much if I say you're right?"

Margit laughed. "Half."

"It's a deal."

She looked around the large, appealing restaurant. It was still packed; a line longer than they'd waited on had formed at the door. Their waitress laid their check on the table, and Margit picked it up. "Major's treat," she said.

Margit handed Lanning the check and money and suggested he go to the cashier. "I have to make a quick phone call," she said.

She went to a booth, inserted coins, and punched in a number she read from a slip of paper from her purse. "Louise Harrison," said the woman who answered.

CHAPTER
TWENTY-THREE

 She left the Pentagon at five, drove across the Arlington Memorial Bridge, and headed in the direction of the Capitol Building. She found a parking space on Sixth and walked toward the Mall, which stretched from the Washington Monument on its western end to the U.S. Capitol on the east. The Mall was at its usual busy best, Frisbees flying, bikes rolling, droves of tourists and natives ("residents" is more accurate) enjoying its open spaces, and the myriad museums of the Smithsonian Institution.

She strolled the Mall's length. After passing the museums of American History and Natural History on her left, she paused at the skating rink and looked across the expanse of grass to the Freer Gallery, known for its collection of Oriental art; to the Hirshhorn Museum and Sculpture Garden; and to the original Smithsonian "castle," which now served as that institution's "Pentagon."

She continued her walk until reaching the National Gallery of Art, its two buildings directly across from the National Air and Space Museum, enjoying, among other features of a fine day, the diversity of architecture in view. The gallery's West Building, designed by John Russell Pope in the 1930s, was, architectural critics noted, the last great building in Washington conceived in the classical style. Next to it, in sharp contrast, was the East Building, completed in 1978, a vision of I. M. Pei; a trapezoid divided into two triangles of pink marble. That the collections housed in each of the buildings reflected their individual designs was to be expected—da Vinci, Degas, Renoir, and Monet in the West; Henry Moore and Noguchi sculptures, Miró tapestries, and Alexander Calder mobiles in the East. It might be nice, Margit thought, if everything in Washington were as appropriate and as well-thought-out.

A cobblestone courtyard spanned the two buildings. Most people used an underground concourse that linked them, but Margit went to the courtyard where she was to meet Louise Harrison, who said she'd wait at the center fountain. Margit admired the fountain, a design that spewed streams of water into the air and, because there was no enclosure, allowed it to flow freely over cobblestones and down terraced concrete to a sheet of glass that formed a wall of the lower concourse.

"Major Falk?" a female voice said from behind. Margit turned. The woman smiled and extended her hand. "Louise Harrison."

"Yes." Margit shook the reporter's hand.

Louise Harrison didn't look the way Margit expected she would. Funny how voices can throw you off. Like having a favorite radio disc jockey for years and building a mental image of the person to whom the voice belongs. Then, meeting the big, booming voice and discovering its slight, slender owner. Margit had pictured Harrison as tall and lanky—somehow British in appearance (because of the name? a female version of Rex Harrison?)—and similarly regal in bearing. Instead, she faced a woman no taller than five feet two inches, with a pug nose, ruddy, fleshy cheeks, and heavy black eyebrows. Her hair was brown and straight, the cut severe.

"I've always loved this fountain," Harrison said. "I can sit for hours and watch the water lift and flow."

"It is beautiful," Margit agreed.

"I appreciate your agreeing to meet me," Harrison said.

"I'm still not sure I should have," said Margit. "I almost changed my mind."

"Glad you didn't." Harrison thrust her hands deep into the pockets of her tan raincoat and looked around. The buildings blocked the sun from the courtyard; it was chilly in the shade of a waning day. Few people were in the courtyard, most passing from one building to the other. Some lingered, including a young man pushing a baby carriage. He stood on the opposite side of the fountain and seemed to be admiring the flow of water over the cobblestones. His carriage was one of those tall British types, but his clothing was pure U.S. campus: jeans, white sneakers, and a black windbreaker. Margit's initial, and fleeting, thought was that it was nice to see a young father taking his infant son or daughter for a stroll, perhaps freeing up the baby's mother for errands, or for time with friends. Modern, and nice.

Harrison noted the young man, too. But he wasn't likely to hear anything they said. He was thirty feet from them, and there was the gurgle of the fountain.

"Look, Major, I know you're uncomfortable meeting with a reporter, and I can understand that." Margit didn't reply. Harrison said, "Then again, maybe I don't understand. Half this town talks to the press on background, no quotes, no attribution. It seems to me that now that Captain Cobol is dead, there wouldn't be any official reason to put a muzzle on you." Again, no response. "Is there? I mean, is there any official reason not to discuss this with me?"

Margit raised her eyebrows. "Common sense, that's all. I'm an officer in the air force. Even though that doesn't impinge upon my First Amendment rights, we do have protocol when it comes to releasing information."

"Let me ask you a question," Harrison said. "You indicated to me when I reached you at Mackensie Smith's house that you might have doubts that your client—is that what they're called in the military, client?—might not have hanged himself the way the official line would have us believe. Why?"

Margit, who'd been relaxed, now felt a tickle of nerves. She said, "I didn't say that to you on the phone."

Harrison said. "No, not exactly, but your tone, and the way you stressed 'alleged,' said a lot more than your actual words. Are you involved in the investigation of Cobol's death?"

"I've been taken off the case."

"You have no continuing interest in it? Officially, that is?"

"That's right."

"Have you changed your mind?"

"About what?"

"About doubting whether Cobol died by his own hand."

Margit looked away from the reporter and focused on the water. There were certain aspects of some people's personalities that invariably annoyed her. One was playing games, like women who use four-letter words and then put their fingers to their lips, saying "Pardon my French." Or men who are always coming close to consummating something—personal or professional—but who keep it going rather than concluding it, never committing. But here she stood, Margit Falk, who had agreed to meet a reporter to discuss what is very much on her mind these days, but who now plays coy. Say good-bye, Margit, or tell her what you're really thinking.

"I don't think Captain Cobol killed Dr. Joycelen, nor do I think he took his own life," she said, looking directly into Harrison's almond eyes. Cobol's note to her was like a large weight in her purse.

"Neither do I," Harrison said.

"Maybe you know more than I do," Margit said.

"What was Cobol like?"

"Very nice."

"A good officer?"

"I think so."

"Was he gay?"

Margit hesitated. The man had been dragged through the mud in ways considerably more savage than revelations about his private sexual life. He died, accused of murdering a scientist, with no recourse, no hearings. Okay, no games. "Yes, he was," she said.

"Joycelen?"

"That's what's been alleged. I don't buy that."

"Cobol was CIA," said Harrison.

"Right," Margit confirmed. "He was on liaison duty at the Pentagon. There are a lot of people from the Company assigned to the Pentagon."

"I thought you had regs against homosexuals in the service."

"We do." Margit didn't like the direction Harrison was taking them. She would not—could not—implicate Major Reich, or others who might have been involved in allowing Cobol to continue in the army despite knowing that his private life blatantly violated regulations. She said, "My guess is that the homosexual population in general is reflected, to some degree, by their percentage in the military."

"Did Cobol keep it private?" Harrison asked.

Did she know something? Was she aware that Cobol had been found out? Reporters, Margit knew, along with lawyers, liked to ask questions to which they already had the answers. "I have to assume he had," Margit answered.

She looked through the water at the young father, who had lowered his head and pushed the carriage toward the glass wall overlooking the underground passageway.

"I really should be going," Margit said. She had a date with Foxboro at seven-thirty.

"Sure. Have you heard that Joycelen might have been a whistle-blower?"

"No," Margit said, realizing at the same time that, in essence, she was on the verge of becoming one.

"You know about Wishengrad's hearing," Harrison said. It was a statement, not a question.

"I read about it," Margit said.

"One of our political-affairs correspondents has a source who says Joycelen was telling tales out of school."

"About DARPA?" Margit asked.

"About Project Safekeep."

"That's news to me," Margit said. She thought about Foxboro.

"Opens up some interesting possibilities, doesn't it?" Harrison said.

Margit chose not to answer. She said instead, "Listen, I really have to go, Ms. Harrison."

"Call me Louise."

"Okay. I wish I had more to offer you. This was wasted time for you." How easy to pull out Cobol's note and hand it to the reporter. She couldn't.

"Not at all," Harrison said. "Just knowing that someone close to the Cobol case shares the same skepticism I have means something."

"Don't read too much into what I've said," Margit said.

"I'll try not to. Could we meet again?"

"For what purpose?"

"Just to talk. Your place, your time. I'll show up whenever and wherever you say."

"Louise, let's leave it this way. If I think I have something to offer you, I'll call."

"Fair enough."

They shook hands. Margit said, "Why don't you leave first."

"You're concerned about being seen with me."

"I guess I am."

"I don't think you have anything to worry about, Major. After all, you're not giving me operational secrets about Star Wars."

"Still . . ."

"We might be able to do somebody some good. Cobol's memory. Joycelen's. The nation? Call me," said Harrison. She walked away.

Margit lingered a few moments. She was alone in the courtyard. She hunched her shoulders against a chill, then headed for her car on Sixth Street. As she approached it, she saw the young father with the baby carriage standing next to his car, which was parked on the opposite side of the street.

Margit got in her Honda, sat a few moments pondering the conversation she'd had with Louise Harrison, started the engine, and slowly pulled away from the curb. The young man with the baby carriage watched her stop at the corner for a red light. Another car that had been parked on Margit's side of the street fell in behind her as the light changed to green, and Margit turned the corner.

The man reached inside the baby carriage, removed a pink blanket, picked up a lifelike doll, and threw both into the trunk. He collapsed the carriage and tossed it, too, into the trunk—on top of his plastic baby.

CHAPTER

TWENTY-FOUR

 Foxboro had cooked spaghetti and made a green salad, which he and Margit ate at a small kitchen table in his Crystal City apartment. Throughout the simple meal, he'd demonstrated intense interest in her activities that day. She'd mentioned lunch with Max Lanning, and Foxboro repeatedly asked what they'd talked about. At one point Margit had laughed. "I can't possibly remember everything we discussed," she'd said. "We just . . . talked. He's a nice young man who works for Bellis, mostly as his driver, and who seems interested in anything and everything."

"How come Bellis has a lieutenant as his driver? I thought enlisted men were drivers."

Margit again laughed. "Not in the Pentagon, Jeff. It may be that way everywhere else in the system, but in the Pentagon, lieutenants are buck privates."

Now, as they sat at the table sipping coffee and eating grapefruit halves, Margit changed the subject. "I read about the hearing into Project Safekeep and Starpath. Did you know it was in the works?"

Foxboro picked up their empty spaghetti plates, took them to the sink, and rinsed them. He said over the sound of running water, "I knew something was brewing."

"Tell me about it," she said. "You must have known earlier."

He shut off the water, turned, and leaned against the sink. "What's to tell? We think there's been some hanky-panky with that weapons system, and we want to get to the facts."

"You must already have facts to justify a hearing," Margit said.

"That's right. Hand me the salad plates."

She assumed he was going to rejoin her at the table, but he left the kitchen and didn't return. She finished clearing, and found him in what would be a small second bedroom, had it been needed for that purpose. Instead, the bachelor had turned it into a home office. A desk lamp cast a muted pool of yellow light on the desktop. Through open blinds the lights of the city flickered across the Potomac. Foxboro was in his chair, his feet propped on the desk.

"Jeff," Margit said from behind, "is something wrong?"

He answered without turning. "Maybe there is."

"Want to share it with me?"

"Maybe what's wrong is us," he said.

"Oh. Maybe you'd like to share your thoughts about *that.*"

He dropped his feet to the floor and turned. "Look, Margit, I've got a ton on my mind. I'm being stretched six ways from Sunday, and it's getting to me."

She came to the side of the desk and sat in a yellow director's chair. "I understand that," she said. "Are you suggesting that I'm imposing additional pressure?"

He shrugged. "I just know I feel trapped."

"Trapped? By me?"

"No, it's just that—look, I don't want to talk about it. Maybe that's what's bugging me, that we get together and we talk shop. The little bit of time I have away from the Hill, I don't want to talk about it."

"Fine. I respect that."

"Then why do you keep asking me about it? About the hearing, for instance?"

"Jeff, you spent the entire dinner pumping me about what I did today, whom I saw, what I talked about. I'm flattered you're interested, but I'd like to think it's a two-way street." When he didn't reply, she added, "Is it?"

His answer was to leave the room. He went to the hall closet and pulled out a tan golf jacket. She stood in the living room and watched him put it on. "Are you leaving?"

"Yeah. I need a walk. I need to be alone."

"Then I suppose I should leave," Margit said.

She wanted him to protest. He didn't. He looked as though he wanted to say something, but no words came from him. He opened the door and left.

Margit returned to his office and sat in the chair he'd occupied, looked across the river at the same lights he'd been watching. Did those lights have the same meaning to him that they did for her at that moment? Washington's light show had always represented beauty to her, a kind of benign grandeur, as it did to millions of other people who lived there, or visited. But now, as she sat in the shadowed small room and gazed at the lights, they represented something dangerous and unwholesome, each light a cynical wink that taunted her, that said: You were better off where you were before. This is not a place for people with ideals, with commitment to Pollyanna concepts of fairness and decency. You don't belong here, Margit, she could almost hear a voice saying. This place—this system—will suffocate you, just as it's doing to your relationship with Jeff. You can't survive it. Either be a good soldier or get out. Go to Bellis and tell him you'd like a transfer somewhere else. He's offered you that. Take advantage of it—before it's too late.

She rested her elbows on the desk and tried to force order into her thinking. Surely, it was possible to inject reason into this situation—into any situation. Nothing is ever solved until the emotional quotient is replaced by hard-nosed cognitive reasoning. She'd always prided herself in having that ability. Law demanded it of you. So did flying a helicopter. She hadn't saved her skin and accomplished those missions in Panama by allowing emotions to fly her chopper.

She wished she'd been been direct and had asked Jeff about the rumor that Joycelen might have been a whistle-blower to the Wishengrad committee. She thought of his pumping her over dinner about her day. He must have had a reason for it, but he hadn't been direct, either. The two of them, supposedly in love (were they?) playing games with each other. Joisting and parrying, like a couple of second-year law students at a mock trial.

She decided to leave. Jeff had made it plain he wanted to be alone. She opened a desk drawer and rummaged through supplies in search of a piece of blank paper, to leave him a note. He could let her know if he ever changed his mind. As she withdrew a sheet of white bond, several scraps of paper came up with it, including one on which was written an address, a phone number, and a series of digits: 2, 2, 5, 5, 10, 2.

Margit stared at it. It meant nothing to her. Yet she felt it was something she'd seen before or at least should connect with. Without much thought, and wanting to be out of there before he returned, she shoved the scrap into her pocket and closed the drawer, rolled the blank page into a typewriter, and typed:

Dear Jeff—

I know you need to be alone at this moment, and I respect that. At the same time, Jeff, I don't think it's accurate, to say nothing of fair, that I should be lumped into the problems that cause you to seek seclusion.

Perhaps I have been too aggressive in trying to find something in this relationship that evidently isn't there, and perhaps never can be. I haven't meant to disrupt you, or us. To the contrary, I've been doing a pretty good job lately of protecting *us,* which, as both of us know, generally ends up a futile exercise. Maybe academic is more apt, because maybe that's what it's been since we first met in school.

I'm sitting here in your office feeling sorry for myself, and not very happy with my current circumstances. I'd thought that coming back to Washington represented a milestone in my life. An assignment at the Pentagon where I could use my legal training. A chance to nurture a relationship with you that has always meant a great deal to me. An opportunity to renew friendships, and to step up to the next plateau in my life. It hasn't worked out that way. It seems that everything I touch these days fails, or dies. But there I go feeling sorry for myself again.

I know I've probably bored you quoting things my father said to me when I was growing up, but I'll add one more. He used to say that *any action is better than taking no action.* It wasn't original with him. Most good psychologists offer the same advice. But it didn't come from a psychologist. It came from him, and because it did, it has additional meaning to me.

Col. Bellis suggested I take leave, get away, put Washington and the Pentagon and Cobol and Joycelen and everything else behind me. I may just do that, although

I'm not sure that running away ever represents an answer. My experience has been that you drag with you whatever it is that churns inside. Still, at this moment sitting in your apartment, it seems an appealing and viable option.

I once had a friend from a small town who took a job in New York City. She stood at her hotel window her first night there and proclaimed in a loud voice, "Gotham I'll conquer you yet." We laughed when she told me that, but the last time I heard from her, she had conquered New York City, at least to her satisfaction. I intended to "conquer" Washington, but the battle turned out to be one-sided. I feel very defeated at this moment and, like all animals, might slip away and lick my wounds.

Enough whining. If, at some point down the road, you want to catch up again, give me a call. If nothing else, I will always consider you a good and valued friend. And, if you feel like going through with our plans for this Saturday, I'm willing.

She signed it, *Love, Margit.*

"I really feel as though I've barged in on you," Margit said to Mac and Annabel as she sat with them in their den.

"Don't be silly," Annabel said. "All you've interrupted was a potential argument over where to take our next vacation. Mac wants to go to London—again—but I'm in the mood for white-water rafting."

"A regular Amazon," Smith said, laughing. "A wild and crazy woman."

Margit smiled. She hadn't wanted to impose upon them when she left Jeff Foxboro's apartment, but it was as though a hand had led her to the phone booth and had punched in their number. They hadn't hesitated. "You sound upset," Annabel had said. "Come on over. I'll put on coffee."

"Jeff and I broke up tonight," Margit told them after Annabel had placed a steaming mug in her hand.

"Oh, I'm sorry," Annabel said.

"I am, too," said Margit. "It was coming."

"Mind if I ask what brought it about?" Smith put in.

"Nothing in particular, Mac. We'd been drifting apart. Jeff was upset. He told me he thought part of his problem was us, and that he needed time alone."

"That doesn't necessarily sound like a breakup," Smith said. "We all need time alone now and then. Too much togetherness can stifle a relationship."

Margit smiled. "Being together too much was hardly our problem," she said. "Maybe if we'd spent more time together, things would have gone smoother."

Smith leaned back and scrutinized her, a gallery visitor examining a painting. "The Joycelen-Cobol mess has a lot to do with this, doesn't it?"

Margit bit her lip. "Yes."

"Jeff wasn't happy with your unwillingness to accept how it ended up?"

Margit thought for a moment before answering. "Yes and no. Initially, he was critical of my involvement with the case. But now that it's over for me, he's been encouraging me to keep pushing."

"What caused that turnabout?" Smith asked.

"I have no idea."

"It's still gnawing at you," Annabel said.

Margit whistled. "That, Annabel, is putting it mildly. I've always considered myself a normally compulsive person. I have my ablutions, like most of us. But in this situation I am totally obsessed, to say nothing of being consumed by it. I must find some answer."

Smith left them to walk Rufus. As he led the beast to a favorite patch of brown grass at the corner, a neighbor called from his front steps. "Evening, Ross," Smith said. "Looks like we might get some rain."

Ross Jepsen, a widower, spent his retirement giving tours at the National Cathedral, and working as a volunteer at the Kennedy Center gift shop. He was a nervous man, especially about the rising crime rate in the city. He had reason. Two years before, he'd been mugged. The mugger hadn't been content to take Jepsen's wallet; he'd beat him, severely enough to leave his victim with a slight speech disorder and a pronounced limp. He beckoned Smith to come closer.

"I was wondering about that car," Jepsen said, nodding in the direction of a green—or gray—sedan parked four or five spaces on the other side of Smith's house.

Smith looked. "Is someone in it?"

"Yes. Been there for an hour," said Jepsen.

Smith grunted. "Probably waiting for someone."

"Waiting a long time."

"Well, Ross, let's keep an eye on it, give it another hour. If he's still there—it is a man? . . ." Jepsen nodded. "Then we'll call the police."

"I think we should do it now."

"If you'd feel better," Smith said.

"I think I would."

"Let me know how it turns out," Smith said, responding to Rufus's urgent tug on his lead.

Smith returned to his house, stood in the doorway of the den, and asked, "What are you going to do about this so-called obsessive-compulsive need to resolve what happened to Cobol?"

Margit sighed. "Keep digging, I guess. I told Cobol's mother at the funeral that there were people who might be willing to help me clear his name. I was thinking of you."

"Flattering," Smith said, sounding as though he didn't entirely mean it.

"It's become a cause with me," Margit explained. "I haven't had many causes in my life, and those I have haven't demanded much of me. I'm involved with DACWITS, a military women's organization. I've worked for local humane societies in some of the places I've been stationed. I feel strongly about many things, but this is different. A man, who happens to be a fellow officer, has died with his name dragged through the mud. He never even had a chance to clear himself. I've done what Colonel Bellis warned me not to do. I became emotionally involved with him, and with his family and friends. I want to clear his name, Mac. I *have* to clear his name."

"Fair enough," said Smith, returned to his recliner. "How do you intend to go about it?"

"I was hoping you could give me some advice about that."

"Do you have any resources left to you within the military?" Smith asked.

"No. Maybe that's what upsets me most. This horrible thing—the murder of a scientist, an army captain accused of the murder, homosexual allegations flying around, the captain found hanged in his cell, allegedly by his own hand—and no one involved has even raised an eyebrow." She thought of Louise Harrison, and debated whether to tell Mac and Annabel about her earlier meeting with the reporter. Smith would be critical of her for talking with the press, and she wasn't anxious to be criticized. But she told them about the meeting, and that Harrison had brought up the question of whether Joycelen had been a whistle-blower to the Wishengrad committee.

Smith muttered, "Interesting. Better: pertinent."

"Jeff must know something about that," Annabel offered.

"I assume he does, but he's not talking," Margit said.

"Joycelen is obviously the key to this," Smith remarked. "And Wishengrad."

Margit agreed.

"What do you want me to do?" Smith asked. He glanced at Annabel, who smiled. Friendly? Chiding? Any smile in a storm.

"Your friend who was here the other night," Margit said. "The private investigator."

"Tony Buffolino," Smith said. "Spelled with an O. He's sensitive about that. What would you like him to do?"

Margit raised her hands in a gesture of helplessness. "I have no idea. I've never worked with a private investigator before."

"Nothing mysterious about it, Margit," Smith said. "Would you like Tony to do some digging into Joycelen's life?"

"Do you think he would?"

A laugh from Smith. "Tony will do anything for money."

Annabel quickly said, "Almost anything."

"Right," Smith said. "Almost anything. I told you he was a good investigator. Is the Cobol family interested in clearing the captain's name?"

"Very much," Margit answered.

"Tony will have to be paid," Smith said.

"Of course," Margit agreed. She sat forward and placed her hands on her knees. "I think Flo Cobol, Robert's mother, would sell hearth and home to clear him."

"I'll talk to Tony," Smith said.

Margit said, "If Flo Cobol isn't willing, I'll pay him out of money my father left me."

Smith sighed deeply before saying, "Are you absolutely sure,

Margit, that wanting to pursue that doesn't represent some—some emotional need of the moment that will naturally pass with time?"

"I've been sitting here wondering the same thing," Margit said. "Is this my feeble attempt to rectify what happened to my father? Maybe. A couple of layers deep? Maybe. But so what? Hopefully, I have a lot of years to live with myself. I didn't go to see Cobol when he called, and I don't want to spend the rest of my years tossing and turning because I didn't do the right thing."

Smith stood in the center of the room. "I'll get to Tony in the morning and set up a meeting. Can you come back tomorrow night?"

"Tomorrow is Thursday," Margit said. "Yes, I can come after work."

"Unless you hear from me, or vice versa. I'll have Tony here at seven."

They stood outside in the tiny front yard that was typical of houses on the block. It was a balmy night; heat and humidity had begun to move in. Summer's last gasp. Low, fast-moving clouds slid silently above them. Smith asked, "Have you thought about taking leave, Margit?"

"Yes, I have, but I think it's better for me to continue working. I might learn more by being in the Pentagon."

"You do realize, don't you," Smith said, "that pursuing this can backfire on you?"

"I've thought about that. I've become a master at rationalization. I tell myself that I'm not going against orders because I haven't received flat-out orders. All I'm doing is a favor for Flo Cobol. I suppose it's the same justification I used in getting you involved with Cobol's defense. The *family* wanted civilian counsel. Now, that same family wants help in clearing the name of a dead son. Does it play?"

Smith put his hand on her shoulder. "Not entirely," he said, "but it isn't outrageous, either. Let's take small steps at a time. No big leaps destined to get you in trouble. Tony will act with discretion."

Margit thanked them and walked up the street to where she had found an almost-legal parking space. Mac and Annabel watched her get into her car, start the engine, turn on the headlights, and pull away. As she did, the car that Ross Jepsen had pointed out to Smith left the curb and fell in behind her. Smith stepped onto the sidewalk and squinted to read the license plate of the receding car.

"What's the matter?" Annabel asked.

"The driver of that car was waiting for Margit to leave. I think she's being followed."

Ross Jepsen approached them.

"Did you call the police?" Smith asked.

"Yes. They came."

"And?"

"I watched from my window. A patrol car pulled up next to the car, and they talked to the driver."

"And?"

"Just like all cops," Jepsen said disgustedly. "They drove away."

"I suppose everything was kosher," Smith said. "Good night, Ross."

"Good night."

Back inside the house, Smith wrote down the plate number. "I want Tony to run down who owns that car first thing in the morning."

"She's in danger, isn't she?" Annabel said.

"All I know is that when people follow you, they aren't handing out winning sweepstakes tickets. Feel like a ride?"

"Where?"

"Bolling. I'll get the car. You call Margit. You'll get her machine. Tell her someone followed her from the house, and to be on the lookout for trouble. Tell her we're on our way."

"You're frightening me, Mac."

"Not my intention. But we should be concerned."

Annabel was waiting at the curb when Mac pulled up after retrieving the car from a rented garage down the street. They said nothing as they headed for the base, where they were stopped by a spit-and-polish young airman and a gate that was lowered.

"Can I help you, sir?" the airman asked.

"Yes," said Smith. "We're here to visit Major Margit Falk."

"Is she expecting you, sir?"

"No. But she'll be happy to see us."

"Excuse me, sir." He returned to the small booth, consulted a base directory, and dialed a number. After a brief conversation, he returned to Smith's car and said, "Major Falk is in BOQ Thirteen Hundred." He directed Smith to the building, stepped back, pushed a button that raised the gate, and stood at attention as the car proceeded beneath it.

Mac and Annabel turned a corner. BOQ 1300 was directly in front of them. As they aproached, they saw two different things. Annabel spotted Margit, who stood on the steps outside the main door. Mac saw the green—or gray—sedan that had been parked on his street an hour earlier. It was metallic blue, and was at the curb across from Margit's building.

Smith headed directly for it.

"There's Margit," Annabel said.

"And there's the car," he said gruffly.

He pulled up next to it and overtly peered at its occupants. They stared back.

"Mac, please," Annabel said.

"How'd they get in here?" her husband asked. He answered his own question. "They belong here." He made a U-turn and pulled up to where Margit waited. The other car drove away slowly.

"Mac, Annabel," Margit said through Smith's open window. "Why are you here?"

"That car," Smith said.

Margit looked at the metallic-blue sedan as its red taillights bled around a corner and disappeared. "What about it?" she asked.

"They followed you."

"Followed me?"

"Yes. They waited in front of our house until you left. Then they fell in behind you."

"I . . . are you sure?"

"Yes. I'll have Tony Buffolino check out the plate in the morning."

Margit's laugh was nervous, disbelieving.

"You okay?" Smith asked.

"Yes. Fine."

"Did you get Annabel's message?"

"What message?"

"I left it on your answering machine," Annabel said, leaning across her husband.

"I didn't listen to messages."

"Margit, why is someone following you?" Smith asked.

"Are they? I don't know why anyone would."

"We're worried about you."

"I appreciate that but . . . want to come up? I'll make coffee."

"Thanks, no," Smith said. "We just wanted to make sure you were all right."

"I'm fine. I really appreciate your coming here. Thank you. But I'm fine."

"Keep your eyes open," said Smith.

"I will. You're both very special people." She kissed Smith on the cheek and grasped Annabel's hand. "Go to bed. Tomorrow is almost here."

As Mac and Annabel drove home, Mac said, "Sorry to drag you out."

"You didn't drag me anywhere. That car. It was the same one?"

"Yes."

"Why?"

"I don't know, although I'm brimming over with speculation. I know one thing for certain, though."

"What's that?"

"That Margit is about to take on the most powerful bureaucracy in the world, the United States military."

"And so are you."

He didn't reply.

CHAPTER
TWENTY-FIVE

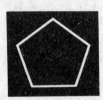

"Margit? Jeff."

"Good morning," she said.

"I acted like a jerk. Forgive me?"

She glanced at Jay Kraft, who was reading that morning's *Early Bird*. "We have to talk," she said.

"I know. I keep reading your note. You said you were willing to hold to our date for Saturday."

"Yes," she said.

"How about dinner tonight? Someplace quiet where we can have a nice, easy conversation."

"I can't. I have plans."

"So soon?" His conciliatory tone had gone flat.

"What do you mean?" she asked.

"Somebody else already?"

"I have to go. I have work to do."

"Okay, okay, sorry. I didn't mean that. How about Friday night?"

"Will call you. Home tonight?"

"Yes. What time?"

"Around eleven."

"I'll be waiting."

Their plans for Saturday involved a dinner-dance at Andrews Air Force Base's Officers' Club, a joint-service social affair sponsored by SecDef's Directorate of Defense Research and Engineering. A "morale booster" was the way it was described around the Pentagon.

Margit had looked forward to it, especially when Jeff had made a point of clearing his schedule in order to accompany her. Now, it did not hold the same appeal, although she was committed to going. You carefully selected what military social events to skip. The invitation had called for an RSVP, but it had the ring of a command performance.

"Good morning, Majors," Max Lanning said from the doorway.

Kraft uttered his predictable grunt. Margit went into the hallway with Lanning and shut the door behind her. "Did you find out anything about that duty roster?" she asked.

"Yup."

"And? Who put Captain Cobol on it that Saturday morning?"

"I had trouble finding out because a copy of that day's roster isn't available."

"Why not?"

"I don't know. They routinely file them, but that one is missing."

"You didn't find out anything," she said.

"Negative," Lanning said. He smiled. "I asked around. I have a couple of civilian friends there, and . . ."

Her expression invited more.

"It was a major in T and E."

"Major who?"

"A Major Mucci. Major Anthony Mucci."

Monroney's aide.

"Thanks," Margit said. "This will help me wrap up my final report."

"Glad I could help. If you want me to find out anything else, just let me know."

"What about my bet?" she asked.

"Bet?"

"HP-5."

"Oh, that." He was whispering. "You both lose," he said.

"We do?"

"Right. That's a top-secret code. CIA."

"Are you sure?"

"Absolutely."

"But you don't know what it means."

"No, and I don't want to. Sorry."

"Nothing to be sorry about, Max. I didn't mean to ask you to look into something top secret."

"I know that. I guess I lose my half of your win."

"Looks like it. Thanks again for checking on the duty roster. I owe you."

When she was again seated at her desk, Kraft asked, "What's the kid got, a thing for you?"

Margit glared at him. "We happen to be friends."

"You should think twice about being friends with lieutenants, especially *that* lieutenant."

"Why especially *that* lieutenant?"

"Because his mind is on vacation, but his mouth works overtime."

Security at the Dirksen Senate Office Building had been beefed up for the arrival that afternoon of Ari Ben Elaha, Israel's ambassador to the United States, who was to meet with Senator Hank Wishengrad. Elaha was escorted by a cadre of American military, supplemented by his own armed escorts.

They met in Wishengrad's private conference room, a large, sparsely furnished space in which an oval antique dining-room table occupied the center. Six chairs lined each side. Wishengrad, two committee colleagues, and Jeff Foxboro and another staff member took one side. Elaha, an official translator—who was seldom needed because Elaha spoke perfect English—and an aide faced them.

Elaha had been lobbying key administration and congressional leaders for the past two weeks. This meeting, he knew, was crucial to his mission. Wishengrad's chairmanship of the Senate committee was a position of indisputable power—especially if you were looking for weapons money.

After a few initial pleasantries Elaha said, "As you know, Senator, I have been meeting with key members of President Beardsley's staff, the National Security Council, and representatives of your Central Intelligence Agency."

Wishengrad smiled. "I am aware, Mr. Ambassador, of those meetings. I hear they went well."

No smile added additional creases to Elaha's avuncular, tan, deeply etched face. "Yes, they have gone quite well," he said. "It is my hope, of course, that this meeting will be as fruitful."

Wishengrad visually involved his colleagues before saying, "We've been reviewing the statements made by your ambassador to the UN, and the formal written requests you've submitted. You're aware, of course, that I've spent years fighting to cut down on the sale of weapons to other countries, including Israel."

"And you've been successful," said Elaha, "much to our chagrin. But despite the stance you've taken in the past, I'm confident that the recent shift in events in our region will create a new and compelling reason to modify your view."

Wishengrad leaned back and pushed his glasses up on his head. "Modify, maybe. Totally change? No chance of that, Mr. Ambassador. Don't get me wrong. It's my view, and that of most of my colleagues on the committee, that we should provide enhanced defensive capabilities for Israel. Hard to argue against that now that your neighbor has proved he can launch a preemptive nuclear strike. How he developed that capability—or, more important, who gave it to him—is the question we'd like answered."

Elaha started to respond, but Wishengrad leaned forward in his chair. "I know what you're about to say. The same thing our own military people have been saying. Finding out *how* it happened is academic in the face of the potential destruction it can deliver. I am also aware that Israel is, and always has been, a staunch ally of the United States."

Elaha nodded.

"What bothers me, Mr. Elaha, is not boosting funding to Israel so that it can defend itself. What sticks in my craw is that you, and your country's lobbyists, have been pushing hard to convince *us* to increase *our* military budget. Sure, they go hand in hand, but the percentage of our defense budget that reaches Israel is small. How we allocate the rest of it to defend *us* seems to me to be out of your purview. At least it should be."

"Why would that bother you, Senator?" Elaha asked. "Israel is in a precarious situation, and has been since its creation. The optimism that abounded following your military defeat of Saddam Hussein was misguided. The valiant efforts of then–secretary of state Baker, and others in that administration, to capitalize on your victory were in vain. To be blunt, the situation has, in some respects, deteriorated rather than improved for Israel. Our proximity to an

Arab nation committed to our annihilation, and one that has demonstrated the nuclear capability to achieve that goal, has turned the usual tense situation into a desperate one."

"Granted," Wishengrad said. "As I've acknowledged to you, my views on increased military funding to Israel have changed. But pushing to increase the defense budget of the United States is another matter."

"Not if you are forced to deploy men and equipment to the Middle East again."

"Which I will do everything in my power to avoid," Wishengrad said. "You've said it yourself. Desert Storm didn't accomplish a hell of a lot except to boost our deficit billions of dollars higher. It didn't buy any security for Israel. It didn't get rid of Saddam Hussein, who slaughtered hundreds of thousands of people, created chaos for Kurds and Shiites in Iraq, and polluted this planet beyond our wildest imagination. About the only good I can see that came out of it was that our president at the time got to flex his muscles as commander in chief. That diverted attention from the problems we were having at home. It also gave the military an excuse to try out its expensive toys, and then come running up here to the Hill for billions more. Frankly, that money is better spent solving problems here at home."

Elaha chewed his cheek before saying, "I don't wish to be brazen, Senator Wishengrad, but I respectfully submit that your view reflects a minority position, even with the more liberal administration currently in the White House."

"I'm aware of that," Wishengrad said. "The military-industrial complex is riding high because of the detonation of that bomb. Strike while the iron is hot. More crime on the streets? Push for a bigger police department. More aircraft accidents? Push for a bigger FAA. Nothing strange about it. The way things work."

"I wish I could share your view," said Elaha, "but I believe in reality. The only hope for peace and security for smaller nations, including Israel, is a strong and committed American military capability. Even if I wish to accept your thesis that we should not be meddling in what is inherently the American budgetary and military process, there is every reason for Israel, and other smaller nations, to champion the cause of an increased United States military budget. Many of the weapons systems that you would see abandoned could be vitally important additions to Israel's military arsenal. Not only would they enhance our ability to defend ourselves, the sale of them would help alleviate your shocking trade deficit. Frankly, it strikes me as a good deal. Much of the increased defense money given us by your country would, in turn, be used to purchase weapons systems from you. You call it 'a wash,' I believe."

One of Wishengrad's colleagues said, "I won't debate your business logic, Mr. Ambassador, but I will be quick to point out that if some of these weapons systems are given the go-ahead, they'll be available for sale to damn near anyone who puts up the cash. You might view that situation as a balance of power—a deterrent—but I don't. If kicking Saddam Hussein out of Kuwait is to have any true meaning for peace in the future, it has to be accompanied by a clampdown on arms sales across the board. That hasn't happened. All the major players in the world's arms business come up with the sleazy excuse that we might as well sell weapons, because if we don't, somebody else will. I don't buy that thinking."

Wishengrad, who'd brought his half-glasses down to his nose, pulled a piece of paper from a folder. "This is a list of weapons systems the Pentagon has been pushing us to fund," he said. "I'll give you one as an example, Mr. Ambassador: Project Safekeep." He glanced up over his glasses. "Israel has expressed quite an interest in it."

"For good reason," Elaha said.

"It won't work," said Wishengrad.

"That conflicts with reports we've received."

"You've received reports from the same sources the Pentagon has, namely those who stand to make big bucks from it. Are you aware that this committee has been investigating that particular project for over a year now, and is about to hold hearings?"

"Rumors. I've heard rumors."

"Why would Israel be interested in buying something that won't work?"

"Whether it will work or not is a matter of opinion, of course. The evaluation of such systems is, unfortunately, tainted by political needs rather than scientific and military considerations. When Mr. Reagan was president, Republicans supported Star Wars. They claimed it would work. Democrats scoffed at the concept. Politics. Hardly the basis upon which to judge sophisticated devices that might one day save a nation."

They debated the issue for another half hour. When the meeting had ground down to an obvious inconclusion, and those at the table had stood and shook hands, Wishengrad said to Elaha, "I promise you one thing. I may have picked up the label of being antidefense, but I don't deserve it. I like to think I call my shots where defense spending is concerned, based upon what I perceive to be real need. No doubt about it, Mr. Ambassador. The sad fact that one of your neighbors is sitting with the nuclear capability to wipe Israel off the earth is not lost on me. I appreciate you coming in, and your candor about your position. Rest assured I'll use my best judgment when it comes to tossing a couple of billion more to our Pentagon friends."

At two, Starpath lobbyist Sam Caldwell left the office of his attorney, Thomas Betterton. He hadn't expected to be there so long. But once seated with the distinguished Washington attorney, whose clients included a veritable Who's Who of prominent Washingtonians called before congressional committees, it was evident that it could not be a short meeting. Or cheap.

Caldwell left Betterton's office aware of two things; his fatigue, and the sober realization that what he was faced with was a lot more serious than he'd anticipated.

His driver took him to the Four Seasons Hotel on M Street, on the fringe of Georgetown. Caldwell went inside and called Joe Maize at the Pentagon.

Maize asked in a hoarse whisper, "How did it go?"

"Piss-poor," Caldwell said. "We'd better talk."

There was palpable fear in Maize's voice. "Did you discuss me?" he asked.

"Damn right we did. I'm at the Four Seasons. I'll settle into the lobby and have a drink. Be here before I finish it."

He'd started his second drink when Maize, looking nervously left and right, handkerchief dabbing at perspiration on his large, round red face, crossed the lobby. Maize wore a tan suit; sweat darkened its armpits. He sat on the love seat next to Caldwell. "Sorry I'm late, Sam. I couldn't just walk out. Had to make an excuse. Traffic was lousy."

Caldwell looked at him with disdain. "What are you afraid will happen to you, Joe, by walking out in the middle of the afternoon? Losing your job?"

"No—I just didn't want people to wonder why I was leaving. I told them I had a personal errand."

"You might call it that," Caldwell said. His eyes were heavy; stubble on his cheeks and chin contributed to his weary look. A pretty young waitress in a long flowered dress asked Maize for his order. "Just club soda. Put a little lime in it," he said.

"Put a lot of scotch in it," Caldwell told the waitress. She glanced at Maize, who nodded. "Scotch and soda. That would be fine."

Caldwell had picked a corner that was partially obscured from the rest of the lobby by potted plants. Both drinks were now on the table. Caldwell shifted his large frame on the love seat and glowered at Maize. "Wishengrad's got more than I thought he had. I figured he was on a fishing expedition, putting on a show for the folks back in Wisconsin. But he's got more gear than just a fishing expedition. He's got himself the kind of case prosecutors kill their mothers for."

"Jesus," Maize said, hunching over and holding his drink in both hands. He asked without looking up, "Betterton told you that?"

"That's right. He had a meeting yesterday with the committee's special prosecutor, that knee-jerk former prosecutor from Wisconsin, Wishengrad's old buddy Harry Love. Love laid it on the table for Betterton—documents, phone tapes, and transcripts, along with everything that son of a bitch Joycelen fed them before he went out."

Maize glanced up. "Did he have those things about me? Tapes and documents?"

"Sure as hell did, Joe."

Maize drained his drink. "Did Betterton tell you when the hearings would start?"

"No. He doesn't know. Love claims it's still up in the air, if you can believe him. I know one thing."

"What's that?"

"That I've got me and my client the best attorney in town. I suggest you try to find the second best."

CHAPTER

TWENTY-SIX

"Some timing, huh?" Tony Buffolino said to Margit as he came up behind her outside Smith's home.

He'd startled her. She turned quickly and saw who he was; relief replaced apprehension. "Right on time," she said.

They sat with Smith in his den. "Where's Annabel?" Margit asked.

"At the gallery." Mac Smith, who was behind his desk, took a sip of coffee, smacked his lips, and looked directly at her. "Still want to pursue this?" he asked.

She didn't hesitate. "Yes."

"Okay. But before we get to that, let's deal with the fact that someone is sufficiently interested in Margit Falk to follow her, or have her followed."

Margit shook her head. "I still have trouble accepting that, Mac. Who? Why?"

"Tony can help with the 'who.'" Smith looked to Buffolino.

"Got to be a government agency, Major."

"Why do you say that?"

"I checked the plate Mac gave me. The car's not registered to anybody. That means government. FBI. CIA. DEA. Military intelligence. The old soldiers' home." He laughed at his own line. "Government agencies got hundreds, maybe thousands a' cars like that. Legal plates, but registered to nobody."

Margit exhaled long and loud.

"Can you inquire into what agency might be behind it?" Smith asked.

"I wouldn't know where to begin," Margit replied.

Neither did Mac Smith. "We can explore this a little later. Let's get to the business at hand. Margit wants to hire you, Tony. To dig into people involved in the Cobol case. It won't be easy. Much of it is inside the Pentagon, or so it seems. I suggested you bone up on it before we met tonight. I assume you have."

Buffolino had worn his best suit, shirt, and tie for the occasion. "I did my homework, Mac," he said. "I figure I don't know everything, but the major here can fill in the blanks."

"I'm sure she can," Smith said. "Margit, what is it you want Tony to do specifically, at least to get started?"

She replied, "Joycelen is the key to unraveling this." She looked at Buffolino. "What I'm trying to do, T—may I call you Tony?"

"Call me whatever," he said.

She smiled. "I'm convinced that Cobol did not murder Joycelen, nor do I think Cobol hanged himself. But the pseudosuicide is not my main concern at this moment. Cobol's family, particularly his mother, who lives in New York, wants very much to clear his name. I hope you can help me."

"I'll do what I can."

"Mac and I felt that the best way to start was to try and gain a better understanding of Joycelen's life, and the people surrounding him, especially those who might have had more of a motive to murder him than Cobol did. Cobol didn't have *any* motive, as far as I can determine."

Buffolino adjusted a white French cuff that extended beyond the sleeve of his midnight-blue suit jacket. "Unless he was a spook. You know, CIA, FBI, one of those organizations. Maybe Joycelen isn't the place to start."

"You have a better suggestion?" Smith asked.

"I just figured it might make more sense to start with Cobol, probe his background a little."

"I don't think so," Margit said. "I'm attempting to do some of that myself within the military, which you couldn't do. The way I see it, with you investigating outside and me working inside we stand a better chance of coming up with something."

"Whatever you say," Buffolino said. He looked at Smith. "You agree, Mac?"

"I suppose so, although it makes me a little nervous to hear you put it that way, Margit. I don't think you should be overtly 'working' at this. You're going far enough out on a limb as it is."

"Let's just say I intend to keep my eyes and ears open."

Smith's grunt was noncommittal, but Margit knew there was displeasure behind it. Maybe concern. She preferred that.

Buffolino said, "Tell me what you already know about Joycelen."

"Okay," Margit said. She ran down what she could from the newspaper clippings, and told Tony of her brief and unpleasant interview with Christa Wren. As far as she knew, she said, Cobol had no more than shaken Joycelen's hand at a CIA briefing.

"You think maybe this Christa Wren had a reason to kill Joycelen?" Buffolino asked.

"Possibly," Margit said. "According to her girlfriend, Joycelen was abusive to her. Wren was at the picnic, and admitted she'd been inside with him."

Buffolino added to notes he'd been taking. "What about his ex-wives?" he asked.

"I never got to speak with them," Margit said. "I intended to, of course, but Cobol's sudden death changed that. Along with a lot of things."

"They can stay on the back burner," Buffolino said. "For now. Anything else?"

"I don't know how far you can get with this," Margit said, "but Cobol saw a psychiatrist in New York. His mother said he came home from visits with the psychiatrist acting a little strange."

"When me and Alicia was seeing a shrink, we came home acting strange, too," Buffolino said. "They make people strange."

"Yes," Margit said, glancing at Smith. "The good ones make some people less strange, too. Maybe you could find out something about him. His name is Marcus Half."

"Funny name," Buffolino said, writing it down. "If you want, I can arrange to bust in, maybe grab Cobol's file. I know this Peterman in New York who . . ."

"Peterman?" Margit asked."

"Yeah. Lock-picker. Safecracker. The best."

"I don't think that would be prudent, Tony," said Smith. "One Pentagon Papers caper is enough. Maybe you could just do a little legitimate investigating into Dr. Half's background."

"Whatever you say." Buffolino stood. "I'll get started soon."

"When?" Mac said.

"Tonight," Tony answered, standing.

Margit flinched. Until that moment it had all been conceptual, a cause to be contemplated. Now, it was rudely real. All she had to do was to change her mind, write off Joycelen and Cobol and everything that had happened to her because of them. All she had to do was to make a simple decision—that she would get back to being a lawyer and helicopter pilot in the United States Air Force, back to the way she'd been before that fateful day at the Pentagon picnic. The Cobol-Joycelen episode had been of such short duration. If she tried, she could excise it from her life.

Never sell out.

She said to Buffolino, "Fine. We haven't discussed your fee."

"Usually, I get three hundred a day. But because Mac's involved—and it's for you—we'll make it a deuce. Okay?"

Smith smiled. "Generous, Tony. I'll remember it the next time you ask for four."

Buffolino flashed Margit a craggy, warm smile and put his hand on her shoulder. "Hey, I know this is important to you. Frankly, if I was you, I'd write it off, but maybe you see this like some kind a' battle. You know, like a warrior. I respect that. I'll do my best. We'll keep in touch. Through you, Mac?"

"Right," Smith said. "You shouldn't have any contact with Margit except in this house." To Margit: "Agreed?"

"Makes perfect sense," she said.

"I won't call you at the Pentagon," Smith told her. "You call me. Your quarter. Spend lots of them."

"See ya," Tony said.

"What's your rush?" Smith asked.

"I'm in no rush. Why?"

"I have an assignment for you aside from investigating on Margit's behalf."

"Shoot."

"I want you to make sure nothing happens to her."

"Mac, please, I don't think . . ."

"Listen to me, Margit," Smith said. "I can't, Tony can't—no one can watch out for your well-being when you're at work or at home. But when you come to *my* home, I want to make sure you get to *your* home, in this case Bolling Air Force Base. An old-fashioned rule of etiquette."

Margit couldn't suppress the smile. "A form of knighthood," she said.

"And I'm your knight," Buffolino said, matching her smile.

"Something like that," said Smith. A vision of Tony in knight's armor flashed into Smith's mind, and was gone as quickly. "Mind if Margit and I have a few minutes alone?" Smith asked the investigator.

"Nah. Of course not. I'll hang outside."

"Thanks, Tony. Only for a few minutes."

When Buffolino was gone, Margit said to Smith, "That drink you offered earlier. Still available?"

He poured two brandies, and they sat quietly in the study. "I want you to know, Margit, that I respect you for what you're doing."

Her chuckle was gentle. "Respect me—but question my intelligence, Prof?"

"Wrong. I don't want to see you hurt. I don't want to see this splendid military career you've forged sputter because of this."

"Colonel Bellis, my boss, told me he felt fatherly toward me."

"I'm not saying the same thing," Smith said. "It would mark me as a lot older than I like to admit." He paused. "But I do care about you. So does Annabel. Chances are, Tony can do his number, and none of your superiors will ever know he has. In the meantime I've been doing some digging on my own. There are certain legal avenues that might be explored to force a reopening of the Joycelen murder. Of course, these are civilian roads to travel. Whether they'll hold up in the military system of jurisprudence is another matter. But I think they're worth pursuing."

"I don't expect that, Mac. Having your moral support and friendship is enough. I just hope you know how much I appreciate this. You could have told me to get lost with perfect justification."

Smith chuckled. "I seriously considered that, Margit. Annabel changed my mind."

"Annabel did? I thought she was against your getting involved in anything nonacademic."

"Oh, she is. But for some reason, you, and this cause of yours, struck a chord with her. I told her I was going to stay out of it. She told me that if I didn't help you, I could sleep with Rufus. No contest. Speaking of the beast, let me throw a line on him, and we'll walk with you and Tony to your car. You can ride him if you'd like."

"Not Tony, I hope."

"I'll have Tony follow you back to Bolling. Once you're inside its gate, keep your eyes and ears open. Assume nothing, Margit. A uniform doesn't automatically translate into kinder and gentler."

"I hate to accept that, but I do. Now. Thanks." She kissed his cheek, and they went to the front steps, where Tony sat smoking a cigarette. Rufus gave him a sloppy lick on his face, which sent Tony scrambling to his feet. "He kisses like my first wife."

Smith told him what he expected him to do.

"Park far?" Buffolino asked.

"A couple of blocks, near Kennedy Center."

As they approached the street where she'd parked, Smith reined in Rufus and stopped. "Don't be obvious, but there's a car over there with a man in it. Parked a few spaces behind you."

Margit glanced sideways in the direction Smith had indicated. "Waiting for me," she said quietly.

"That's my bet."

"I'm—I have to admit I'm shaken by this."

"Understandable. Try to ignore the car. Drive straight home. Don't indicate you're aware of him. Tony, get your car and come around to here. When he falls in behind Margit, you get behind him. Okay?"

"Right."

Buffolino headed for his car, which was around the corner. Smith said to Margit, "Not too late to cancel. I can tell Tony to forget the whole thing."

"The government is following me," she said in a low voice.

"Looks that way."

"My own people."

"Maybe not exactly. But whoever is doing it draws a paycheck from the same taxpayer pool."

She reached in her purse and handed Smith a piece of paper.

"What's this?" he asked.

"A note I received from Cobol after he died. Please keep it for me. It might help explain why I have to do this, and not let it fade away to become a footnote to my life."

Smith jammed the note into his pants pocket.

"I'll call you tomorrow, Mac. Maybe we can have another meeting, and Tony can report what he's found."

"Fine."

"Mac."

"Yes?"

"Tony wouldn't just go ahead and hire this Peter person, would he?"

"No. He'll do as he's told."

"Good night, Mac."

Lieutenant Max Lanning examined his shoeshine as a means of averting Colonel Bellis's eyes. But he couldn't escape the voice. They were in Bellis's office. Lanning had just returned him to the Pentagon after a series of meetings across the river.

Bellis, who'd done all the talking—more like subdued shouting through clenched teeth—stopped for a breath. Lanning looked up and said, "Sir, I didn't think I was doing anything wrong. All I did was . . ."

"All you did was stick your nose into things that aren't any of your goddamn business. The fact that Falk asked you to do it doesn't mean squat."

"Yes, sir."

"Did she tell you why she wanted to know about the duty roster, and this HP nonsense?"

"No, sir. I mean, yes, sir, she did. She wanted to know about the duty roster to help her write the final report on Captain Cobol. She had a bet with a friend about HP."

"A bet?"

"That's what she said."

Bellis stood, which enhanced his threat fourfold. He seemed to the young lieutenant to be forty stories tall. "Anybody ever tell you, lieutenant, about the dangers of fraternization with higher-ranking officers?"

"Yes, sir."

"I understand you spend a lot of time with Major Falk."

"Not true, sir. We just talk sometimes."

"Stop talking."

"With . . .?"

"With Major Falk."

"Sir, wouldn't that look kind of strange?"

Bellis came around his desk and sat on its corner. He now hovered only two feet above Lanning's face. "*I* will speak with Major Falk about this. I will tell her that she is not to pursue any questions about the Cobol case. It's closed. Do you understand me?"

"Yes, sir. Sir?"

"What?"

"You won't tell her that I told you what she asked me to do—will you? I mean, sir, you called me in and asked me about it. I've been truthful. But I wouldn't want her to think that . . ."

"Get out of here, Lieutenant. Give Major Falk the same general respect you'd give any officer. But keep it at that. Understood?"

"Yes, sir."

Lanning went to the door. He could feel Bellis's eyes boring into his back. He slowly turned and said, "Sir, I'm sorry."

"So am I," Bellis said. "Make damn sure you don't have any more reasons to have to say you're sorry—or you'll learn the meaning of terminal sorrow."

TWENTY-SEVEN

 After seeing Margit drive safely through the main gate at Bolling and watching the other car pass through, too, without incident, Buffolino headed for home. Alicia had been complaining about the number of nights he was out working cases; he figured it was good domestic politics to spend this night with her.

But as he drove toward the modest home they'd recently purchased in Rockville, he suddenly turned off the highway and headed in the direction of the address he'd been given for the late Dr. Richard Joycelen.

Joycelen had lived in what turned out to be a nondescript apartment building on New Hampshire, a few blocks from Dupont Circle. Buffolino parked at a hydrant in front of the building and took a walk around the block. He returned to the front and approached the doorman, who sat in the foyer reading a newspaper. His name tag read WILLIE.

" 'Evening," Buffolino said pleasantly.

Willie looked up.

Buffolino pulled out his wallet and flashed his P.I. license. Willie reached for his glasses. By the time he had put them on, Buffolino had returned the wallet to his pocket. "I'm on a special investigation detail on the Joycelen murder," he said.

Willie stood. He was a lot bigger than he'd appeared sitting down. He had a high, raspy voice, and talked rapidly. "That's over and done with," he said.

"That's what we want the general public to think, Willie. But we're still investigating. Lots of loose ends."

"I thought that army guy who hung himself did it."

"Probably so," Buffolino said, shifting from one foot to the other. "The doctor was a real big shot." Buffolino looked left and right, then leaned closer to Willie. "Lots of top-secret stuff. I don't know why I get stuck with all the cleanup, but that's what my orders are. Take one last look around his apartment, see if anybody missed anything." Buffolino suddenly looked at Willie as though he'd had an unpleasant thought. "You haven't rented it yet, have you?"

Willie shook his head. "It's empty. Nobody's even looked at it. Too many empty apartments on the market."

"Yeah, I understand. I'll just go up, look around, then get out. My wife'll kill me if I get home late again tonight. Let me have the key."

"Police, you said?" Willie asked, narrowing his eyes and leaning closer to Buffolino's face as though to verify something in it. "Let me see that badge again," he said.

"It isn't a badge," Buffolino said. "Like I said, I'm private." He showed Willie the license. In the same movement his thumb and forefinger pulled out a fifty-dollar bill. Inflation. Oh, for the good old days of ten-dollar bribes to doormen.

"As long as you're official," Willie said. "Looks like you are." He took a key from a rack and handed it to Buffolino.

"I won't be long," Buffolino said.

Joycelen's apartment was on the top floor of the ten-story building, one of four penthouses. Buffolino let himself in and closed the door behind him, then flipped on the overhead light. The apartment was bare. Everything had been moved out. He opened sliding glass doors and stepped onto a balcony that overlooked the city. A gentle rain fell. There was fog on the horizon. Buffolino liked this kind of weather; Alicia was happy only when the sun was shining insanely. This kind of night better reflected Tony's inner self—not particularly impressed with the state of the world as it existed, nor with the reality that came with getting older: Yes, Virginia, there is a finish line.

He went back inside, slid the doors closed, and walked from room to room, trying to picture what it had looked like when there was furniture, pictures on the walls, rugs on the floors, and somebody living there. From what he'd read, Joycelen was a strange-o. But weren't all scientists? They'd said he was gay. But he'd been married a couple of times, and had a girlfriend, this woman Wren. What kind of guy was he? Kinky? Into porn videos? Ritualistic? Kind to furry little animals, or wishing he were back in school pulling legs off frogs? You never know about people, he thought. That was what made police work so interesting. You just never knew. The minute you thought you did, you were in big trouble.

He wished there were at least one chair left to sit in. He felt like hanging out a while. Sometimes Buffolino thought he had psychic abilities. He could sit in an empty room and close his eyes, and the room would come to life for him, including the people in it. But there wasn't a chair, and he thought of a pouting Alicia. "Pack it in," he told himself.

He opened the door. Staring at him from across the hall was half a face, the other half obscured by a partially closed door.

" 'Evening," Buffolino said, not taking his eyes off the other eyes.

"Who are you?" The voice belonged to an older female.

"A visitor," Buffolino said. "Who are you?"

"Did Willie let you up?"

"Yes, ma'am, he did. Police."

The woman opened the door a little further, and Tony now saw a mosaic of sags and bags. Hair that could use a good shampooing hung loosely down the sides of her face. She wore a pink-flowered housecoat and powder-blue terry-cloth slippers.

"Sorry about your neighbor, Dr. Joycelen," Buffolino said.

The woman said nothing.

"Must have been a shock what happened to him, huh?"

"Nothing about him shocked anybody," she replied.

Buffolino hesitated, then decided to encourage the conversation. He stepped toward her, which caused the door to close slightly. "Name's Buffolino. Anthony Buffolino." He extended his hand. Her eyes looked down at it, but she didn't reciprocate.

"He must have had a lot of visitors, huh?" Buffolino said. "I mean, being a famous scientist and all."

"Not so many," the woman said. "Who'd want to be with him?"

"How come you say that?"

"You don't know?"

"I know he's dead."

"He was a miserable, vile, rotten, evil person."

"I heard he wasn't a great guy," Buffolino said. "You can call me Tony. What's your name?"

A painful moment of indecision. "Marge."

"Well, Margie, a pleasure to meet you."

"You're the police?" she asked.

"Yeah."

"Let me see your identification."

Buffolino smiled, and showed her his P.I. license.

"A private investigator."

"Yes, ma'am."

"Like in books? I read a lot of books about crimes and murders."

"I never been in a book," Buffolino said. "But maybe we'll both be. Hey, Margie, let me ask you something. You say Dr. Joycelen didn't have many visitors. Anybody special come here all the time, like a man or a woman?"

"A few. There was a woman, a blonde. Good-looking but cheap-looking. She used to come a lot. And there was the man."

"The man?"

"Came as regular as clockwork, every Tuesday night at midnight."

"That's interesting," Buffolino said. "At midnight? Every Tuesday?"

"That's what I said."

"He stay the night?"

"I wouldn't know about that," she said. "I don't spy on my neighbors."

"That's a good trait."

"He didn't stay overnight."

"How long would he hang around?"

"An hour. A half hour."

"You get his name?" Buffolino asked.

"I told you I don't snoop on my neighbors."

Buffolino smiled warmly. "Just in these few minutes with you, Margie, I know you're not the kind of lady who would, and I admire that. I just figured he might have introduced himself to you like I did tonight."

"I don't usually stand out in the hallway at midnight," she said haughtily.

"What'd he look like?" Buffolino asked.

"Pretty young, but from what I read about Joycelen, I suppose he would like young men. Real young."

Buffolino asked her to give him a description of Joycelen's regular midnight visitor. She started to, but he interrupted. "Tell you what, Margie. I got a good friend who does composite sketches for the MPD. I could get him over here sort of on a free-lance basis. He moonlights. He's a fine artist. Paints pretty pictures, but pays his rent doing police sketches. You know artists. Always broke. Anyway, if you described this guy to him, he could put it on paper."

She hesitated, but Buffolino knew that the contemplation of providing a description to a police artist was too compelling to dismiss. "I suppose I could," she said.

"Great. If I can get him over here tomorrow morning, that be okay with you?"

"What time?"

"Whatever time you say."

"I sleep late. I don't sleep so good. I'm up most of the night, so I sleep late."

"Noon okay?"

"I could see him at noon. Will you be with him?"

"Of course. I wouldn't want a stranger knocking on your door, Margie."

When Buffolino got home, and after explaining to Alicia that he'd intended to be there earlier but had a last-minute job, he called his artist friend, Maurice Woodson.

"How much?" Woodson asked.

"She's a nice lady, Maury. Maybe she'll make us sandwiches."

"Sandwiches I can always get. How much?"

"A hundred."

"A hundred and a half."

"Whatever you say."

CHAPTER

TWENTY-EIGHT

 Charene Maize did what she did every weekday morning after getting up at six. In bathrobe and slippers she went to their large kitchen that overlooked a small Japanese garden, made coffee, squeezed oranges, and split two English muffins in preparation for toasting. She turned on a tiny television set, not because she was interested in the financial program that aired each morning at that hour but because the voices kept her company.

Such routine, she thought. She glanced at the clock: six-fifteen. Fifteen minutes before her husband, Joe, would get up at the buzz of a second alarm setting. She would hear him walk heavily from bed to bathroom, her signal to put the muffins in the toaster oven.

The routine seldom varied, even when he'd come home late and drunk as he had last night, too tired to brush away the heavy odor of alcohol from his mouth, stumbling as he tried to get out of his pants, cursing, and then attempting to slip into bed so as not to awaken her. Which, of course, he always did.

She heard the alarm's second buzz, automatically reached for the muffins, and listened for his footsteps. None. She put the muffins in the toaster oven, listened again, then went outside to retrieve the newspaper from the driveway.

Back inside, there was still no sign that he'd got up, and she was gripped with a spasm of fear. Her husband had been told by their family doctor two years ago that he perfectly fit the medical profile of a potential coronary victim. He had to lose a lot of weight, the doctor had said, and cut down on his drinking and smoking. Work less and learn to relax. Joe Maize hadn't done any of those things, and Charene had tired of nagging him.

She went up the stairs and looked into the bedroom. He was on his back in bed. His eyes were open, hands folded on his chest. A coffin pose.

"Joe, the muffins are on," she said.

"Later, maybe," he said, not moving.

She approached the bed and looked down at the face she'd awakened to all these years. He could infuriate her, and often did, but he'd been a good husband, and a good father to their grown children. She could be angry that he stayed out too many nights and drank too much, but she also knew it went with the territory. Hard drinking. Male bonding. Buyer-seller. Contacts. Vestiges of a lifestyle that had pretty much gone by the boards in this day of bottled water and skinless chicken. She loved him.

"Joe, are you feeling okay?"

He'd been staring at the ceiling. Now, he moved his eyes to take in her. "I thought I'd take the day off," he said.

She hadn't heard those words in years. "Why?" she asked, realizing the question in no way reflected what she was feeling. How wonderful. Maybe they could take a drive, or do some gardening. The garden certainly needed it.

He derricked his bulk up against the headboard and rubbed sleep from his eyes, then ran his fingers through tousled hair. "Just tired, that's all. The muffins are in? I'll be down in a minute."

She sat on the edge of the bed and placed her fingers on his folded hands. "Sleep as long as you want. No rush to get up if you're not going to work."

"I can't sleep," he said. "Don't let the muffins burn."

They sat in a sunny nook in the kitchen.

"Want part of the paper?" Charene asked.

"No. Doom and gloom. That's all they write about these days."

She judged his mood. He was quiet, somber, but not angry. "What did you do last night?" she asked. "Who did you go out with?"

He named colleagues from the Pentagon. "I stayed too long," he said. "Had one drink too many."

Three or four too many, Charene thought. It remained that, an unstated thought.

Were there other women? Probably not anymore. There had been some early in their marriage, flings when out with the boys, nothing more serious than that. They'd had bitter words about it early-on, but then profound pragmatism set in. So what? she'd decided. She would be perceived with scorn for carrying that attitude into the era of feminism, but, again, so what? Charene Maize had never carried a brief for the feminist movement. She did carry a brief for survival.

"What do you want to do today?" she asked.

"Hang around. I thought I'd see if I can get the model working again."

He'd become interested years ago in flying radiocontrolled model planes. He'd got good at it, and had spent many weekends at local aerodromes putting his pride and joy, a red-and-white model Cessna 172, through its graceful airborne paces. Sometimes when Charene went with him, he'd allow her to take the controls. She knew she would never be as skilled as he, especially at landing it in one piece, but she loved being with him at those times. He was always so relaxed. And enthusiastic. A boy again.

Which was why she was disappointed a few years ago when he'd lost interest, and relegated the model to a workshop that took up half of the garage.

"That's a great idea," she said. "Would you like to go out for an early dinner? Nothing fancy."

"Sure. Okay."

He dressed in old clothes he'd worn when painting the house; large dabs of color testified to his amateur standing. "More on you than on the wall," Charene had kidded. He hadn't lifted a paintbrush since.

He went to the garage-workshop, and Charene cleaned up the kitchen, then showered and dressed. She had nothing special on the agenda, although she had tentatively accepted an invitation for lunch at the home of one of her friends. Just a gabfest, woman chatter—"Can you imagine what my husband did yesterday?"

Much giggling. She would cancel that plan if Joe showed any last-minute interest in their having lunch together.

At eleven she decided to pay him a visit. She made more juice, his favorite beverage after scotch and bourbon, and loaded a plate with cookies she'd bought the previous evening at a church fund-raiser. She stopped to admire plantings in the garden, then looked toward the garage; the door to the workshop was closed. It was a beautiful Friday in Washington; why hadn't he left the door open to allow the pristine air to circulate? As she approached, a tray with the juice and cookies balanced in one hand, she noticed that the door was open a few inches. Had she been wearing shoes, the click of her heels on the flagstone walk would have been heard inside. But she still wore her slippers; her steps were cushioned silence.

She paused at the door. Ordinarily, she would have pushed it open and walked in, but she suffered the same feelings she'd had earlier when he hadn't got up. Instead, she placed her fingertips against the door and slowly pushed. Her husband was seated on a stool at the workbench, his back to her. Next to the red-and-white model plane was a shotgun, its barrel propped up on books so that it was pointed at his face. He held the weapon down tight on the books with one hand, and was extending a piece of wood toward the trigger.

"Joe!" Charene screamed. The juice and cookies fell to the stone walk. Her sudden presence startled him. The shotgun fell off the books, and he almost fell off the stool.

"Joe. What are you doing?" A rhetorical question. He was about to kill himself.

She wrapped her arms around his large frame, nestled her lips to his neck. Tears ran freely down her cheeks. "Honey, honey, what's the matter? What could be so bad that you would want to . . . ?"

She felt his body heave, and she pressed tighter, as though to draw him inside the protective shell that was her. "Joe, Joe, Joe," she repeated. "Tell me. Please, oh God, tell me."

He said through labored breathing, "It's over, Charene. It's all over."

"*What's* all over?"

He went to the far corner of the workshop and placed his beefy hands against the wall. She maintained the distance between them. Eventually, he turned and looked at her with the eyes of a small boy asking forgiveness of a parent. "They know," he said.

"Know what?"

"They know that I've been—that I've been taking payoffs from Sam Caldwell to doctor the audit reports on Safekeep."

She asked, "What are you talking about?" Because she didn't know what he was talking about.

"Charene," he said, extending his hands, "I took money from Caldwell. I took the money because—because, I wanted us to have more." He stepped outside into the garden, which he embraced with extended arms. She followed. "I wanted good things for you and the kids," he said. "It's so expensive. Putting them through college. Cars. Vacations. This house. I wanted better things." He turned. "I'm a liar. Not just for you and the kids. I've been a fraud my whole life. I wanted better things for *me.* I'm a goddam civil servant. There's so much money being made in defense. So much money, Charene, going into people's pockets instead of building better weapons. Payoffs passing hands every minute of every day of every goddam year, and I finally wanted some of it. That's all. Just some. Not much. A tiny portion for you, for me. And—they know. It's over."

Charene put her arm over his shoulder and shepherded him into the house. The big man who had been her husband for so many years was now reduced in size, as though a leak had developed. He slumped at the kitchen table.

"I'll be right back," Charene said, going quickly to the bar in the den, where she poured a glass of bourbon. She handed it to him. He looked up, managed a small smile. "I don't need this," he said.

"Take a sip. It will calm you." He did as he was told.

They said nothing to each other, birds feeding outside the window the only sound. Finally, she said, "You didn't have to do it for us, Joe. But most important, you don't have to end your life because of it."

"I don't know what else to do. I don't want to disgrace you and the family. Joycelen had been feeding the Wishengrad committee everything about the project for a long time. They know—everything."

"So what?"

He couldn't help but laugh, but it was mirthless. "So what? Do you realize what this means? I'll go to jail."

"We'll fight it. People in this rotten city break the law every day and don't go to jail. Presidents. Cabinet members. Advisers to the high-and-mighty. We'll fight it with everything we have, Joe. We'll fight it, and we'll win. When we do, we'll sell this house and the Japanese garden and the cars, and we'll go someplace simple and plain, a place the Washington phonies don't even know exists. You'll fly model airplanes, and I'll plant a garden with vegetables. We'll eat them instead of having them cooked by a fancy foreign chef in a fancy foreign restaurant." She took his hands in hers. "Ending your life is not the answer, Joe, because if you end your life, you end mine. I need you."

That evening, they went to dinner at a neighborhood steak house. "Order the biggest steak on the menu," Charene said. "Tomorrow, we'll start a whole new life. We'll eat healthy, take long walks, and enjoy being alive. You hear me, Joe? Alive!"

Later that night as they sat up in bed, Maize said, "I'm afraid."

"Don't be," she said.

"Not about being charged with a crime. I think Joycelen was murdered because of this."

"Who?" she asked.

"Caldwell."

"Stay away from him. Go over to the other side. Who can you talk to about providing evidence in return for immunity, protection?"

"I have no idea. I should get a lawyer."

"Then get one. Get a good lawyer and have him approach whoever is in charge of this investigation. Tell them everything. Do whatever you have to."

Smith had called Margit and suggested she come to his house that evening at seven, which didn't pose a problem for her. She'd spoken with Jeff Foxboro the previous night and had said she needed Friday to herself. Would they attend the dinner-dance at Andrews Saturday night? They'd agreed they would, although she now questioned that decision. Had she had more time to think it out, she probably would have canceled, but her total focus was on the previous meeting with Smith and Buffolino, the realization that she was being followed, and the urgency in Smith's voice when he asked her to come to his house this evening.

She was late. Buffolino and Smith were seated at the kitchen table. A large envelope was in front of Tony.

"Drink?" Smith asked.

"Glass of water, please, Mac." She looked at Buffolino. "You've already come up with something?"

He gave her his best toe-in-the-sand expression. "I got lucky," he said.

She sat next to him. "What do you mean, you got lucky?"

"First of all, I started the ball rolling with this Dr. Marcus Half in New York. I got a friend up there who—"

"Not that Peterman," Margit said.

"Nah. A guy who used to be a shrink. He got bagged for hitting on his female patients, which didn't go over big with the AMA. Anyway, he does work for malpractice lawyers and knows his way around the medical business. I'll run up there tomorrow and see what he comes up with."

"Fine," said Smith.

"It won't cost much. The plane, a lunch. I'll be back tomorrow night."

"Okay," Margit said. She tapped the envelope. "What's this?" she asked.

"Well, I don't know whether it'll help or not, but maybe it will. I figured I'd show it to you and let you decide."

"Fill me in," she said to Smith as he placed a glass of water in front of her. "What's going on here?"

Smith sat on the opposite side of the table. "Tony went to Joycelen's apartment last night after he left us. He talked to a neighbor, who told him that a young man had visited Joycelen with surprising regularity. Every Tuesday at midnight. Tony, being the inventive person that he is, went back there today with a composite-sketch artist from the police department. The neighbor gave what Tony says was a hair-by-hair, pore-by-pore description of this regular midnight visitor, and the artist drew the sketch. We thought you should see it."

Margit stood and paced the kitchen. Were she truthful, she would have admitted that she did not want to see it. The reality was—and it caused an ache in her belly—she was afraid it would be a picture of Robert Cobol. The possibility that Cobol had lied to her, and had, in fact, a homosexual relationship with Joycelen, had occurred to her. That would be a blow she wasn't sure she could weather, not after all she'd committed to in the interest of clearing his name. She said to Smith, "I'm not up to surprises, Mac."

"Maybe it won't be," he said.

She rejoined them at the table. "Go ahead," she said. "Open it up. Let's see this mysterious midnight caller to the eminent Dr. Joycelen."

Buffolino undid the envelope's clasp, slid his hand inside, slowly removed the paper, and placed it in front of Margit.

"It's Jeff," she said flatly.

"Looks that way," Smith said.

Buffolino said, "Mac told me this was somebody you know, somebody kind of special in your life. I'm sorry."

Margit looked at Smith. "You seemed to sense at dinner a month ago that Jeff had more of a connection to Joycelen than he was admitting."

"Right. But he denied it. This might not mean anything, Margit. You mentioned rumors that Joycelen was a whistle-blower to Wishengrad and his committee. If so, it wouldn't be unusual for Jeff to function as a go-between."

Margit folded her hands on the table and looked down at them. "I know that, Mac, but I wish he'd been more honest with me." She sat back. "Is that asking too much, to be honest with someone you wake up next to, someone who says he loves you?"

"In Washington? It often is," Smith said gruffly.

Margit glanced down at the envelope. Buffolino had scribbled many notes on it, including an address. She said, "That's Joycelen's address, isn't it?"

"Right," Buffolino said. "Look, I gotta get going. Alicia's been on the warpath. Women! You marry 'em, they right away put in a time clock, and you gotta punch in and out." He then realized he had an obligation to see Margit safely back to Bolling and said so.

"No need," Smith said. "I'd enjoy a ride. Get home and punch in, Tony. You don't want to be docked."

"Thanks, Tony," Margit said.

"My pleasure. I'll check in with Mac when I get back from New York."

As Smith walked Buffolino to the door, Margit pulled from her purse the piece of paper she'd taken from Foxboro's desk. "I knew the address was familiar," she said when Smith returned, handing the paper to him.

"Another note," he muttered. "That note from Cobol to you was upsetting. Believe what he said in it? That he was set up?"

"Yes."

He examined the paper from Foxboro's desk. "What do these numbers mean?" he asked.

"I don't know," Margit said.

"Where did you get this?"

"From Jeff's desk."

"Does he know you have it?"

"I assume not, unless he's looked for it and found it missing." Smith frowned.

"What's wrong?" Margit asked.

"Nothing. Unless . . ."

"Unless Jeff had something to do with Joycelen's murder." The words came out easily. It was no ad-lib; she'd written the line earlier. "I prefer not to have to evaluate that possibility at the moment," she added. "Is the Smith escort service available? I don't have a headache yet, but I guarantee one will be arriving any moment."

TWENTY-NINE

A fourteen-piece group culled from the Bolling base band provided music for Saturday night's "morale booster" at Andrews Officers' Club. If the success of the swing-era event could be measured by the size of the crowd, it was a resounding triumph. Whether the intended lift in morale was to be sustained beyond the weekend would be evident on Monday.

It was eleven. The dance floor had been full all evening, especially when slower ballads were played. Margit and Jeff were leaving the floor after moving softly and slowly to "Polka Dots and Moonbeams" when the bandleader kicked off a faster tempo, an arrangement of Glenn Miller's "In the Mood."

"Game?" Margit asked.

"Sure," Jeff said.

Margit's father had been a jitterbugger, and had taught his daughter all the moves. Foxboro was overtly uncomfortable, which only enhanced Margit's appreciation of his good-natured participation all evening. His movements were wooden, but he was there—her dancing straight man—content to sway a little and, if nothing else, give her a reference point. And a partner. Despite what passed for much contemporary dancing, it was always nice to have a partner on a dance floor.

Margit's smooth footwork was the center of attention until Major Anthony Mucci and his date, a pretty blonde who at first glance looked to be in her teens but who at second glance wasn't, took to the floor. The other dancers stopped and formed a loose circle around them. The major was a superb dancer; the girl was no robot, either. Everyone clapped to the rhythm. When the song ended, it turned to applause.

"That was fun," Margit said as she and Jeff headed for the last table they'd sat at during the evening. Threading the crowd, Margit saw that Bill Monroney was now seated at the same large table, and that Mucci and his date were about to be. Monroney, who seemed to be stag, had greeted her earlier in the evening, and she'd introduced Jeff to him. When they'd parted after a brief conversation, Foxboro asked about him.

"Just an old friend," Margit answered. "We were stationed together in Panama." She knew what had prompted the question. Monroney had an intense way of looking at women. Foxboro had picked up on it, but hadn't pressed for details.

"Feel like some air?" she asked, having decided to avoid the table.

"I feel like sitting after that workout—yours, I mean." He took her hand and led her to the table.

After they were seated, Margit said to Mucci, "You're quite a dancer."

"Thanks," he said. His date, whose name was Jill, smiled, pretended to be exhausted, and said, "He wears me out."

Monroney bought a round of drinks for the table. He said to Margit, "Beautiful dress."

"Thanks," she replied. "Left over from the prom." She wore a shell-pink, almost knee-length cotton piqué dress, scooped low in the front and with a front-to-back portrait collar. Her shoes had been dyed to match. Foxboro, whose wardrobe consisted primarily of sports jackets and slacks, had dragged a gray suit from the recesses of his closet, one with permanent wrinkles. He might walk the corridors of power, but a power dresser he was not.

The conversation at the table was spirited, and took many turns. At one point a Marine captain asked, "Everybody got their desert boots out and ready?"

"You really think Beardsley will order it?" Monroney asked.

"Why not?" the marine said. "Bush didn't hesitate—and it made him King for a Day."

"Yeah, but criticizing Desert Storm, and the mess it left, helped Beardsley get into the White House," Monroney offered.

"Beardsley doesn't have any choice," Mucci said. "He knows

we'd better get over there before the second bomb goes off, and this time it won't be a test, or a warning."

"How do you feel about it, Margit?" Monroney asked.

She shrugged. "He gives the order. We go," she said.

The rumor that the United States would once again deploy troops to the Middle East had been circulating for weeks. Yesterday, the United Nations Security Council had passed a resolution condemning the detonation of the nuclear device. The resolution went on to demand that any remaining nuclear weapons be identified to a UN commission, and that those weapons be placed under the commission's irrevocable control.

"You might lose your friend here," Mucci said to Foxboro, looking at Margit.

Foxboro replied, "They won't need lawyers in the Middle East."

"Maybe they won't need lawyers," Monroney said, "but they'll need chopper pilots."

"And grave-diggers," said Foxboro.

"Oh," the marine said. "Do I detect a nonbeliever in the crowd?"

"Jeff is on Senator Wishengrad's staff," Monroney said.

"The bane of our existence," said the marine.

"The voice of reason," Foxboro said.

"I love all you guys on the Hill," the marine said, thrusting his jaw in Foxboro's direction. "You ever put your ass on the line for this country?"

"This is silly," Margit said.

"No, it's not," Foxboro said. "Have I ever been in the service? I haven't. But you don't have to lie in mud to know when a pig farmer's making bad decisions about his stock."

"You guys make me sick," the marine said.

"Throw up someplace else," Foxboro said, his own jaw extending.

Margit was relieved when another officer at the table said, "Aren't you the major who was defending Dr. Joycelen's murderer?"

"One and the same."

"Cobol's a head case who won't be missed," the man said.

Margit looked past him to where her boss, Jim Bellis, and his wife were enjoying seconds from the dessert buffet. A few feet from them was a knot of unaccompanied single officers, including Max Lanning.

Margit had forgotten about Lanning. When she and Jeff had arrived, the first familiar face she'd spotted was Lanning's, and she'd warmly greeted him, adding, "Max, this is Jeff Foxboro."

Foxboro had extended his hand. Lanning took it, said, "Excuse me," and was gone. Margit had looked down at her dress to see whether she'd suddenly displayed a sign warning of contagious disease.

She brought her attention back to the table. Mucci was staring at her.

Foxboro stood, put his hand on Margit's shoulder, and said, "Be right back." He headed for the rest rooms.

Monroney said, "Nice young man you have there." Before she could respond, he added, "Shame he works for Hank Wishengrad. Like breaking bread with the enemy."

She faced him. "I don't view it that way. We're all part of one big country, with the same goals. Americans."

"Some more than others. You and I should have a talk."

"Why?"

"Because I think you could use some good advice. By the way, Celia and I are getting a divorce."

"I'm sorry to hear that."

"Inevitable. A long time in coming. No black or white hats, just a relationship gone sour. Not especially good for the career, but I'm not looking for stars on the shoulders anymore."

"Why do you think I need advice?"

"Because rumors around the Palace say you've been stepping on big, big toes."

"That's ridiculous," she said, turning away. When he said nothing, she faced him again. "What rumors?"

"That's what I want to talk to you about. I won't bug you, Margit. Call me when you have time, and an open mind. Don't wait too long." He smiled. "Have to run," he said, standing. "Good night, everybody." His fingertips rested on Margit's shoulder. He squeezed, and walked away as Foxboro returned to the table.

The band started another slow number. "Dance?" Foxboro asked. "I'm a master."

She shook her head. "I'm beat. Had enough?"

Foxboro looked at the marine, who'd glowered at him since their exchange. "I've had plenty. Ready any time you are."

"Cinderella's going home," Margit announced to the table. "Have to be back here tomorrow at two for a flying date. Good night."

She made a point of stopping on their way out to say good night to Bellis and his wife, to whom she'd introduced Foxboro earlier in the evening. The colonel smiled and shook Jeff's hand again. "Tell your boss on the Hill that we're all in the same game," he said pleasantly.

Foxboro said, "I think he knows that, Colonel. He just sees the game being won with a different playbook. Nice meeting you."

"Take good care of this special lady," Bellis said, smiling at Margit. "I know she's a good lawyer, hear she's a hell of a chopper pilot, and now I've seen she's a world-class dancer."

"Tonight, I'm a dancer," Margit said. "Tomorrow, I'm a chopper pilot. And Monday? The law beckons again. Nice life. Good night Mrs. Bellis, Colonel Bellis."

"Feel like a nightcap? Coffee?" Foxboro asked as they left the parking lot.

"Coffee would be nice," she said. She'd decided while at the table that she would not wait to bring up what she'd learned about Foxboro's regular Tuesday night visits to Joycelen's apartment. She'd also decided to return to him the note she'd taken from his desk. Enough shadows. Time to get everything out in the sunshine.

She'd assumed they'd stop at a late-night spot for coffee, but he headed for Crystal City, evidently intending to serve up coffee at his apartment. Fine. It didn't matter where, just as long as the setting was conducive to a heart-to-heart.

"Regular or cappuccino?" he asked after they'd arrived.

"Fancy," she said. "When did you get a cappuccino maker?"

"This morning. It took me a couple of hours to figure it out, but I think I have it down now."

"Cappuccino, by all means."

As he worked in the kitchen, she stepped out onto the small terrace. Clouds that had hovered above all day were now far out to sea. The sky was intensely black, the stars distinct. She stood at the railing, identifying constellations to escape the earth, when he came up behind. She wasn't aware he was there and continued looking up at the heavens until he put his hands on her shoulders and pressed against her.

"You startled me," she said.

"Jumpy, aren't you?"

He stepped back. She turned, rested against the railing. "I suppose I am. I have reason to be."

"Feel like talking about it?"

"I would like that very much."

"I'll be back in a minute," he said. "Hopefully with something that approximates cappuccino."

Sitting in one of two chairs, she opened her purse, and her fingers found the note she'd taken from his desk. Should she start with that, or first mention the sketch Buffolino had provided? That decision was taken from her when Foxboro placed two cups on the table and said, "Here. At least it's brown and liquid. Before you get into what's got you uptight, let me ask you a question. Did you take a piece of paper from my desk the last time you were here?"

He knew—she hadn't expected it. "Yes," she said, pulling the note from her bag. She handed it to him.

"Why?"

"I don't know. . . . You'd left, and I was unhappy. I started looking for a piece of paper to type my note on, and this came up with it. The address looked familiar, but I didn't know why. So, I took it. I shouldn't have. I'm sorry."

"It's okay."

"You knew Joycelen pretty well, didn't you?" she said.

"I didn't know the man at all," Foxboro said.

"Then why a note with his address on it?"

"No reason."

"Jeff, that doesn't make sense." He said nothing. She continued. "Joycelen was providing information to Wishengrad and the committee. Right?"

"Where did you hear that?"

"Doesn't matter. It's going to come out. A reporter . . ."

Foxboro leaned forward. "What reporter?" His expression was stern.

No more shadows. All sunshine from now on. "Her name is Louise Harrison. She's with *The Washington Post.* She's part of an investigative team looking into Cobol's so-called hanging and Joycelen's whistle-blowing."

"You've been talking to the press?"

"Only once, and I offered little."

"What else have you learned?"

"That you—that you had regular contact with Joycelen. Tuesday nights at midnight."

He cocked his head and nodded. "I'm impressed," he said. "Excuse me." He went inside. Should she follow? She didn't have time because he reappeared. "How did you find that out? This reporter?"

"No. She doesn't know anything about it. But I do, and it upsets me. Were you the contact with Joycelen for Senator Wishengrad? Did Joycelen hand over materials for the committee to you?"

"Right again." He drew a deep breath. "Your cappuccino is getting cold," he said.

She stood. "Jeff, whatever went on between you, Senator Wishengrad and Joycelen is of no concern to me. At least it wouldn't be if Joycelen hadn't been shot, and I hadn't been handed the lousy job of defending his accused murderer. Cobol didn't kill Joycelen. I know that as surely as I know my own name. But someone did."

"Are you suggesting that I might have?"

She shook her head. "Of course not. But if Joycelen's death had something to do with the fact that he was providing sensitive information to your boss and his committee, then it might have had something to do with his being killed, and with Cobol being accused. I want to clear Cobol's name. Not only have I made that pledge to his mother, I've made it to me. I don't make many promises to myself, but when I do, I keep them, even if it means trouble for me."

"Which it will."

"I don't doubt that," she said. "What do those numbers mean on the paper?"

"Since you're batting a thousand, you tell me what they mean."

"I have no idea. A code of some sort. They can't be dates. Dollar figures? Hundreds? Thousands?"

"Thousands," he said.

Margit's eyes opened wide.

"Joycelen was selling us the information. Every time I paid him off on a Tuesday night—a thousand, three thousand, whatever—I noted it on that piece of paper to keep track." He scrutinized her.

"Does that satisfy your curiosity about the Foxboro-Joycelen connection?"

"Is there more?"

"Sure. Joycelen fed us enough to make a strong case against Project Safekeep and its California contractor, Starpath. There've been enough payoffs on that project to cut the national debt by half. The people involved are going to have their asses handed to them, and with pleasure. But Joycelen died too soon. He had more to give—correction, to *sell* us—bigger fish, tangible information about that wonderful organization you work for that'll blow it out of the water, or at least bring it back to civilian control."

"Organization? The military? The Pentagon? Information about what?"

"About selling out this country." Now there was fire in his eyes. She saw it for the first time. A zealot's eyes. An evangelist preaching something distinctly not religious, but an equally powerful metaphor. Patriotism. By his definition.

"I'd better go," Margit said.

"I think you'd better stay," he said.

"Why?"

"Because there's more to talk about."

"Not if it's military-trashing time. I heard enough of that at the table tonight."

"Fair enough. Feel like watching a video?"

"No."

"Come." He took her hand, led her to the living room, and indicated she should sit on the couch in front of the TV. "Just a short piece," he said, inserting a cassette into the VCR. He sat next to her and hit Start on the remote control. A color grid appeared on the screen, then static, then—the desert erupted as the nuclear bomb that had been detonated in August lifted earth into the heavens, followed by the familiar-shaped cloud. The screen went black.

"Why did you show that to me?" she asked.

"To remind you."

"Of what? That a bomb was tested? Hard to forget."

"Not so hard for some people. Have you seen what's happened since the demonstration?"

"Lots of concern. The UN . . ."

"Military muscle," he said. "Billions more for arms in case the next bomb is aimed at somebody. Weapons systems that will bankrupt this country. The president's about to deploy troops there again. Nice. Like the policy was written by the beneficiaries."

"The military?"

"Right again, Major."

They looked at each other before Margit broke their silence. "Are you suggesting that the United States—at least its military arm—*planned* this?"

He laughed. "You could make a living as a fortune-teller."

"No."

She went to the sliding doors to the terrace and looked through them.

"*Yes,*" he said from the couch. "Your folks planned it. Sold the weapons to our friendly Arab dictator."

She spun around. "This is insane," she said.

"It happens to be true."

"That was what Joycelen told you?"

"That was what he started to tell us."

Margit returned to the couch. "Why did Joycelen decide to cooperate with you? With Wishengrad and the committee?"

"The numbers on the paper. He was a whore. Money."

"He sold cheap."

"For Project Safekeep information. His price was considerably higher where the bomb was concerned. Actually, he wasn't in much of a position to make demands of us. Once he'd sold out on Safekeep and Starpath, we had him."

"Had him?"

"Right. Had him. All we had to do was leak his actions to DARPA and the Pentagon, and he was dead meat. We pointed that out to him, and he saw our logic."

"I—I find this incredibly distasteful," Margit said.

"Why?"

"You work for a United States senator, not a district attorney. You sound as though you were out to put a mobster away."

"What's the difference? The people in the military who arranged for the bomb—bombs—to be delivered to the Mideast are no different from any mob organization. Arranging to deliver nuclear weapons to another country is against the law in this land of ours, Margit. The military mafia. Thugs. Traitors. Different uniforms."

"Some of them, maybe. Damn few. Can you prove it?" she asked, unable to control the rising emotion in her voice.

"Not yet. Will you help?"

"Me? Help betray the United States?"

"Wrong, Margit. Help *save* the United States."

The next question wasn't easy for her, but she said anyhow, "Or to advance the career of an ambitious young man named Jeff Foxboro?"

He ignored it. "Ever hear of an organization called Consulnet?" he asked.

She didn't reply.

"Arms dealers. A consortium. One of the shadowiest, biggest, and most powerful in the world."

"So?"

"So—they pulled in the plum of their shady existence. Provide nuclear weapons to one nut in the Mideast so that this country will panic and pump billions into the Pentagon."

"Proof?"

"Help us find it."

"By being a Joycelen?"

"Yup. You're inside. You're sitting at the right elbow of what makes the Pentagon tick. You've also proved with this Cobol thing that you have all the investigative zeal of a TV Columbo. Maybe a Miss Marple is more apt."

She sprang to her feet, grabbed her shawl from where she'd tossed it on a chair, and went to the door.

"Aren't you overreacting?" he asked.

"You should see this Miss Marple when she really overreacts. Good night."

"Sleep on it," he said. "We'll talk tomorrow."

"Wrong. I am spending tomorrow by myself. I fly at two. That's because I am a commissioned officer in the United States Air Force, and damned proud of it."

"Wait. I'll drive you home."

"I think I'd rather find my own way—home."

"Margit, please listen to me. We could work together. Joycelen is gone. You're not."

"Why don't you add 'not yet'?"

"At least let me drive you."

"No," she said. "I know where I'm going now. And I think I know how to get there."

CHAPTER
THIRTY

 Zero-five-hundred hours. The next morning. Sunday.

The helipad at the Langley, Virginia, headquarters of the Central Intelligence Agency had been dark. Now, as an army colonel in flight suit, a master sergeant in coveralls, and an army major in a tan, short-sleeved summer uniform approached a waiting helicopter, floodlights washed the area with harsh white light.

They climbed into the chopper, received permission to lift off, and headed in the direction of Andrews Air Force Base.

Their sudden and unannounced appearance in Andrews Ops took the duty officer by surprise. He'd been lounging in a chair behind the flight desk reading the paperback edition of Ronald Reagan's autobiography, although the reading resembled sleeping. He stumbled to attention as the major approached.

"Good morning, Lieutenant," the major said. He pulled a set of orders from a slim briefcase and placed them on the desk. The lieutenant read carefully. "Two choppers tonight?" he said.

"Right. Overnight."

"Yes, sir." The orders had been drawn by the Central Intelligence Agency's director of clandestine services, and had been signed by the director of the CIA himself, Thomas Hickey. That's clout, thought the Ops officer.

"Let me see today's flight schedule," the major said.

"Yes, sir." The lieutenant slid a clipboard across the desk. The major studied it. "Mind if we choose?" he asked.

The lieutenant laughed. "No, sir." Where does a gorilla sleep?

The major jotted down two aircraft numbers—617 and 439. "We'll take those," he said. "Don't want to interfere with your schedule today. Busy. Looks like both are due back by sixteen hundred hours. They're fully operational?"

"Yes, sir."

The major nodded at the sergeant who'd accompanied him from Langley. "This is Sergeant Chilton," he said. "Line chief for our fleet. He'll check these two choppers out now, and give them another look after they've been flown this afternoon." Chilton was a burly man with large, hairy hands, a shaved head, and a beer belly that he worked hard to suck in.

"Yes, sir—Major Reich," the Ops officer said, reading off the major's name tag.

Margit awoke at seven Sunday morning with a pulsating headache. The taxi she'd called last night from a pay phone in Jeff's lobby had taken its time to arrive. Eventually, after she'd got across to the Egyptian driver where she wished to go, they headed for Bolling. A boxy gray sedan had fallen in behind them.

"Pull over," she told the driver. He didn't. "Stop!" she shouted.

He understood that simple command and pulled over. The sedan slowed, then started to pass them. Margit, who'd kicked off her pink pumps in the cab, opened the door and jumped out. In stockinged feet she shook her fist at the sedan's driver, who turned his head away and continued up the street.

She was dropped off at the main gate to Bolling, and wearily walked the rest of the way to her BOQ. Sleep did not come easily. When it did, it had been interrupted by a succession of dreams, none of them pleasant.

She lingered in bed Sunday morning, but eventually tired of trying to find a comfortable position to alleviate the pain that shot up the back of her neck and spiraled around her skull. She made tea and pretended to clean her quarters, but her mind worked overtime. What Foxboro had claimed—that the United States had provided nuclear weapons to an Arab dictator in order to create a military budgetary feeding frenzy—was preposterous. Wasn't it? She hated the idea that such a question would even occur to her. Foxboro's accusations were spun of fantasies, self-serving needs to justify the importance of his existence. And Wishengrad's existence, too. America was obviously, and as usual, at war with itself—Congress versus the Pentagon, hawks versus doves, everyone puffed up with moral right. It was wrong. It wasn't the way it was supposed to be. It was not the America she'd pledged to defend.

The phone rang three times that morning, but she let her answering machine respond, and she monitored the calls.

The first:
"I have to see you, Margit. There are things you just don't understand because you don't want to. I know you're there, damn it. Pick up the phone."
Foxboro slammed his phone down.

The second was from Mac Smith:
"Good morning, Margit. This is Mac. I trust you're out doing something pleasant. I'm just calling to let you know that Tony came back and has some interesting, but maybe not terribly useful, information about our psychiatrist friend in New York. Give me a call, and I'll fill you in or arrange for you and me to get together with Tony at the house. Have a good day."

The third call was another familiar voice:
"So, I can't be trusted," Bill Monroney said. *"I didn't wait for you to call me because I think it's too important that we talk, and do it fast. Now that I'm a bachelor, please call me at my BOQ at Andrews."*
He left his number.

There was the natural temptation to answer the calls, but she resisted. The conversation with Jeff had been unsettling, at best. She hadn't realized just how upset she was until getting out of bed and reflecting upon it in the morning light. As reluctant as she was to admit it, Foxboro's principal interest in her seemed to be as a potential source of information for his boss, and for the committee his boss chaired. Could anyone be that callous, that *driven* to ignore the basic rules of decency in a relationship in order to advance a career? That was the only way she could read it. The personal aspects of their coupling obviously meant little to him, which was a bitter pill for her to swallow, not so much because it had happened, but because she had been so incapable of judging another person.

She spent time in Building P-15, where she sweated out anger and frustration. Showered, and dressed in her jumpsuit, she felt better. As tricky as flying a helicopter might be, the machine was more dependable than the human beings with whom she'd been recently interacting. Or, in Pentagon management, interfacing. You push a button in a chopper, and unless something is broken, a familiar reaction occurs. Not so clear-cut with people, she thought as she checked her flight bag one final time, got in her car, and headed for an hour with the copter to which she'd been assigned.

" 'Afternoon, Major," the Ops officer on duty said as Margit approached the desk.

"Hi. Did you order this day?"

He grinned and looked out the window. "Couldn't be nicer," he said. "Perfect VFR weather. You filling squares today? You've got Huey four-three-niner."

She shook her head. "No, just logging a pleasant hour. I thought I'd play tourist, maybe fly over to Turkey Island." She pointed on the chart to a group of six small islands in the Potomac, northwest of Andrews.

"Pretty out there," he said.

"Any chance of getting clearance into prohibited area Fifty-six Alpha?" The center of Washington—specifically the White House and close-by buildings and monuments—was designated as prohibited airspace. The charts called it P-56 A.

"Shouldn't be a problem, Major. I'll clear with my c.o."

The necessary forms completed, she went to where Huey 439 stood at the end of a row of choppers. It was a busy day at Andrews; every other copter in line was spoken for, and pilots were going through their preflight, or postflight, checks.

A line chief, one of two, whose name tag read CHILTON chatted with a pair of pilots as they drank coffee from Styrofoam cups. Margit was pleased to see a different chief from the young man who'd been so uncaring the last time she was there. She introduced herself to them.

Some of the other pilots had scheduled an hour of formation flying, something Margit had considered doing, too. She hadn't flown close formation since Panama. Too late for that now. You had to plan and schedule far in advance. Besides, it had been a late night. She was in the mood only for joyriding this day.

She asked Chilton, "Everything shipshape?"

"Yes, ma'am," he said. "They're all ready to go."

"Have fun," one of the other pilots said.

"You bet," Margit tossed at him.

She carefully conducted her preflight using the checklists. Everything looked to be in order, but as she was about to climb into the right seat, she hesitated, then returned to the roof of the chopper and eyeballed the blade-root laminations. Her father would be proud of her. Every chopper pilot checked the Jesus Nut, but too many ignored the possibility of hairline cracks in the blades themselves. "The J-Nut might be okay," her father had told her, "but it doesn't do a pilot any good if the blades split away."

These blades looked fine. "Thanks," she said under her breath to the man who'd been such a positive influence in her life and who she wished were alive to dispense his wisdom—and his love. Lord knows, she could use both.

She'd plugged her mike cord into the chopper's radio system, and put her helmet on the seat. She removed the helmet, replaced it with her body, adjusted the helmet on her head, pulled shoulder straps down and secured them, and followed the internal checklist.

Margit listened to the ATIS Charlie report, then tuned to the tower frequency at Andrews. "Air force four-three-niner ready to go," she said crisply into her microphone. "Request chopper route two." Route two was one of many prescribed helicopter routes across the city.

"Roger, four-three-niner," the controller in the tower replied. "Request to fly through prohibited area Fifty-six-Alpha has been granted. Helicopter route two approved. Contact Washington TCA at Marlow Heights. Squawk five-two-seven-five."

"Roger."

"Air force four-three-niner cleared for takeoff."

"Roger."

She followed a northwest compass heading, overflying the town of Morningside and paralleling the Suitland Parkway until changing heading to a northerly direction over Washington National Cemetery.

When she reached Fort Dupont Park, she slowed airspeed, then increased power so that she was in a virtual hover over the park. She slowly regained airspeed and followed her original compass heading. Directly ahead, across the Anacostia River, was the nation's capital, the splendid sun painting the imposing government buildings and monuments even whiter than they were. Below, in the park, families dotted the green countryside. A perfect day for a picnic—and for flying. A sudden recalled vision of being in Jeff's apartment last night hit her, and she realized she hadn't thought about it since walking into Ops. "Forget it," she told herself aloud, adjusting power to provide more forward momentum in the direction of the city.

She crossed the Anacostia and flew a route that took her between DC General Hospital on her left and RFK Memorial Stadium on her right. After passing those familiar landmarks, she turned due west and flew north of the Capitol Building, then slowed the aircraft to look down at the Mall. Evidently, half of Washington had decided it was a good day for a picnic, or for jogging and bicycle riding, for browsing the myriad museums of the Smithsonian, or for just lying on a blanket and soaking in the rays of a waning summer.

What a wonderous thing a helicopter was, she thought, able to hang in midair as though tethered to an infinite cord anchored somewhere high above. She was again in a hover at fifteen hundred feet above a multitude of people on the ground. She knew that some of them were probably looking up at her and wondering what this military helicopter was up to. Had to be official business, they would think. Surveillance in anticipation of the arrival of a dignitary? Part of a training exercise? She smiled. None of those. Just doing the same thing you are, she thought, enjoying myself on this beautiful Sunday.

She inched the Huey forward, which moved her in the direction of the imposing white obelisk that was the Washington Monument, D.C.'s Eiffel Tower, the tallest man-made creation on earth when its capstone was laid in 1884, now merely the District's tallest structure and the world's loftiest piece of solid masonry.

Immediately beyond was the oblong, glass-surfaced Reflecting Pool, which ended at the stately and inspiring Lincoln Memorial.

She made a decision to fly north of the Lincoln Memorial, then follow the river over Theodore Roosevelt Island and continue northwest until reaching the small group of islands that were her destination.

A voice crackled in her earphones. "Chopper four-three-niner, DC Control. Have you cleared P-Fifty-six Alpha yet?"

"Negative, but about to," she replied.

"Roger. Please advise."

"Will do."

She gave the Huey more forward speed and circumvented the Washington Momument. She adjusted her heading to bring herself back over the Reflecting Pool, and was pointed directly at the Lincoln Memorial.

The craft suddenly jerked to its left. Margit tried to adjust using the antitorque pedals, but her efforts had no influence over the chopper's erratic behavior. It continued to pull wildly to its left, as though trying to turn itself into an airborne corkscrew. Nothing she did corrected the out-of-control situation. The tail rotor ran wild, spinning at top speed on its own and sending the copter into a precarious attitude. It began to tip over on its side as the tail wagged the dog. "Damn!" Margit exploded, her hands and feet fighting the vibrating pedals, cyclic, and collective.

"Mayday, Mayday!" she barked into the mike.

She looked out her door. Below, surrounding the Reflecting Pool, were hundreds, perhaps thousands, of people. She didn't have much time—seconds—to do something to keep the chopper from hurtling down into their midst.

She smelled fire. Electrical. The hydraulic lines. A wisp of acrid smoke reached her nostrils.

The altimeter read one thousand feet. She changed pitch on the freewheeling main rotor above, guiding the Huey down in an autorotation. She descended fast, faster than she wanted to, but she knew she would land safely. More important, those on the ground would not be hurt, because her path of descent took her directly into the middle of the Reflecting Pool.

She killed the power. With the sudden cessation of it to the tail, the violent yawing lessened, and the craft began to right itself in her skilled hands.

Hopefully, no one was breaking the rules against swimming in the Reflecting Pool.

Huey 439 hit the water and threw up a wave. She was thumped hard but didn't have to worry about drowning; the pool was only a few feet deep. When the chopper had settled, she threw open the door on her side and sat there. Hundreds of people lined the pool and applauded. She felt no sense of accomplishment. Embarrassment was the feeling of the moment. And anger. What kind of maintenance mayhem had been the result of carelessness that had killed all control to the tail rotor?

"Air Force four-three-niner," the familiar voice of the TCA controller said.

Margit activated her mike with the floor switch. "Roger," she said.

"We have a report of a chopper down on the Mall. That you?"

"Yes, sir," she said.

"Are you okay?"

"I'm fine," she said.

"Condition of chopper?"

"Rusting."

"We've dispatched a rescue team. Suggest you remain with aircraft, unless there is danger in doing so."

"No danger. Not at the moment. But there will be once I get out of the rig and find out who screwed up with this bird. Out!"

CHAPTER
THIRTY-ONE

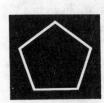 By the time rescue crews from National Airport, Bolling AFB, and Andrews AFB showed up, the crowd surrounding Margit's downed chopper rivaled July Fourth on the Mall. The press had arrived in droves; still photographers shot the scene from every conceivable angle, and television remote trucks, their antennae extended high into the air, transmitted the tragicomic scene to their studios for later, and repeated, airings.

A military jeep transported Margit back to Andrews, where she underwent a two-hour debriefing. She recounted in detail every aspect of the emergency she'd faced, and the steps she'd taken to save herself, the people on the ground, and the aircraft.

She came out of the small debriefing room behind the Ops desk and stopped to talk with other pilots, who were naturally curious about her experience. They asked what she thought had caused the mishap. She told them she didn't know, but offered that the runaway tail rotor had to have been the result of incredibly sloppy maintenance.

Or . . . tampering?

She couldn't help but wonder about that.

She'd successfully exorcized that troubling thought until, while saying good-bye to her fellow pilots, she heard the Ops officer ask someone whether Major Reich had been informed of the chopper's loss. The other officer replied, "No need. Reich canceled the mission a couple of hours ago."

She approached the desk. "Excuse me," she said. "I heard you mention a Major Reich. Did he cancel because of the accident?"

The officer who seemed to know answered, "No. A change in orders. At least that's what he said when he called."

Margit laughed. "I'm glad to hear that. Wayne would be furious with me for losing a chopper he intended to use."

"Happens all the time," said the Ops officer. "You know the Company. Always canceling something."

"Just as well," Margit said. "I got it down. Maybe they wouldn't have."

"Something out a' sight must have really fouled up in your chopper," the Ops officer said to Margit. "Our line chief signed off on it, and so did Reich's."

"Oh. I'll have to ask Wayne about that. Who was his line chief?"

The officers looked at each other. "What was his name? Wilton? Chilton? Something like that."

Margit remembered the chunky line chief who was there before she took off. His name tag had read CHILTON.

"Well, sorry to screw up the fleet," Margit said. "I'll be anxious to find out what the problem was."

Her mind was so clotted with what she'd learned about Reich and his "mechanic" that she had trouble concentrating on the road and drove to Bolling in a fugue state.

As she walked into her BOQ, the phone rang. She looked at the digital numbers on her answering machine that indicated the number of calls recorded. There were nine, including three from that morning. She waited until the obligatory four rings had sounded. The machine went into action, giving out her message. Then, through the speaker, came a male voice.

"I'm trying to reach Major Margit Falk. This is Sergeant Davis. It's important that I . . ."

She yanked the receiver out of its cradle. "This is Major Falk. You're the one who called my base locator and told me Captain Cobol wanted to see me."

"Yes, ma'am."

"But there is no Sergeant Davis at McNair Detention Center."

"Yes, ma'am, I know that. Davis is not my real name."

"Then what the hell is your real name?" she snapped.

"Ma'am, I'm not looking for any trouble. That's why I'm using a false name. I was a friend of Bob's. We were—we were close once."

"Look," Margit said, unable to put the reins on her cumulative frustration and anger. "Let's skip the euphemisms. You say you were close. Do you mean you had a homosexual relationship with him?"

"Yes."

"You delivered that note to my BOQ?"

"Right."

Margit sat in a chair and wished she had a cigarette to light. She hadn't smoked since high school, but she now understood the appeal. She said, "Okay, I've had enough of all the games. Why are you calling? What do you want to tell me?"

"That Bob—Captain Cobol—was set up to take the blame for the murder of Joycelen."

"How do you know that?"

"He told me."

"Who set him up?" she asked.

"The CIA. Elements within the CIA, as he put it."

"Could he prove it?"

"No. He said they'd given him last-minute duty at the Pentagon that Saturday morning to put him in place at the scene of the murder."

"Who put him there? Name!"

"He said Major Mucci made the change on the roster."

"Was he alleging that Mucci killed Joycelen?"

"I don't know."

"Well, Sergeant Davis, or whoever you are, I'm a little tired of hearing 'He said,' and, 'He told me' without attribution. You're assigned to the detention center?"

There was a pause.

"Did you hear me?" she asked.

"I was. I'm leaving the service."

"Why?"

"Reg Thirteen-Thirty-Two. They don't like us to dishonor the uniform." There was, at once, sadness and anger in his voice.

"Can we meet? After you're discharged? When will that be?"

"Tomorrow. They gave me a choice. Get out nice and quiet, or face a court-martial. Who needs that?"

"Tell me how I can reach you," she said.

"I'll call you again."

"Promise?"

"Yes, ma'am. Bob told me you were okay, a stand-up lady. He said he trusted you."

She felt a small lump form in her throat, and talked through it. "Were you there when he hanged himself?"

"Major Falk, he didn't hang himself. They hanged him."

"Are you sure?" she asked.

"Did I see it? No. They sent a medic in the day before, who shot him full of something. He slept nearly twenty-four hours. Then they found him with a sash around his neck. No way!"

"Thanks for calling," she said. "Call me again."

She listened to her other messages. They were all from reporters wanting to follow up on the accident. Her fifteen minutes of fame. She could do without it.

She adjusted the shower as hot as she could stand it and stood beneath the sharp needles of water in the feeble hope that it would cleanse her of everything that had happened in her life recently.

It didn't.

Wrapped in a robe, she sat at her desk, pulled out a yellow legal pad and pen from a drawer, and wrote:

> Foxboro—Tells me we sold nuclear weapons to an Arab dictator to boost military budget. Bagman for Wishen-grad with Joycelen. Wants me to spy for him in Penta-gon. No thanks.

> Reich—Orders chopper I am scheduled to fly. Has a Company mechanic work on it before I go up. Malfunc-tion. Reich was Cobol's supervisor at CIA. Let him off the hook when discovered he was gay. Goes undercover. Surfaces just when I'm about to fly. Come on!

> Monroney—Says he has to talk to me. Tells me it's im-portant. Tells me I'm stepping on big toes. Where did he hear that? What does he want to say to me? Best way to find out is to let him say it.

> Mucci—Changed duty roster to make sure Cobol was in Pentagon morning of Joycelen murder. Sour person.

Would do anything he was ordered to do. Good dancer. Creep!

All the above—Foxboro exception, but barely—tied up with military. What about civilians? Christa Wren? No. Doesn't have the resources to have me followed. Tony said car was government-issue. Still, best motive for murder is personal. Passion. Jealousy. Fed up with being abused? Can't blame her.

What about Joycelen?—Selling secrets to Wishengrad committee. Selling bigger secrets about nuclear weapons, if I can believe Jeff. I don't. Joycelen. A brilliant whore? Or a dedicated American? Fed up with waste and excess? Did we give bomb to Arab? Enough to turn Joycelen? If so, he had redeeming qualities.

She stared at what she'd written, then picked up the phone. Mac Smith answered on the first ring.

"I just heard," he said, excitement in his voice. "They had a piece on TV about a chopper coming down in the Reflecting Pool, and there you were. Are you all right?"

"Physically, I'm fine," she said. "It was hairy, but the only real damage was to the chopper, and to my ego. I got your message this morning. Sorry I didn't return the call. I was here, but didn't feel like picking up for anyone. Even you."

"The beauty of answering machines," he said. "I'm not offended. I've done it myself. More than once."

"I have to see you."

"Because of the accident?"

"Because I need to talk to somebody about what I've experienced the past few days. I can't think of anybody better able to sort things out for me."

"I'm easily flattered."

"Not flattery. Haven't you heard it gets you nowhere? Any chance of us going to dinner tonight? My treat."

"Annabel and I were just talking about going out. As usual, we have conflicting viewpoints about where to go. You can arbitrate."

"A place quiet, private, and without ears. Some sloppy restaurants suffer from bugs. In D.C., building permits automatically call for bugs in every light fixture."

"I used to think the same thing when I was trying cases in this town. The wrong people always seemed to know what was going on before the right people did. You've answered the question about where to have dinner. Right here at Chez Smith. No microphones in the light fixtures, although I can't vouch for Rufus. Big ears. Can you head over now?"

"On my way."

The delivery boy from the American Cafe, who carried what would be their dinner that night, arrived at Smith's house as Margit walked up the street. "Give it to me," she said, reaching in her purse and handing him money. "Keep the change."

Annabel answered the door, looked at the bags in Margit's arms with AMERICAN CAFE printed on them, and said, "Moonlighting?"

"The way things are going, I might consider it as full-time career."

They spread the food on the kitchen table. Smith said, "Feel like talking about the accident?"

"Sure." She replayed it for them, concluding with the overheard conversation about Major Wayne Reich, reminding them that he'd been Cobol's supervisor at the CIA and had given Cobol a break when his homosexuality had been discovered.

"What do you make of that?" Smith asked.

"Reich brought along his own mechanic, who, according to the guys at Ops, checked out the one I flew."

"Do you think this mechanic deliberately tampered with it?" Annabel asked. Her wide eyes reflected her fear for Margit.

"I'll know more about that after they tear down the chopper and see what caused the tail rotor to have a life of its own. Then again, maybe they won't give out the straight scoop, at least to me."

Smith asked, "Any other reasons to think the accident resulted from a deliberate act?"

"No. Maybe yes." She told them about her evening with Foxboro, and his claim that the Pentagon—at least a unit within it—had provided the bomb to the Mideast madman.

She shifted to Monroney. "He's a colonel at the Pentagon. We were stationed together in Panama and—we were close for a while.

Anyway, he told me at the dinner-dance last night that he had to talk to me because he'd heard I'd been stepping on big toes. That was the way he put it to me."

"And?" Smith said.

Margit continued. "A young lieutenant named Lanning who'd always been friendly—the one who found out for me who switched the duty roster to place Cobol at the Joycelen murder scene that morning, and who told me that the 'HP-5' designation on Cobol's personnel file was top secret—gave me the cold shoulder at the dance. All I can figure is that he was told to stay clear of me."

"Could be," Smith said. "You damn near died today. Anything more to support our worry that somebody deliberately caused it?"

"Maybe there is," she said. "I got a call before I came here. From a Sergeant Davis. That isn't his real name, but he's the one who called me the night Cobol supposedly hanged himself, and who delivered the note to me." She described the conversation.

Annabel, who'd left the room for a fresh supply of napkins, rejoined them. "Have you told Margit what Tony found out about Dr. Half in New York?"

"I'll take care of that now." He said to Margit, "Tony couldn't be here tonight, but I said we'd call him so that he could fill you in." He dialed Buffolino's number. The erstwhile D.C. cop came on the line. Smith handed the phone to Margit.

"I didn't come up with much," Buffolino said. "What I did find out is that this Marcus Half is a controversial guy." He laughed. "So what? You work for the CIA, you gotta be controversial."

"Wait a minute," Margit said. "Half is a CIA psychiatrist?"

"Not exactly. The way my friend tells me, the CIA's got all kinds a' civilian doctors cleared to treat agents. My friend says that if you're an agent who knows secrets, and you have to go under the knife for an appendix or somethin', the surgeon doin' the cutting has gotta be cleared. And there's another spook in the operating room to hear what you say while you're out."

Margit knew that Cobol had been sent by the CIA to Marcus Half in New York, at least according to Cobol's mother. Flo Cobol's assumption was that before her son could be given his sensitive assignment, his psychological stability had to be determined.

"Anything else?" she asked.

"Well, this Dr. Half has made a pretty good name for himself in hypnosis. Lemme see. I made notes. Oh, yeah. Half didn't invent the thing he uses—that was another shrink named Spiegel, my friend says—but Half is one of the gurus, at least where the CIA is concerned."

"What is this *thing* you're talking about?" Margit asked.

"Lemme see. Right. He uses a thing called the Hypnotic Induction Profile. The way I get it, you test people to see how hypnotizable they are. It's like a chart. If you come up a 'five,' you're a real patsy for a hypnotist. If you're like a one, or a two, there ain't nobody can make you take your clothes off."

"I see," said Margit.

HP-5, she thought. Could that be what the handwritten notation on Cobol's personnel file had meant? Cobol's hypnotic profile, as determined by visits to Dr. Half in New York? Was Cobol a "five" on the scale?

"This is more interesting than you imagine, Tony. Anything else?"

"Not really, Major, except that Half was in the news a couple a' years ago. Maybe you remember. I never noticed. A CIA agent who was cracking up came to New York to see him, and ended up jumping out his hotel window."

"I do remember it," Margit said.

"My source brought me some articles about Half. He was accused of being part of a group of doctors playin' around with trying to control people's minds with drugs and hypnosis and crap like that. I don't think anybody ever proved anything, but that's what the stories said."

Margit nodded at Mac and Annabel. She said to Buffolino, "Good work, Tony. I'm impressed."

"Glad to hear it." He laughed. "I wish my wife was. Oh, by the way. I checked out Joycelen's two ex-wives. They hated his guts, but both have solid alibis. Well, got to run. Say hello to the professor and that gorgeous woman who was dumb enough to marry him."

Margit cracked her first smile since arriving. "I might not pass that comment along," she said. "Thanks again. My best to your wife."

She told Smith and Annabel what Buffolino had said—excluding his final comment.

"What do you make of it?" Smith asked. "If your thesis is correct—that the 'HP-5' on Cobol's record indicates he was highly suggestible—do you think it played a role in his being accused of murdering Joycelen?"

"It could, couldn't it?" Margit said. "Cobol claimed to his friend, this Sergeant Davis who isn't Sergeant Davis, that he'd been set up. He said the same thing in the note to me. I don't know anything about hypnotism. Would it be possible to program him to take the rap?"

"I thought he proclaimed his innocence to you," Annabel said.

"He did. How perfect is hypno-programming? Maybe you can get someone to act against their basic nature and morals through hypnosis, but when it comes down to facing a firing squad, the effect might wear off. I don't know. I remember a psych professor talking about it. He said you don't tell someone under hypnosis to do something wrong. You change the visual, is the way he put it. You don't tell a loving husband to shoot his wife. But if the husband is highly hypnotizable, you can convince him that his wife is a raging killer bear when she comes through the door. Same thing with that old schooldays rumor that boys could hypnotize a girl to take off her clothes. She won't do it—unless she's told under hypnosis that she's alone in a room, and it's become unbearably hot in that room."

Margit slapped her hands against her thighs and let out a stream of exasperation. She said with energy, "That's the problem with this whole thing. All kinds of tantalizing bits of information, but never enough to know anything for certain."

"What's next?" Smith asked.

Margit stood defiantly, hands on her hips. "I want to lay this out on the table for the right people."

"Who are the right people?" Annabel asked.

"I can start with my boss, Colonel Bellis."

"Margit, do you think that's wise?" Smith asked. "Maybe we should wait until you and Tony come up with more tangible information."

"I don't want to wait. I *can't* wait. I've been told I was thrown to the wolves by being assigned to defend Cobol, a sacrificial lamb. I was almost killed today because—and I know I can't prove it—because somebody played with the helicopter I was flying, somebody who knew I was scheduled to fly. I have a boyfriend—strike that!

former boyfriend—who wants me to spy for him and his senator to help prove what he claims was a sellout of this country by my own people. Some of these people have been following me day and night. I'm snubbed by a lieutenant who, until last night, kept stumbling over himself to be close to me. I'm almost splashed all over D.C. concrete. And I get this veiled warning about 'stepping on toes.' No. I think somebody owes me an explanation, and I intend to ask for it. I'm not going to . . ."

She fought emotions that threatened to overwhelm her, her fists clenched at her sides. "They won't do to me what they did to my father."

CHAPTER
THIRTY-TWO

Helen Matthei, Bellis's administrative assistant, looked up as Margit entered the colonel's reception area at eight-thirty the following morning. "Good morning, Major Falk," she said in her usual cheery tone.

"Good morning, Helen. Is the colonel in?"

"No." She raised her eyebrows. "Called to a last-minute series of meetings. Which gives me a chance to catch up on those things I never seem to when he's around."

"When is he expected back?" Margit asked.

"Not until five." Helen saw the disappointment in Margit's face. "Anything I can do for you?" she asked.

Margit said, "I really need to see him. It's important. Could you pencil me in at the end of the day?"

"I don't know what his schedule is when he gets back, but I'll leave a great big note on his desk."

"Thanks, Helen. I appreciate it."

"Glad to see you in one piece this morning," Helen said. "That was some near miss."

"But only a near miss. Could have been worse. Thanks again. I'll be in my office all day."

Had she lingered a few minutes more, she would have been there when Bellis called. Helen told her boss that Major Falk urgently wanted to meet with him, and that she'd told her he would be back at five. "I damn well want to see her, too," he said. "Make it six."

After receiving Helen's call confirming the six o'clock meeting, Margit hunkered down and tried to get back into the Project Safekeep files. It was difficult, not only because her thoughts were elsewhere, but because she now knew of the investigation. Would it involve her? Not likely. She hadn't been on the project long enough to know anything, at least officially.

Each time the phone rang, she thought it might be Jeff. Her thoughts were ambivalent. On the one hand, she wanted him to call and apologize—and mean it. On the other hand, the more pragmatic, and certainly wiser, side of her said that it was over, and that she was better for it.

A number of calls that morning were from media following up on the accident story. AF CHOPPER CRASH-LANDS ON MALL. PILOT ALL WET. She referred them to the I.O. By eleven her earlier thoughts were under control, and she was able to concentrate on the material at hand.

Until the next call. From Bill Monroney.

"I left a message at your BOQ yesterday," he said.

"I know. Sorry, but I wasn't in the mood to return calls."

"I'm glad you're alive," he said. "You sure picked an interesting place to set down."

She couldn't help but smile. Once the trauma of the near-fatal accident had passed, she was able to appreciate the less serious aspects of the event. Humorous, in retrospect. Certainly not on anybody's Sunday schedule.

"I meant what I said Saturday night," he said. "I have to talk to you."

"About what? Those big toes I supposedly stepped on?"

"And more. I'm not your enemy—I wish you wouldn't treat me like one." An operator asked for additional coins. Why was he calling from a pay phone?

"Have lunch with me. We'll get away from here, take a drive in the country. If you don't want to do it because of personal feelings, do it for professional ones. I'm not kidding when I say that, Margit. We need to talk."

"All right," she said.

"Take the Metro to Pentagon City. I'll pick you up in front of the new Ritz."

She was tempted to ask why the clandestine meeting but didn't. It added urgency to the invitation.

They'd agreed to meet at twelve-fifteen; Pentagon City was only one stop away from the Pentagon. She left her office at noon, came up into the bustling mall that was Pentagon City, entered the elegant hotel through a rear entrance, crossed the lobby, and stepped outside through the front doors. Monroney, dressed in civilian clothing, was waiting in a blue Chrysler convertible. The top was down.

Margit slid into the passenger seat. Monroney smiled and said, "Ready for a ride?"

"Not too far," she said. "I have work to do."

"I thought we'd go to Occoquan. Thirty, forty minutes."

"Okay," she said. "I've been meaning to visit there. Supposed to be pretty."

"Pretty, quaint, touristy, and enough distance from here to make me comfortable."

He took Route 395, the infamous Shirley Highway known for its massive traffic jams during rush hours, and headed south toward Richmond. Midday traffic was light; ten minutes later they were out of Alexandria and turning onto 95. Another ten minutes and they'd crossed the Occoquan River into Prince William County, and were in the popular commuter town of Woodbridge, with its commercial strips of gas stations, fast-food outlets, auto dealerships, and mini-malls. He took local roads in a northerly direction, doubling back toward the river. Fifteen minutes later they came down a hill into Occoquan, developed as a mill town in the eighteenth century. An annual crafts show was in progress; the narrow main street that paralleled the river was clogged with cars and pedestrians. They got lucky. A car pulled away from a legal parking space, and Monroney moved into it. He put up the top, and they walked a block to a restaurant on the river called the Sea and Sea. Monroney had taken the day off; Margit envied his civvies.

Their luck continued to run. A window table overlooking the river had opened up.

"It's good to see you again," he said after diet soft drinks had been served.

"We saw each other just the other night," Margit said.

"But I wasn't alone with you. I hate crowd scenes."

"Did you have a good time without Celia?" Margit asked.

"No, but it had nothing to do with Celia. You? Did you have a good time with your beau?"

Margit smiled. What a nice, old-fashioned term. "Yes, I did."

Monroney said, "You're a great dancer. I didn't know that about you when we were in Panama."

"There wasn't much opportunity to dance there," she said. "Unless dodging bullets qualifies."

He said, "I love you."

She sat back and looked around the restaurant, not in search of anything but to avoid visual contact with him. Finally, she squared herself in her chair. "Is this the reason you wanted to have lunch today?" she asked. "If so, you've done it under dishonest circumstances. Your comment to me Saturday night about stepping on toes, and the tone you took today on the phone, said something different than what's happening here."

"I suppose it looks that way, but you're wrong. Actually, what I'm about to say will seem even less genuine. The fact that it happens to coincide with my feelings for you can't be helped. Ready?"

She looked at him.

"They've got you targeted, Margit. You're in their sights."

"Who are you talking about?"

"The brass."

She began to respond, but a waitress asked for their order. They opened menus and made quick choices—a seafood salad for her, club sandwich for him.

"You were saying," she said.

"I was saying that Margit Falk is walking in harm's way."

"Because I'm being followed?"

"Followed? Are you?"

"You know nothing about that?"

"No. Why should I?"

"Because you seem to know a lot about what's happening to me—or *could* happen to me."

"I know nothing about you being followed. I do know, though, that there are heavy hitters who aren't happy with Margit Falk."

"Including you?"

"I'm no heavy hitter, and you know it. Hey, I started off by telling you I wasn't your enemy. I'm not. I want to help you."

"Who sent you to deliver a message?"

His laughter was of exasperation. "Look, I don't fault you for being suspicious, but don't extend it to me. Nobody has sent me to tell you anything. If they'd tried, I would have told them to go to hell. I'm like anybody else at the Pentagon. Unless you're deaf and blind, you can't help but pick up on rumors that fly around the building. Besides being the seat of national defense, it's the most efficient gossip mill in history."

Monroney came back to his reason for asking her to lunch. "Nothing spooks the military mind more than seeing its own hang out with the wrong people." He paused for her reaction. She didn't have one, because she didn't know what he was talking about. "I don't know anything about your boyfriend, Foxboro," he said, "except that he's a key member of the Wishengrad staff. I said to you Saturday night that it was like breaking bread with the enemy. I wasn't kidding."

Could it be this simple? This mundane? That her superiors at the Pentagon were upset because she dated a staff member of a liberal senator who'd devoted most of his elected life to chipping away at the military budget? She expressed this.

Monroney sipped his black coffee, then said, "As I told you, what I had to say to you works in my favor. I would love to see you break it off with Foxboro because, frankly, I'd like to try to make something out of you and me. But that isn't my motive. Believe me when I say that."

"I'm trying."

"Keep trying. I don't know how much you know about Project Safekeep. You've certainly heard that Wishengrad is launching a full-scale investigation into it. That has a lot of meaning to me. T and E is in a tough position. We've had people in our department who've been verifying test results all along. The question has to be asked whether they were paid off."

"Like Joycelen," she said.

His expression said that he didn't know.

"The Wishengrad committee paid Joycelen for providing information about Safekeep."

"I didn't know that," said Monroney. "No altruism involved?"

"None whatsoever."

Monroney laughed. "Looks like the rumors are hotter and heavier in your end of the building than in mine. What other nuggets can you give me?"

"I think I've already given you too much. Your turn."

"Simple. Back off."

"Back off from what?"

"From this crusade you're on about the Joycelen murder, and Cobol. It's over and done with. Joycelen and Cobol are buried."

She wondered whether he was mouthing the words and thoughts of someone else. She asked; he assured her it wasn't the case.

"I'm concerned about this lovely creature sitting across from me," he said. "You and I, and everyone else like us in the Pentagon, are not supposed to know more than we need to know to perform our jobs. People who try to know more than that make other people nervous. Trust me, Margit. I'm giving it to you straight. I'm putting my own neck on the line by sitting here with you and telling you these things."

He was right. Still, she didn't trust him. Was that what happened to people after going through what she had for the past few weeks? Trust no person? View everyone with whom you come in contact as having a hidden agenda? If so—if she'd reached that stage in her own life—she didn't like it. She was raised to give people the benefit of the doubt, and to believe in them until they proved themselves to be unworthy of trust. This was the antithesis of that. She couldn't—wouldn't—live and work that way. She had to believe in those with whom she shared common goals, professional or personal.

She wanted to believe Monroney. She needed a friend. He was someone with whom she'd shared intimate moments years ago, and who now seemed eager to reenter her life. But he was a colonel. He worked in the Pentagon. That combination, as unlikely as it would have been for her a scant few months ago, now represented something ominous.

"Let me ask you a simple question, Bill. Are you saying that the scrutiny I've come under from my superiors has solely to do with the fact that Jeff and I went together?"

He raised his eyebrows. "You put it in the past tense."

"No comment. But if it is, it's not because someone in authority told me it had to be."

He thought about what she'd said. "It isn't just Foxboro," he said. "It's the Cobol thing."

"What about the 'Cobol thing'? I've been taken off the 'Cobol thing.' "

"Let's take a walk."

They left the restaurant and strolled the riverbank. When they'd reached a secluded spot, Monroney said, "Believe me when I say I don't know specifically what importance Cobol had regarding Safekeep. I do know that he must have had some significance. He's dead, and they prefer it that way. You're trying to keep him alive. That goes against policy."

"Policy? What policy?"

"Whatever policy the elephants have concocted. The problem is, you never know where this kind of policy directive originates. There are no memos. There are Pentagons within Pentagons. The Company seems to be pulling more strings these days. They've got moles in every office in the Pentagon, including mine."

"Oh?"

"Tony Mucci. I just found out he's CIA. Not on the books, but everything that happens in T and E gets fed back to the Company, compliments of Major Mucci."

"How do you know?"

"Doesn't matter. The point is, Margit, make damn sure you know the person you're talking to. *Really* know him." He frowned. "Maybe you can help me understand something. Why are you pursuing the Cobol case?"

"Because an innocent man died accused of murdering another person. He didn't. I think it's only fair and decent and human that somebody rectify that. People shouldn't go to their graves like that."

He said quietly, "Your father?"

"Yes." She'd told him about her father when they were in Panama.

"It's that important to you?"

"What happened to my father? Of course it is, but nothing can ever be done about that. But here's a young and dedicated officer who's gone to his grave as an accused murderer. Leaving a legacy that he murdered a top U.S. scientist is something his family shouldn't have to bear for the rest of their lives."

"Is it important enough to put your career—maybe your life—on the line?"

No one had asked it so directly, but she'd thought about it. She had no trouble saying, "Yes."

They walked farther, stopping under a tree whose long, graceful branches beckoned at the river. "You won't back off," Monroney said.

"Absolutely not."

"I respect you," he said.

"Thank you."

He looked across the river. It flowed slowly and was brown—not especially pretty but pleasantly tranquil. "How can I help you?" he asked.

"Bill, I'm not asking anyone in the service to help me, at least not someone with something to lose."

He faced her. "I told you I'm not looking for stars on my shoulders any longer. Am I looking to make waves? Hell, no. I have two years to the pension, and have big plans for that money. Classic case. Retire at colonel's pay, and young enough to start a second career. Appealing, and I won't do anything crazy to screw it up. At the same time, what I said at the table stands. I love you, and have since Panama. You hated me—no, that isn't in your nature. You had no respect for me when you found out that I was married and had kids. I can't blame you, but I didn't use you. I was sincere. If you hadn't ducked out so fast, things might have turned out different. I think—I know—I would have divorced Celia and married you. Things weren't good even back then. I want to be your friend—and more than that. Whether that develops is your choice. All I ask is that you give it a chance. In terms of the trouble you're facing, I'm here to lean on, to talk to, maybe even to come up with some advice, some perspectives that you haven't considered. Will you remember that?"

She was touched by his words. The pervasive feelings of distrust she'd felt earlier had faded. Not completely, but enough. "Yes," she said, "I will."

CHAPTER

THIRTY-THREE

 "So, here we are," Bellis growled. "You wanted a meeting. You've got it. The floor is yours." He'd removed his jacket, rolled up his sleeves, and loosened his tie.

Bravado is always so much easier in its contemplation. Margit had considered many ways to gently slide into her presentation to soften its impact. Bellis's hard stare said to get to the meat of it—fast.

"Sir, there are many questions I need to have answered."

His expression didn't change. "Go on," he said. "I'm listening."

"I was almost killed yesterday."

"I know that. I read the newspapers, watch TV. You did a hell of a good job averting a disaster."

"Yes, I did." She paused. "I'm still trying. I think my chopper was tampered with."

"That's a heavy charge. Who are you accusing?"

"No one specifically. A number of people knew I intended to fly yesterday."

"Including me."

"That's right, sir. I don't know who it was, but somebody was behind it."

"Proof?"

"Not the kind that you, as an attorney, would accept. But there's more."

"I'm all ears," he said, settling back and bringing his feet up on the edge of his desk. She resented the pose.

"A number of months before Dr. Joycelen was killed, a Major Wayne Reich at the CIA learned that Captain Cobol was a homosexual. As you know, that means dismissal from the service under Reg Thirteen-thirty-two. But Reich made an exception in Cobol's case. He told him he could remain on active duty because he was such a good officer."

Bellis's expression was nonresponsive.

"Cobol had been sent to a CIA-cleared psychiatrist in New York named Marcus Half. Half, according to my information, was deeply involved in the CIA's mind-control experimentation a number of years ago. He works with something called the Hypnotic Induction Profile. It runs on a scale from one to five. A 'five' means you're extremely hypnotizable, maybe to the extent of being capable of being programmed."

"Go on."

"Somebody added to Cobol's personnel file the symbol 'HP-5.' I think that meant that Cobol was a 'five' on Half's hypnotizability scale."

"You aren't about to rewrite *The Manchurian Candidate*, are you?"

His comment struck her as unnecessarily snide, but she ignored it. "Major Anthony Mucci, an aide to Colonel Monroney in T and E, changed the duty roster for the Saturday morning Joycelen was killed. He put Cobol on it at the last minute. Convenient, wouldn't you say?"

"Maybe necessary for staffing reasons."

"I don't think so. Mucci is wired into the CIA."

Bellis smiled. "One of hundreds floating around these halls. The Pentagon has its own mole corps all over D.C."

Margit said, "It's my contention that Captain Cobol was set up to take the rap for someone else in the Joycelen murder, and that the same person—or people—arranged to foul up my helicopter."

"This Major Reich?"

"A good bet." She recounted Reich's visit to Andrews with his mechanic.

"Why do you think Reich, or anyone else, would want to kill you?"

"Because of what I've learned."

Bellis drew a heavy breath, looked above her head at an antique wall clock, removed his feet from the desk, and sat up. "Why?" he asked.

"Why what, sir?"

"Why are you so damned driven to chasing what you only think is true about Joycelen and Cobol?"

She stiffened against an encroaching set of nerves and started to answer, but he interrupted. "You and this commitment, Major— this crusade you're on—have become a nasty thorn in my side. I spent half of today in meetings because of you."

"I'm sorry, sir. Meetings about me?"

"Right. I was ordered to straighten you out, get you off your white horse so you'd let Cobol and Joycelen stay where they are—in the ground."

"I've been followed," Margit said. "Were you made aware of that at these meetings?"

"I've known about that since it started," he said.

"Sir, I—that disappoints me."

"Why should it? It wasn't my decision. It wasn't done on my orders. But I am in the loop. At least that one."

"I don't like that my own people consider me so untrustworthy that they follow me day and night."

"It doesn't matter a hill a' beans what your feelings are about it," Bellis said. "It was considered operationally necessary."

"And who made that determination?" Margit asked.

"To be truthful? I don't know. But it sure as hell came from above me."

She said, "Sir, you asked before why I feel this commitment to clear Cobol's name. I know it isn't in my job description to do that, but I promised Cobol's family that I would do whatever I could to give them some dignity and peace. I can't walk away from that commitment. And by the way, Colonel, I don't buy for a second that Cobol hanged himself."

Bellis stood and stretched, then yawned. He went to a corner cabinet, opened a small refrigerator, and took out a bottle of diet soda. "You, Major?" he asked over his shoulder.

"No, thank you."

He returned to his chair. "Have you exhausted your list of accusations?" he asked.

"No. I've also decided that I was chosen to defend Cobol because

I was considered expendable. Because I'm a woman. Because I wouldn't make waves."

"If I did assign you to the case for those reasons, I sure was wrong." He checked the clock again. "It's six-thirty," he said. "We have until nine. Got any more to say?"

Margit's brow furrowed. "Until nine?"

"The people I met with today told me to resolve this matter with you before the day was over. I told them I didn't think I could, because Major Margit Falk has what I perceive to be an ingrained stubborn streak."

She shrugged and avoided his eyes. "If I do, it's never caused me to balk at an order."

"A first time for everything," he said. "I am ordering you to drop any further inquiry into Joycelen and Cobol."

She bit her lip. "Sir, I respectfully tell you that I cannot do that."

"See what I mean?"

"You knew that would be my answer."

"Yes, I did."

What happens at nine? she wondered. She asked.

"I told my colleagues that I was meeting with you at six, and would issue a direct order to drop what you're doing. But because I didn't have any faith you'd accept that order—and, by the way, you do realize that by not obeying it, you face a dishonorable discharge for insubordination?"

The words hurt but came as no surprise. She nodded.

"I told them you'd probably refuse to follow my order, even if it meant your commission and career. I told them that if it came to that, the only thing it would accomplish would be to turn you into one angry civilian lady who'd go public with her accusations, get plenty of press, and occupy everybody's time trying to refute your claims. I suggested that if my suspicions were correct, *they* meet with you tonight. It's scheduled for nine. I suggest you attend."

"Is that 'suggest' as in 'order'?" Margit asked.

"I'll leave it up to you."

"I'll be there," Margit said.

"Quarter of nine. Right here. Before you leave this office, is there anything else you plan to vent? I hate surprises."

Margit hesitated, but not long. She'd gone this far; might as well go the distance.

"Dr. Joycelen was murdered because he was a whistle-blower to Senator Wishengrad's committee. He was selling information about Project Safekeep."

"So I understand. Paid?"

"Yes, sir. But I was told something else, something much more important."

"What's that?"

"I was told—and I prefer to keep the source to myself—that the nuclear weapon tested in the Middle East was provided by us."

Bellis's face didn't change. He said flatly "identify the source of this allegation."

Margit ignored him. "Dr. Joycelen, I was told, had started to provide information to the Wishengrad committee about that charge."

Bellis came around the desk, stood over her, and said, "I think our nine o'clock meeting has just moved from important to crucial." He walked to the center of the room and stood with his back to her, hands on his hips, obviously deep in thought. When he faced her, he said, "Every bit of common sense, every ounce of my training, tells me to place you under house arrest. But another side says that won't be necessary, that you'll be back in this office at quarter of nine. Which side should I go with?"

The words "house arrest" jarred her. She seemed to be making a habit of this lately—forging ahead, aware of the potential consequences. Unable to put on the brakes. She'd stepped over the line. No, leaped over it was more accurate. But facing house arrest? Dishonorable discharge for insubordination? How could this happen to her? Bellis was waiting for an answer. "I don't need to be placed under house arrest," she said. "I'll be here."

He fastened his top shirt button and pulled his tie neatly up to his neck. He opened the door. Margit thought of many more things to say but said none of them. He closed the door behind her with symbolic force.

Margit went to her empty office and slumped behind her desk. A flyer on it caught her eye. There was a DACWITS meeting at seven in the auditorium that she'd planned to attend. Might as well, she thought. It was more palatable than sitting alone until her scheduled execution.

As she entered the auditorium where hundreds of uniformed women had gathered, she wondered whether she'd be able to concentrate on the evening's agenda. That didn't prove to be a problem. The group was addressed by Representative Pat Schroeder, the Democratic congresswoman from Colorado who'd co-sponsored a bill some time back to amend the forty-year-plus exclusion statutes prohibiting women from serving in combat roles. The Senate, too, had looked favorably upon such a bill. But the Bush administration had referred the notion to the inevitable committee, in this case a "blue-ribbon presidential panel" that was to ponder it and report its findings some time in 1993—or 2003—or beyond.

"The fact is," Schroeder said, "the military cannot do without its women, and that means in every conceivable role, without consideration of gender. In 1968 there were only forty thousand women in the armed forces. Today, that number is well over a quarter of a million, and it's growing rapidly. You're well aware of the hypocrisy inherent in the statute that prohibits you from going into combat. Many of you have already been in combat—even if it was called something else."

The audience applauded.

She continued. "You put your lives on the line in the Persian Gulf, and you gave your lives. Now, because of the threat of nuclear war in that region, it appears that you will again be called to serve side by side with your male colleagues, and you will do it with the same honor and excellence you've demonstrated in the past. I was extremely proud to have co-authored a crucial bill with Representative Beverly Byron, and potentially to have been able to play some small part in bringing about full equality for women who have helped defend this country's Constitution since its inception."

The applause was louder. Many rose to their feet.

Schroeder concluded her remarks by running down laws of other nations regarding women not only in combat, but in the military service itself. She mentioned Italy and Spain, which totally exclude women from military service. In Germany a handful of women are restricted to service in health-care services. Canada and Denmark train women as fighter pilots; the British have moved in the direction taken by the Schroeder-Byron bill; and Israel conscripts women into its military forces and assigns them to combat units, but withdraws them if those units are sent into battle.

"Thank you for allowing me to be here this evening. The tireless work of this organization has proved instrumental in reaching the goal of allowing women to fight shoulder to shoulder with men. You are to be congratulated."

Margit was, at once, stirred and saddened by what she'd heard. She believed in what the bill represented, and was especially proud of the air force, the only service that had openly embraced the notion of women in combat during recent hearings. At the same time, she was achingly aware that she stood on the threshold of losing a career to which she'd been dedicated for so many years.

She checked her watch: eight-thirty. Time to return to Bellis's office and face the music. Music? Face the enemy? She was sorely tempted to call Mac Smith and ask his advice. Show up? Walk away? No. It was beyond his kind of help. This was now her show, and the show must—would—go on. No esoteric legal issues involved. She was an air-force officer and had been called upon the carpet for disobeying orders, as tacit as they might have been.

She sat in Bellis's empty reception area. He walked in at ten to nine and disappeared into his office. He emerged moments later. "Let's go," he said.

She fell in step, staying to his left and slightly behind as her lesser rank dictated. She wished her heels didn't make so much noise on the bare floor as they headed for the second floor of E ring, where the Joint Chiefs' suites were located. It was carpeted there, and quiet. Lights in the hallway had been lowered as an energy-conservation measure. A few people were still at work, but compared to the usual hustle-bustle of the Pentagon, the hall had a surrealistic, almost dreamlike, quality.

They stopped in front of a door on which a sign read BRUCE A. MASSINGILL, UNDERSECRETARY FOR POLICY. "Wait here," Bellis said. He knocked, heard "Come in," and went through the door, leaving Margit alone. He was gone for what seemed to her a long time. Then the door opened, and Bellis said, "Come in, Major."

A captain and a bird colonel sat at desks in the reception area. The captain stood, went to a door and knocked, opened it slightly, and poked his head inside. "They're here, sir," he said. Without another word he pushed the door fully open and stood at attention as Bellis, followed by Margit, entered the undersecretary's private conference room.

The lights in the large room were even lower than in the hallway. Seated at the far end of a highly polished and very long cherrywood table was Undersecretary Massingill. She'd seen many pictures of him and had heard about his considerable power, as well as his overt enjoyment in exercising it.

He looked small at that distance. Gray hair was cropped close to his temples; he wore a dark suit and tie. A V of white shirt showed. His nondescript face was deadpan. Flanking him were three officers. Margit was introduced to two of them—General Walker Getlin, vice chairman of the Joint Chiefs; and Joseph Carter, the CIA's assistant director for foreign policy. She indicated that she needed no introduction to Major Anthony Mucci.

"Sit down," Massingill said, indicating chairs on either side of the table. Margit took one next to Carter; Bellis sat across from her. "Nice of you to come here at this late hour," Massingill said. The kindness inherent in his words surprised her. She didn't expect it because of his reputation, and because of the circumstances.

"It is my understanding, Major Falk, that Colonel Bellis has been direct with you today about our displeasure with actions you have taken of late. He has ordered you to cease taking those actions. Am I correct?"

Margit cleared her throat. "Yes, sir, that is correct."

"It is now my understanding that you have informed Colonel Bellis that you do not intend to obey his order. Am I correct again?"

"Yes, sir."

"I'm certain you're aware, Major Falk, that the military service cannot, and will not, tolerate such insubordination."

Margit nodded.

"Perhaps you can explain why you would take what has been an outstanding career in the United States Air Force and place it in such jeopardy."

Margit drew a deep breath and looked at Bellis, then down at her hands, which rested on the table. She wasn't sure she was up to trying to explain once again her motivation to clear Cobol's name. She'd already made different versions of the speech to Foxboro, Mac and Annabel Smith, Bill Monroney, and, only hours earlier, to Bellis.

"Major Falk," Massingill said. "I asked you a question."

"Sir, I believe Colonel Bellis has told you why I have placed myself in this position. I did it knowingly, and accept full responsibility. I never asked to be involved in the murder of Dr. Joycelen, but I was by being assigned to defend his accused murderer, Captain Robert Cobol. I asked not to be given that assignment but was overruled by Colonel Bellis. I followed his order despite my serious reservations. As a result, and because I was determined to do the best possible job as a defense attorney, I came to know a young man, a good soldier, a decent person, and that young man's mother. I came to believe that Captain Cobol did not kill Dr. Joycelen. I do not waver in that belief, even at this moment. I also do not believe that Captain Cobol hanged himself. He was terminated to protect someone, or something, that was responsible for Joycelen's death. Cobol's mother lives with the nightmare that her dead son went to his grave accused of murdering a leading U.S. scientist. I don't know whether, if I were a mother, I could live with that. I've had to live with watching my father be unfairly forced to leave the service because someone lied and a superior officer carried a grudge.

"I am, and have always been, a proud and committed officer. My record reflects that. I believe orders are to be followed, unless, of course, they are illegal. In this case, the order to stop probing what happened with Joycelen and Cobol is not in and of itself illegal. But the accusation against Cobol is certainly, if I am correct in my thesis, illegal. Murder always has been."

The room was eerily silent. The men stared at her. In that quiet moment a question hit her. Here she was, sitting with some of the top brass in the American military establishment, who presumably were there to inflict the ultimate punishment, her dishonorable discharge from the service. But if that were to be the outcome, why do it here, at nine o'clock at night, in the presence of such powerful men?

General Getlin, the Joint Chiefs' vice chairman, said, "It is my understanding that you are aware that Dr. Joycelen was providing information to the senator from Wisconsin and his staff that would seriously jeopardize our ability to develop a vitally important weapons system, Project Safekeep."

"Yes, sir, I am aware of that," Margit replied. "I am also aware that it is said to be vital."

The CIA's Joe Carter spoke. "Colonel Bellis informs us that someone has filled you with the absurd notion that this country, this government, this administration, has provided a nuclear weapon to a madman, with the goal of achieving an increased military budget."

Margit had hoped that wouldn't come up; she was sorry she'd mentioned it to Bellis. She stood. "Sir, I have been told that Dr. Joycelen not only sold information detrimental to Project Safekeep, he was in the process of providing information to that same senator about the very accusation you've just raised. I don't know whether that's true or not. If it is, it renders my crusade, as you call it, on behalf of Robert Cobol's name insignificant. If it is true, it is not what my country, my government, or my military service is supposed to represent. That, like a murder, is also illegal."

Margit saw in the room's dim light a thin smile form on Massingill's face. He raised his head and took her in with downcast eyes. His smile did not provide warmth. Instead, it sent a beam of frost in her direction. He said, "Major Falk, we are not here tonight to punish you for your indiscretions. We don't like losing good officers, and it is our policy—my policy—to go that extra yard to see that good officers like you are retained. But sometimes even a well-meaning officer becomes mired down in false information and ill-advised causes. I believe it is our obligation to correct such false information, and the assumptions that naturally follow. Do you understand me?"

What Margit understood was what Bellis had said earlier—that if she were drummed out of the service, she would become a civilian loose cannon, capable of, at least, complicating the lives of the men in the room, and others. She also thought of Cobol breaking Reg 1332, and being told he would not be punished because the service did not want to lose a "good officer."

She said, "Sir, I would be pleased and relieved to have it shown to me that I'm wrong. I wish none of this had ever happened, and that it would just go away. If you accomplish what you have just stated, I will be grateful. It would mean I could return to my duties with renewed commitment and dedication."

"Please sit down," Massingill said. He nodded at Mucci, who went behind Massingill and slid open doors that were part of the wall, exposing a large television monitor. He turned it on, and did the same with a VCR. He took a videotape from a briefcase that had been on the table in front of him, inserted it in the VCR, used dimmers to bring down the lights to a dull copper glow, and pressed Play on the VCR.

Margit wondered whether she was about to see another tape of the nuclear-weapons test in the Middle East. But the monitor's screen came to life, and a scene that had been recorded from a high angle played out for her eyes.

A man stood next to the purple water fountain in the basement of the Pentagon. He checked his watch, mumbled something under his breath. Joycelen! It was Richard Joycelen.

The camera continued to relentlessly record what was happening. He—Joycelen—checked his watch again. Then, footsteps. Another look at his watch. A second man entered the scene. He pointed a gun at Joycelen. Neither man said anything. The second man fired. The bullet shattered Joycelen's eyeglasses and pulled skin and bone into the gaping hole it had created between his eyes. A word formed on Joycelen's lips but was never sounded. The scientist slumped to the floor, his back riding down the purple fountain, his face washed in a grotesque, velvety red.

The screen went black. Mucci removed the tape, returned it to his briefcase, and turned up the lights to their previous level. The men in the room observed Margit's reaction, like physicians peering down on an exotic operation in a medical arena. They saw her begin to tremble, eyes wide, horror frozen on her face.

"Satisfied?" Massingill asked.

She was numb, speechless.

Joycelen had been murdered by Captain Robert Cobol.

"You don't have to worry about clearing his name any longer, Major," Massingill said. "His name is tainted because it deserves to be. My suggestion is that we all go home, get a good night's sleep, and wake up in the morning ready to continue the daunting challenge of defending this nation against those who would see it destroyed. Oh, by the way, Major Falk, I've personally reviewed your father's file. It seems he was the victim of an unfair process. I've ordered that he posthumously receive a commendation, and a promotion."

Margit fought back bitter tears. She stood and said loudly, "If Cobol did it, he was told to do it. Programmed to do it. He was blackmailed, brainwashed." Her brief proclamation drained all energy from her. She sat.

"That active imagination of yours will snap back to reality pretty quick," Massingill said. He came around behind her and placed a hand on her shoulder. "I'm glad we could resolve this for you, Major Falk. I think you'll find your next assignment to be the sort of job every chopper pilot dreams of. Colonel Bellis will fill you in. Major Mucci will accompany you from the building."

He removed his hand and went to the door, Getlin and Carter following. "Good night," he said. "Please turn off the lights when you leave."

Mucci stood at attention by the door. Margit looked across the table at Bellis, who seemed to have aged. "I'd like to leave," she said.

Bellis stood. His shoulders sagged; his eyes missed hers.

She said to Mucci, "No one, especially you, will escort me anywhere."

He remained in his silent brace.

"Please excuse us, Major," Bellis said. When Mucci didn't respond, Bellis said in a louder voice, "Leave the room, Major Mucci. We will be out shortly."

"Yes, sir," Mucci said.

When he was gone, Bellis said to Margit, "I'm sorry."

"Sorry about what? That I was wrong—but am right— about Cobol? That I've been offered a blatant bribe to be a good little girl and keep my mouth shut?"

"No," Bellis replied. "I'm sorry that this night ever happened. What will you do?"

"Tomorrow? I don't know. Tonight? I have some phone calls to make."

"I admire you, Major," Bellis said.

"Admire me? For what?"

"For having a set of convictions that run deep. Get those convictions from your father?

Her eyes misted. "I guess so," she said in a voice on the verge of breaking.

"Sometimes our convictions get pushed aside by pragmatic needs," Bellis said. Margit raised her eyebrows. "Career, family, just getting through," he continued. "And sometimes because of a belief in something that doesn't hold up to hard scrutiny. Like tonight." He sat in his chair, the room's dim light leaving half of his face in shadow. "Go make your phone calls," he said. "I think I'll just sit here awhile. I have some thinking to do."

She walked to the door, stopped, and turned. He smiled, and tossed her a small salute. She left.

Mucci stood at attention just outside the door. Despite Margit's objections, he followed her from the meeting and to one of the Pentagon's exits. He held the door open for her. "Take the advice," he said, his eyes black, his mouth barely moving.

She came to attention. "No, you take *this* advice, Major. You ever touch me—you ever come near me—and you'll end up singing in a boys' choir."

CHAPTER

THIRTY-FOUR

March of the Following Year

Wisconsin senator Henry "Hank" Wishengrad looked down from his chairman's chair of the Senate Armed Services Committee. His glasses poised precariously on the tip of his nose. His unsparing expression was matched by his voice.

"The testimony you have given here today is shocking in its ramifications. Naturally, I wish you could have brought us more tangible evidence of the charges you level. On the other hand, with the way most of our military and intelligence establishments function under a dark blanket of secrecy, I wouldn't be surprised that the physical elements you describe have long ago felt the shredder's teeth. We've subpoenaed the videotape you've told us about, but we're told no such tape ever existed. We subpoenaed the psychiatrist in New York, Dr. Marcus Half, but he refuses to testify because of his doctor-patient relationship. The medical corpsman who visited Captain Cobol in his cell will say only that he administered a sedative because the captain was highly agitated, and the corpsman was afraid he posed a danger to himself. Why a medical corpsman is free to make such judgments, and to administer injections, is something else this committee should look into.

"Whether we ever get to the bottom of this remains conjecture. I will say, however, Ms. Falk, that you are one courageous lady to have stood by your principles, abandon a sterling military career, and come before this committee and the American people to call for righting what is, if it can be proved, a tale of gross abuse of power. I'll go further. Anyone, civilian or military, who would take the law into their own hands, and for their own purposes, is stealing our country right out from under us. They're our own people, but every last one of them is a traitor."

Margit smiled weakly at Wishengrad. Her eyes went to Jeff Foxboro, who sat behind and to the left of the senator. He'd become her ally because of the hearing. What personal feelings remained between them were relegated to memories.

"May I make one final statement?" Margit asked.

"You make as many statements as you wish, Ms. Falk."

"The saddest day of my life was the day I resigned my commission in the United States Air Force. Every morning I put on that uniform, I felt a sense of pride and purpose. But I don't think I've ever felt as patriotic as I do today. This country, this government, and the armed services that serve both, are made up of thousands of dedicated and qualified men and women. They carry out their daily assignments believing that what they do benefits their country and its people. But there are within this group of good people those who would subvert the laws and regulations in order to fulfill their own prophecies. They believe, I suppose, that what they do is right and good. It isn't. We are a nation of laws, which led me to become a lawyer. These people—and my solace is that there are so few of them—ignore the very thing they are charged with protecting. They burn the village to save it, as we all heard from Vietnam. They take it upon themselves to decide what is right for this country, ignoring those with legal authority who say otherwise. It was my misfortune to be put in direct contact with this minority when I was assigned to the Pentagon. My life has changed dramatically because of it, and I will, for the rest of my days, regret my bad luck. But I wish to leave this committee with the understanding that I have been proud to serve with the men and women of our armed forces, and will always view them with that same pride." Her eyes filled up, and concluded with a broken voice, "Thank you very much."

Wishengrad's female colleague on the committee said, "May I say, Ms. Falk—no, I think I'll call you Major Falk—may I say that you are an exemplary young woman. The air force, and this country, have lost a valuable person, and I rue the circumstances that led to your resignation. But rest assured that the service you do here today, while condemned by those involved in this outrageous episode in our history, deserves our everlasting gratitude."

It was eleven in the morning. Wishengrad called a twenty-minute recess.

When the committee returned, and the next witness was seated at the witness table, Wishengrad smiled down at Margit. "I'm pleased you chose to remain, Major Falk," he said. He looked at the new witness, who sat next to her. "You, sir, are obviously cut from the same cloth. You have had an esteemed career in our military service. You have served this country admirably and unselfishly. Yet, because you place principle at the top of your priority list, you sit before this committee to testify against some of the same men you so faithfully served. I commend you for this action."

Colonel James Bellis, in full uniform, sat hunched over the table, elbows pressed into it, face leaden. Margit glanced at him. You're a good man, she thought. You and my father would have gotten along.

Wishengrad adjourned that day's portion of the hearing at six, with Bellis scheduled to return the following day. The colonel had told everything he knew about the plan hatched by Bruce Massingill—and carried out by a small core of believers within the Pentagon—to provide nuclear weapons to the Arab dictator for the purpose of creating panic within the United States and forcing the hand of Congress to substantially increase the military budget. His testimony was detailed and compelling. He'd been present at many key meetings, and had kept his own personal and confidential diary, which he had shared with the committee prior to his appearance. Because those involved with the plan had been meticulously careful not to leave tracks, tangible evidence to support his and Margit's allegations was slow in coming. But come it did, in dribs and drabs, one piece leading to another, each bit of testimony sending committee investigators down new paths of inquiry. And the nation sat glued to its collective TV set as the hearings were broadcast in all their shocking and tawdry truth.

Members of Consulnet who'd been subpoenaed had refused to appear, and there was no way to enforce the subpoenas. All of them, with the exception of Potomas, were foreign citizens. Potomas, learning of the probe into Consulnet's activities, had packed up and moved to Greece. But Foxboro had told Margit—"Your ears only"—that the British member of the arms-dealing consortium, Sanford Sheffield, was weakening under intense pressure from his own government, and was close to testifying.

Wishengrad's final comment to Bellis and Margit as he closed the session was, "I find something uplifting about the two of you choosing to remain together throughout these proceedings. There is a feeling of solidarity that gives credence—at least to this senator—to your testimony. I wish you a pleasant evening, and look forward to continuing in the morning."

The sharp rap of his gavel signaled the day was over.

Mac and Annabel had their choice of two favored tables at Mac's favorite D.C. steak house, the Georgetown branch of Morton's of Chicago. There was the table in "Rosty's Rotunda," where Dan Rostenkowski, Democratic chairman of the House Ways and Means Committee, often camped; or "The Box," a table below a large portrait of former House Democratic whip Tip O'Neill. They chose the Box. Mac knew, and was fond of, the retired Boston pol.

Annabel enjoyed Morton's, too, which made it easier for Smith. She was generally quick to turn down his suggestion to dine at other temples of beef, but not Morton's. The lighter side of the menu appealed to her, and there was the unfailingly warm greeting they received as semiregulars.

"Will Margit call tonight?" Annabel asked after shrimp cocktails had been served. It had been the first day of the Wishengrad committee's hearings.

"I don't know. If I were her, I'd go straight home to bed," Mac answered.

"She's a remarkable person," Annabel said. "To give up her career because of what she believes in—such idealism ought to have been taught to every yuppie her age who came out of college looking to make money in investment banking."

"And in the law," Smith added. "There are few of her class. And she seems happy. The fact that Bellis decided to stand up with her made a big impression on her. What did you think of Bill Monroney?"

"My jury's still out on him. Obviously crazy about her. What's your verdict?"

"It's Margit's verdict to come to, not ours. I trust her judgment. She was taught by the best." He sat back and smiled wryly.

That day's edition of *The Washington Post* was on the banquette next to Smith. He glanced down at the front-page headline: TROOPS IN BORDER SKIRMISHES—THREE AMERICANS DIE.

The fourth in a series of articles by Louise Harrison also occupied page 1. It was accompanied by a photograph of Margit and Colonel Bellis as they left the Russell Senate Office Building the previous day after having met with Wishengrad's staff. The first three articles laid out every detail of the Cobol-Joycelen story as recounted to her by Margit. Now, it had shifted to the story of Consulnet and the Massingill conspiracy, with Colonel James Bellis quoted extensively.

"Watergate. Iran-contra. October surprises. Now this." Annabel sighed. "At least it's coming out in the open."

"I think Beardsley acted too soon sending troops to the Mideast," Smith said.

"Maybe Margit's and Bellis's testimony will help bring them back."

"Not a chance. Beardsley needs a war the way Bush did. We're not exactly reveling in an age of prosperity here. Besides, it's good for the yellow-ribbon manufacturers."

Annabel smiled. Her husband was at his cynical best.

She asked, "What do you think will happen to Margit when this is over?"

"I'd say she'll do just fine. That start-up helicopter service knew a good thing when it saw her. Three days a week as its legal counsel, and two days captaining one of its choppers. She'll never be totally happy out of the military. She bleeds blue, only it isn't for the Dodgers. But she'll be okay. She had no future there. I think the toughest thing she had to do was face Cobol's mother. I knew when Margit told Mrs. Cobol the truth that we'd hear from her again. If she'd decided to fade away and not pursue what happened through Wishengrad and his committee, she would have lied to Mrs. Cobol, told her she was unsuccessful in clearing her son but that she still believed in his innocence. She never intended to let it drop. Not from Day One."

Their steaks were served Pittsburgh style—black-and-blue.

She took a bite. "Excellent," she said.

He did the same. "Excellent," he said.

"Mac," Annabel said.

"What?"

"Has this episode with Margit changed you?"

"In what way?"

"Has it caused you to—to want to get back into the arena? Take on bigger challenges than teaching law?"

"No," Smith said, enjoying another piece of steak.

"I'm glad," Annabel said.

Their eyes met, and knowing smiles came to their lips.

Annabel's smile turned into a cynical laugh. "You lie," she said.

Smith shook his head. "I'm not looking for action or challenge anymore, Annabel. I happen to be contented with the bland, peaceful, uneventful life I currently lead. You provide all the spice I need."

"Really?"

"Absolutely."

"I like that. I didn't know you considered me spicy."

"All I'll ever need."

"Good."

Their waiter passed the table. "Anything I can get you?" he asked.

"Some horseradish, please," Smith said. "Make it the hot stuff."

MARGARET TRUMAN, the author of ten successful mystery thrillers, was born in Independence, Missouri. She now lives with her husband, Clifton Daniel, in New York City.

They have four sons and two grandchildren.